ID0953742

THE ROBIN & THE KESTREL:

BARDIC VOICES

BOOK II

Baen Books By Mercedes Lackey

Bardic Voices: The Lark & The Wren
If I Pay Thee Not In Gold (*with Piers Anthony*)
The Ship Who Searched (*with Anne McCaffrey*)
Reap the Whirlwind (*with C.J. Cherryh*)
Wing Commander: Freedom Flight (*with Ellen Guon*)

Urban Fantasies
Born to Run (*with Larry Dixon*)
Wheels of Fire (*with Mark Shepherd*)
When the Bough Breaks (*with Holly Lisle*)
Knight of Ghosts and Shadows (*with Ellen Guon*)
Summoned to Tourney (*with Ellen Guon*)

Bard's Tale™ Novels
Castle of Deception (*with Josepha Sherman*)
Fortress of Frost and Fire (*with Ru Emerson*)
Prison of Souls (*with Mark Shepherd*) (forthcoming)

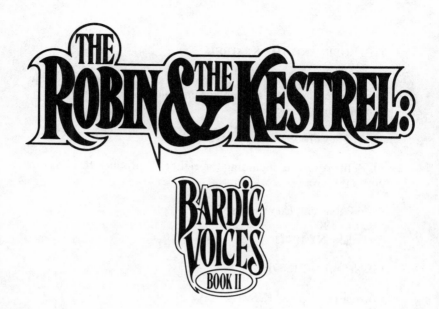

THE ROBIN & THE KESTREL:

BARDIC VOICES

BOOK II

MERCEDES LACKEY

THE ROBIN AND THE KESTREL

Baen Publishing Enterprises
P.O. Box 1403
Riverdale, NY 10471

ISBN: 0-671-72183-6

Cover art by Darrell K. Sweet

Distributed by Simon & Schuster
1230 Avenue of the Americas
New York, NY 10020

***Dedicated to**
Dr. Paul Welch, and the other
avian veterinarians who keep
the namesakes of our Free Bards,
wild and tame, alive and well.*

THE ROBIN & THE KESTREL:

BARDIC VOICES

BOOK II

CHAPTER ONE

Jonny Brede — aka "Free Bard Kestrel" — shook mud and cold, cold water out of his eyes. He grunted as he heaved another shovelful of soft mud from beneath the wheel of their foundered travel-wagon. And the hole immediately filled up with water. This was *not* how a honeymoon was supposed to be conducted. Not in a blinding downpour, with more mud on him than even this flood of rain could wash away. Not with their wagon stuck in a pothole the size of Birnam. What happened to "and they lived happily ever after"?

It's stuck at the end of tales in stupid Guild ballads, that's what happened to it. Real people get stuck in potholes, not platitudes.

Jonny Brede grinned at that, in spite of the miserable situation; it had a good ring to it. A nice turn of phrase. He'd have to tell Robin; she could store it away in her capacious memory and put it in a song some time. She was the one with a talent for lyrics, not he. They hadn't been out of Birnam for more than a week when she'd already crafted a song about the two of them, "The Gypsy Prince." "If I don't, someone else will," she reasoned, "and if it isn't Rune or Talaysen, they'll probably get it all wrong. Never trust your story to someone else."

Well, she had a point. Though he simply could not think of himself as "Sional," much less as "Prince Sional" — not anymore.

Not when the "Prince" was in command of no more than himself, two mares, and a shovel. Better "Jonny," or better yet, "Free Bard Kestrel."

He shoveled a little more muddy gravel under the wheel of their caravan-wagon and took a cautious peek at his bride of a few scant weeks through a curtain of rain. The last time he'd looked at her, she'd been giving the wagon a glare as black as the thunderclouds overhead. She'd been standing to one side of their patient, sturdy, ebony mares, fists on her hips, gaudy clothing pasted to her body by the rain, with her ebony hair flattened down on her head and her lips moving silently. He did not think she was praying. The look on her face had boded ill for the King's road crew, if she ever discovered who had permitted this enormous pothole to form and fill with soft, sucking mud.

Her temper did not seem to have improved in the past few moments. She held the bridles of their two well-muscled horses and murmured encouraging things into their ears, but the scowl on her face belied her soft words. Hopefully her temper would cool before she actually needed to find a target for her anger other than the storm itself. Robin had a formidable temper when it was aroused.

Kestrel sighed, and stamped down on the gravel to make it sink into the mud and hopefully pack down. *He* was happy, despite being soaked to the skin, cold and muddy. Their horses had shied at a lightning strike, running off onto the verge of the road and now their wagon was mired at the side of the road. So what? It was not an insurmountable problem. The wagon had not been hit, their horses had not broken legs, neither of *them* were hurt. It was just a matter of hauling the thing out themselves, or waiting until someone came along who could help them.

So what? He wasn't going to let a little accident

upset his cheerful mood. In fact, he thought he had never been so happy before in all his life. Certainly not during his best-forgotten childhood.

He shoveled in another load of gravel, which splashed into the yellow mud and sank. *Prince Sional, huh. Oh, it's a great thing to be a Prince, when your father sticks you in a so-called palace that's half derelict, with one servant to care for a child, an invalid Queen do all the char work, and deal with leaky roofs and cracks in the walls. It's a great thing to be royal, when your kingly father trots you out only for special occasions when a live son is useful. It's a fine thing to be a Prince, when you've got snow on your satin bedspread in the winter, leaks onto your head in the summer, and the servants at the Crown Palace eat better than you do. When your only friend is a Guild Bard who should have retired a hundred years ago . . .*

He'd been ignored by his wastrel father, who was too busy debauching himself to pay attention to his son *or* his land, and willfully neglected by his father's underlings. The only thing good in that childhood had been his mother and tutor, a Guild Bard of Birnam, one Master Darian, who had been father, mother, and mentor to him. Master Darian had taught him about honor and about care. And within his own specialty, first the love of music, then the means of making it.

Kestrel's eyes misted over and a tear or two joined the rain on his cheeks. *Darian, my good Darian, faithful one. Oh, Master, I wish you could see me now. I think you'd be pleased. You always said it was the music that should be important, and the skill of those who played it. I think you'd like Robin. I know you'd like Talaysen.*

King Charlis' royal chickens had come home to roost with a vengeance. When he had wrung his land near-dry to support his self-indulgence, some of his subjects could bear no more. One, Charlis' own brother, was willing to act on their desperation. He staged an uprising; flooded the palace with his own men, and killed his brother, taking the throne for himself.

Now, at long last, Kestrel knew why his uncle had taken those drastic steps. And he knew now what neither he nor Darian had known then; that Rolend had no intention of harming his nephew, and that the orders that night had been to stay away from the Dowager Palace. Then in the morning, after the situation had been resolved, Rolend had planned to bring Sional to the Crown Palace to be installed with his cousin and his cousin's tutors.

Whether he would have given me preference for the throne over Victor — well, that hardly matters. He wasn't going to kill a child.

But Sional had been snooping, as a young boy would, in places he shouldn't have been; he had seen his father's assassination and the beginning of the uprising, and had run to his tutor in terror. Old Darian, not knowing any of the plans afoot, had assumed the worst, and had smuggled them both out of the palace, out of the city, and out of Birnam through the terrible fens between Birnam and Rayden.

As a Guild Bard from Birnam the old man was given a certain respect, even though he had been in the scant train of the Queen until she died, then had chosen to live in obscurity as Sional's tutor for her sake. But the Guild in Rayden was not minded to see any prize places go to some outsider, and Jonny and his ailing mentor had been shuffled off to the Guild Hall at Kingsford and left to rot.

Kestrel wiped away a couple more tears; of anger this time, at the arrogant bastards who'd politely jeered at the brave old man, and had accounted his stories of revolt and assassins to be a senile fool's meanderings. They had never questioned the boy that Darian called "Jonny Brede."

I was sick with marsh-fever. And they wouldn't have believed me, anyway. The marsh-fever had taken his memory and left him thinking he was no more than a peasant boy that Darian had chosen for his apprentice despite the "obvious unsuitability" of the boy; either the fever or the trauma of flight had also left him with a stutter he still suffered.

He scrubbed the back of his hand across his mouth and tasted grime and dilute salt. *Damn them. Darian should have been covered with honors, and what did they do? They stuck him in the worst room in the Guild Hall, a room they wouldn't even put a servant in, and left him to die. If it hadn't been for me, he would have died within a week. He was too old and too tired to flee across two countries with a sick boy.*

He had to keep reminding himself that it was all in the past. Otherwise he'd get too angry about things he couldn't change. That was what Master Wren kept telling him, and he was right.

He shoveled in another load of gravel, packing it down savagely. Oh, that was what everyone told him, but *forgetting,* now — that was the hard part.

The Guild had a lot to answer for. When Master Darian died, it was their own law that he be found a new Master. He was, after all, a full apprentice, and had anyone been watching out for his rights, he would have gotten that new Master. But no one wanted to be bothered with a stuttering apprentice — and one who was a "legacy," chosen by a Bard from another kingdom, at that. There would be no grateful parents sending gifts as there would have been if he had been born well-off. There would be no gifts from the boy to the Master who had discovered him, if and when he achieved fame, for that Master was Darian. There was no one to insist that the boy's rights be observed, for that troublemaker, Master Talaysen, had vanished after tossing all his honors into the face of the Guild Master.

In short, there was no profit in taking the boy, and it would mean a great deal of wasted time trying to train him out of the stutter.

So the Guild Master and his chosen cronies told him he was feebleminded, a half-wit; told the same tale to anyone who looked the least bit curious. Then they had thrown him out into the street with only the clothes on his back and those few personal possessions he still had, denied his rights to a new Master, denied even the old harp his Master had left when he died.

Something Talaysen had said made him smile in spite of his anger. "The irony is, they trained *plenty* of half-wits in there, and they are still doing so. It doesn't take wits to play without any sense of the music. Half-wits are conscious only of form and style, not content — and form and style are all the Guild cares about."

If I'd had that harp, I could at least have made some kind of living as a street-busker. That had been the worst of it; he had no skills, and he was too old to find another Apprenticeship in a trade. *If I'd had the harp, I would have found the Free Bards earlier — or they would have found me, the way they found Rune. They'd have told me I wasn't worthless. . . .*

Still, there was no point in dwelling on *that.*

No, he certainly had no pleasure in looking back at *those* years. Nor at the ones that followed; with no harp to play to make a living, and no way of ever getting one, he had been forced to look for whatever work he could find as an unskilled laborer. He worked himself to the bone in the worst of conditions, stealing when there was no work.

That was when his life had truly fallen to pieces. His uncle, King Rolend, had gotten wind of the fact that he was still alive. The King's own grasp on the throne was as shaky as his predecessor's had been; he could not afford a pretender to it, however young. And a young boy, had anyone *known* what he was, would have been easy to manipulate. There were plenty of people in Birnam who would have been very pleased to get their hands on a figurehead for a counter-rebellion.

So King Rolend had made the cruelest decision of his life. To have seeking-talismans made, and send out hired killers bearing them, to find Sional, now only fifteen or sixteen, and kill him.

Since Sional had no inkling of who and what he was, this was even crueler than it seemed. He was now caught in the heart of a senseless nightmare. Hired killers were after him, and he had no notion *why*. Their mere existence made it impossible for him to accept a permanent job even when one was offered, for he dared not stay in one place for too long.

He shook rainwater out of his eyes, and glanced over to his beloved Robin again. She had that knack for dealing with animals that all Gypsies seemed to have; the mares were listening to her and had calmed considerably.

Flickering light overhead made him cock his head to look at the sky. An area of clouds just above him lightened again, and a distant mumble of thunder followed the light.

Good. All the lightning was up in the clouds. *May it stay there.* This was a bad place to be caught by lightning, here in an area of road lined by oaks. Oak trees seemed to attract lightning, for some reason, and several of the huge trunks nearby bore mute testament to that.

He had done all he could for this wheel. He moved

to the other, and started in again, his thoughts returning to the past. *If anyone wanted to devise a hell for someone,* he thought, packing the gravel as far in under the wheel as he could, *It would surely have been a life like mine!* Able to find only the most menial of work, watching over one's shoulder for the mysterious killers — and not knowing why they pursued, much less how to get rid of them!

He had taken a job as a goat-driver, a job that brought him to the edge of the Downs and the little town of Karsdown. What he had not known was that this late in the season, there would be no further work in Karsdown for an unskilled laborer. He found himself trapped in a tiny sheep-herding town with no work in it, without enough money to buy himself provisions to get to someplace else, and without the woods-knowledge needed to live off the land. He had been desperate; desperate enough to try to pick the pocket of a tall man with graying red hair, who appeared to have enough coin that he would not miss a copper or two. His target was a man he had not then known was a Bard, since he was not carrying an instrument, nor wearing the Guild colors of purple and silver or gold. He had tried to pick the pocket of one known both as "Master Wren" and — by a chosen few — as the great Free Bard Master Talaysen. Wren was the same man who had fled acclaim and soft living to form the loose organization known as the "Free Bards" — but before he had done that, he had won Guild Mastery as well, under the far-famed name of Master Gwydain. The songs and music of Gwydain were famed in every kingdom — though the songs and music of Free Bard Talaysen bid fair to eclipse that fame.

Funny — Wren outshines even himself!

All *he* had known at the time was that the man was

accompanied by two young and attractive women, and to Jonny's eyes was spending a great deal of money. He had assumed that the man was — well — their "honey-papa," as the shepherds would say, an older man who bought young ladies nice things and received most particular and personal attentions from them in return.

That he had been mistaken was his good fortune rather than his bad, for that was when his streak of horrible luck finally broke. Talaysen had caught him, but had not sought to punish, but to *help* him. The young women had been his wife, the Free Bard Rune, and a Gypsy Free Bard named Gwyna, but far more often referred to as "Robin."

Kestrel grinned at *that* memory. Robin had first loaded him down with all her packages to carry, without so much as a "by-your-leave," and then had marched him off to get a bath in the stream and had made it very clear that either *he* would bathe, or *she* would bathe him. And her expression had told him wordlessly that if she did the bathing, it would be thorough, but not pleasant. He opted to scrub himself down, and change into some old clothing of Rune's rather than his own rags.

Amazing how much better being clean for the first time in months can make you feel. And she certainly thought I cleaned up well enough.

He stole another glance at her, and it seemed to him as if she looked a trifle less angry. Perhaps talking to the horses had calmed her. He hoped so; there was no reason to be angry, after all. Even though the pothole seemed to be the size of Birnam, the wagon that was stuck in it was *theirs*, the horses that drew it were *theirs*, and it all was a gift of his uncle —

The same uncle who had tried to kill him, true, but King Rolend wasn't trying to kill him anymore.

He grinned again. Poor Uncle Rolend! He had been no match for the wits of Talaysen, the magic of the Gypsies, and the determination of his three new friends to see him *out* of the mess!

One of the Elves who'd come to his wedding, one of those who were allies of both Talaysen and King Rolend, had told him that it was no accident, his being in Karsdown at the same time as the other three. "Your Bardic magery was awakening," the Elf had said, with lofty off-handedness. "It called to them, as theirs called to you, If you had not met then, you would have met soon."

He rubbed his nose, uneasily. He wasn't altogether certain about this "Bardic Magic" business. It was easy enough for Wren to be blithe about it; *he* was a Master twice over, in the Guild Bards and the Free Bards, and a nobleman to boot. *He* was used to power of all sorts. Kestrel was far from comfortable with the idea that he could influence people and events just by thinking and singing. . . .

Well, right now that hardly mattered. No magic, Bardic or otherwise, was going to get this wagon out of the muck. It was going to take nothing more esoteric than muscle of man and beast.

But was that really why Talaysen had so readily "adopted" him? Master Wren said not, no matter what the Elf said. "All it took was to hear you play," the Bard had said, simply. "I knew you were one of us, and that we had an obligation to help you."

He grinned, through the rain dripping down his back, and in spite of the aches in his muscles. To hear that, from the one he admired most in the world —

I wouldn't have blamed him if he'd gotten rid of me that night in Ralenvale when the killers caught up with me. . . .

Though no one had been hurt except the killers

themselves, it had been a terror-filled night, both for Kestrel, who had hoped to escape his pursuers, and the Gypsies they had camped with.

But before that, he had been having the time of his life, for the Gypsies treated him as one of their own, and made him feel at home with them. That was when Jonny had earned his Bardic nickname of "Kestrel" from the Gypsies; he had said, in disgust, that his stutter made him sound like a kestrel. The Gypsies had seized upon that and promptly dubbed him "Free Bard Kestrel." They'd included him in their music, their dancing — and never once teased him about the way he sounded when he talked.

Then the attack had come. One of the assassins had died, challenging a magical trap set by the Gypsy mage, Peregrine. The rest had fled when their weapons missed their target.

I thought for certain when they realized how much trouble I was bringing to them that they would tell me to make my own way. But instead, Wren had decreed his lost past must be plumbed — to find out why he was the target of such attacks, so that something could be done to prevent or evade them.

Peregrine had performed the magic that unlocked Kestrel's lost memories, and *then* "Jonny Brede" learned who and what he really was. It had been a shock to all of them, but it had been Talaysen who decreed they must go to the source of those memories, to discover the truth of the matter, and what, if anything, they should do about that truth.

From the first, *he* had never really entertained fantasies of being the "lost Prince" returned to reclaim his throne — or not for long, anyway. He wasn't certain what the others had in their minds. But the further into Birnam they got, and the more questions they had asked, the more the truth about the current and past

King emerged, although they had more questions on the whole than they had answers. So, at last, they had taken the risky chance of summoning Elves to answer what had become a series of vital questions.

And the answers the Elf gave them had not been in keeping with any fantasy of "lost Princes." Kestrel's father Charlis had indeed, even by Elven standards, been a terrible King; he had wasted the resources of his land on his own pleasure, and had taken no thought to truly governing it. King Rolend had acted in part to keep his brother from destroying his own lands and people with his greed. Rolend was the very opposite of his brother, and had, through sacrifice and hard work, brought Birnam back into prosperity.

The obvious question then was why had such an apparently good and honorable man been sending killers to rid himself of a child?

The Elves had an answer to that as well, for they were privy to Rolend's counsels and many of his secrets; Rolend believed that the King's concern lay with all the peoples of his realm, and not just those who were human.

Rolend, they said, had learned that the Prince had survived his flight into Rayden and had become more and more nervous, as the boy grew older, that one day someone might use the Prince as a front in an attempt to regain the throne. He was, after all, the "rightful" heir to his father. And there were plenty of folk who had profited when Charlis sat the throne, who now were not profiting in the reign of his honest brother. These folk, a mixture of dishonest Priests of the Church, discontented Dukes and Sires who had enjoyed considerable autonomy in their own holdings under Charlis, and the Birnam Bardic Guild who had lined their pockets with Birnam's gold, would have been overjoyed to have a

figurehead to use for a counter-rebellion, particularly one as romantic as a "lost Prince." *Most*
particularly, one who could be manipulated, as a
young, and presumably naive, child could be.

So King Rolend had gritted his teeth and sent assassins, armed with tokens that would lead them to the
Prince.

He would never feel safe until "Prince Sional" had
been taken out of the picture, permanently.

Intellectually — well, I could understand that. Kestrel stood for a moment to ease his cramping
shoulders, then went back to his work. *And now that
I've met with Uncle — all I can say is, I'm glad things
worked out this way. The trouble with Uncle Rolend is
that he is very good at convincing himself that he is
doing something for the best possible reason. It's awfully easy for someone like that to think that the end
justifies the means.*

Kestrel did not *want* the throne; he knew, deep in
his heart, that he was a good musician, but would
make a terrible King. He knew nothing of governance
outside of the little gleaned from a few ballads, which
was hardly the best source of information.

Oh, Rune would have made a better King than me!

The only way to stop the assassins, short of dying
or taking the throne, was to find a way to renounce
his heritage. So, with the help of Talaysen, Rune,
and the Gypsy named Robin whom he had come to
love, he had taken himself out of the picture.
Permanently.

A midnight incursion into the palace was in order;
they held Rolend "hostage" briefly while they
explained themselves and worked a little Bardic magic
to make him *believe* what they were saying. That was
followed by a sunrise abdication — a very public abdication — on Kestrel's part.

And then Kestrel sealed his "unsuitability" by publicly proposing marriage to a Gypsy . . . and being accepted.

The corners of his mouth turned up in a smile he could not repress. The look on her face when he had proposed!

It probably matched the look on mine when she accepted.

No King could ever wed a commoner; the Dukes, Barons, and Sires would never permit it. No nobleman could *ever* wed a Gypsy; by doing so he had rendered not only himself, but all his future offspring, completely ineligible for the throne of Birnam. By that single action he had ensured his safety and that of those with him, no matter how suspicious his uncle might become.

So here they were, riding off to make their way in the world as "mere" Free Bards in a gypsy caravan complete to the last detail and as luxurious in its appointments as it could be and not attract robbers and brigands —

Well, we were "riding" up to an hour ago, anyway.

— the wagon itself a gift of his uncle, who had been only too obviously relieved to see the last of him.

With Talaysen and Rune now safely installed as Rolend's court Bards, and Talaysen actually appointed Laurel Bard to the throne, hopefully Rolend's fears would *stay* safely buried.

But Kestrel had always preferred to hedge his hopes with defenses. *A man who fears shadows can sometimes manufacture enemies, as Gwyna's people say.*

Besides, there had been no point in courting trouble or giving King Rolend any cause for more sleepless nights. The best way to show him that "Prince Sional" was dead and *not* lamented, was to keep as far from Birnam as possible.

Not exactly a hardship, to keep his distance from one little pocket-kingdom when he had all the wonders of Alanda to roam in. He had always been fascinated, even as a very tiny child, by the stories about all the myriad races and cultures of this strange and patchwork world. Now he had the chance to see them firsthand. *All* of them, or at least as many as he could in a single lifetime.

I am far more likely to thank my uncle than hold a grudge against him. This time he didn't bother to hold back the grin. *He is stuck on that stupid block of a throne for the rest of his life, and he will never move more than twenty leagues from his own castle. He will never see the Mintaks and their step-pyramids, the canal-streets of the Loo'oo'alains, the walled fortress-city of the Deliambrens! Why, he probably won't even go under the Elven Hills with the Elves in his own little kingdom!*

Birnam had never been a home to him; in fact, he had never really known a home, nor did he have a clear recollection of a time when he had owned more than he could carry in a thin rucksack on his back. A luxurious wagon was home enough for him! And the road was all the country he needed. Besides, now he need no longer watch his back for the mysterious men who had kept trying to murder him.

His grin widened. Altogether, this was a *wonderful* life, mud, stuck wagon, and all!

"What *are* you grinning about?"

Robin came around the side of the wagon, and scraped a draggle of wet hair out of her eyes as she spoke. Jonny seized her wrist and pulled her over to him, giving her a muddy hug and a passionate kiss, both of which she returned with such interest that he began to think he might steam himself dry in her arms. He let go with reluctance.

"I'm g-g-grinning at th-this!" he said, waving his hand at the wagon, the horses, themselves. "I m-m-mean, think ab-b-bout it! We may be s-s-stuck, but we c-c-can just unhitch th-th-the horses and g-g-get inside if w-w-we want! Th-th-there's nothing s-s-stopping us, if w-w-we d-decide to g-g-give up for a little. It's *ours.* Y-y-you s-s-see?"

She nodded, finally, and a ghost of a smile appeared as her frown of worry faded. "You know, you're right. We don't have to be anywhere. We've got anything a Gypsy could ever want, we *can* get out of the wet if we get tired of trying to fish this thing out of the mud, and the horses will survive a soaking."

He nodded vigorously. "You s-s-see? We aren't even b-b-blocking the r-r-road! W-w-we can w-w-wait unt-t-til someone c-c-comes along who c-c-can give us a h-h-hand! And if anything is b-b-broken, w-we have the m-money to f-f-fix it! Th-th-that's m-m-more than I've ever been able to say b-b-before!" He lowered his eyelids suggestively. "Th-th-there's lots of w-w-ways to get w-w-warm."

Now she grinned right along with him, and tossed her head to get her wet hair out of her eyes. "True," she agreed. "But I would like to think I'd at least tried to get this thing out of the muck before we give up and go inside. The horses are ready any time you are." Her smile turned wistful. "I don't think either of us thought we'd be spending part of our honeymoon trying to boost a wagon out of a pothole."

"A m-m-muddy p-p-pothole," he said, ruefully, looking at the state of his clothing. Impossible now to tell what color it had been, as mud-soaked as it was.

She shrugged, and put her shoulder to the other wheel. "Still, I'll keep telling myself that it is our wagon. We have options I never had before. A year ago I'd have been huddling under a rock overhang if I was lucky, or trying to stay warm under a fallen log if I was not."

He bent to his wheel and she whistled to the horses, who strained forward in their harnesses while the two of them pushed the wagon from behind.

Indeed. This was *their* beautiful, if mud-splashed, wagon. They were safely in Rayden again, and on their way out, after which dear Uncle would have no clue as to where they might have gone. And shoving away at his side was the loveliest — if muddiest — lady he had ever known in all his life. And she had picked *him.*

All right, I'm prejudiced, he admitted, as the wagon rocked a little in place, but otherwise refused to move. *But I'm also not blind, and I think I've seen enough lovely ladies to know true beauty when I spot it!*

After several attempts, the wagon was not budging, the horses were straining, and the rain showed no signs of abating. Robin panted, bending over with her hands braced against her knees, her wet hair dangling down. Kestrel massaged his hands and again tried to see if anything was obviously wrong.

He was beginning to think that there might be something broken or jammed; this wagon had axles built into the body to protect them. A good idea, but it made it difficult to judge what might have gone wrong without the tedious business of taking off the bottom plate.

He sighed, and Robin turned her head and caught his eye.

"Are you s-s-sorry you d-d-didn't get the K-K-King of B-B-Birnam after all?" he asked, ruefully. "You w-w-wouldn't be standing in the m-m-mud if you had."

But Robin only grinned, her good nature restored by the exertion. "Powers forfend!" she replied. "The

King of Birnam would be fair useless getting this blasted wheel out of the mud! Let's try that notion of yours, of heaving up and trying to shore up the wheel while it's up."

It had been a faint hope more than an idea, but if Robin wanted to try it he was game.

"You d-d-do the c-c-counting," he said, with a self-deprecating laugh. "If I d-d-do, we'll b-b-be here all d-d-day!"

CHAPTER TWO

Gwyna shoved little bits of wood under the wheel, using a larger piece to protect her hands in case the wagon slipped back. *Damn the rain. Always comes at the worse possible time.* A rain-soaked lock of hair fell down across her nose in a tangled curl again, and she didn't have the hand to spare to push it out of the way. It tickled, and it got in the way of her vision.

It was hard to stay cheerful when you were dripping wet, your hair was snarled and soaked, and there was mud everywhere the rain didn't wash it away. But there was Kestrel, laboring manfully beside her, for all his slight build, and *he* wasn't complaining. Poor thing, he wasn't much taller than she, nor much more muscled, though regular feeding had put a *little* more weight on him. He still inspired women to want to take him home and feed him pastries and milk.

And then feed him something else entirely, girl, she told herself, and grinned, in spite of the cold rain dripping down her back and the certain knowledge that at the moment she looked more like a drowned kitten than a seductress. Well, he was *hers.* The others would simply have to look and wish.

Even soaking wet and muddied to his ears, he was a handsome piece, though he hadn't a clue that he was, bless his heart. Long, dark hair, as dark as a Gypsy's, now plastered to his head, but luxuriant and wavy when it was dry, set off his thin, gentle face with its huge, innocent dark eyes and prominent cheekbones — definitely a face to set maidens' hearts a-flutter. And when you added in the promise in the sensual mouth and clever hands, well, it set the hearts of no-longer-maidens aflutter, too. And he looked fine, very fine, in the flamboyant colors and garments favored by the Gypsies. He did most of his "speaking," when he could, with eloquent gestures and with his eyes. Right now, they held a cheer that not even their dismal situation could quench. And relief that once again, she had affirmed that she would rather have Kestrel the Free Bard than all the Kings in the Twenty Kingdoms.

And what would I do with a King, if I had one? Thank you, no. She was nothing if not practical. *A King has all of his duties, and little time for pleasure, if he is a good King. I should see him for perhaps an hour or two in the day. I have my Kestrel with me as much as I like.*

The horses stamped restively; she went up to the front of the wagon to reassure them. Thank the Lady that King Rolend had the sense to fling gold at Gypsy Raven with which to outfit a wagon and buy horses for it, rather than trusting such a task to his own stablemen. Not that the King's stablemen were unfit to choose horses, but a pair of pampered highbloods would be ill-suited for tramping the roads in all weathers. No, these mares were as sturdy as they were lovely; two generations out of the wild horses of the Long Downs, and crossbred to Kelpan warmbloods for looks and stamina. Truly a wedding present fit for a Prince, for all that he was Prince no more. A Prince of the road, then.

Why would she ever trade a life bound to one place for her free life on the road, anyway? She'd had a dislike for being tied to one spot *before* her unfortunate encounter with the dark-mage Priest, an encounter that left her with a horror of cages and being caged; now she was positively phobic about the notion.

Kestrel did not know about that, beyond the bare bones, that a renegade Priest-mage had turned her into a bird and caged her. He did not know how she had refused the Priest's demand she be his mistress, and that he had not only turned her into a bird, he had turned her into a bird too heavy to fly! He'd put her in a cage just barely large enough to hold her, and had displayed her by day for all the Kingsford Faire to see as his possession, and by night to the guests at his dinners.

Only the intervention of Rune and Talaysen had freed her; only Talaysen's acquaintance with a decent mage-Priest had enabled them to break the spell making her a bird. It had then rebounded upon its caster, who was still, for all *she* knew, languishing in the same cage he had built for her, in the guise of the ugliest and biggest black bird she had ever seen.

But ever since, the thought of staying in one place for too long brought up images of bars and cages. . . .

No, thank you. No Kings for me! No matter how luxurious, a cage is still a cage.

The horses calmed, she went back to her task of shoving wood wedges under the wheel. Trying to, at any rate. It was awfully hard to tell if she was getting anywhere at all; the mud was only getting worse, not better, as the rain continued to pound them.

"'Ware!" Kestrel warned her with a single word; he could usually manage single words without stuttering. She snatched her hands and board out of the way, called to the horses, and the wagon settled as Kestrel and the mares let it down.

He closed his eyes and sagged against the back of the wagon. She appraised him carefully, trying to measure with her eyes just how exhausted he was, how strained his muscles. *We can't manage too many more of these attempts,* she decided. *He hasn't got them in him, and neither do I.*

She thanked her Lady that he was *not,* like so many men she knew, inclined to overextend himself in the hope of somehow impressing her. That sort of behavior didn't impress her and it inevitably led to the man in question hurting himself and *then* pretending he was not hurt!

Kestrel, on the other hand, was naive enough about women to take what she said at face value — and bright enough not to do something stupid just for the sake of impressing her.

And I am just contrary enough to say precisely what I mean, so all is well. She had to shake her head at herself as she admitted that. *I would not have him change for the world and all that is in it. I am no easy creature to live with. He would not change me, either. So he says, and so I believe.*

She leaned against the wagon, and tried to knot her wet hair at the nape of her neck, but little strands kept escaping and straggling into her eyes. She gave it up as a hopeless cause.

This naivete of his was something to be cherished — if that was precisely the right thing to call it. Perhaps it was simply that he had no one to teach him that women were anything other than *persons.* Truly, he had no one to teach him that women were *anything!*

After all, his childhood was spent with that old Master of his, and not even a female servant about — and the rest of his time was spent trying to earn enough to keep fed and running to save his life.

For whatever reason, he was one of the few men she knew, Free Bards and Gypsies included, who simply *assumed* that she was his partner — his equal in most things, his superior in some, his inferior in others. She had met a few men who were *willing to accept* her as a partner, but Kestrel was only one of three who simply *assumed* the status, and the other two were Raven and Peregrine. There was a difference, subtle, but very real to her, between that *acceptance* and *assumption.* It was a distinction that made a world of difference to her.

He never asked her to prove anything; he simply assumed that if she claimed she could do something, it was true. When she said she could not, he worked with her to find a way around the problem. When he knew how to do something, he asked her opinion before he simply *did* it — and she gave him the same courtesy.

Like this situation that they found themselves in now; neither of them knew a great deal about wagons, at least of this type, and neither of them were large and muscular. Without any arguing, they had each tried the other's suggestions, and when things didn't work, they simply went on to try something else.

Oh, they had arguments; everyone did. But when it counted, they were partners. Arguments were for times of leisure!

In a peculiar way, even standing in the pouring rain, wet and miserable, cold and besmeared with muck, was a wonderful and rare experience. It proved something to her that she had hoped for all along; that she was his friend, companion, the person he trusted, as well as his lover. She could count the number of couples who could say that on one hand, and have fingers left over.

"Ready?" she asked, when it looked as if he had recovered as much as he was going to. He nodded tiredly.

"C-c-can't d-d-do this m-m-much l-longer," he said, simply. "I'm ab-b-bout gone."

"So am I," she admitted. "And so are the mares. But let's give it what we have, yes?"

He nodded. She counted. On *four,* she shouted to the horses, and they all strained to the limit.

Nothing happened. Just as nothing had really happened all the times before, no matter what they had tried.

" 'Ware!" she shouted, and they both let go as the horses slacked the harness. The wagon did not even move a great deal as it settled back.

Her good temper finally broke under the strain. She clenched fists and jaw, and glared at the wagon, the pothole, the mud that now reached halfway to the wheel-hub. "Damn," she swore under her breath, as she backed off and stared at the cursed thing. "Stupid, stubborn, blasted, demon-possessed pile of *junk!*" It was pretty obvious that there was nothing they were able to do alone that was going to free the wheels. They were *not* going to get it out, and everything they did now that it *was* obvious was a wasted effort.

She muttered a few Gypsy curses at the wheels under her breath for good measure. Kestrel just pulled the hair out of his eyes and leaned back so that the rain washed the mud from his face. After a few moments with his mouth open, drinking the fresh rain, he lowered his head and looked at her apologetically, as if he thought that *he* was somehow responsible for the situation.

"It's really s-s-stuck, isn't it?"

She nodded and, in a burst of fading annoyance, kicked the wheel.

As she had *known* it would, this accomplished nothing except to hurt her toe a little.

"Damn," she swore again, but with no real vehemence; she was too tired. Then she sighed. "It's really, really stuck. Or else something is broken. Let's get the horses under whatever cover we can, and try and dry off before we catch something."

As if to underscore the triumph of nature over the hand of man, the skies *truly* opened up, sluicing them with rain that seemed somehow *much* colder than the downpour that had already drenched them.

The horses cooperated, but their harness didn't; stiff leather, soaked with water and heavy, met cold stiff fingers. It took so long to unharness the mares that Robin's temper was well on the way to boiling by the time they had the two sodden beasts hobbled under the scant shelter of a low tree, wrapped in woolen horse-blankets.

They did *not* tether the team under an oak. And they did spread a canopy of canvas over the branches above, giving each beast a nose bag of grain to make up for their sad excuse for stabling.

Robin and Kestrel finally took shelter in the wagon, involuntarily bringing at least four or five buckets of rain in with them through the open door. By then, they were so cold that Robin despaired of ever feeling warm again. The charcoal stove in the wagon took time to heat up; that made it safer in a wooden wagon, but it meant it took a while to make any difference. In the meantime, they huddled in blankets that didn't seem to help very much even though they were dry.

Robin stared at the tiny stove, willing it get warmer. The rain showed absolutely no sign of stopping; she'd had a forlorn hope that once *they* gave up, the rain might, too. She'd even seen a patch of blue to the east, but it had closed up again before it had ever fulfilled its promise.

She and Jonny were too far from any village to walk to shelter, even assuming they would be willing to leave the horses, the wagon and everything in it.

Neither of them were, of course. She didn't know if the mares were broken to saddle; if they weren't, trying to ride them would probably end in someone getting dumped on his head.

Besides, only a fool would walk or ride off and leave everything he owned unprotected. She pulled the blanket closer around her shoulders, and shivered. Rain pounded the wooden roof, making it very hard to hear anyone who wasn't shouting.

If I can just get warm again, this could be pleasant. . . .

Oh, the frustration that a little prosperity could bring! And the unexpected discomforts!

The more you have, the more you have to lose, and the less willing you are to let go of it.

Back when she was on her own, traveling afoot, burdened only by her pack and her instruments, she would never have found herself in such a fix. It seemed so long ago that she had been so footloose, and yet it was no more than a few months ago! Hard to believe that this was the first really *bad* rain of late fall — and she had begun journeying with Lark and Wren at the very end of summer. They didn't even meet Jonny until the first of the Harvest Faires.

If I was still alone, I would be sitting beside a warm fire right now —

Her conscience, which had a better memory than the part of her that controlled wishful thinking, sneered at her and her pretensions. A warm fire? Maybe. *If* she had been clever enough to read the weather signs and *if* she had been lucky enough to get a place at an inn. And even *if* she met both those conditions, there was no guarantee that the fire would be a warm one, and she would probably not be sitting right beside it, but rather off to one side. The paying customers got the flame; more often than not, the entertainers had to make do with the crackle.

Anyway, it would be under a solid roof —

Solid? Maybe. Maybe not. Her conscience called up a long litany of leaking roofs, inns without shutters, stinking little hovels without *windows,* dirt-floored, bug-infested places with only a hole in the center of the roof to let the smoke from the fire in the middle of the room escape. Which it mostly didn't. . . .

Maybe, if she hadn't even found that kind of scant shelter, not a roof at all.

In fact, if she hadn't been clever or lucky, she *could* be shivering in the so-called "protection" of her travel-tent right now, a lot colder and wetter than she was, or even be huddled under a bush somewhere. The wagon was solid, the fire was their own, and they were entitled to the flame and the crackle, once the stove warmed up.

If it ever does.

But memory did supply some honest memories of sitting on the clean hearth of a good, clear fire, in a good quality inn; sipping a mug of spiced cider or even wine, listening to the rain drum on the roof while she tuned her lute. In fact, she had spent whole seasons in such venues, the valued fixture of the tap room who brought in custom from all around.

Will this stove never heat up?

"Th-they s-say a w-w-watched p-pot never b-boils," Kestrel said, his voice muffled under his blanket. "D-do w-watched s-s-stoves n-never heat?"

"I'm beginning to think so," she replied. "I —"

"Hello the wagon! Having trouble?"

The clear tenor voice from outside carried right over the drumming of the rain on the roof. She was out of her blanket and had poked her head out of the door at the rear of the wagon before Kestrel could even uncurl from his "nest." That voice was more than welcome, it sounded familiar!

Another vehicle had pulled up on the road beside them, a wagon much, much larger than theirs. So large, in fact, that it probably had to keep to the major roads entirely, for the minor ones would not be wide enough for it. As it was, there was just barely room for a farm-cart to pass alongside of it. Anything larger would have to go off to the side of the road and wait.

It had tall sides, as tall as a house, and rather than wood, it was made of gray, matte-finished metal. It had glass windows, *real glass,* covered on the inside by shutters. Below the windows were hatches, perhaps leading to storage boxes. It was drawn by four huge horses, the like of which Robin had only seen when the Sires held one of their silly tournaments and encased themselves in metal shells to bash each other senseless.

As if they weren't already senseless to begin with.

The huge beasts stood with heads patiently bowed to the wind and weather, rich red coats turned to a dull brown by the rain, white socks splattered with mud, "feathers" matted. They were beautiful beasts, but she did not envy their driver, for they would eat hugely and be horribly expensive to keep. That was why only the Sires could afford such beasts, although their great strength would be very useful to any farmer. Then again, anyone who could afford a rig like *this* would have no trouble affording the feed for these four huge horses.

Their little Gypsy caravan would easily fit inside this colossus, with room for two or three more.

The driver sat in sheltered comfort inside a porch-like affair on the front, enclosed on the left and right, roofed and floored. He leaned out around the side, just as she tried to make out who or what he was —

and as soon as he saw her, his face was lit by a mixture of surprise and delight.

"*Old Owl!*" she exclaimed, jumping from the back of the wagon to the ground. "By our Lady, I can't think of anyone I'd rather see more!"

Kestrel poked his head out of the door of the wagon just in time to hear Robin address the driver of an utterly amazing vehicle as "Old Owl."

Both made his eyes widen. The wagon was like *nothing* he had ever seen before in his life. It seemed as alien to this road and forest as a coronet on a rabbit. The driver was as astonishing as his wagon, and he certainly saw why Robin — and presumably the other Free Bards — would call him by that name.

He looked *quite* owllike, although he was more human than a Mintak or a Gazner — but much less so than an Elf. While Kestrel stared, the driver grinned down at them both, perfectly protected from the rain by the roof over the driver's box. Kestrel simply gaped at him, unashamed, since he didn't seem to mind.

"Welladay, I can think of places and times I'd *rather* see you in, other than mired in a morass, Gypsy Robin," the driver replied cheerfully, cocking his head to one side. "I suppose now I shall *have* to get you out. If I don't, you'll write some kind of nasty little ditty about me and I shall never be able to show my face in polite company again."

"I?" Robin made innocent eyes at him, and pretended shock. "Why should I do anything like that?"

"Because you are the Gypsy Robin, and no male, human or not, escapes your charm without regretting it." The strange being bowed from the waist, and winked at Kestrel. "Give me a moment to change and I will be down beside you."

Robin snorted, and shook her head. To Kestrel's

bemusement, Gwyna was now as cheerful as if their wagon was safely on the road and the sun was shining overhead. What magic did this man have to make her suddenly so certain he would be able to fix all their problems? "Still a clothes-horse, now as ever! Your wardrobe, no doubt, is the reason for the size of your wagon!"

"How not?" he countered. "Why not?" and disappeared inside.

Kestrel blinked. "Old Owl" — whoever and whatever he was, had been one of the oddest attractive creatures he had ever seen. His face and body — what Kestrel had seen of the body, anyway — had been fairly human. But that was where the similarity ended. He had long, flowing, pale hair growing along his cheekbones, giving his face the masklike appearance of an ancient owl. These were not whiskers or a beard; this was hair, as fine and silky as the shoulder-length hair on his head, and it blended into that hair on either side of his face. To complete the image of an owl-mask, his eyebrows were enormous, as long as Kestrel's thumb, and wing-shaped.

The hair on his head had been cut in some way that made parts of it stand straight up, while parts of it lay flat, all of it forming a fountainlike shape. It gave the man's head a fantastical appearance, and his clothing —

Well, what Kestrel had seen of it, left him dazzled and astonished, and quite, quite speechless. It had certainly rivaled anything he'd seen on any Gypsy; not only was it brightly and brilliantly colored and cut in fantastic folds and draperies with flowing sleeves and a capelike arrangement at the shoulders, but parts of it gleamed with a distinctly metallic sheen, and some had the look of water, and still other parts were as iridescent as an insect wing.

No wonder he had not wanted the mud to spoil it!

First and foremost — who *was* this person, this "Old Owl"? And what was he to Robin? "Wh-wh —" Jonny began.

"Who is that?" Robin asked, turning around to give him a lopsided grin. She waded back to the wagon through ankle-deep mud. "Well, we call him 'Lord' Harperus, or 'Old Owl' since he is something of an honorary Free Bard, he's pulled so many of us out of fixes like this one. No one knows if he's really entitled to the 'Lord' part, but he has piles and piles of money, as much as any Sire, so everyone calls him 'Lord.' He's a Deliambren."

A Deliambren! Kestrel blinked, and his interest sharpened considerably. The Deliambrens were top of the list of beings Kestrel had always wanted to see. They were reputed to be wizardly mechanics, building clockwork creations that could do almost any task. You found their constructions in the homes of the wealthiest of the Barons and Dukes, and the palaces of Kings. Very few Sires could afford the handiwork of Deliambrens, and very few merchants, even Guild Masters. Those who *could* afford them boasted about it.

The Deliambrens knew how to make magical lights that illuminated without creating heat or needing any oil to fuel them. They created boxes that produced music, melody after melody, fifty tunes or more without repetition, boxes no bigger than a wine cask. It was even said they could build wagons that did not need horses to pull them, and conveyances that could fly!

They lived, so Kestrel had been told by his tutor, in a place called "Bendjin." It was a "Free Republic," whatever the hell *that* was; there were no Kings, Sires, Dukes, or anything else there, he'd been told. How they were governed, he had no notion; it sounded completely chaotic to him.

And that was all he knew of them, other than the fact that they had something so complicated it was akin to magic that they used to create their toys. And the toys answered to anyone, mage or not.

"I've n-n-never s-s-seen a D-Deliamb-b-bren," he managed to get out. "D-d-do they all l-l-look l-like th-that?"

Robin laughed, and reached up and hugged him. "Old Owl is not the only one you'll see on the road, and that is just about the only place you ever will see them," she told him, all her good cheer back, now that the stranger had offered his help. "Unless you earn an invitation to Bendjin, that is. They don't make very many of those, so don't get your hopes up. I don't know if they all look *quite* like that, but they are all pretty flamboyant. We call him *Old* Owl because Erdric back at Kingsford is an Owl too, but Harperus is his senior by a century or so."

Kestrel tried not to goggle at that. "*How* old is he?"

She shook her head, as the rain slacked off a little. "I don't exactly know," she replied, after a moment of thought. "Wren said he was at least a hundred years old, and guessed from records and stories that he might be as old as two hundred. That was the best guess he had, but Wren said he couldn't be sure."

He hopped down off the back of the wagon to join her; she gave him a flirtatious kiss. "We'd better get things ready so when he comes out, all he has to do is use our chains to pull us out." Kestrel nodded, and waded through the mud beside her. They were already so wet and mired that a little more wouldn't matter.

"I've been inside Bendjin," she offered, as they got the tow-chains out of the box on the back of the wagon where they were kept safe from rusting in an oiled bag. "Once, when I was very small. They brought in my Clan to entertain for a festival of some kind. I don't think they let anyone but Free Bards and Gypsies inside the walls; I don't think they trust anyone else." She chuckled. "I suppose they know we have no reason to covet their powers, since no Gypsy would ever own anything he couldn't repair himself in a pinch, and no Free Bard would care about anything other than making music."

"W-was it l-like they s-say?" he asked, fascinated by the mere idea of being inside the Deliambrens' mysterious fortress-city.

Robin took her end of the chains and fastened them carefully to the loops built into the frame of the wagon before she answered. "I wasn't very old, but it was rather amazing, even to a child. It was quite dazzling, that's all I can tell you," she said reminiscently, as he copied her movements with the chains on his side. "Lights; that's what I mostly remember. Lights everywhere. Not candles or lamps or anything of that sort. They have lights outside that glow when darkness falls, and little light-globes inside that light up and grow dark again at the touch of a finger. All the colors of lights that you can possibly imagine. They do have wagons that move by themselves, without horses. And they have boat-shaped things that fly. I only saw the little ones; Old Owl told me there were bigger ones that they use for their special trading missions outside Bendjin, and some even bigger ones that they only use once in a while, because they kind of break down a lot."

Kestrel grimaced. He couldn't imagine anything involving a Deliambren *breaking down* —

"I wish I could describe what I saw for you," she concluded, with a little shrug of apology, "but I was only five or six years old. I don't remember much

more than that. Oh, I do recall one other thing; they
had some pet birds that were just as flamboyant as
their costumes, birds that sat on your shoulder and
talked! I played with one for hours, and I really
wanted one, but Old Owl told me that they just
couldn't stand cold, and it would die in the first
winter."

"I'll f-f-find you one th-that w-w-won't," Kestrel
promised, and was rewarded with a smile. A warm and
lovely smile, that said, *You understand.* And he did.
He truly did.

Besides, it was not all that difficult a promise to fulfill. With all of the creatures of Alanda, surely there
was a bird like that somewhere. . . .

"Well!" said Harperus, popping his head out of the
door of his vehicle. "Are you ready?"

"I think so, unless you want to come down here and
look things over first," Robin called up to him.

He nodded; that amazing hair was all tucked under
a shiny hood, the hood of a coat made of the same
shiny blue material. Water slid right off it without
soaking in, as if it were made of bright metal like the
wagon itself. "Good idea. I probably know a bit more
about wagons than you do, little one. Unless you've
studied them since I saw you last, or this young man is
an expert — ?"

Kestrel shook his head, not trusting his voice. He
would surely stutter, and look a fool.

Robin laughed. "This 'young man' is my *vanderlan,*
Old Curiosity."

"You? *Vanderie?*" Harperus seemed as delighted as
he was surprised, which was something of a relief to
Kestrel. "It must be a true-love match then, for *you*
would never settle for less! My felicitations and blessings, my children! Not that you need either, from me,
or anyone else —"

He leapt down to the ground with remarkable agility for someone who was a hundred years old —

Or maybe two hundred!

He held out his hand to Kestrel, who took it and shook it gingerly. Then Harperus kissed Gwyna chastely on one cheek. "And that is all you shall get from me, you young minx!" he said, when she pouted. "Forget your flirtations, please! I have no wish to make your young man jealous or he will begin to look daggers at me!"

When Kestrel grinned shyly, and managed, "R-R-Robin c-can t-t-take c-c-care of hers-s-self," the Deliambren laughed with pure delight.

"I see you have yourself a wise partner, pretty bird," Harperus said with approval. "Now, let me have a look at this bit of a predicament —"

He continued talking as he peered under the wagon, then extracted an object from his coat and did *something* around the axle. Flashes of light came from beneath, and Kestrel wondered what he could be doing under there. . . .

"Are you new to the Free Bards, youngster?" he asked Kestrel, his voice emerging from beneath the wagon as if from the bottom of a well. "I don't recall anyone mentioning someone of your description before —"

Now Kestrel was in a quandary; he wanted desperately to talk to this man — but he was afraid that his stutter would make him sound like a fool.

But then Harperus cocked his head just enough so that he could look out and Kestrel could see one intelligent eye peering up at him. The color of that eye was odd — not quite brown, not quite yellow. A metallic gold, perhaps, with the soft patina of very old metal. "Take it slowly, lad, and take your time in answering. I'm in no great hurry, and you mustn't be ashamed if you have a trifle of trouble speaking. Plenty of intelligent people do; it is often because they are so intelligent that their thoughts run far ahead of their mouths. Simply work with one word at a time, as if you were composing a lyric aloud."

Kestrel was momentarily speechless, but this time with gratitude. "I — have only b-been w-w-with the F-F-Free B-Bards since f-first H-Harvest F-F-Faire."

"We found him, Wren and Lark and I, I mean," Gwyna put in. She gave Kestrel an inquiring glance; he nodded vigorously, much relieved that she wished to tell their story. Better she tell the tale. If he tried, they'd be here all day.

She summed up the entire mad story in a few succinct sentences. Harperus made exclamations from time to time, sounds that were muffled by the fact that he was halfway under the wagon by now. Finally he emerged, amazingly mud-free and dry.

"Fascinating," he said, eying Jonny as if he meant it. "Absolutely fascinating. I must hear more of this, and in detail! I must have a record of all this — it could be very significant in the next few years."

Robin laughed at him. "You and your *datas*," she mock-scolded. "That's all you people are interested in!"

"*Data*," he corrected mildly. "The singular is the same as the plural. It is *data*."

"Whatever," she replied. "You Deliambrens are the worst old maids I ever saw! You can't ever hear a story without wanting *every single detail* of it! Like sharp-nosed old biddys with nothing more on your minds than gossip!"

To Kestrel's surprise, Harperus did not take any-offense at Gwyna's words. "It is all information, my dear child," he told her. "And information is yet another thing that we collect, analyze, and sell. Somewhere, some time, there will be someone who will want to know about this story, for there will be all manner of rumors and wild versions of it before the winter is over. And we will tell him, for a price. And he will trust *our* version, for he will know it to be composed of nothing but the facts. Facts are what we sell, among other things."

"Just so long as you don't sell him who we are and *where* we are," Robin replied sharply, suddenly suspicious. "Those same people could be more interested in using Jonny than in *facts,* my friend. You people —"

"You know better than that," he said, with immense dignity. "Now, however, is not the time to discuss the ethics of information-selling. Firstly, it is very wet —"

"Tell me something I *don't* know!" Robin exclaimed, tossing her sodden hair impatiently.

"— and secondly, I have some bad news concerning your wagon. I fear you have cracked the axle." He *tsk*ed, and shook his head as Robin winced and Jonny bit off a groan. That was something they could not fix themselves; not without help, at any rate. "It is just as well that you could not budge it. You might have caused more damage. If you had attempted to drive on it, that would break it, within a league." He nodded, as Gwyna grimaced. "You must go somewhere there is a cartwright; I do not have the equipment to fix a vehicle such as yours."

"I know where there's a cartwright, and it isn't that far from here but —" Robin began, biting her lip anxiously.

He brightened. "Ah! Well, then in that case, there is no true problem. I can get you out without further damage, and I can tow your wagon without breaking the axle."

Kestrel gaped at him. "How?" he gasped.

Harperus laughed. "Watch!" he said. "And see! Am I not a Deliambren? There will be wonders! Or at least" — he amended, with a sheepish smile — "there will be *winches*."

CHAPTER THREE

There were, indeed, winches; just as Harperus promised. Or *a* winch, with a hook on the end of a cable, a winch that swung out from the back of Harperus' vehicle. Once Gwyna had an idea of what he intended, she made him wait while she extinguished the fire in the charcoal stove; there was no point in risking coals spilling and setting fire to the entire wagon. It was quite a powerful winch, although not at all magical, simply very well made. Harperus maneuvered his huge wagon so that the winch was as close to the back of their wagon as possible without the wheels of his vehicle leaving the firm roadbed. Then he unwound the cable, fastened the hook of his winch to the chains they already had in place, and enlisted the help of both Bards with the business-end of the winch.

It required hand-cranking; if there were any of the magical machines legend painted anywhere in or on the wagon, they were not in evidence. As the two Bards helped Harperus turn the capstan, the cable and chains slowly tightened; then, the rear rose with a wide and amusing variety of odd noises as the mud fought against releasing the wheels.

The mud was no match for Harperus' winch. Jonny was relieved at how relatively easy it was to crank it up by hand. He knew a little, a very little, about machinery. This winch must have some clever gearing to make it so easy to use.

As the wagon creaked and groaned, the wheels pulled free with a sucking sound, and rose above the muck. Blobs of thick mud plopped back into their parent pothole.

They didn't stop there. Harperus continued to winch the wagon higher, until the damaged rear was well above the roadbed. Jonny hoped that everything was stowed away properly in there. If it wasn't — well, there was no hope for it. It was going to be a mess inside, with things tumbled everywhere.

A small price to pay for getting out without losing the axle while moving. *That* would have caused more than a mess; they might have lost the whole wagon. They surely would have been injured, perhaps seriously, depending on how fast they would have been going when the axle broke.

The rain finally slacked off, and by the time Harperus was ready to actually haul their wagon up onto the road, it had thinned to a mere drizzle.

They fastened the halters of the mares to the front — now the rear — of their wagon, stowed the harness away in the exterior storage boxes under the driver's seat, but left the blankets on them, and put away the tarpaulin and nose bags. The mares didn't look unhappy about moving; they couldn't have been very comfortable in the rain and chill wind. Before too very long, everything was ready.

Harperus checked and double-checked everything, from the set of the hook to the lock on the winch, before he had convinced himself that all was as it should be. Then, with a self-satisfied grin, he handed them both up to the driver's bench on his wagon. Jonny admired the arrangement as he took his place; there was a clever set of steps built into the front of the wagon, and the front panel had a door set into it. Harperus took his place beside them, handling the reins of all four horses with the confidence of long practice.

He clucked to them and shook the reins. The four huge horses leaned forward into their harnesses, pulling with a will.

The wagon crawled forward; the wheels creaked and squealed, and more creaks and groans came from the Gypsy wagon behind them as Harperus sought to pull it free.

Sucking mud made obscene sounds that sent Robin into giggles. Kestrel leaned around the side of the driver's box and gazed anxiously back at their precious wagon.

But Harperus knew what he was doing. The wagon was fine; protesting, but fine. Inch by inch, bit by bit, Harperus pulled it free of the mud that had held them trapped for most of the day. As the front wheels rolled up onto the roadbed with a rumble and a crunch of gravel, Kestrel let out a sigh of relief, and pulled his head back in under the shelter of the roof.

Harperus regarded him with faint disappointment. "You doubted me!" he accused.

"N-not y-you," Kestrel protested. "I w-w-wasn't sure ab-b-bout *our* w-w-w-wagon!"

"Ah." Harperus beamed with the pleasure of accomplishment, then his expression changed to one of concern. "Oh, you two look near-frozen. And you're certainly soaked. There are blankets under the bench; wrap yourselves up in them before you catch something."

Kestrel was a little disappointed; he wanted, badly, to have a look inside the fascinating vehicle, and it would have been nice if Harperus had invited them to go inside to warm up. He sighed as he fished around under his seat with one hand until he encountered something soft that felt like cloth.

He pulled it out; it was a blanket, with no discernible weave, of a tan color nearly the same as all the mud. It seemed awfully light and thin to do any good, but it was better than nothing. Or so he thought, until he actually wrapped it around his shoulders and head.

Suddenly he was warmer; *much* warmer. And — was he getting drier, as well? It seemed so! He stared at Harperus in surprise; the Deliambren returned his look blandly.

Maybe all the wonders weren't inside the wagon after all!

He began examining the "driver's box" covertly, while pretending to watch the horses.

They were under as much shelter as most porches on a house provided. The driver's seat was well-padded and quite soft, covered with something that looked superficially like leather, but didn't feel quite like leather. And now that they were moving, there was a gentle stream of warm air coming from underneath it, drying his feet.

The box itself was quite spacious, with a great deal of room behind the driver's bench, more than had been apparent from the ground. There was quite enough room for all three of them on the bench, side-by-side, and there was enough room for a second bench behind the first. Maybe Harperus intended to put one in some day, for passengers who would rather not ride inside the wagon. . . .

Then he noticed something else; now that they were on the move, the horses did not seem to be leaning into their harness at all. In fact, on a closer look, he would have said, if he were asked, that they were guiding the wagon rather than pulling it. They certainly weren't straining in the least.

Could it be that the wagon propelled itself, and their presence was a deception?

It was certainly a very good possibility —

But his curiosity would have to go unappeased; he had no way of checking his supposition, and if Harperus did not want them to know something, then that was his business.

Still, that didn't help assuage his curiosity in the least.

The Deliambren was the first nonhuman being Kestrel had ever seen up close, with the exception of the Elves who had attended the wedding. There had been both a Mintak and a Gazner at King Rolend's palace, but they were ambassadors of some kind, and he had not wanted to approach them.

That had been more caution on his part; he could not have gone near them without causing new suspicions in his uncle's mind just when it had been settled.

He had been very, very careful how he looked and acted around Rolend's court. Why would he be talking to a foreign ambassador after he had renounced his title? Rolend would have immediately suspected he was intriguing. Perhaps plotting with nonhumans, looking for a way to get power again. Surely, that is how Rolend would have thought of it.

He had told himself that he had the rest of his life to talk to anyone he wanted. What would have been the point of creating trouble when eventually he would find other nonhumans to talk to freely?

He wanted to ask Lord Harperus thousands of questions. Harperus seemed amazingly approachable, and quite affable. Gwyna had closed her eyes and was settling back for a nap, so he wouldn't be interrupting anything *she* had planned. "Wh-what are y-y-you d-doing out here, L-L-Lord?" he asked, trying to frame each word carefully. Gwyna snuggled into his shoulder, and gave him a little smile and a nudge of encouragement.

"What is my reason for being on the road, do you mean?" Harperus replied, and chuckled, as Robin grimaced a little. "Collecting information. As your dear lady will tell you, we Deliambrens do an inordinate amount of that. This *is* a much more elaborate vehicle than I am wont to use, however, as I assume our Gypsy Robin has noted. I am also acting as an advance scout, of a kind, this time. My people will be embarking on a most ambitious project shortly, and I am establishing contacts for them, so that they will never lack for allies on the ground in the initial part of the journey."

"Ambitious project?" Robin said. "Just what do you mean by that?" She sounded suspicious again, and her eyes opened, but narrowed thoughtfully. "Are you planning something we Gypsies ought to know about?"

"Nothing sinister, my dear," Harperus replied soothingly. "In fact, it is something that your people will find useful, I think. We intend to make maps — maps of all of Alanda, eventually, and those, like the Gypsies, who assist us will get maps for their efforts. Road maps, terrain maps, population maps, resource maps — we intend to build something we call a 'data base,' so that if someone has an abundance of corn or copper, coal or pre-Cataclysm artifacts, we will be able to find a buyer for him."

"Which information you will no doubt give him for a price," Robin said dryly. But despite her heavy irony, she had relaxed again, and was braiding her hair.

"And, if he does not have the means to transport his product, or fears being cheated, we can act as broker," Harperus replied, just as blandly. "Why not? We also have an *honorable* intent, though you might not believe it, Gypsy Robin," he added. "We intend to see to it that those with superior forces do not take those resources that do not belong to them. I mean this," he finished, his voice suddenly without any hint of humor. "I am quite, quite serious about this. Before the Cataclysm, my people acted as a policing force among the stars. Presumably, the rest of them still do, somewhere. Now that we have stabilized our position and regained our mobility, our mission can be resumed, albeit on a smaller scale. It is, after all, in our interest to see that no culture is exploited. They are all potential customers, when all is said and done."

"Huh," Gwyna replied. "So now you're looking for more allies than just the Gypsies?"

"Allies on the ground, yes," Harperus replied. "We cannot do everything. We will need folk we can trust in or near every land we travel through, in case there are things we need, or repairs we need to make."

Allies on the ground? An interesting choice of words. Did they imply that this "project" would involve people traveling through the air? Were they going to bring one of those air-wagons Robin had described out into Alanda?

How much dared he ask, without becoming impolite?

Or worse; perceived as dangerous? Harperus had power, money, and resources he could not even dream of. It would be very foolish to make Harperus think he might be a threat of any kind.

"H-h-how long h-h-have you kn-known R-Robin?" he asked, instead of the questions he *wanted* to ask. Perhaps, after feeling the Deliambren out, he could ask them later.

"Oh, since she was very young," Harperus told him, turning to wink at him. The skin around the Deliambren's eyes crinkled when he smiled, and he pulled back the hood of his coat and shook his hair free. "I first met her when her Clan came to perform at the

Four Worlds Festival. She was always getting into places she was not supposed to, and I was detailed to keep an eye on her."

"Me?" Gwyna exclaimed. "I never —" Then she began to cough, as if she had not intended to say anything.

"Most adventuresome was her foray into the upper reaches of the butterfly conservatory; I had no notion that a five-year-old could climb so high," Harperus continued as if he had not heard her protest. "Most interesting was when she decided that the fountain in Hazewood Square required fish, and began transporting them, in her bare hands, one at a time, from the view-ponds in the Aquarium nearby. Amazingly, they all survived the trip! It was quite a surprise to the fountain-keepers, however."

He turned to Gwyna, who was blushing furiously. "How *did* you catch them, anyway? I have never been able to figure that out."

"I tickled them," she said, in a small, choked voice.

"You tickled them." Harperus shook his head, and peered ahead through the curtain of rain. "Some sort of obscure Gypsy secret, I suppose." He turned back to Kestrel. "At any rate, I have been the 'adopted uncle' for any number of Gypsy youngsters, and she is one of them. Although I must admit that our dear Robin is one of my favorites."

Kestrel relaxed a trifle; if Robin had known him *that* long ago, then certainly he was not one of the odd creatures you heard about from time to time whose behavior was so bizarre you never knew whether they considered themselves your dearest friend or your worst enemy. "D-d-do you d-d-do m-much tr-traveling?" he asked.

"I would say that I am probably on the road for about half of the year," Harperus said, after a moment of thought. The wagon swayed slightly beneath them; nothing like the rough jouncing of their own little caravan. "Some of us enjoy traveling, trading, and gathering information, and those of us who do spend as much time out and about as we may. Usually we travel in wagons about the size of yours, and there is very little to distinguish it from a Gypsy caravan. Frankly, dear boy, I would *not* have taken this vehicle if it were not for two things, and one of them is that it can defend itself from an unpleasant visitor. It is far too conspicuous for my liking."

A little shiver ran down Kestrel's back at that. *It can defend itself . . .* He could not even begin to imagine what that could imply. He did not want to find out at first hand. And he was very glad that Harperus did not consider them "unpleasant visitors."

"Have you made any good bargains lately?" Gwyna asked casually. Harperus brightened at that, and began rattling off a number of trades that he considered to be something of a coup. A "laser imaging system" ("still functional, if you can believe it!") for a small glass-smelting furnace; a "complete cache of memory crystals" for an equal number of precious stones. Or rather, Kestrel assumed they were precious; Harperus referred to them as "cultured" pearls, rubies, and sapphires. Kestrel was not certain just what "cultured" meant. Perhaps they were better educated than other gems. Something else Harperus said made him feel a little better.

"You know, value lies in rarity, really," the Deliambren told Gwyna, when she raised her eyebrow and asked who had gotten the *real* bargain. "They were using the memory crystals for jewelry, and valued them no more than quartz. We simply gave them something better suited to display — and tripled *our* library. To us, memory crystals are rare. To them, our cultured stones are. Everyone benefits, and no one feels cheated. That is the essence of a good bargain."

Gwyna laughed and told him he would never make a horse-trader, and then settled back for a *real* nap against Kestrel's shoulder as the rain changed to a dismal drizzle. He held her with an arm around her shoulders, supporting her so that she could nap, as the unknown source of warmth beneath their seats dried them all and made her drowsy.

Harperus patiently waited through Kestrel's stuttering, and answered all of his questions, though Jonny could not tell just how much of what he said was evasion. Finally he turned the tables on the Free Bard and began his own series of questions.

Mostly, he concentrated on Kestrel's own story, and seemed particularly fascinated by the intervention of Rune and Talaysen and the latter's discovery of the power of Bardic Magic.

"I have often suspected something of the sort existed among you humans," Harperus said thoughtfully. "Particularly in light of some things I have seen Gypsy Bards do — calming crowds that were in an ugly mood, or charming coins out of the previously unwilling. Fascinating. And you have this power?"

"Wren s-s-says s-s-so," Kestrel replied, but with uncertainty. "And he says G-G-Gwyna does too. I th-think he's r-r-right. B-but I d-d-don't know if I w-w-w-want t-t-to use it s-s-since it c-can c-cause as m-much t-trouble as it s-solves."

Harperus nodded, his face very still and sober. "I can understand that — but you may be forced to. You should at least master this power before it masters you. Not learning to use it could be more hazardous than mastering it."

Jonny shook his head.

"If you do not learn how to control this 'magic,' it

may act without your knowledge or control," Harperus amended. "Let me give you an example. Some peoples we have encountered have the power to read the thoughts of others — and if they do not learn how to do this at their will, it happens without control, and they can be overwhelmed by intruding thoughts so that they do not know who, where, or even *what* they are. Do you understand now?"

Kestrel nodded, then. And Harperus was right; if he did not learn how it "felt" to invoke this magic, he might use it when he didn't want to, and that could have some unfortunate consequences. Especially if he was using it on someone who had the ability to *tell* when magic was being used, and had a reason to resent it being used on him!

"If I may bring up a possibly delicate subject?" Harperus said, carefully. "Your — ah — difficulty in speaking?"

Kestrel flushed. "Wren th-thinks it's b-because of the f-f-f-fever I c-c-caught when w-w-we esc-c-caped B-B-Birnam."

Harperus shook his head. "I would think not. From all that I know, such a problem is more because of some kind of extreme upset in the past. Your escape, I would say, is itself to blame, and the fear and stress you went through. Not the fever. My people have been known to treat such things, and they are usually successful. May I offer some advice?"

Jonny nodded eagerly. Wren had some advice to give, but he had been no expert, and admitted it. No one else had anything to say on the subject. Robin didn't seem to care — but it would have been so wonderful to tell her all the things she deserved to hear without falling all over the words!

"As I said, this is sometimes the case of your mind running ahead of your words. First, you must learn to relax, and think about the *words,* not about what your listener is going to think when he hears you." Harperus smiled as he saw Jonny's eyes widen with surprise. "You see, some of this is also from tension. You wish to make a good impression, so you tense up. Your mind runs on ahead, and ceases to control your speech, so the tension makes you stammer. You stutter — you fear you are making a bad impression — you grow tenser — and you stutter more. You try to speak faster, to get your words out through the stuttering, and this makes you more tense, which makes it worse yet. If you relax, and take things at their own, slow pace, you will find your problem easing. Think of each word as a note in a melody, and pronounce it with the care you have in singing, and *do not think* about your listener. When you sing, what are you thinking of? The audience, or the song?"

"The s-s-song!" Kestrel replied in surprise. "I alw-w-ways r-relax when I s-sing!"

"And you do not stutter, I wager." Harperus shrugged. "This is how I would begin to overcome the difficulty. The rest is much, much patience. It will take a very long time, and you must not be discouraged. It took, perhaps, ten years to establish this pattern in you. It cannot be unlearned in a day, or a week, or even a year, necessarily. But you will improve, a very little, every time you speak, and people who have not heard you for some time will be astonished at what you think is no progress at all."

Kestrel bit his lip and stared at the ears of the nearest horse. He *wanted* a magical cure; for Harperus to touch his lips with a machine, and make the stutter go away.

But something that could take the stutter away might not keep it away. And understanding it might. . . .

He raised his eyes and stared at the road ahead, misty in the steadily falling rain, and followed the Deliambren's advice, concentrating on each word.

"Thank you, L-Lord Harperus," he managed, with a minimal stammer. "I will t-try your adv-vice."

"I hope that it works," Harperus replied earnestly. "And try to keep this in mind, every time you are tempted to hurry your words. It will take *longer* to get them out if you stammer than if you took your time with them. You are a good young man, and a bright one. You do not speak without much thought. A wise man will be willing to wait to hear your words, and you need not waste them on a fool."

He might have said more, except that at that moment there was a polite tap on the wall of the driving box behind them.

Kestrel's head snapped around, as the back of the box slid open. So *that* was how Harperus had gotten in and out of his wagon! And evidently Harperus was not alone on this "collecting" mission of his —

"Harperus," said a deep, resonant voice from the darkness beyond the open door, "I wonder if I might join you and your guests?" The opening was shrouded in shadow, and all Jonny saw was a vague, humpbacked shape in the darkness. But the voice sent a thrill of pleasure down his spine. It was a pure delight simply to hear it; a deep bass rich with controlled vibrato.

"Certainly, T'fyrr," the Deliambren replied immediately. "There are no xenophobes here. I'm sure my friends would welcome meeting you and your company."

"I am pleased to hear it," the voice replied, and the shapeless figure, who was shrouded in fabric, or an all-enveloping cloak, ducked its head and came out into the light.

It was *not* wearing a cloak.

As it carefully closed the door at the rear of the box behind it with one taloned hand, and folded down a hitherto-invisible seat from the side of the box, the "shrouding cloak" proved to be a set of wings, and the hood, head-feathers. Gwyna woke from her half sleep to glance at, and then stare at, Harperus' road companion; T'fyrr was nothing more or less than a *true* nonhuman, an enormous bird-man.

As the being arranged himself on the seat with a care to those folded wings and a tail that must have made most chairs impossible for him, Harperus made introductions. "T'fyrr, this is Gwyna, who is also called Robin. She is a Gypsy and a Free Bard, and I believe I have mentioned her before. This is her husband, Jonny, who is called Kestrel; he is also a Free Bard. As you know, T'fyrr, all Free Bards have trade-names, so that the Bardic Guild will never know precisely who they truly are. In public, you must call them 'Robin' and 'Kestrel.' My friends, this is T'fyrr."

The huge beak — quite obviously that of a raptor — gaped open in what was very likely T'fyrr's attempt at a smile. "I see from your expressions that you have never met one of my kind before this. You should not be surprised, since the Haspur do not travel much outside their own land, and few wish to venture into it. My land is very mountainous, and since we fly, we have not made such niceties as *roads* and *bridges*. This makes it difficult for the wingless — and thus, the harder to invade."

"So you keep it that way." Robin had recovered enough to show her sense of humor. "As a Gypsy, I approve. Our way to keep from being hunted and hounded is never to stay in one place for more than a day or two. The best defense is to let something besides yourself provide the 'weapons' and barriers."

"So we say. Much talk of weapons and dangers, but our world is not a kind one," T'fyrr said towards Harperus in what must have been a private joke. The avian had very little difficulty with human speech, despite his lack of lips, and Jonny was completely fascinated. How could something with that huge, stiff beak manage human words?

He watched closely as T'fyrr spoke. "Your t-t-tongue!" he blurted aloud, without thinking.

T'fyrr intuited what he meant with no difficulty, and laughed, a low, odd sort of caw. "It is very mobile, yes. A kind of finger, almost. This is a good thing, for I, like the two of you, am a singer of songs, and I am thus not limited to those of my own people."

"You're a Bard?" Gwyna exclaimed. "Do they have such things among your folk?"

"A kind of Bard, indeed, though I am far more like the Free Bards; we do not have anything like this 'Guild' Harperus has told me of." He made a clicking sound that expressed very real disapproval. "They seek to cage music, or so it would seem. I like them not. It is a pursuit for fools; a waste of intellect."

Gwyna grimaced. "We don't like them either. Free Bards don't believe in caging anything, music, people, or thoughts."

Within moments, the two of them were immersed in a deep discussion of freedom, thought, the politics of both, and other philosophical considerations, much to Harperus' amusement. Jonny was completely content with the situation, since it gave him the opportunity to study T'fyrr to his heart's content.

The only thing at all human about the bird-man was his voice and his stance; upright on two legs. He had just told them that the wings he bore on his back were entirely functional, and Jonny would have given a great deal to see him in flight. As large as he was, his wingspan must be very impressive.

He was as completely feathered as any bird Jonny had ever seen, from the top of his head to his "knees." His "hands" were modifications of his "feet"; both had sharp talons on fingers and toes, and scaled skin stretched over bone, with prominent thin, strong muscles beneath the skin. Those feet and hands were formidable weapons, Kestrel was quite certain — and he was just as certain that, in a pinch, T'fyrr would not hesitate to use his strong, sharp beak as a weapon as well.

T'fyrr's chest was very deep, much deeper than the chest of a human, and probably accounted for the resonance of his voice. In color he was a gray-brown, with touches of scarlet on the very edges of his wings and tail.

He wore "clothing" of a sort; a close-tailored wrapping that covered his torso without impeding the movement of any limbs or his wings and tail. It did not look very warm, and Jonny did not blame T'fyrr for staying in the shelter of the wagon until now. An odd, spicy scent came from his feathers — or perhaps, from his clothing — when he moved, very pleasant and aromatic.

But it was his voice that interested Jonny — as a musician. There were over- and under-tones to his speaking voice that made Jonny sure his singing voice would be incredibly rich. It would surely sound as if it were three people singing in close harmony rather than one.

"I am a folklorist," he said at last, when the discussion of philosophy ended in mutual agreement. "I am collecting songs, most particularly songs of what my people refer to as the 'outreach era,' when we first ventured outside of our borders after the Cataclysm. We have long known of the Deliambrens and in fact have traded with them for certain rarities. When it became obvious that to complete my quest for certain knowledge, I would have to go outside the Skytouching Mountains and the aeries of my people, I knew whom I must recruit to my efforts."

He nodded at Harperus, who chuckled and bowed. "I think it was a matter of mutual recruitment," Harperus said modestly. "After all, there are things even Deliambrens cannot do, and that is to fly without a machine. We are trading in skills. He originally pledged to aid me in return for Deliambren aid. When I asked if he would aid me now, he agreed. He is to scout by air for me; I am to help him continue his musical quest —"

"He and his people have a way of capturing music and sound and holding it. We had this ability before the Cataclysm, but we have lost the skill of making the devices, as well as the tooling," T'fyrr said, before Harperus could finish his sentence. "So there you have it. We aid each other, and we each have skills the other does not. I had been learning the songs I did not know from Harperus' collection; at about the time I had learned all that he had, he decided to go out on this collecting venture and asked if I would pay my debt by accompanying him. When I learned he would be visiting some of the lands where my songs originated, I agreed, of course."

Jonny was completely fascinated, and a bit dazzled. After years of *hearing* about exotic creatures and never meeting one, he had just encountered, not one, but *two* in the same day!

So, while Gwyna engaged both Harperus and T'fyrr in yet another discussion, this time concerning politics, he simply sat quietly and watched and listened with every nerve.

❖   ❖   ❖

Gwyna was charmed by Kestrel's open fascination with both Lord Harperus and T'fyrr, although she did not share it — or at least, not to the same extent. She had been around nonhumans all of her life, after all. Her Clan had often been asked to perform by Harperus, and there were any number of talented linguists in her family, so they were often requested as translators wherever they went. While she had never seen a bird-man before, and she was intrigued by the sheer novelty of such a creature, the novelty wore off fairly quickly. She was far more interested in what Harperus and his companion had seen and heard so far on this trip.

And in the philosophies of an avian race, which to her seemed very complimentary to the Gypsy way of life.

Harperus' wagon astounded and intrigued her far more than either Harperus or his friend. She didn't often lust after anything material, but she had the feeling that the more she saw of this wonderful conveyance, the more she would want it.

For one thing, it was quite obvious to anyone who knew horses that this thing was propelling itself. The horses were only there for guidance. And she had not missed the fact that Harperus had disconnected some esoteric device *before* he had asked for their help in winding up the winch. If she and Kestrel had not been present, he probably would not have used that capstan at all. Doors appeared in walls that seemed solid, seats could be folded down out of nowhere. The wagon itself had glass windows, with metal sides that obviously required neither painting nor maintenance. What a time-saver that would be! There was none of the jouncing around associated with their vehicle, and she rather doubted that Harperus would ever suffer the inconvenience of a broken wheel or a cracked axle.

The heated air coming up beneath their seat must be coming from somewhere, and only gave a hint of how comfortable the interior of this vehicle must be. She already knew about the Deliambrens' "magical" heating and lighting, and she could not imagine Harperus doing without either.

And Harperus' little dropped comment about how the wagon could "defend itself"—

There must be wonder upon wonder inside this vehicle, and she wanted to see the inside, badly.

And yet, if she did — she would *have* to try to calculate just how much it would take to get the Deliambrens to part with enough of their precious "technology" to give her something like the luxurious appointments in this thing. And she had the horrible suspicion that it would require selling herself, Jonny, and any children unto the ninth generation into virtual slavery to acquire it.

But wouldn't they thank you for it every time they woke in warmth or cool comfort?

Maybe if she saved Harperus' life, or something . . .

Even as part of her was thinking these thoughts, the rest was aghast. How could she *want* anything that badly? Wasn't she a Gypsy and a Free Bard? How could she even think about becoming tied down to anything or anyone for the sake of a mere possession?

But — ! that interior voice of greed wailed.

To get her mind off that greedy little inner self, she turned the subject to politics. The Deliambrens always wanted to hear about politics, for politics affected trade, and trade was a large part of their life.

And there were serious changes occurring, changes that seemed minor and subtle, but could build to devastating results.

"It isn't just the Bardic Guild, though it's the worst of the lot. What Talaysen thinks is that the Guilds are trying to get as much power as the Dukes," she said, after describing some of the troubles the Bardic Guild had been causing for the Free Bards. "And the High King seems to be letting them get away with it."

Harperus looked troubled. "I fear that is because the High King has lost interest in governing the lesser Kings," he said, after a moment. "There is much unrest among the Twenty Kings, and more still among the nobles. Many of them have gone back to feuding, quarrels which would have been strictly squashed a few years ago. There is something amiss in the High King's court."

"What is worse, to my mind, is that the Guild and the Church seem to be working together to cause problems for anyone who does not agree to the rules of the Guild and Church," Gwyna said. "And the High King is letting them get away with this."

"But the twenty human Kingdoms are but a small part of Alanda," T'fyrr objected, flipping his wings impatiently. "They are insignificant in scale! Surely, Harperus, you concern yourself too much with them —"

"They are a small part, it is true, but they are strategically placed," Harperus pointed out. "If there is war among them, as there was in the days before the High King, they can effectively cut us off from many things that we need."

"And as you have often pointed out to me, humans breed like rabbits," Gwyna interjected with some sarcasm. "They may only be the Twenty Kingdoms, but they have spread out to occupy a great deal more territory than they held originally. We aren't a peaceful species, Harperus. And I don't care *how* superior your weapons are, my friend, enough bodies with spears and swords can take over that precious Fortress City of yours, either by treachery or by siege. While they may not have the stomach for losses that great, they can certainly lock you inside that Fortress for ever and aye."

"That had not escaped our notice," was all Harperus said. But though his tone of voice was mild, she detected an edge to it. "This is the other of the reasons why I was willing to take this particular vehicle. I can leave small devices now that can collect more information without the need for human agents. I fear that we will have need of such information."

Gwyna sighed. "Are we heading for the Waymeet between Westhaven and Carthell Abbey?" she asked. "If we are, that would be a good place to talk to people and to leave one of your little 'collectors,' both. I'm certain that the Waymeet family will give you no difficulty over leaving such a thing."

At Harperus' nod, T'fyrr asked with puzzlement, "What is a Waymeet? You have not told me of this."

"I did not tell you because we were not going there until we encountered our two young friends," Harperus replied. "But Robin tells me that there is a cartwright there, and a cartwright is what they most urgently need at the moment."

"The Gypsies created the Waymeets," Gwyna told the Haspur. "We created them, and we continue to run them, even though now there are a number of non-Gypsies who know about them and use them." She thought for a moment; she had lived with the knowledge of Waymeets all her life, and had never needed to describe them to anyone before. "You find them just off the major trade roads," she continued, finally. "They're a special, permanent camping-place, with a caretaker, certain things like bathhouses and laundries, a small market, and a population of craftsmen. One thing is pretty important; they're all on land that doesn't *belong* to anyone, not Duke nor Sire, not

Guild nor Church. And another; no one stays there more than a few days at a time, except when bad weather really bogs things down. I know there will be a cartwright there, which solves *our* problem, and there will be people for Harperus to talk to with fresher news than ours."

T'fyrr nodded as he followed her words. "And the caretaker charges a certain amount for the amenities?" he hazarded. "Such things would make camping there more attractive than camping in the wilderness. Civilized."

"Exactly so," she said, nodding. "They're also, as the Old Owl here well knows, excellent places to pick up information, gossip, or both. People speak more freely there — and if *I* pass the word," she added, a little arrogantly, "they will speak very freely to him."

Harperus smiled. "I am certain of that, Gypsy Robin. For all of us, this Waymeet will be most productive."

CHAPTER FOUR

Stillwater Waymeet lay just off the main trade road, down a lane of its own that was — currently, at least — in better repair than the trade road. The Sire had not been keeping up his road repairs lately; another sign that the King of Rayden had become lax in seeing that his nobles attended to their duties. Probably the road would remain in poor repair until a Guild Master or a high Churchman had to pass this way. Ruts were the least of the problems along the trade road; much worse were the potholes at the edge of the road that gradually crept into the right-of-way and formed an actual hazard to traffic. By contrast the Waymeet lane was smooth, graded gravel, well-tended, and potholes had not been permitted to form on the edge.

There was a single sign at the joining of the lane and the road, a sign that said *Stillwater Waymeet* and had little carvings of a bucket of water, a caravan, and an ear of wheat, signifying that water, camping, and food were available. As large as it was, Harperus' wagon negotiated the turn easily, although the wagon filled the entire lane and the wheels were a scant finger length from the edge of the gravel.

Robin yawned discretely; it had been a very long day, and trying to get their wagon out of the mud had pretty much done her in. As thick as the clouds were, there had been no real "sunset," only a gradual thickening of the darkness. It *was* dusk now, though; a thick, blue dusk with darker blue shadows under the trees, and she was going to be very glad to stop, get something hot to eat, and get to sleep.

"How long is it to the Waymeet itself?" Harperus asked, probably puzzled by the fact that the long tunnel of trees arching over the lane gave the illusion that it went on without any end. Most of the leaves had fallen from the seasonal trees, but there was a healthy percentage of evergreens along here that kept the lights of the Waymeet from showing. Despite the constant rain, the bitter scent of dead leaves hung in the air along the lane, and the gravel was covered with a carpet of fallen leaves that muffled the steady clopping of the horses' hooves.

"Not far," Robin assured him. "There's a slight, s-shaped bend up ahead that you can't see from here; it keeps this from being a straight line to the road. Keeps people from driving up like maniacs and running someone over."

The Gypsies were responsible for the creation of the Waymeets, building them up from a series of regular camping grounds along the roads. When a camping site always seemed to hold at least two Gypsy families and never was completely unoccupied, people would naturally begin to improve it. After a while, permanent, if crude, amenities (protected fire pits, stocks of wood, bathing and laundry areas, wells) were built at such places, slightly more elaborate than similar arrangements at large Faire-sites. With people always at a site, there was little chance that such amenities would be vandalized, and incentive to take care of them. Then the next logical extension was for someone to decide he was tired of living on the road, but did not want to live in a town —

That unknown Gypsy had settled instead at one of those camping grounds, and had built not only living quarters for himself and his family, but a bathhouse, a laundry, and a trading post, and had begun selling odds and ends to the others who came to camp. This had the result of bringing in more campers; after all, why take the possibly dangerous step of camping alone when you could go somewhere, not only safe, but which boasted some small luxuries? From that moment, it was only a matter of time before others who wished to retire in the same manner found other such sites and did the same thing.

Then someone had the bright notion to open the sites up to *anyone* who traveled the trade-roads, for a fee.

The results of these enterprises were varied. Some Waymeets wound up resembling an inn, but without a building to house travelers. Some turned out, as was the case with Stillwater, rather along the lines of a village, without the insularity.

Robin had been to Stillwater many times. The camping grounds were laid out in sections for wagons and for tents, and patrolled by the proprietor's two tall sons and three of his cousins, to discourage theft and misbehavior. There was clean water in both a stream and a well. It also boasted a bathhouse and laundry, a cartwright, a blacksmith, and a carpenter. A small store sold the kinds of things people who traveled often broke, lost, or forgot; it served as a trading post for those who had goods to trade or sell. The fee to camp was minimal, the fees charged for the other services reasonable. Virtually all of the permanent residents were Gypsies, since generally any Gypsy who wished to retire from the road but still wanted the excitement of life on the road looked for a Waymeet that needed another hand about the place. At a Waymeet it was possible to have most of the excitement and change of traveling without ever leaving your home.

Waymeets were well known, and their locations clearly marked on most maps, since most experienced travelers with their own wagons used them — often in preference to the Church hostels set up for similar purposes. Most merchants would rather pay the higher fees of the Waymeets rather than endure the lodging-with-sermons one got at the hostels. Only in truly vicious winter weather were the hostels more popular than the Waymeets.

The result was a peculiar village where the entire population changed over the course of a week — more often than that in summer, when travel was easier.

As they rounded the first curve, the lights of the Waymeet began to glimmer through the screening of trees. As they rounded the second, the Waymeet lay spread out before them.

Right on the lane at the entrance, surrounded by lanterns on posts, was the building housing the laundry, bathhouse, store, and proprietor's quarters. A tall, handsome young Gypsy was already waiting for them beside the lane as Harperus pulled up. He wore a cape of oiled canvas against the rain, but he had pulled the hood back, and mist-beads glistened in the lantern light as they collected on his midnight-black hair.

"Not full, are you?" Harperus asked anxiously, as the young man strolled over to the driver's box after appraising the horses with an admiring eye.

"Fullish, Old Owl, but not full-up," the young man replied. "It's about the last chance of the season for traders, an' we got folk comin' home from Harvest Faires. Ye don't recognize me, I reckon, but I'm Jackdaw, *Guitan* Clan. I mind I met you when I was knee-high —"

"You're the lad with the knack with penny-whistles!" Harperus exclaimed, to the young man's delighted smile that the Deliambren had remembered him. "Dear heavens, has it been *that* long since I saw you last? How did you come here? I thought you and your family were somewhere near Shackleford!"

"Sister went *vanderei* with Blackfox, he got Stillwater from his nuncle, reckoned he could use some hands an' tough heads." Jackdaw shrugged, and grinned, his teeth gleaming whitely in the gathering dusk. "Not much call for a penny-whistle carver, and never could carve naught else. Fee's ten copper pennies for th' two wagons, indefinite stay, you bein' Free Bard an' all —"

He peered through the gloom, and Robin spoke up to save his eyes. "Robin of *Kadash* Clan, *vanderei* with Free Bard Kestrel. I hope the cartwright isn't full-up, we've got a cracked axle, or so Old Owl says. The road has gone all to pieces since I was here last."

"Nay, nay, nothin' he can't put aside, anyway, since he's a cousin." Jackdaw looked the pair of wagons over with an expert eye. "Kin come afore *gajo*. I'll tell him t' come look you over as soon as this blasted rain clears. Right about the road, though, an' the Sire ain't done nothin' about it. Prob'ly won't, 'till he breaks his own axle. Tell you what, there's two sites all the way at the end of the last row left; pull both rigs into the first site, drop the little wagon, then pull the big 'un up into the second site. You'll both be right an' tight t' pull straight out when y' please."

Robin had already pulled out her purse and passed the ten coppers over to Jackdaw before Harperus had a chance to protest or pay the lad himself. "You pulled us out and towed us here, so let me discharge the debt and cover your fee," she said firmly. Harperus had known Gypsies more than long enough to understand the intricate dance of "discharging debt," so he did not argue; he simply followed Jackdaw's instructions and drove the horses to the next-to-last path on the left, then all the way down to the end. The lanes were also marked clearly with lantern poles, with another set of poles halfway down, and large white stones marking the place to pull into each site.

Parking the wagons was as simple as Jackdaw had stated, which was a relief; Robin had known far too many Gypsies who would try to wedge a wagon into a space meant for a one-man tent-shelter. The camping sites were on firm, level grass, with trees and bushes between each adjoining site, and a rock-rimmed, sand-lined fire pit for each site as well. Robin didn't get a chance to see much of the Waymeet, however, for by the time they were parked and the horses unhitched, night had fallen, and a thick darkness made more impenetrable by the mist had taken over the area.

Kestrel took all six horses to the common corral and stable area; shelter was provided, and water, but food must either be bought or supplied from their own stores. Just as he left, the mist thickened, and then the rain resumed, pouring down just as hard as it had during the day.

Robin cursed under her breath, and Harperus looked annoyed. "T'fyrr, you stay in the wagon," he ordered. "There is nothing worse than the smell of wet feathers, and I don't want to chance you catching something in this cold. Robin and I can deal with unhitching her caravan and pushing it back."

He did *something* at the side of the driver's box, and soft, white lights came on at the rear and the front of his wagon. Robin's eyes widened, but she said nothing. The lights looked exactly like oil lamps, and if you had not seen them spring to life so suddenly and magically, you might have thought that was what they really were. A flamelike construction flickered inside frosted glass in a very realistic manner.

But the "flames" were just a little too regular in their "flickering;" there was certainly a pattern there. And besides, oil lamps required someone or something to light them, they simply didn't light themselves.

Then she shrugged, mentally. If Harperus wanted to make things look as if he was driving a perfectly normal — if rather large — wagon, that was his privilege. If he wanted to pretend that he had no Deliambren secrets in there, that was his problem. No one who had ever seen Deliambren "magic" was going to be fooled for a second. The glass in the windows was enough to show this was no ordinary wagon, and the smooth metal sides were too unlike a wooden caravan to ever deceive anyone.

Together they cranked the winched-up caravan down; it was no problem for only two to handle, even in the downpour, since it was always easier to get something *down* than it was to get it *up*. And it was not as hard as she had thought it would be, to push the caravan back a few paces from the rear of Harperus' wagon. The wheels moved easily on the wet grass. Harperus climbed under the damaged rear end again and poked and prodded, and created his mysterious little flashes of light, then finally emerged and shook water and bits of leaves off his hands.

"That axle will hold your weight, I think," he said, as Robin's nose turned cold and she shivered in the light breeze. "I wouldn't worry about sleeping or moving around in the wagon. I wouldn't trust it to take the abuse of the road, but sitting here on grass there should be no problems."

She had no idea how Harperus could tell all of this

just by looking at the axle — or what little could be seen of the axle inside its enclosure — but she was quite confident that he was right. Deliambrens were seldom, if ever, wrong about something that was physical or structural.

"Thank you, Old Owl," she said with gratitude. "I don't know how we'd have managed if you hadn't come along —"

He cut short her speech of gratitude with a wave of his hand. "You are freezing, little one, and all this can wait until morning. I will go and see to our horses while you get something warm to eat and some sleep. Think of it as trade for the rumors you are going to track for me. You can thank me in the morning. All right?"

She nodded, with a tired sigh. Deliambrens as a whole were not very good at judging the strength of human emotions, nor the strength of the actions that emotions were likely to induce, but this time Harperus had gauged her remaining reserves quite accurately. "Right," she said, without any argument. "Talk to me in the morning and let me know what you want me to listen for tomorrow, what you want me to say to the others."

Harperus nodded and turned back to his own wagon, hurrying through the rain to the front, which was the only place on the vehicle with an entrance. The exterior lights went out as abruptly as they had come on as soon as she reached the door of her own little caravan. No matter; she knew where everything was, and lit the four *real* oil lamps by feel, filling the interior of the wagon with a mellow, golden light, and very grateful for the stock of sulfur-matches that had come with the wagon. They were precious and hard to come by; she only used one, then lit the rest of the lamps from a splinter she kindled at the first lamp.

Once again she lit the tiny charcoal stove, and waited for the place to warm up. The interior of the caravan was well-planned as far as usable space went. Their bed was in the front, just behind the driver's seat, and the door there slid sideways rather than swinging open, so that someone could lie on the bed and talk to the driver while the wagon moved down the road. And on warm nights, a curtain could be pulled across the opened door, giving privacy and fresh air. A second curtain could be pulled across the other side of the bed, giving privacy from the rest of the wagon. It *was* possible to sleep four, in a pinch; an ingenious table and bench arrangement on the right-hand wall under the side window could be made into a bed just wide enough for two. But the arrangement would not be good for long periods, unless the people in that bed were children.

There was storage for their clothing under the bed, more storage above it. The stove was bolted away from the wall in the rear beside the rear door, and had a cooking surface on the top of it. Storage for food was nearby and their pans and utensils hung from the ceiling above it. There were small windows surrounded by shallow storage cabinets on either wall, where they kept everything else they needed, from instruments to harness-repair kits. The table and benches, bolted to the wall and floor, were beneath the right-hand window, and a built-in basin above a huge jar for fresh water with a spigot on the bottom, were beneath the left-hand window. The basin could be removed from its holder, to be emptied out the window or filled from the jar.

Harperus' suggestion of hot food was a good one. How long had it been since they'd eaten? Certainly not since noon.

Still shivering, she made the simplest possible hot

meal, toasting thick slices of bread and melting cheese over the top of them — and putting a kettle for tea on top of the stove. The activity kept her from feeling *too* cold, and by the time Kestrel returned, the wagon had begun to warm.

"I — got the h-horses — put up," Kestrel told her, as she stripped his sodden clothing from him and wrapped him in a thick robe made from the same material as their blankets. "And f-fed."

"Good — here, eat this, you'll feel better." She put a slice of toast-and-cheese in his left hand and a mug of tea well-sweetened with honey in his right. With a smile of gratitude, he started on both. "And next time, I can put the horses up and you can make dinner."

"D-done," he agreed, as he joined her on the bed.

"Thank goodness Harperus came along," she sighed. "We'd still be out there if he hadn't."

Jonny nodded. "I've n-never seen a D-Deliambren before. Are th-they all like h-him? So c-courteous?"

"Most of them." She sipped her tea, carefully; it was not that far from being scalding. "All of them would stop to help someone they knew, and most would stop to help a stranger. They can afford to. With their magic, there aren't too many people who would be a threat to them."

"Ah." He shifted a little more, and tucked his feet in under his robe. "I w-was w-wondering if they all are so — so — d-d-detached."

"As if Harperus is always observing the rest of the world without really being part of it?" she asked in reply, and at his nod, she pursed her lips. "They really are pretty much all like that," she told him. "All the Deliambrens I've met, anyway. They just don't understand our emotions, but they're completely fascinated by them. I think that's why they enjoy being around the Free Bards and the Gypsies. They like to hear the songs that we sing that are full of very powerful emotions, and they like to watch the emotional reactions of our listeners. It seems to be a never-ending source of entertainment for them."

Kestrel made a face of distaste. "L-like we're s-some kind of b-bug."

"No, not at all," she hastened to tell him. "No, it's something like the fascination I have for watching someone blow glass. I can't do it, I don't understand it, but I love to watch. This fascination of theirs gets them in trouble too — they are *very* apt to go running off into a bad situation just because it looks interesting. Wren had to pull Harperus out of a mob once, for instance, and another Deliambren we know nearly got disemboweled for asking one too many questions about a particular Sire's lady." She hoped Harperus had more sense than that. "It's not that they don't feel things, they just don't express them the way we do. Harperus has a very good sense of humor and tells excellent jokes — but he can't always tell when things have turned serious, and he can't always anticipate when serious things have turned deadly. They seem on the surface to be very shallow people, and I've heard some Churchmen call them 'soul-less' because of that."

Kestrel's expression grew thoughtful. "Th-the things the Church is s-saying, about th-the n-nonhumans? H-having no souls? And b-being d-damned?"

"Could be very, very dangerous for the Deliambrens," she said, catching his meaning. "And they don't even realize it. They have no idea how very emotional people can be when it comes to religion, and how irrational that can make them."

Kestrel finished his bread, took the last sip of his tea, and put the mug down on one of the little shelves built above the foot of the bed. "M-maybe. And m-maybe he d-d-does. He asked *you* t-to listen for r-rumors."

She licked her lips thoughtfully, then nodded, as a sudden flash of lightning illuminated the cracks around the doors and the shutters. The thunder followed immediately, deafening them both for a moment.

"You might be right," she admitted. "If so, it may be the *first* time he's been able to figure out when he's treading on dangerous emotional ground! But —"

"It c-can wait unt-til tomorrow," Kestrel said firmly, and took her mug away from her. He put it down beside his own, and then took her in his arms. "I m-may be t-tired, b-but I h-have other p-plans."

And he proceeded to show her what those plans were.

Afterwards, they were so exhausted that not even the pounding rain, the thunder, or the brilliant lightning could keep them awake.

Jonny woke first, as usual; he poked his nose out from under the blankets and took an experimental sniff of the chill air.

Clear, clean air, but one without a lot of moisture in it. Maybe the rain had cleared off?

He opened up one eye, and pulled back the curtain over the door by the bed. Sunlight poured through the crack, and as he freed his head from the bedclothes, he heard a bird singing madly. Probably a foolish jay, with no notion that it should have gone south by now. He smiled, let the curtain fall, and closed his eyes again.

In a few more minutes, Robin stirred, right on schedule. She cracked her eye open, muttered something unintelligible about the birds, and slowly, painfully, opened her eyes completely. Jonny grinned and stretched. Another day had begun.

He crawled past Robin, who muttered and curled up in the blankets. She was never able to wake up properly, so he was the one who made breakfast; he got the stove going and made sausage, tea, and batter-cakes, while she slowly unwound from the blankets. He ate first, then cleaned himself and the tiny kitchen up while she ate. And about the time her breakfast was finished, Robin was capable of speaking coher-ently. About the time she finished her second mug of tea, the cartwright arrived.

Kestrel left her to clean herself up, and joined the cartwright in the clear and rain-washed morning.

There was no sign of life in Harperus' wagon, but it was entirely possible that the Deliambren and his guest were up and about long ago; there was enough room in there for six or eight people to set up full-time housekeeping. Certainly it was possible for Harperus to be doing anything up to and including carpentry in that behemoth without any trace of activity to an out-side watcher.

The cartwright was a taciturn individual, although not sullen; he seemed simply to be unwilling to part with too many words. Clearly another Gypsy by his dark hair and olive skin, his scarlet shirt and leather breeches, he nodded a friendly greeting as Jonny waved to him. "Free Bard Kestrel?" he asked, then crawled under the wagon without anything more than waiting for Kestrel's affirmative reply. He had brought a number of small tools with him; he took off the pro-tective enclosure on the offending axle while Kestrel watched with interest. He studied the situation, with no comment or expression on his dark face, then replaced the cover and crawled back out.

"Right," he said then. "Cracked axle. Not bad. Start

now, done by nightfall. Fifty silver; good axle is thirty, ten each for me and Grackle."

Robin poked her head out of the wagon as he finished, and Kestrel blanched at the price of the repair. They *had* it; had it, and a nice nest-egg to spare, but all the years of abject poverty made Kestrel extremely reluctant to part with *any* money, much less this much. He looked to Robin for advice. Was this fair, or was the man gouging them?

Robin shrugged. "It's a fair price," she said. "An axle has to be made of lathe-turned, kiln-dried oronwood, and the nearest oronwood stand that *I* know of is on the other side of Kingsford."

The cartwright (whose name Kestrel *still* did not know) nodded, respect in his eyes, presumably that Robin was so well-informed. Kestrel sighed, but only to himself. There would be no bargaining here.

"G-go ahead," he said, trying not to let the words choke him.

The cartwright nodded and strode briskly off down the lane towards the cluster of buildings at the front of the Waymeet, presumably to get his partner, tools, and the new axle.

"D-do we s-stay here?" he asked Robin. "Are w-we s-supposed to help?"

"Not at that price," she replied, jumping down out of the wagon. "I heard him out here, so I locked everything up, figuring if he could start immediately, we could go wander around the Waymeet for a while, and see if there's anyone I know here. We can't do anything in the wagon while he has it up on blocks, changing out the axle."

She reached up and locked the back door, then slipped the key in her pocket. The bird in the tree above them, who had been silent while the cartwright was prodding the wagon, burst into song, and she looked up and smiled at it.

That smile lit up his heart and brought a smile to his lips. He reached for her hand, and she slipped it into his. "Th-there's lots of n-news t-to tell, and m-more t-to hear. L-let's at least g-go tell Gypsies and F-Free B-Bards ab-bout Wren and L-L-Lark. And th-the w-welcome to Free B-Bards in B-Birnam. Th-that's g-good news."

"Surely," she agreed. "And we'll see if there's anything of interest to us in what the other folk here have to tell us in the way of news."

To Robin's delight, the first people they encountered, cooking up a breakfast of sausage around their fire, were people she knew very well. It was a trio of Free Bards: Linnet, Gannet, and Blackbird. Blackbird jumped up, nearly stepping into the fire, when he spotted Robin, and rushed to hug her.

Linnet was a tiny thing, with long, coppery-brown hair that reached almost to her ankles when she let it down. Gannet's hair was as red as flame, his milky face speckled with freckles; Blackbird's red-gold hair was lighter and wavy rather than curly, like Gannet's. All three had sparkling green eyes, and slight builds. They made a striking group, whether they were dressed for the road or in their performance costumes.

She made the introductions hastily; none of the trio had ever seen Jonny or even heard of him, so far as she knew.

"Linnet is flute, Gannet is drum, and Blackbird is a mandolin player," she told him, concluding the introduction. "Kestrel is a harpist, and he's learning lute —"

"Well, if Master Wren declared he's one of us, that's good enough for me," Blackbird declared. "No other qualifications needed. Now, we heard there was some kind of to-do over in Birnam — but how did you end up mixed in it, and *how* did you end up wedded?"

She glanced over at Kestrel, who shrugged, and settled down on one of the logs arranged as seats around the open fire. "Finish your meal and we'll see if we can't get it all sorted out for you," she said, following his example. "We've already eaten, so go right ahead."

Jonny didn't say a great deal, but he did interject a word or phrase now and again; enough that it didn't look as if she was doing all the talking. Linnet and her two partners kept mostly quiet, although by their eyes, they were intensely excited by the whole story. They passed sausages and bread to each other, and filled tea-mugs, without their gazes ever leaving the faces of the two tale-tellers.

"— and then, well, it was just a matter of getting wedded," Robin concluded.

Kestrel grinned wryly. "And s-so p-p-publicly that K-King R-Rolend c-couldn't th-think I w-was g-going to b-back out of my p-p-pledge. S-s-so here w-we are."

"Lark and Wren are still in Birnam, and King Rolend made Wren his Bard Laurel, so he said to pass the word that Free Bards are welcome in *any* place in Birnam," Robin added. "That's the biggest news, really. Apparently the Bardic Guild in Birnam was one of the biggest benefactors of the old King's spendthrift ways, and they are *not* happy with Rolend."

"And th-the f-f-feeling is m-mutual," Jonny pointed out. "Th-things th-that Wren w-wants, he's h-happy t-to g-give. P-politely th-thumbing his n-nose at the G-G-Guild."

"Like the right for any musician to work anywhere, and take anyone's pay, at least in Birnam." Gwyna made no secret of her satisfaction, and the other three looked so satisfied that Robin wondered if they had been having trouble finding a wintering-over spot.

"Well, that's the best news I've had since the Kingsford Faire!" Linnet exclaimed. She glanced over at her two partners, who nodded. "I think the situation in Birnam is well worth crossing those damned fens, even at this late in the year. We haven't found a *single* wintering-over job, and we've been looking since the first Harvest Faire."

Robin blinked in surprise at that, as Gannet carefully poured the last of the tea-water over the fire, putting it out. Steam hissed up from the coals and blew away in the light breeze. "That's odd," she said carefully.

"Odd? It's a disaster!" Blackbird never had been one to mince words. "No one will take us. There's Guild musicians in every one of the taverns we've wintered over in before. The innkeepers just shrug and wish us well — elsewhere. They won't tell us why they hired Guild when they couldn't afford Guild before, and they won't tell us why they *don't* want us, when the Guild musicians aren't as good as we are."

But Gannet looked up with shadows in his dark eyes. "Got a guess," he offered. "Just now put it together — been a lot of Priests around, preaching on morality. We're a trio."

Robin shook her head, baffled, but Linnet put her hand to her mouth. "Oh!" she exclaimed, looking stricken. "I never thought of that! We're —" she blushed, a startling crimson. "We've always shared a room, you see —"

Robin grimaced. "If the Church Priests are going around the inns, threatening to cause trouble if there are 'immoral people' there, you three would be right at the top of their list, wouldn't you?"

"I never thought it necessary to announce that we're siblings every time we ask for a job," Blackbird

said, with icy anger. "It doesn't exactly have anything
to do with *music*."

"Well, maybe it does now," Gannet said, his jaw
clenched. "Church's poking its nose into *our* lives,
time we went on the defensive, maybe —"

"Or time we went into Birnam, where we don't
have to make excuses, just music," Linnet said firmly.
"No, *I* don't like running away any more than anyone
else, but the Church scares me. It's too big to fight,
and too big to hide from."

She stood up and shook out her skirts decisively. "If
they decide not to believe that we're siblings, we have
no way of proving that we *are!*" she continued. "And
for that matter, a nasty-minded Churchman can make
nasty assumptions even if they accept our word! Call
me a coward, but there it is."

Gannet rose, nodding, as Robin and Kestrel got to
their feet, leaving only Blackbird sitting. He stared up
at them, stubbornly, for a long moment. Then he finally sighed and rose to his feet as well.

"We're too good a trio to break up," he said, with an
unhappy shake of his head. "I think you're overreact-
ing, but if it makes the two of you happy to head for
Birnam, then that's where we'll go."

Robin let out the breath she had been holding. "I
think you're being wise," she said. "It's just a feeling I
have, but — well, incest is punishable, too, and the
punishments are pretty horrible. It might be worse for
Church Priests to know you *are* related, and sharing a
room."

"Better to be safe," Linnet said, with twitch of her
skirts that told Robin that she was not just nervous,
she was actually a little *afraid*, and had been the
moment that Gannet mentioned the Church.

And that was not like Linnet.

Not at all.

Something had frightened her, something she hadn't even told her brothers. Threats from some representative of the Church?

Or some Priest deciding he liked her looks and promising trouble if she wouldn't become his mistress. It had happened to Robin, and the trouble had come. Small wonder Linnet would rather leave the country than come under Church scrutiny again. Robin would make the same choice, in her place.

She and Kestrel found several more Gypsies, and two more Free Bards, besides a round dozen wandering players who were not associated with either the Guild or the Free Bards. To all of them she passed the news that any musician was welcome to play wherever he could find work in the Kingdom of Birnam. Some of the ordinary musicians were interested, most were not — but they were folk who had a regular circuit of tiny inns, local dances and festivals, and very small Faires. They had places to play that no Guild musician would touch with a barge-pole, and while the living that they eked out was bare by her standards, it was enough for them.

The Free Bards were, like Linnet, *very* interested in her news, and had similar tales of finding Guild musicians — or, at least, musicians in Guild badges — playing in the venues where no Guildsman had ever played before.

But it was not until they found another musician who was both a Gypsy and a Free Bard that they had anything like an answer to the question of *why* this was happening.

The ethereal strains of a harp drew Kestrel across the clearing and into the deeper forest beyond the immediate confines of the Waymeet. Dead leaves

crackled underfoot, and the scent of tannin rose at his
every step. This was no simple song; this was the kind of
wild, strange, dream-haunted melody that some of the
Gypsies played—though Robin never would, claiming
she had no talent for what she called *adastera* music.
She said it was as much magic as music, and told him it
was reputed to have the power to control spirits and
souls, to raise ghosts and set them to rest again.

Robin followed him under the deep shadows of the
trees, as the bare branches above gave way to thick,
long-needled evergreens, a voice joined the harp,
singing without words, the two creating harmonies
that made the hair on the back of his neck stand on
end. This was music powerful enough to make even
Harperus weep! The harpist must be a Gypsy, but who
was the singer? It did not sound like any human
voice. . . .

The path they followed seemed to lead beside the
stream that watered the Waymeet; it led through deep
undergrowth, along the bottom of a rock-sided ravine
that slowly grew steeper with every twist and turn of
the path. The stream wound its way through a tangle
of rounded boulders, but its gurgle did not sound at all
cheerful, although it was very musical. It held a note a
melancholy that was a match for the sadness in the
music floating on the breeze ahead of them.

"Nightingale," Robin muttered. "She's the *only* person I can think of who plays like that! But who is the
singer?"

They had their answer a moment later, as the
stream and path brought them to a tiny clearing made
by the toppling of a single tree that bridged the water.
There, beside the tree, was the harpist, seated on a
rock with her harp braced on her lap. And standing
beside her was T'fyrr.

Not even the birds were foolish enough to make

any sound that might disturb these two. The Haspur stood like a statue of gray granite in the twilight shadows of the forest, only his chest moving to show that he was alive, with his eyes closed and his beak open just enough to permit his voice to issue forth. Nightingale's eyes were closed as well, but most of her face was hidden in the curtain of her hair, as she bent over her harp, all of her concentration centered on her hands and the melodies she coaxed from the delicate strings.

Both of them were too deeply engrossed in the music to notice their audience — and Robin and Kestrel stopped dead to keep from breaking their concentration.

The song came to its natural end, a single harp-note that hung in the air like a crystal raindrop; a sigh from T'fyrr that answered it.

For a long, long moment, only silence held sway beneath the branches. Then, finally, a bell-bird sang out its three-note call, and the two musicians sighed and opened their eyes.

T'fyrr caught sight of them first, and clapped his beak shut with a snap.

"T-T'fyrr —" Kestrel said, softly, "th-that was w-w-wonderful."

The bird-man bowed, graciously. "It was an experiment —" he offered. "It was not meant to be heard."

"But since it was . . ." The Gypsy that Robin had identified as "Nightingale" cocked her head to one side.

Robin evidently knew her well enough to answer the unspoken question. "As critique from two fellow harpists — you've found the best match to your harp and your music I've ever heard," Robin replied. "I know Kestrel agrees with me, and he's a better harpist than I am. That was nothing short of magical."

Nightingale's mouth twitched a little, as if she found Robin's choice of words amusing. "Well, we had agreed, T'fyrr and I, that this song would be the last of our experiments this morning. And while my heart may regret that you found us and are about to make us cleave to that agreement, my hands are not going to argue." She began flexing them, and massaging each of the palms in turn. "A forest in autumn is not the best venue for a performance. It is very damp here, and a rock makes a chilly, and none-too-soft cushion." Her eyes met Kestrel's, sharp and penetrating, and just a little strange and other-worldly. "T'fyrr said that you would turn up eventually, and that you had some news?"

Once again, the two of them passed on their own news, with the added tales from Linnet's trio and some of the other musicians. "We started out with only good news," Robin concluded, ruefully, "but we seem to have acquired news of a more sober flavor. I feel like a bird who just finished the last song of summer, and sees the first storm of winter coming —"

Nightingale nodded. "And now you will hear why *I* am here, and not in my usual winter haunt. And I think I may have the answer you have been looking for, as to why there are fewer places for Free Bards, and Guild musicians crowding into our old venues."

As Robin took a place on the fallen tree, and Kestrel planted himself beside her, Nightingale glanced up at T'fyrr. "I think that some of what I have to say will affect you, my new friend," she said. "But — listen, and judge for yourself."

When Nightingale had found her usual winter position as the chief instrumentalist at a fine ladies' tea-shop closed to her, taken by a barely tolerable Guild violist, she did more than simply look for work, she began looking for the cause. And just as Gannet had, *she* had found clerics from the Church posted on street-corners, preaching against "immorality." But unlike Gannet, she had *listened* to the sermons.

"Time after time, I heard sermons specifically against *music*," she said. "And not just any music — but the music performed by what these street preachers referred to as 'wild and undisciplined street players.' They *always* went on to further identify these 'street players' as people no Guild would permit into its ranks, because of their lack of respect for authority, their immorality, and their 'dangerous ways.'"

"Us, in other words," Robin said grimly. "Free Bards. Just what were the complaints against us, anyway?"

Nightingale's mouth had compressed into a tight line, and Kestrel sensed a very deep anger within her. "According to what they *said*, directly, our music is seductive and incites lust, our lyrics licentious and advocate lust, and we destroy pure thinking and lead youths to rebel against proper authority. To hear them talk, the Free Bards are responsible for every girl that ever had a child out of wedlock, every boy that ever defied his parents, and every fool who sought strong drink and drugs and ruined his mind and body. But it wasn't only what they said directly, it was what they implied."

"Which w-was?" Kestrel prompted, quickly.

"That we're using magic," she said flatly. "That we're somehow controlling the minds of those who listen to us, to make them do things they never would ordinarily. He was full of examples — boys that had been lured into demon-worship by a song, girls that had run off with young brigands because of a song, folk who had supposedly been incited to a life of crime or had committed suicide, all because of the 'magic spells' we Free Bards had cast on them through our music. They even had the titles of the songs on their tongues, to prove their lies — 'Demon-Lover,' 'Follow Come Follow,' 'Free Fly the Fair,' 'The Highwayman's Lady.' As if simply by knowing the title of a song, that proved there was evil magic behind the singing of it. *That* is why there are no jobs for Free Bards. Not because we're 'immoral' — but because no one wants to risk a charge that some patron did something wrong because the musician at the hearth somehow cast a sinister spell upon him and took control of his mind. Most especially they do not want to risk an accusation that such a spell had been cast against a minor child."

Kestrel felt cold. That was too close to the truth, as Wren had uncovered it. *Some* Free Bards *could* influence the thoughts of others. Not to any sinister purpose, but —

"And the Guild, in its infinite wisdom and compassion, has been offering an option to the owners of the better taverns and those citizens of modest wealth who may hire a musician or two," Nightingale continued, her voice dripping with sarcasm. "They have been recruiting what they call 'Guild-licensed' musicians — players who are not good enough to pass the Guild trials, but who may be barely competent musicians on one or two instruments. These people are certified *by the Church* and licensed by the Guild as being capable of entertaining without corrupting anyone. They wear Guild colors and double-tithe to the Church, plus pass back a commission to the Guild."

"Brilliant," Robin muttered, bitterly.

"This, of course, does leave us the street corners, the very poor inns and taverns, the common eating-shops, and the patronage of younger people who usually don't have a great deal of money," Nightingale concluded. "And, of course, the country-folk, who haven't gotten the word of our immorality and possible corrupting magic-use yet."

T'fyrr, who had remained silent through all of this, finally spoke. "I like this not, lady," he said, his voice echoing oddly through the trees.

"No more do any of us, friend," Robin answered for all of them.

They finished making their rounds of the other, non-musical "residents" of the Waymeet at just about the time that the cartwright (who they now knew was called "Oakhart") and his helper were taking the wagon down off the blocks. "She'll hold now," Oakhart said, with satisfaction. They shook hands on it, and the cartwright departed with his promised fifty pieces of silver. Kestrel let Robin pay the man; it gave him pain to see that much money leaving their hands.

Harperus appeared just as Oakhart was leaving, and invited them to dinner and a conference around the fire he had just built. He had quite a civilized little arrangement there; folding chairs, a stack of baskets, each containing a different, warmed dainty, and plates to eat from. "T'fyrr told me what your Gypsy-harpist friend said," the Deliambren told them, as they accepted plates full of food that obviously had never been prepared over a fire, tasty little bits of vegetables and meats, each with different sauces or crisp coatings, or sprinklings of cheese. "This is some of what I had heard, the rumors that I wanted you to track for me, but not the whole of it."

Gwyna picked up a bit of fried something, and bit into it with a glum expression. "I don't know how we're going to fight the Church, Old Owl. I don't know how anyone could."

"I h-heard some other things," Kestrel added casually, after popping a sausagelike thing into his mouth. "I

d-don't kn-know if it m-means anyth-thing. Or if th-the
Ch-Church has anyth-thing t-to d-do with this. N-no one
else s-s-seems t-to think it m-means anyth-thing. J-just —
th-that n-nonhumans are h-having a h-harder t-time of it,
just l-like the F-Free B-Bards. All of a s-sudden it's all
r-right t-to s-say y-you d-don't t-trust 'em, th-they're
th-thieves, or sh-shifty, or l-lazy. Th-that it's h-harder for
'em t-to g-get any k-kind of p-position, any k-kind of j-job,
and even t-traders are f-finding it h-harder t-to g-get
c-clients, unless th-they've g-got something ex-exclusive.
And th-there are s-signs showing up, at inns and t-taverns
and l-lodgings."

"What kind of signs?" Harperus asked, sharply.

"Ones th-that s-say 'Hu-humans only.'" He
shrugged. "N-not a l-lot of them, th-they s-say, b-but
I've n-never heard of th-that b-before."

"Nor have I." Harperus was giving him a particularly penetrating look. "You seem to think this is
nothing terribly important, certainly nowhere near as
important as these preachers and the apparent backing of the Bardic Guild by the Church."

Kestrel shrugged again. "It's j-just a c-couple of
b-bigots," he said. "Wh-what h-harm c-can they do?"

"Could they express their bigotry so openly if they
did *not* have some sanction?" Harperus countered
sharply. "And if there are signs reading 'Humans only'
now, how long will it be, think you, before there are
signs that say, 'Citizens only,' 'Guild Members only,' or
even 'No one permitted in the gates without Church
papers and permissions'?"

Kestrel blinked, and his level of concern rose mark-
edly. "D-do you th-think the Ch-Church is behind
this, too?"

Harperus stroked his cheek-decorations with a
thoughtful finger. "I find it peculiar that a Church
whose scriptures speak of love and tolerance should

suddenly have words of hate and intolerance in its collective mouth," he said. "I find it disturbing that it is
effectively sanctioning things that should be repugnant to any thinking being. And I do not think that it is
any accident that this should be happening to the two
main groups who escape the Church's authority — the
nonhumans, who do not share this human religion of
the Sacrificed God, and the Free Bards and Gypsies,
who have no address and cannot be followed, controlled, or intimidated."

"I find it significant too, my friend," boomed T'fyrr
out of the darkness. "What is more, I have been speaking in greater depth with Nightingale, who tells me
that the Church has never before preached against the
use of magic — but now finds reasons to condemn
even such beneficial magic as healing, if they are not
performed by a Priest. And I wonder, how long before
use of magic is declared a crime — and how long before anyone that the authorities wish to be rid of is
called a magician?"

"A very good question, T'fyrr." Robin's face was
grim, and Kestrel felt a cold and empty place in his
stomach that the excellent food did nothing to fill. "A
very good question. And I am beginning to wonder if
the answer to your question can be measured in
months."

"That," Harperus said, "is precisely what I am afraid
of."

CHAPTER FIVE

Kestrel thought about the revelations of the day long into the night, and in the morning, while Gwyna took their mud-stained garments to the laundry to try to scrub them clean again, he waited for Harperus to make his appearance.

It was another clear, cold day, with a bite in the air that warned that winter was not far off. Kestrel's thin fingers chilled quickly, and he stuffed his hands into the pockets of his coat to warm them. The Deliambren came out of his wagon from the door at the front, looked around, and greeted Kestrel with some surprise. "I didn't expect to find you here, still," Harperus told him. "I expected that you and Robin would be on your way as soon as the sun rose. Have some breakfast?"

He had his hands full of something, and offered Jonny a very odd object indeed; a thin pancake folded around a brightly colored filling. Strange-looking, but Kestrel already knew that Harperus' odd-looking food was very good, and he accepted his second breakfast of the day with alacrity. There had been too many days in the past that he had had no breakfast, no lunch, and no dinner. Old habits said, "Eat when you can," so he did.

"W-we have ch-chores," Kestrel offered, after first trying a bite and discovering that it was as good as dinner had been last night. "Th-things w-we didn't g-get to. L-laundry, a l-little cl-cleaning. Re-s-stocking. And w-we hadn't d-decided where w-we w-were g-going, yet. S-South, that w-was all w-we knew. W-we needed t-to look at s-some m-maps."

There was still hot tea left in their wagon; he turned and got mugs well-sweetened with honey for both of them. Harperus accepted his with a nod of thanks. The warm mug felt very good in Kestrel's cold fingers.

"So. You'll be going out of Rayden, I take it, given the word you gathered yesterday?" Harperus regarded Kestrel shrewdly over a mug of steaming tea. "Obviously, you can't go back to Birnam, so where are you thinking of heading?"

"D-don't know." He finished Harperus' offering, and dusted off his hands. "Th-this b-business w-with the Ch-Church; I g-got the f-f-feeling you'd heard m-more than you t-told us l-last night."

"And if I have?" the Deliambren asked levelly.

Kestrel studied the odd, inhuman face. It was very handsome, the more so as he became accustomed to it; the swaths of silky hair only added to the attraction. There was no sign of aging at all; certainly no sign of the years Robin had claimed for the Deliambren. And there was no sign of any emotion that Kestrel recognized. Harperus' odd-colored eyes studied his, seeming more coppery this morning than yellow.

"Y-you've b-been w-watching th-things for a l-l-long t-time," he said, finally. "C-collecting inform-m-ma-tion. S-so maybe you kn-know. H-how c-can wh-what the Church is d-doing b-be j-j-justified?"

"One of the characteristics of organized religion is that no action it takes has to be justified from outside, if it is justified by the religion itself, Kestrel," Harperus said, patiently. "That is a truism for nonhuman as well as human religions. No matter how irrational an action is, if it is done in the name of the religion, that alone serves the organizers."

Jonny shook his head. "I d-don't understand," he said, plaintively.

Harperus sighed. "Neither do I. But then, I have never claimed to be religious."

Both of them wore coats against the chill in the air, and once again, Jonny shoved one of his hands into his pocket and wished that he were somewhere warm that had never heard of the Church. "Wh-when I asked the tr-traders wh-why these th-things were happening, th-they d-didn't know either. And th-they didn't s-seem worried." He tried to make his glance at Harperus an inquiring one, and evidently Harperus read it that way.

"That seems to be the prevailing attitude." Harperus looked up at the sky, broodingly. "The only human folk who are worried are the Free Bards and the traveling musicians — and they seem concerned only with the immediate effect these sanctions are having on their livelihood. No one seems at all concerned about what could happen next, or the sanctions against nonhumans. To be honest with you, Kestrel, those worry me the most. And not because I am Deliambren, either."

Jonny had formed some ideas of his own last night, and he wanted to see how they matched with the Deliambren's. "Why?" he asked.

Harperus smiled thinly. "You pack many questions into a single word, youngster." He leaned back against the side of his vehicle. "I am not concerned for myself and my race, because there is no one in the Twenty Kingdoms who can effectively threaten us, my earlier protestations notwithstanding. We can simply *outlive* human regimes. We have the capability of closing up the Fortress and outliving this current generation. We have done so before, and are always prepared to do so again. It is simply not our policy to boast of that ability."

Jonny's eyebrows rose. He had not expected Harperus to be so frank. . . .

"However, the reason that these little, petty annoyances worry me is that they seem to have been formulated, by accident or deliberately, to undermine a great deal of the progress that has been made here in the last few centuries. Progress in cooperation, that is." The Deliambren's expression was a brooding one. "Each little action seems designed to strike in such a way that the group that is acted against is *quite* certain that the actions against them are far more important than the petty annoyances of other groups." He leaned towards Kestrel, his mouth set in a thin, tight line. "Look at you — the Gypsies think there is no problem at all, because it is only happening in the settled places, and they pay very little heed to anything done in towns. They assume that if trouble spreads, they can simply drive away from it. The Free Bards are more concerned with the restriction on their ability to make a living, and not on the reputation they may be getting thanks to the tales spread by Churchmen —"

"N-not N-Nightingale," Kestrel protested.

"True. Not the Nightingale. But she is unique among all the Free Bards and Gypsies I have spoken to." He shook his head. "None of them are at all thinking about what is happening to the nonhumans, because they think their own problems are much greater. I have not heard from the nonhumans themselves — and that alarms me. Are they being harassed? Are they being arrested and taken off into oblivion? Are they being deported? Or is there nothing happening at all? I have heard nothing, and when I hear nothing, I worry more than when I hear rumors.

I only *know* that the few nonhuman traders I know have simply turned over their routes in Rayden to human partners. The human traders frankly see this in terms of less competition and more profit. The nonhumans are gone, and I cannot question them."

Kestrel blinked. He had not considered the possibility that there might actually be bad things happening to the nonhumans. "Do you th-th-think —"

"That any of that has happened?" Harperus' grim expression lightened a little. "Not yet, Kestrel," he said gently. "But I greatly fear it *may*."

"M-m-me t-t-too." Jonny was serious about that; he had seen too many "insignificant" things turn out to be dangerous, had things that should have been no more than annoyances turn out to be life-threatening.

"There is a last 'why' that I have not answered," Harperus continued. "That is because I do not know. Why is this happening? I honestly have no idea, partly because my people do not think like yours. It would seem to me that the Church is doing very well without all this nonsense. Or it is, if you take the Church's primary goal as being the saving of souls and directing people to act in a moral and responsible manner. But if the Church's goal has changed to something else —"

"Th-then th-that m-may b-be the *why*." Jonny licked his dry lips, nervously, and ventured his thought on the matter. "M-maybe it isn't j-just a wh-why. M-maybe it's also a *who*."

Now it was Harperus' turn to raise his eyebrows. "This might be the work of one person? Perhaps a person in a position of power within the Church? Or — someone who wishes to use these changes as a means of gaining more power for himself?" At Jonny's nod, he pursed his lips, thoughtfully. "An interesting speculation. I will look into this."

Harperus handed Jonny his mug, then shoved away

from the side of the wagon, turned on his heel, and headed back to the door, vanishing inside. Jonny turned and went back to his vehicle, walking slowly and thoughtfully.

He was not offended by Harperus' abrupt departure; he knew better than to expect human behavior or even what a human would think of as "politeness" out of a nonhuman. In fact, he was rather gratified; it meant that the Deliambren took him and his speculations seriously.

But Harperus was not the only person who now had that particular speculation to "look into." Jonny had decided last night that if the Deliambren thought enough of his idea to take it seriously, *he* would see what he could do to track down the center of all these troubles.

As he had told Harperus, there often was a *who* in the middle of something like this, and if you could find him and deal with him, before he had become so protected that it was impossible to get near him, you could actually do something. In fact, you could effectively stop the movement before it had gained its own momentum and had, not one, but many people devoted to keeping it alive. It was like extracting the root of a noxious plant, before it spread so far and had sent up so many shoots it was impossible to eradicate.

He had learned a great deal about politics in the short time he had been in Birnam, watching the way the people opposed to his uncle's rule had operated. He had probably learned more than anyone else had ever guessed.

Ordinary people, he had noticed, tended to do what they were told, as long as they were given orders by someone who was a recognized authority. Or, as long as the orders did not affect their own lives very much, they would support the orders through simple inaction. If you made changes gradual, and made them seem reasonable, no one really cared about them.

And the changes mounted, imperceptibly, until one day people who had been "good neighbors" — which basically meant that they had not disturbed each other and had no serious quarrels with each other — were now deadly enemies. And it all seemed perfectly reasonable by then.

As long as nothing bad happens to them, people they know, or anyone who agrees with them — "Atrocities" only happened to your own kind. "Just retribution" was what happened to other people. A cult or a myth was someone else's religion. *Your* religion was the right and moral way.

Or as the Free Bards put it, "One man's music is another man's noise." As long as people were able to listen to what they called music, they didn't care if "noise" was banned. . . .

Well, this all might be something the Free Bards could do something about, at least if it was at a controllable stage. Maybe *that* was another "why" — why the Free Bards had come in for the greater share of trouble so far. They poked fun at pompous authority; they made the strange into the familiar. It was very difficult for a person who had heard Linnet's "Pearls and Posies" to think of Gazners as "cold-blooded" for instance — or Wren's own "Spell-bound Captive" to believe that Elves truly had no souls. The Free Bards opened up the world, just a little, to those who had never been beyond their own village boundaries. Jonny knew that Master Wren had wider ideas for the Free Bards than most of them dreamed at the moment. Wren saw his creation as a means to spread information that others would rather not have public — and perhaps he might even have a greater goal than that. But that was enough for Jonny, at least at the moment.

So, this whole situation just might be a state of affairs that Free Bards could do something about. It *definitely* was something they should know about if it turned out there was a single person behind the persecution!

So — the first thing to do would be to see if he and Robin could track the sermons to their source.

He thought about that for a moment. There were only two of them, and they could only go in one direction. There was Harperus, who would be "looking into things" as well. But what about asking Nightingale as well? She was the one who had stopped to *listen* to the preachers in the street. She was the one who had given them the most information. She was already observing. If she was willing to expand that a little —

He locked up the wagon, and went in search of Nightingale. He would find out what direction she planned to go when she left the Waymeet. They would go in the opposite direction. Perhaps this little group of Free Bards would be able to find some answers to all their questions. And — dare he hope — solutions as well?

Kestrel sighed, and took up the reins as the first fat drop of rain plopped down on the gravel lane in front of the horses. "An-nother b-beautiful d-day," he said sardonically.

"It could be worse," Robin replied, and patted his knee. "At least the rain held off long enough for our laundry to dry."

"And w-we d-did get that n-nice h-hot b-bath," he admitted. Although it had been something more than a mere "bath" — the bathhouse proved to be the kind that had several small rooms, each furnished with a huge tub, fully large enough for two. It had been well worth the money, all things considered.

"We did. We are clean, the wagon is clean, all our clothing is clean — we just might be presentable enough that they won't throw us out of Westhaven," Robin said, cheerfully.

The horses stamped, showing their impatience, but Kestrel was not going to let them move out just yet. Not until —

A sharp whistle behind him told him that Harperus was about to pull out. The Haspur had once again vanished into the depths of the wagon; Kestrel doubted that more than a handful of people had even glimpsed him during the three days they all camped here. It had been T'fyr who had spoken to Nightingale and obtained her agreement to reverse her planned course and return to Kingsford, to see if the strange Church activities originated there, or elsewhere. "But then I am going to Birnam," she had said firmly. "I must eat, and I cannot eat if I cannot play."

Kestrel got the feeling that if it hadn't been for T'fyr, she wouldn't even have agreed to that much.

Harperus' huge vehicle moved slowly into the lane parallel to theirs. Once they reached the trade road, Kestrel planned to follow him for the short period when they would both be going in the same direction. A few leagues up the road, a minor, seldom-used trade-road branched off this one. This was the road to Westhaven, which just happened to be Rune's old home, and that was the direction he and Robin were going, while Harperus and T'fyr took the main road.

It was Robin's notion to spy on Rune's mother, if she was still there. She wanted to be able to tell Rune *something* about what was going on in her old haunts;

she had told Jonny that she thought Rune would feel less guilty over leaving if she knew her mother was all right.

Personally, Jonny hadn't detected any concern for her mother on Rune's part, but he wasn't a female. There might have been things the two of them said to each other that made Robin think Lady Lark felt guilt over leaving her mother to fend for herself. And one road was as good as another, really — at least, when the road led eventually to Gradford. *That* particular city had a High Bishop in residence, which made it another logical candidate for information about the Church.

What was more so far as he was concerned, there was an abbey, Carthell Abbey, lying on that little-used road that linked Westhaven and Gradford. Priests and the like who lived in isolated abbeys liked to talk to visitors; they might say something to give Kestrel a place to start.

How Harperus maneuvered that huge wagon so easily, Kestrel had no notion — but he brought it around smartly and was already on the lane leading to the trade-road by the time Kestrel got his mares in motion. The rear of the wagon was a blank wall; peculiar sort of construction. Wagons were dark enough that most people cut windows everywhere they could.

The new axle performed exactly as Oakhart had promised; they jounced along in Harperus' wake, but thanks to the Deliambren, their course wasn't as bumpy as it could have been. Harperus' wagon was much, much heavier than theirs, and his wheels much broader, although the distance between his left and right wheels was about the same as between theirs. That was why Jonny was letting him lead; as long as he kept their wheels in the ruts left by the Deliambren's wagon, their ride was relatively smooth.

At about noon, they all stopped at the crossroads for a meal; Harperus supplying more of his odd, but tasty food, and Robin offering fresh honey-cakes she had bought at Waymeet.

"Be careful out there," Robin said, as they made their farewells. "If we see you at Gradford, I *don't* want to see you in trouble!"

"I?" The Deliambren arched an eyebrow at her. "I am a well-known and respectable trader. You, on the other hand, are a disreputable Gypsy, and a Free Bard to boot! I am far more like to see *you* in a gaol of one sort or another!"

Jonny shivered; after the things that Nightingale had told them, that was no longer very funny. "D-d-don't even j-j-joke about th-that," he said. "L-let's j-just s-say w-w-we'll s-s-see y-you b-b-before M-M-Midw-w-winter."

"So we shall. May your road be easy, friends," Harperus responded, gravely. "Now — if you are to make Westhaven before nightfall —"

"We had better be off." Robin swung herself up into the driver's seat, leaving Jonny to accept Harperus' clap on the shoulder and T'fyrr's handclasp —

— or clawclasp. Or whatever.

Then they parted company; Harperus to take his wagon onward, and Robin to turn theirs down a much smaller road, one covered with wet, fallen leaves and shaded by sadly drooping branches, with undergrowth so thick that once they were on the lane, it was no longer possible to hear or see the larger vehicle. In moments, they could have been the only people in the entire world. There was no sign of any human, nothing but the forest, the occasional birdcall, and the steady drip of water from the bare branches.

Kestrel sighed. In some ways, he was glad that the

two of them were alone again, but he had enjoyed Harperus' company, and he wished he could have heard T'fyrr sing a few more times.

But most of all, he liked the feeling of security he'd had, being around the Deliambren and his formidable wagon. No one was likely to give Harperus any trouble, and if anyone did, against all common sense, he was probably going to regret doing so.

He only wished that the same could be said for them.

They reached the village of Westhaven quite a bit before nightfall. The fact that the road was considerably less traveled meant that it was, conversely, smoother than the main road. Less traffic during all this bad weather had made for fewer ruts, though there were erosion cuts to rattle across. The mares made much better time that he or Robin had any right to expect.

"If I recall, the inn is on the other side of the village," Robin said. There wasn't much there, really; a few buildings around a square, although there did seem to be a farmer's market going on. This was the kind of village that Jonny Brede would have passed by, if he'd had the choice. There was no room for an outsider here, everyone knew everyone else. Still, though strangers might not be welcome, their coin was, and spending money usually brought some form of speech out of even the most taciturn of villagers.

"W-we should g-get some bread," he said. "M-maybe ch-cheese. S-S-Stillwater d-d-didn't have either."

Robin glanced at him out of the corner of her eye, and smiled. "So we can find things out without asking questions, hmm?" she replied. "Oh, I can think of a few more things we could use. Roots, for one; and more feed for the horses. Even at the 'good price' they gave me for being a Gypsy, the price for grain at Still-water was outrageous."

By that time, they were actually *in* the village; virtually everyone in the square or the stalls along one side stared at them as they drove in. Robin pulled the horses up to the single hitching post with ostentatious care, then jumped down and tied the mares up to it. Kestrel climbed down on his side, trying to look as formidable as possible.

The village square was centered around a well. No great surprise there, most small villages were. There were four buildings on three sides of the square, with two larger buildings, one clearly a small Church and the other a Guild Hall, on the fourth side. A joint Guild Hall from the look of it; there were boards with the signs for the Millers', the Joiners', the Smiths' and the Tanners' Guilds up above the door. No Bardic Guild harp, though, which was a relief.

The stalls had been set up along this side, and Kestrel followed Robin as she opened the back of the wagon, got a basket, and made her way directly towards them. It looked as if the rain that had plagued their travel so far had scarcely touched Westhaven; the dust of the street was damped down, but had not turned to mud, and beneath the dust, the street itself was packed dirt that must surely turn into a morass every time it rained heavily.

Now I remember why I like cities, Kestrel thought. Paved streets, and regular collection of refuse, were two very good reasons.

As Robin approached the first stall, looking determinedly cheerful, he decided he did not like the faintly hostile way the woman minding it and the two loitering in front of it were staring at her. He steeled himself for trouble.

But it never came. At least, not in the form of outright "trouble."

Instead, the thin, disagreeable-looking wench, who had a face like a hen with indigestion and hair the color and texture of old straw, completely ignored them. She began chattering away at her two cronies at such a high volume and rate of speech that it would have been impossible for anyone to "get her attention" without interrupting her forcibly and rudely.

But Kestrel knew that Robin had no intention of doing anything that would give the stallkeeper an excuse for further rudeness. And if the wench thought she was going to outmaneuver a Gypsy —

Instead, Robin silently surveyed the contents of the stall with a superior eye, counterfeiting perfectly the airs of a high-born nobleman. She raised one supercilious eyebrow, then sniffed as if she found the selection of baked goods *vastly* inferior to what she was expecting, and sailed on without a single word to any of the three.

At the sound of a smothered giggle from just ahead of them, Robin smiled, and exchanged a quick glance with Kestrel. He nodded slightly in the direction of the giggler, an older woman in the next stall, one with a plain but merry face, who was selling eggs, sausage, and bacon.

Although none of these things had been on their tentative shopping list, Robin headed straight for her, and engaged her in a spirited bargaining session. As Robin put her purchases in her basket, she cocked her head to one side, and paused for a moment.

"Is there any place here in Westhaven where I can get *fresh* bread?" she asked, loudly enough that the women at the first stall could hear her clearly. "Properly made bread?" The disagreeable hen-woman flushed, and the egg-seller's mouth tightened as she held back another giggle.

"Well, Mother Tolley isn't a baker, precisely, but she sells the *freshest* bread on market-days," the egg-seller said, with a slightly malicious sparkle to her eyes that told Kestrel there was a petty feud, probably of long standing, between her and the hen-woman. "It's from an old family recipe, and her own yeast, and I buy it myself. She's got the last stall in the row."

"Thank you *so* much," Robin replied, with a warm smile. "I really appreciate *your* courtesy."

She made her way past the next four stalls, still smiling, and paying no outward attention to the varied expressions of shock, amusement, and hostility the women there displayed. Interesting that there were only women in the market today. Perhaps the harvest was late.

Or perhaps the men did not consider market-day to be within their purview.

Now, Kestrel was no stranger to small villages or the behavior people who lived in them exhibited, particularly to outsiders, but the feeling here was — odd. By their clothing, by the condition of the buildings, and by the unused state of the road leading to Westhaven, this village was not exactly prospering. The women with stalls here *should* have been falling all over each other to attract the money Robin was so willingly spending.

But they weren't. The first woman had been actively hostile, and only the woman with the sausages seemed at all friendly — and that was simply because of the quarrel she had with the first stall-keeper. What was going on here?

The last stall held something they could actually

use; some nice, freshly dug root-vegetables and two round, golden loaves of bread — obviously the last of a large baking, by the blank places on the cloth where they sat. "Mother Tolley" behaved in the way Kestrel had expected — she was obviously pleased to see them and their coins, and was only too happy to sell them whatever they wanted. Robin chatted with her about the weather, the terrible state of the roads, revealed the fact that they had come from Birnam by way of Kingsford and that they were on their way to Gradford.

"My, how you've traveled! And you've been through Kingsford! Oh, I wish I could see it some day," Mother Tolley said, brightly. "I hear the Kingsford Faire is something to behold!"

"It is, indeed," Robin replied, nodding. "I have been there as a performer every year since I was a child of ten."

"Truly?" Mother Tolley's eyes widened. "What is it like? Is it as great as they say?"

Robin spread her hands wide. "Absolutely hundreds of people attend the Faire, from Dukes to Guild Masters to every manner of peddler you can imagine. If there is anything in the world that can be sold, you'll find it at Kingsford Faire. All the best performers in the world come there, and the Holy Services at noon on Midsummer Day are beyond description."

"All the world comes to Kingsford Faire." Mother Tolley repeated the old cliché as solemnly as if she had made it up on the spot. "Well, say, since you are so well-traveled, and a musician and all —" she hesitated a moment, then, with a sly glance at the other women, continued on "— there was someone I knew once who had a hankering to go to the Kingsford Faire. It was a local child, with so many dreams — well, there aren't too many folk who believe in dreams, especially not

here. I don't suppose you've ever heard tell of a fiddler
girl named Rune?"

By now, Kestrel would have had to be a blind man
not to notice how *all* the women, even those who were
feigning indifference or displaying open hostility, were
stretching their ears to hear Robin's reply to that question. And by the look in her eyes and the set of her jaw,
Robin was about to give them more than they bargained for.

"Rune? Lady Lark?" she said brightly. "Why, of
course I have! Everyone in all of Rayden and Birnam
knows all about Free Bard Rune! Why, she's the most
famous Free Bard in two kingdoms except for Master
Wren!"

Mother Tolley blinked. Apparently that was not
precisely the response she had expected. Kestrel figured she had hoped to hear something good about
Rune, but not this. "Rune! Famous!" she said, blankly.
"Why, fancy that —"

But Robin wasn't finished, not by half. "Oh, of
course!" she continued, raising her voice just a little, to
make certain everyone in the market got a good
chance to hear. "First there was her song about how
she bested the Skull Hill Ghost — I don't think there's
a musician in Rayden that hasn't learned it by now."

"She — actually —" Mother Tolley was still trying
to cope with the notion that Rune was famous.

"Oh, indeed! And she still has the Ghost's ancient
gold coins to prove it!" Now Robin was getting beyond
the truth and embroidering . . . and that made Kestrel
nervous.

"Gold? The Ghost has gold?" That was one of the
other women, her voice sharp with agitation.

"He did, but he gave it all to Rune, for her fid-
dling," Robin said brightly. "But that was just the
beginning. Then she became an ally of the High

King of the Elves for getting the better of one of the Elven Sires."

"Elves?" said another, in a choked voice. "She —"

Robin ran right over the top of her words. "But of course, what *really* made her famous was that she won the hand of Master Bard Talaysen himself with her talent and her musical skill — in fact, *she* was the one who saved him from that Elven Sire she bested. He wedded her, and now the two of them are the Laurel Bards to the King of Birnam, King Rolend, not just Laurel Bards but his personal advisors —"

Mother Tolley's face had gone so completely blank from astonishment that Kestrel couldn't tell what her feelings were. He guessed she would have been pleased to learn that Rune was doing well — but that this was something she wasn't prepared to cope with.

"I was at the ceremony, myself," Robin rattled on, in a confidential tone, as if she was a name-dropping scatterbrain. "As one of Lady Lark — that's what we call her, Lady Lark — one of Lady Lark's personal friends, of course. My! Even a Duke's daughter would envy her! She has twelve servants, all her very own — *three* of them just to tend to her wardrobe!"

Kestrel elbowed her sharply; she'd already gone too far three lies ago. She ignored him.

"The King himself gave her so much gold and gems that she couldn't possibly spend it all, and the weight of her jewelry would drown her if she ever fell into a river wearing it!" Robin gave him a warning look when he moved to elbow her again. "She wears silk every day, and she has three carriages to ride, and she bathes in wine, they say —" Robin simpered. Kestrel did his best not to laugh at her expression, despite his unease. He hadn't known she could *simper*. She was a better actress than he'd thought. "Our wagon and the horses and all — that was her present to me. You know, she gave wagons and horses to all her Gypsy friends who came to the ceremony. *So* sweet of her, don't you think?"

Mother Tolley had gone beyond astonished. "Yes," she said faintly. "Yes, very sweet. Of course."

Calling *Rune* one of King Rolend's Laurel Bards and a personal advisor was not exactly the truth — and the picture Robin had painted of Rune and Talaysen wallowing in luxury and wealth was not even *close* to being true. But Kestrel watched the faces of those who had been so eager to hear some terrible scandal about their prodigal runaway, and their puckered expressions told him that some of the good citizens of Westhaven were less than thrilled to hear that she was doing well. And the more sour those expressions became, the more Robin embroidered on her deceptions. He didn't think he had ever seen her look quite so smug before.

But while this was all very amusing to her, he was beginning to worry more than a little that she might be digging a hole they both were about to fall into.

"W-we must g-go," he said, firmly and loudly, before she could make up any more stories, this time out of whole cloth — either about Rune or about their supposed importance to her. Or worse yet, told the whole truth about *him*! He didn't know what was worse — to have these women believe Robin's tales, or to have them think her a liar.

"Ah," Robin said blankly as he completely threw her off her course for a moment with his interruption; then she regained her mental balance, and blinked, as if she had suddenly figured out that she might have gone a little too far. "Of course, you're right! We have a long way to go before we stop tonight."

She tucked her purchases carefully in her basket and allowed Kestrel to hurry her off.

"What w-were you th-thinking of?" he hissed, as they followed the sausage-woman's stammered directions to the mill.

"I'm not sure," she said weakly. "I got kind of carried away."

He refrained from stating the obvious.

"It was just — those sanctimonious prigs! You saw how they wanted to hear that I had never heard of Rune, that she was a nothing and a failure! I wanted to *smack* their self-satisfied faces!"

"Y-you d-did that all r-right," he replied, a little grimly, as they arrived at the mill.

The miller himself was busy, but one of his apprentices handled their purchase of grain for the horses. It took a while; the boy was determined that he was going to give them exact measure. By the time they returned to the wagon, the stalls were deserted, and the women gone from the marketplace.

Kestrel's stomach told him that there was no sinister reason for the empty market — it was suppertime, and these women had to return home to feed their families.

But the silence of the place unnerved him, and for once even Robin didn't have much to say. She unlocked the back of the caravan quickly and stowed her purchases inside; he went to one of the storage bins outside to put the grain away. Suddenly he wanted very much to be out of Westhaven and on the road.

Quickly. He felt eyes on his back; unfriendly eyes. The women might be gone, but they were still watching, from their homes and their kitchens. The sooner he and Robin had Westhaven behind them, the better.

He had put the last of the bags of grain away in the bin and locked the door, when he heard footsteps behind him.

"Hey!" said a nasal, obnoxious male voice. "What kinda thieves do we have here?"

CHAPTER SIX

He turned, but slowly, as if he had no idea that there was anyone at all there, pretending he had not heard the voice or the not-so-veiled insult. They weren't in any trouble — yet. An official, even in a tiny, provincial village like this one, would not be as young as the voice had sounded. Obnoxious, surely. Officious, of course. But not young. So this must be some stupid troublemaker, a village bully and his friends.

He knew as soon as he turned that he had been right, for the young men wore no badges of authority. There were three of them, none of them any older than he. All three were heavily muscled, and two of them had teeth missing. All three were taller than Kestrel. He looked up at them, measuring them warily. Definitely bullies, else why have three against two?

Don't do anything. Maybe they'll get bored and go away.

"So, Gyppo, what'd ye steal?" one asked, rubbing his nose across the back of his hand. It was a very dirty hand, and the nose wasn't exactly clean either. Dirty hair, pimpled face, a sneer that would have been more appropriate on the lips of a bratty little six-year-old.

Then again, I doubt his mind's grown much beyond six.

Kestrel ignored them, and moved to the front of the wagon. Robin was already there, untying the horses

from the hitching post. Bad luck there; they would
have to lead the horses around to turn the wagon, and
the three bullies were purposefully blocking the way.
The horses were well-trained, but it would be easy
enough to spook them.

"He's a Gyppo, he *had* ta steal sumthin'," said the
second. The troublemakers moved in a little closer,
blocking any escape — unless they left the wagon and
horses and fled on foot. And they were trapped
between the wagon and the blank wall of the Guild
Hall. Even *if* anyone here might be inclined to help,
there would be no way to see what was going on.
"Mebbe he stole th' wagon."

"Mebbe he stole the horses," said the third. "They's
too good a horse fer a Gyppo."

"So's the wagon," replied the first. "Mebbe he stole
both. Hey, Gyppo! Ye steal yer rig? Thas more likely
than that tale yer slut spun, 'bout Rune given it to ye!"

Something about the bully's tone warned Kestrel
that Robin's stories about Rune had brought them the
trouble he feared. This fool had been no friend to
Rune while she'd lived here — and he held a long-
standing grudge against her, like the hen-faced
woman.

"Yah," said the third, sniffing loudly and grinning.
"*We* know all 'bout Rune! Her mam's a slut, she's a
slut, an' I reckon her friends'r all sluts, too." He stared
at Kestrel, waiting for an answer, and became angry
when he didn't get one. "How 'bout it?" he growled.
"Ain't ye gonna say nothin'?"

Kestrel had been watching them carefully, assessing
them, and had concluded that while they were very
likely strong, and probably the town bullies, they also
didn't have a brain to share among them. They were
slow, and moved with the clumsy ponderousness of a
man used to getting his way through sheer bulk and

not through skill. And the way they held themselves told him they were not used to having any real opposition. They wanted to goad him into anger, into rushing them like an enraged child. They would not be prepared for someone who struck back with agility and control.

Still, if they could get away without a physical confrontation —

He simply stood his ground, and stared at them, hoping to unnerve them with his silence.

Stalemate. They stared at him, not sure what to do since he wasn't reacting to their taunts in the way they were used to. He stared at them, not daring them to start anything, but not backing down either.

Robin made a movement toward the slit in her skirt that concealed her knife. He put his hand on her wrist to stop her.

Unfortunately, that movement broke the tenuous stalemate.

"Yah, Rune's a slut an' her friends'r sluts!" said the first one, loudly. "Right, Hill, Warren?" He grinned as the other two nodded. "Hey, boys, I gotta idea! We got our fill'a her — so how 'bout we get a taste'f her friend, eh? They say Gyppo women is real hot —"

And he made the mistake of grabbing for Robin — who had fended off more bullies in her time than there were people in this village. As she launched herself at her would-be molester, Kestrel sprang at the one grabbing for him.

Fighting off assassins for most of your life tends to make you a survivor; it also teaches you every dirty trick anyone ever invented. Kestrel turned into a whirlwind of fists and feet, and Robin was putting her own set of street-fighting skills into action. He hadn't wanted this to turn into a physical confrontation, but the bullies had forced it on him, and now they were going to find out that the odds of three large men against a tiny man and woman *had* been very uneven — but not in *their* favor.

He kicked the legs out from beneath the one nearest him by slamming his foot into the fool's knee before the man had a notion that he had even moved. The bully went down on his face and started to scramble up, putting his rear in perfect target-range. Kestrel followed his kick in the rump with one to the privates so hard that the bully could not even scream, only gasp and double up into a ball. Robin had already done the same to the fool who had grabbed her, except that she hadn't bothered to knock his legs out from under him first. And she hadn't hit him with the knee, either; he was expecting that. He had backed out of knee range, laughing. She had snap-kicked him as she had intended all along, and the laugh turned into a gasp as she put her full weight behind the kick. She had followed up *her* foot to the groin with a backhanded blow in his face with the hilt of her dagger that put him to the ground with a bleeding nose and a few less teeth.

They both converged on the third bully, the one who seemed to be the leader, slamming him up against the side of the wagon before he had quite comprehended the fact that his two friends were no longer standing.

They knocked the breath out of him, and Robin had her dagger across his throat before he could blink. Kestrel grabbed his wrists and twisted his arms back while he was still stunned, holding him so that no matter how he moved, it would *hurt*. And the more he moved, the more it would hurt.

"Now," breathed Robin, as the bully's eyes bulged with fear and the edge of her blade made a thin, painful cut across his throat, "I think you owe us an apology. Don't you?"

Kestrel jerked the bully's arms so that they wrenched upwards in their sockets. He gasped, and nodded, his eyes filling with tears of pain. Now the very fact that nothing of this confrontation could be seen from the square or the houses around it worked in *their* favor. So long as no one missed these fools and came looking for them, if things went well.

Then again — they probably won't come looking for someone who might be beating the pulp out of two strangers. No one wants to know what these three are doing, I'll bet.

"I *also* think it would be very wise of you to make that apology, like a gentleman, and say nothing more about this," she continued. *"Don't you?"*

Frantically, he nodded, his eyes never leaving her face. The bloodthirsty expression there would have terrified a denser man than he.

"Just a few things I want you to think about, before you make that apology," she said harshly. "You might have what you *think* is a clever idea, about claiming how we attacked you, after we drive off." She shook her head, as he broke out in a cold sweat. "That would be a very, very stupid idea. First of all, you'd end up looking like a fool. Why, look how *small* we are! We weigh less than you do, the two of us put together! Think how *brave* you'd look, saying that two *tiny* people attacked you and beat you up, and one of them a girl! You would wind up looking like a weakling as well as a fool, and everyone from here to Kingsford would be laughing at you. What's more, they'd say you can't be any kind of a man if you let a girl beat you up. They'd say you're fey. And they'd start beating *you* up, any time you left home."

The sick look in his eyes told Kestrel that her words had hit home, but she wasn't finished with him.

"There's another reason why that would be a very,

very stupid idea," she continued. "We're Gypsies. Do
you know just what that means?"

He shook his head, very slightly.

"That means that we have all *kinds* of ways to find
out what you've been doing, even when we aren't
around. It means we have even *more* ways of getting at
you afterwards — and all of them will come when you
aren't expecting them." Her eyes widened, and her
voice took on a singing quality —

And Kestrel sensed the undercurrent of music in
the mind, music that could not be detected by the
ears, the music he only heard when someone was
using Bardic Magic.

Robin's voice matched that music, turning her
sing-song into a real spell, a spell meant to convince
this fool that every word she said was nothing less
than absolute truth. "We'll come in the night, when
you're all alone — catch you on a path and send
monsters to chase you until your heart bursts! We'll
send invisible things, night-hags, and vampires to
your bed, to sit on your chest and *squeeze* the
breath from your lungs while you try to scream in
pain and can't! We'll come at you from the full
moon, and set a fire in your brain, until you run
mad, howling like a dog!"

The bully was shaking so hard he could hardly stand
now.

"Or — we'll wait — and one night, when you're sitting at your ease —"

Her eyes widened further, and he stared at them,
unable to look away.

"— watching the fire — all alone — no one around
to help you, or save you —"

He was sweating so hard now that his shirt was
soaked.

"— suddenly the fire will *flare*! It will grow! You'll

be unable to move as it swells and takes on a form, the form of a two-legged beast with fangs as long as your arm and talons like razors! You'll scream and scream, but no one will hear you! You'll try to escape, but you'll be frozen to your chair! You'll watch the *demon* tear out your heart, watch as it eats your heart still beating, and howl as it takes you down to hell!"

At the word "hell," a burst of flame appeared under his nose, cupped in the hand that was not holding the dagger.

A slow, spreading stain on the front of his pants and a distinctive smell betrayed just how frightened he was. The bully had wet his breeches with fear.

Kestrel let him go in disgust, and the man dropped to the ground, gibbering incoherently. Robin stepped back and smiled at him sweetly.

"Now," she said, "do you apologize for calling me a slut?"

He nodded frantically.

"Do you apologize for calling Rune a slut?"

His head bobbed so hard it practically came off his shoulders.

"Are you going to keep your filthy tongue off Rune and any other Free Bard? Are you going to take your two playmates and go away, and never say *anything* about this again?" She smiled, but it was not sweetly. "Are you going to pretend all this never happened?"

"Yes!" the bully blubbered, through his tears. "Yes! Oh, please —"

"You may go," Robin said, coolly, sheathing her dagger so quickly it must have looked to the man as if she had made it vanish into thin air. He fled.

The other two were just getting to their feet, but they had heard and seen everything Robin had said and done. And they had been affected by her Bardic spell too, just not as profoundly or immediately as

the first bully. The one Kestrel had kicked helped
the one with the bloodied face to his feet, and the
two of them supported each other, getting out of
sight as quickly as possible.

Which was precisely what Kestrel had in mind, as
well — getting away before some other variety of
trouble found them! He jumped into the driver's seat
and picked up the reins, giving Robin just enough
time to scramble into the passenger's side before turning the mares, and heading out of the village at a brisk
trot, thanking whatever deity might be listening for
the thickening dusk that hid both them and their erst-
while attackers, and for the emptiness of the village
square.

"Wh-why d-did you *d-d-d-do* that?" he asked, as
Robin arranged her skirts with a self-satisfied little
smile.

"What?" she asked, as if he had astonished her by
asking the question. "Why did I use the Bardic Magic?
I wanted him to believe me! If I hadn't, he'd have gotten another dozen of his friends and come after us!"

"N-not using th-the B-Bardic M-Magic!" he
scolded, guiding the mares around a tricky turn.
"M-making th-them th-think w-we w-were evil m-m-
mages! R-remember wh-what the Ch-church has
b-b-been saying ab-b-bout m-mages?"

"Oh, that," she replied, indifferently. "What difference does it make? He won't tell anyone *anything*
now. He'll be sure that the moment he opens his
mouth, a demon will come after him."

"*N-now*," Kestrel retorted. "You kn-know the
m-magic w-wears off! H-how l-long b-before he t-tells
a P-p-p-priest?"

"So what? We're never coming back." She had
something cradled in her skirts; a moment later, he
heard the distinctive clink of coins. "Hah!" she said, in

the next moment, as the wagon jounced a little. "We actually came out ahead!"

"*Wh-what?*" he yelped. He knew exactly what *that* meant; she'd not only beaten and terrified those bullies, she'd *picked their pockets.* "Y-you d-d-d-didn't!"

"Of course I did," she said, calmly, taking the coins and pouring them into her belt-pouch. "Why not? They deserved worse than that! Didn't you hear them? I'll bet those louts absolutely terrified Rune while she lived here! They should be grateful that I was in a good mood! I almost made the three of them eunuchs while I was at it!"

"B-but —" he protested. "Th-that m-makes us n-no b-better th-than th-they are!"

"I don't think so." She folded her arms stubbornly across her chest. "I think we were simply the instrument of proper justice."

"B-but —" He gave up. She would never admit she was wrong, even if he managed to convince her of it — and even if he did, she would only think he was worried about the possible consequences. That wasn't what made him so upset, but how could he make her understand that she had just acted in as immoral and irresponsible a manner as the *Church* claimed Free Bards were?

How could they honestly refute the claims of the street preachers when they actually *did* what the street preachers said they did? Even though they had been provoked —

Never mind. Right now, the best thing he could do was drive. Maybe this would sort itself out later.

He hoped.

Darkness had fallen by the time they reached the next building on the road. The Hungry Bear inn — distinguished as such by the sign over the door, a crudely painted caricature of an animal that *could* have been a bear — or a brown pig — or a tree-stump with teeth. The sign was much in need of paint. The *inn* was much in need of repair.

Even in the fading twilight and the feeble flame of a torch beside the door, that much was all too obvious. It was clean, superficially at least, but so shabby that Gwyna would have passed it by without a second thought if they were really looking for a night's work.

But they weren't, so when Kestrel pulled the horses to a halt outside the front door — which didn't even have a lantern, only that crude pitch-and-straw torch — she hopped down to see if she could find the inn-keeper.

She had barely one foot on the ground before a round blob of a woman dressed in clothing more suited to a coquettish girl came hurrying out to see if they might be customers.

As she came out of the darkness of the tap room and into the flickering light from the torch, Gwyna felt her eyes widen in surprise. Was *this* Rune's mother?

She must be — certainly the lavish use of cosmetics, and the straw-blond hair, the low-cut blouse and the kilted-up skirt matched Rune's descriptions. But if this was Rune's mother — either Rune's memory was horribly at fault, or the woman had doubled, or even tripled her weight, since Rune had left!

"Welcome to the Hungry Bear," the woman said, her eyes taking in their equippage, and probably evaluating it to the last penny. "My name is Stara, and I am the innkeeper's wife — how may I serve you?"

Well, that certainly clinched it. This *was* Rune's mother, and she had evidently managed to wheedle, connive, or blackmail her way into more than Jeoff's bed.

Well, Rune was right about that much. And since I

don't see any other helpers around, I suspect they either can't afford more help anymore, or no one will work for them. So Rune was right there, too, in thinking Stara would have turned her into an unpaid drudge, given half a chance. If Rune had stayed, she'd have found herself shackled to this shoddy inn for the rest of her life, with music taking second place to whatever her mother wanted her to do.

"We are musicians, Innkeeper," Robin said, in a carefully neutral voice. "We hadn't really expected to find an inn here, but we usually offer our services in return for a room and a meal —"

Not that I'd sleep in any bed you had anything to do with. You probably haven't washed the sheets in months.

The balding and middle-aged innkeeper himself appeared at the door as Robin finished her little speech, but he held back, diffidently saying nothing, quite obviously very much the henpecked husband. Stara looked them over critically, and her eyes sharpened with mingled envy and greed at their prosperity. No one who drove a rig like theirs, new, and well-made, would be an inferior musician or poor. . . .

And given the general air of abandonment, when Rune ran off, most of the business went somewhere else. There should be at least a handful of customers in there, and the tap room is empty. I don't smell anything cooking, either, which means they don't get enough customers of an evening to have a regular supper ready.

So, *if* they stayed, there'd be an empty tap room, a poor meal and a cold and musty bed. And given what had just happened back in the village —

It probably wouldn't be a good idea to stop here. No matter what else I could find out about Stara. I think I've seen enough to tell Rune all she needs to hear.

Enough to make her glad that she got out while she could.

"Uh — Stara —" the innkeeper said, timidly. "We don't know these people. We don't know anything about them. Remember what the Priest has been preaching? These people aren't wearing Guild colors. So many of these free musicians sing that licentious music, that music that makes people do sinful things —"

Stara started to wave him to silence, but it appeared that on this subject, at least, he would not be henpecked. He raised his chin and his voice stubbornly. "You know very well how sinful we were when that daughter of yours was playing her music here! And every night the tap room was full of people dancing, singing, taking no thought of their souls —"

"I know," Stara muttered resentfully, no doubt thinking how full the cashbox had been back then.

"Well, what if these people are the same kind?" he asked her, his voice rising with a touch of hysteria. "I'm sure the Sacrificed God has been punishing us for our sin of letting people like that play here while that daughter of yours was here. Worse than that, what if they're magicians? I don't think we should let anyone play here who hasn't been approved by the Church!"

Harperus' words rang at her out of memory. *"How long before the signs say, 'No one permitted without a Church license'?"*

She grimaced, her expression hidden in the shadows of the wagon. *Not that I'd want to play here, with or without a license.*

"I would not want to make anyone uncomfortable, much less give them the impression that they were sinning by simply listening to music," Robin said, smoothly. "I personally have never heard of any such nonsense as musicians who were magicians, but since your Priest evidently has, I will take his word that such things exist. And since obviously you don't want us, and no one can prove he *isn't* a mage, we'll just be on our way. We would never want to play where we were under suspicion, or where our music wasn't wanted." She raised her voice a little more, and pitched it to make certain that it carried. "We are really in no great need of lodging, as you can clearly see, so do not concern yourselves for us on that score."

Not that you would care, but it's a nice little dig, isn't it?

Stara looked disgusted and stormed back into the tap room. The innkeeper followed, wearing a look that mingled triumph and apprehension in equal measure. Triumph that he had his way, no doubt — and apprehension for the way that Stara was going to make him pay for getting his way. The door shut behind them.

Kestrel looked over at her, holding the reins quietly. "Interesting," he said.

She nodded. "I really think we ought to try camping somewhere down the road. Between the bullies and Priests with tales of music that leads you into sin, I'd sooner trust myself to wolves than Westhaven."

"But would ye trust yerselves to ghosts, young friends?" asked a hoarse voice from the shadows of the rear door, across the inn-yard from the sorry excuse for a stable. "An ye would not, turn back 'round and take the long road — or follow th' right-hand fork o' this one."

A stolid woman with a round, red face moved out of the shadows and into the uncertain light of the torch. "*She* wouldna tell ye, an' *he* would be just's pleased t'see a sinner come t'grief, but yon's the road over Skull Hill. There be a Ghost there, a murderin' Ghost. It's taken a priest in it's time, no less, so it don't care a tot fer holiness. Yer safe enough by day, but by night, ain't nobbut safe on Skull Hill."

Kestrel nodded, gravely. "Th-thank you, l-lady."

The cook looked pleased at being called "lady." "Tush. Tain't nothin' no *decent* person wouldna pass warnin' 'bout."

Robin looked closely at the woman; they knew all about the Ghost from Rune, of course, but Rune had described someone very like this woman — one of her few supporters after the innkeeper's first wife had died. The cook —

"Are you Annie Cook?" Robin asked. The woman stared at her, and nodded, slowly, her expression turning to one of apprehension.

"How d'ye know —" Annie began, clearly suspecting Robin of an uncanny, unnatural method of learning her name.

"Rune told me about you," Robin replied quickly, not sure how long it would be before Stara or Jeoff came to chase them off. "She said you were a good friend to her while she was here."

The uneasy expression turned again to one of pleasure. "Rune! I hope th' child's well! She did aright t' run off from here."

Impulsively, Robin decided to tell Annie a more edited — and truthful — version of what she had told the villagers. "Rune is doing wonderfully; she is a Master Free Bard herself, she's wedded Master Bard Talaysen, and they are both in the service of the King of Birnam. She is *very* happy, and she and Talaysen are expecting their first child in the summer."

Annie gaped at her, then the gape turned into a smile. "Ye *don't* say! Welladay!" The smile widened. "Why good for the girl! If ever there was a child deserved a bit'a luck, it was that 'un!" She glared at the closed door of the inn. "Not like 'er mother. That bit can't get nothin' without it bein' through some man's bed. An' had Rune stayed here, she'd'a been slavin' away i' that tap room while her mam sat on 'er fat rump an' held th' cashbox."

"*Annie?*" the voice from within was muffled, but clearly Stara's. Annie rolled her eyes, waved a friendly, but silent farewell, and retreated to her kitchen.

Dark as it was, the road was smooth enough to permit them to travel by night, at least for a while. Kestrel held the horses to a walk. It wasn't as if they had to fear pursuit from the village. It wasn't likely that, even if by some miracle the three bullies got over their fright, any of them would come pursuing the Gypsies in the dark. "S-so that w-was S-Stara," he said. "N-n-nasty, p-petty piece."

"I'd have run off long before Rune did," Robin said thoughtfully. "Long, long before Rune did. That woman can't see past the end of her nose, and if she ever had a generous bone in her, it's long since gone."

Kestrel chuckled. "S-sunk in f-fat."

It was still barely warm enough for crickets, which sang a melancholy tune in the grasses beside the road. Overhead, thin clouds obscured the stars; the overcast was blowing off, but the moon was not yet out. No way to see past the dim lanterns on the front of the wagon, but the underbrush was so thick on either side of the road that there was no chance of the horses wandering off. And this road, according to the maps, went straight to Carthell Abbey without forking.

By way of Skull Hill.

That was according to the map; according to Rune and Annie Cook, the road forked a little way ahead, and while the old road still went over Skull Hill, the locals had cut another, cruder path around the dangerous place. Passable, she had said.

"I th-think, that c-compared to S-Stara, the Gh-Ghost m-must have been a p-pleasant audience," he said, trying to make a small joke.

Robin chuckled. "Certainly more appreciative. And the Ghost *rewarded* talent instead of stifling it."

"T-true." The horses clopped on, through the thick darkness, carefully feeling their way. Kestrel had been watching for roadside clearings, but there didn't seem to be any. He was beginning to wonder if they ought to stop and camp along here, even if they had to camp in the center of the road. After all, it wasn't as if it got very much use — they were hardly likely to block any-one's travel! By the old tracks they had seen, they might have been the only wagon along here in the past week.

"Th-that p-place where the r-road f-forks should b-be around here s-soon," he said. "What if w-we —"

"What if we go up Skull Hill?" Robin asked, sud-denly.

For a moment he wasn't certain he had heard her right. "Wh-what?" he blurted.

"What if we go up Skull Hill?" she repeated. "Con-front the Ghost, just like Rune did?"

He *had* heard her correctly. "Are you c-c-c-crazy?" he spluttered. "Why?"

She laughed; she didn't *sound* crazy. She did sound rather determined, however. "Why not?" she replied. "Rune did, and she wasn't even fully trained! We already know it likes music, and it might have another silver hoard or something equally interesting to swap for our music. We might be able to get him to grant unmolested passage to Gypsies and Free Bards, and that would be worth a night of playing, alone — we might need a road some day that no one will take."

He chewed on his lip, fiercely, and thought about it. She had a point. She had a very real point. The old road ran this way for a reason; it was a shorter route than the one that Harperus and T'fyrr were taking. If Gypsies and Free Bards knew it was safe for them to use, it could take a couple of days off their trips in this part of the world.

And if no one else would use the road for fear of the Ghost — it made a very neat escape route in case of trouble. From here to Stillwater was no great distance, and Stillwater could be held against even armed men if necessary.

"Let me get a lantern and walk ahead of the horses, so I can spot the place where the road forks," she said, while he was still thinking about it.

He pulled the horses to a halt; she wriggled back over the bed, and popped out the back with a lit lantern in her hand. She trotted up to take the halter of the right-hand horse, and held the lantern over her head to keep from getting glare in her eyes.

Well, that was all very well for her, but nothing saved him from the lantern-glare! He squinted, but he couldn't quite make out the road. He let the reins go slack; she was the one who could see where they were going —

And he realized a few moments later that she was leading them down the left-hand fork of the road. The overgrown, but obviously older, fork of the road.

"*Robin!*" he yelped. "Wh-what are you *d-d-doing*?"

She stopped the horses, and looked back at him, a little defiantly.

"I told you!" she said. "I want to climb Skull Hill to meet this Ghost face to — whatever!"

Robin left the mares and brought her lantern back to the Kestrel, placing it at his feet. She looked up into his face, carefully gauging his expression. "I don't think there's any real danger," she said, calmly and reasonably, watching his eyes. "Honestly, or I wouldn't even consider this."

He didn't seem frightened. Of course, he could be hiding his fear. "N-no d-d-d-danger," he repeated sarcastically. "Wh-when wh-who kn-kn-knows *how* m-m-many p-p-p-people have d-d-died up th-there!"

She took a very deep breath and got a firm grip on her temper. He wasn't saying she was stupid — wasn't even implying it. "When have I ever done anything really reckless?" she asked him.

He looked as if he was about to say something — but thought better of it, and closed his mouth again. "G-go on," he said grimly. "I'm l-l-listening. If y-you have a r-r-real argument, b-b-besides c-curiosity, I w-want to h-hear it."

"I've known something about magic for a long time," she told him. "At least, about some of the tinier magics. Not Bardic Magic, but little things Gypsies take for granted; healing, animal-charming, that kind of thing. And I think I know how this Ghost kills. I am pretty sure that his only real *weapon* is fear, and he can't do anything unless you're already afraid of him."

Kestrel looked skeptical, but a little less grim. "S-so?"

She licked her lips, and stared at the lamp flame for a moment. "If you're afraid of him, he can turn that fear against you — he can make it so overwhelming that — that it becomes something the human body just can't deal with. The heart races until it just gives up, he chases you until you drop dead of exhaustion, that kind of thing. Maybe some people don't die — maybe *most* of them don't die, they just run mad in this wilderness until they die of thirst or starve, or wild beasts get them."

"Th-that's v-v-very c-c-comforting," he said with heavy irony.

"But the point is that if you *aren't* afraid of him, he can't hurt you," she insisted. "Or if you interest him, he won't use that weapon of his! Rune wasn't completely terrified of him — and she interested him. So she was able to stand up to him. I don't know why we can't!"

Kestrel shook his head. "Wh-who s-s-said w-we aren't af-f-fraid of h-him?" he muttered. "N-n-not m-m-me."

She chuckled, as if he had made a joke. "Jonny, do you think I would have suggested this if you weren't a Master Bard in your own right? Think a minute! Rune managed to entertain this Ghost before she was even *trained* — when she was just a little better than a common traveling musician like all those people back in the Waymeet. Just think for a moment what we might be able to find out from him! Jonny, you're going to be the best thing he's heard in — well, since he got stuck up there!"

The only thing he was vain about was his talent and his ability as a musician. He began to soften as she appealed to that vanity.

"I think we can do this with no danger," she said, persuasively. "I think *you* could do this all alone, but with two of us there, we can keep from getting too exhausted."

Finally, the stubborn line of his jaw softened, and he sighed. "You r-r-really want t-t-to d-do th-this, d-don't you?"

"Yes," she replied, firmly. "I do. Call it — a sort of test. I want to measure myself against the same stand-ards as the best musicians I know. This is one of them."

He shook his head. "All r-r-right," he replied.

"Th-this m-makes m-more s-sense than wh-what you d-did back in W-Westhaven, anyw-w-way."

And as she led the horses up to the top of Skull Hill, she was left to wonder —

What in heaven's name did he mean by *that*?

CHAPTER SEVEN

Gwyna was just as glad that Jonny was not as familiar with Rune's history as she was. It had not been easy to convince him to go along with her scheme, but her appeal to his only point of pride had turned the trick. If he had known as much about the Ghost as she did — he might not have agreed even under a threat to their lives.

Robin knew she had a distinct advantage over Kestrel; she had heard Rune tell the story of the Skull Hill Ghost in detail, several times. Jonny had only heard the song. She knew pretty much what to expect, and when to expect it; she knew all there was that Rune had been able to put into words about the *effect* the Ghost had on people. She had paid very close attention to that story each time Rune had told it, because even before she had ever met Jonny or had learned that she, too, had the gift of Bardic Magic at her disposal, she had intended to come to Skull Hill one day.

Not just because she was determined to prove — if only to herself — that what Rune could do, she could duplicate. No, that was the easy answer, the one she thought Jonny would best understand.

Robin had spent her life in the pursuit of answers for the questions that plagued her. The story of the Ghost had created more questions for her than answers, and had powerfully aroused her curiosity. What *was* this spirit, anyway? The impression she'd gotten from Rune was that it was not, and never had been, human. So what was it? Was it really a spirit at all, or something more like an Elf, except that it was both more limited and more powerful? If it was a spirit, then why was a spirit bound to Skull Hill? And if it was the spirit of some creature that had not been human when alive, then what had brought a nonhuman creature *here,* to the heart of a human kingdom, and what had bound its spirit here after death?

And why was it killing people with fear? Rune's story made it very clear that the Ghost was deliberately *trying* to murder his victims; the deaths that had occurred were as a result of the Ghost's deliberate use of his powers to kill. By that definition it was a murderer.

But the fact that he — it — had also let Rune "buy" her way free with her music implied that the Ghost could spare people when it chose to do so. The things it had said implied that it was not free to leave. Those implications only opened up a horde of questions so far as Robin was concerned.

Before she had ever met Jonny, curiosity had driven her to do things and go places when nothing else would have. Questions would burn inside her until they found an answer. Talaysen often said it was her greatest strength and her greatest weakness, and she didn't see any reason to disagree. But her curiosity had gotten her information that might never have come into the hands of the Free Bards or the Gypsies otherwise, and many times, that information had been important to their survival.

This time both intuition and curiosity had combined forces. *This is important,* that was the message she was getting from both. She didn't get many "hunches," and she tried hard to follow them whenever she did; they were right more often than they were wrong.

She kept the lantern over her head to keep her eyes from becoming dazzled by the light, and led the horses up the untidy, long-neglected track. It wasn't as overgrown as she would have expected, though; no bushes or trees, only weeds, and those looked sickly and were no taller than her calf, even after a summer's worth of growth. She knew what *that* meant; there was a road underneath this track, one of the Old Roads, the ones no one knew how to build anymore. If she got out a shovel and dug, she knew she would hit the hard surface of one of the roadways that dated back to the Cataclysm; it would be a lightless black substance, like stone but yielding, like tar but much harder. Nothing could grow through it; that was why there was nothing growing on this track but short weeds. The earth and loam that had covered this road couldn't be more than an inch or so thick; just enough for grass and weeds to take root in. There would be no cracks or imperfections in it, unless she came to a place where an earthquake had split it, or the edge of a Cataclysm-boundary, where it would be cut off as if by a giant knife.

The Old Roads usually connected two or more important places — or at least, places that *had* been important before the Cataclysm. There were often ruins along them. The Deliambrens always wanted to know about Old Roads, so the Gypsies kept track of the ones they ran across. Did Harperus know this one was here?

Probably not. Whatever this segment had connected before, it certainly connected nothing of any import now. Gradford was a very minor city-state despite its pretentions otherwise, and what was Westhaven? Nothing, full of nobodies. A dead-end, dying,

and not even aware it was in its death-throes. Too stupid to know that its days were numbered.

*The only thing that makes it important is that Rune
came from there*, Gwyna thought cynically, thinking of
the women in the marketplace and the three bullies
they had left damaged. Of course, she had — she
hoped — inflicted some emotional damage on the
women who deserved it, with her descriptions of
Rune's fame and prosperity. *I hope that hen-faced
bitch is so envious of Rune that she chokes on her dinner. I bet* she's *the one that set those bullies on us. I
hope she nags her husband about silk gowns and carriages until he beats her senseless. I hope that fool I
scared into incontinence is her husband, and I scared
him into impotence as well!* She kept her feral snarl to
herself. *Vindictive? Oh, a tad.*

She knew better than to say any of this out loud.
Jonny, bless his sweet little heart, was *not* vindictive.
He believed that concentrating on revenge simply
reduced you to the level of your persecutors. Gwyna
believed in an old Gypsy proverb; *Get your revenge in
early and often. You might not have another chance.*

Maybe that was why the Ghost fascinated her so.
Was he somehow working out some bizarre scheme
for revenge? If so, on who, and why? Was he choosing
to let *some* people by, people they never even heard of
because they were unaware that they had been in any
danger at all?

Or was he a strange revenant from the distant past,
from the time when this Old Road had been in use?
Could something have called him up out of that past
to haunt this stretch of roadway? Could his reasons
and motives, or need for revenge, be buried so far in
the past they no longer had any relevance?

Or if this creature was strange enough, could they
even understand his reasons, much less his motives?

An owl called up above her, and she sighed. No point in following that line of speculation. He had to be understandable; there was no point in this, otherwise.

Well, he's enough like us to enjoy our music.

The track grew steeper, and she felt the strain in her calf muscles. Too bad she couldn't ride, but if she let the horses try to pick their own way, they might get hurt. She glanced back at Jonny; he was watching all around them, nervously expecting the Ghost to pop up at any moment.

She didn't think that was likely; the Ghost and things like him often picked specific times to appear. Sunset, midnight, moonrise, or moonset seemed to be the most often chosen. Since people had been caught out on this track by the spirit after dark, not knowing that it was there, and since Rune had climbed Skull Hill without seeing the Ghost and had to actually wait for it to appear, Robin guessed that it probably appeared at midnight or moonrise. Tonight the two would be almost simultaneous; midnight and moon-rise within moments of each other.

And they would be at the top long before either. There would be plenty of time to rest her aching legs and eat a little. Time enough to park the wagon and ready the instruments. Time to think about what they were going to play, what they were going to say. Every-thing needed to be perfect for this performance.

After all, it was going to be the performance of a lifetime . . . and it had better be the best performance of their lives. She had the feeling that the Ghost would not accept anything less.

"You might as well eat something," Robin observed, biting into her bread-and-cheese with appreciation. Mother Tolley did, indeed, make very good bread; firm and sweet, with a chewy crust. *About the only thing good in that whole town,* she decided. *Unless Annie Cook's skills match Rune's memory.* The tasty bread settled into her stomach comfortably, and she took another bite.

"C-c-can't," Jonny replied, nervously fingering the tuning-pegs on his harp as he watched the shadows for any sign of the Ghost. There was nothing, and had been nothing since they had parked the wagon here. And if Rune's story was accurate, there would be plenty of warning when the Ghost *did* arrive; it was not going to sneak up on them when they weren't looking. *Likes to make an impressive entrance. I wonder if it was an actor once?*

They were at the very top of the hill, with the slash of the road going right across the clearing at the very peak. As overcast as it was, even with the lamp burning, you couldn't see a thing beyond the darker forms of trees and shrubbery against the slightly lighter sky. A cool breeze blew across the clearing, but it held no hint of moisture, and no otherworldly scent of brimstone or the fetor of the grave, either.

Robin shrugged as she caught Jonny's eye. "This would steady your stomach," she suggested. "It's going to be a long time until dawn. You're going to need a little sustenance before the night is over."

"I g-guess s-so," he said, after another long moment. But he groped after her hand, then seized the slice of bread-and-cheese she handed him without looking at it, and wolfed it down without tasting it, his eyes never leaving the clearing in front of their wagon.

With the help of the lantern, Gwyna thought she'd identified Rune's rock — that is, the one Rune had been sitting on when the Ghost appeared to her. They had parked the wagon with the tail of it facing that rock and the clearing in front of it. She figured it was the most likely place for the Ghost to manifest. Now it was just a matter of waiting.

Jonny was not taking the waiting well. He was as tight as a harp strung an octave too high, and if she hadn't *seen* him in crisis situations and *known* that he handled them well and settled once the crisis was upon them, she'd have been very worried about his steadiness.

Her stomach was fluttery — hence the bread-and-cheese — and her shoulders were tight. But her senses seemed a hundred times sharper than usual, and everything happened with preternatural slowness. She heard every cricket clearly and knew exactly where it was; she knew where the owls were hooting, and about how far away they were. She felt the breeze across her skin like a caress; she tasted the bitter tannin of dead leaves, the promise of frost in the air. All of it was very immediate, and very vivid.

She *wanted* this to happen; she had not felt so alive for weeks. That was what performance nerves did to her; she'd felt exactly like this when they'd gone in to confront Jonny's uncle, King Rolend. Afterwards, she might shake and berate herself for doing something so risky — but now, there was only the chill tingle of anticipation and —

And the moon was rising!

She caught the barest hint of it, a mere sliver of silver at the horizon, before it was covered by the clouds. But that was enough — and enough to tell her that the chill tingle she felt along her nerves was *not* anticipation. It was something else entirely.

Magic? The crickets!

The crickets stopped chirping abruptly, with no warning. They had not faded away; no, they had stopped entirely, leaving behind a hollow and empty silence that seemed louder than a shout. The breeze dropped into a dead calm.

Then, in the very next moment, a wind howled up out of nowhere, just as Rune had described, a wind carrying the chill of a midwinter ice-storm. It flattened their clothing to their bodies and if Robin had not taken the precaution of binding her hair up for travel, it would have blinded her with her own tresses. This was not a screaming wind — no, this wind *moaned.* It sounded alive, somehow, and in dire, deadly, despairing pain. A hopeless wind, a wind that was in torment and not permitted to die. A tortured wind, that carried the instruments of its own torture as lances of ice in its bowels.

It whirled around them for a moment, mocking their living warmth with deathly cold, as they huddled instinctively close together on the wagon-tail. There was more than physical *cold* in this wind; the hair on her arms rose as she realized that this wind also carried *power.* Not a power she recognized, but akin to it. The antithesis of healing-power . . . malignant, bitterly envious, and full of hate. The horses were utterly silent, and when she looked back at them, she saw them shaking, sides slick with the sweat of fear, and the whites of their eyes showing all around.

She didn't blame them. *Now,* now that it was far too late, she realized what an incredibly stupid thing she had done. Whatever had made her think she could bargain with this thing? This wasn't a spirit — it was a force that was a law unto itself. She shook with more than cold, she trembled with more than fear. She had walked wide-eyed into a trap. Her own confidence had betrayed her. Her guts clenched, and her throat was too tight to swallow; her mouth dry as dust and her heart pounding.

The wind spun out and away from them; in the

blink of an eye it swirled out into clearing, gathering up every dead leaf and bit of dust with it. In a moment it had formed into a column, a miniature tornado, swaying snakelike in the middle of the clearing.

There were eyes in that whirlwind; not visible eyes, but something in there watched her. She felt those eyes on her skin, felt them studying her and searching for weaknesses, hating her, hating Jonny, hating even the inoffensive horses. Hating every living thing, because *they* were alive and it was not.

She couldn't take her eyes off the whirlwind, and Rune's description quite vanished from her mind. All she could think of were the words of the song.

> *. . . then comes a wind that chills my blood*
> *And makes the dead leaves whirl. . . .*

But the song had said nothing about how the leaves glowed with a light of their own. Nor about the closing in of malignant power as it surrounded her and increased until it choked her.

Each leaf glowed in a distinctive shade of greenish-white, the veins a brighter white against the shape of the leaf, somehow calling to mind things rotting, things unhealthy. The leaves pulled together within the center of the whirlwind, forming a solid, irregular shape in the middle of the whirling wind and dust, a shape that was thicker at the bottom than the top, with a suggestion of a cowl crowning it all.

The shape grew more distinct by the moment as the wind whipped faster and faster until the individual leaves vanished into a glowing blur. Then the odd shape at the top of the column *was* a cowl, and the entire form was that of a hooded and robed figure, somehow proportioned in such a way that there was never any doubt that this *thing* was not, and had never been, human.

Exactly as Rune had described.

> *. . . rising up in front of me, a thing like shrouded Death. . . .*

Oh, it looked like Death in his shroud, all right — worse, it *felt* like Death. The wind died; it had, after all, done its work and was no longer needed. Robin had never felt so cold, or so frightened. Her heart seemed lodged somewhere in her throat, and her fingers were frozen to her instrument —

It's doing this, not you! The thought came sluggishly, up through a thick syrup of fear. *This thing is making you afraid! Didn't you feel the power? Fight it! Fight it, or you won't be able to speak! And if you can't speak, you can't bargain, and you certainly can't sing!*

With the thought came determination; with the determination and the sheer, stubborn will came the realization that the fear *was* coming from outside her! She clenched her jaw as momentary anger overcame the fear —

— and broke it!

It was gone, all in that instant, and once broken, the spell of fear did not return. She sat up straighter; she was free! Her stomach unknotted; her heart slowed. Her throat cleared, and she was able to breathe again.

The last of the leaves settled around the base of the robe. The figure within that robe was thin and dreadfully attenuated; if it had been human, it would have been nothing but bone, but bone that had been softened and stretched until the skeleton was half again the height of the average human male. *Elongated.*

That was the description she was searching for. And yet, there was nothing fragile about this thing. The cowl turned towards them, slowly and deliberately, and there was a suggestion of glowing eyes within the dark shadows of the hood.

The voice, when the thing spoke, came as something of a surprise. Robin had expected a hollow, booming voice, like the tolling of a death-bell. Instead, an icy, spidery whisper floated out of the darkness around them, as if all the shadows were speaking, and not the creature before them.

"How is it" — it whispered — "that you come here? Not one, but two musicians? Have you not heard of me, of what I am, of what I will do to you?"

Robin felt the pressure of *magic* all around her, as the Ghost tried to fill her with fear and make her flee. But the fear failed to touch her; she sensed only the power, and not the emotion the Ghost sought to use against her. So it did not know she had broken its spell!

Time to enlighten it.

"Of course we have heard of you!" she said, clearly and calmly. "The whole world has heard of you! Listen —"

Her fingers picked out the introduction to "The Skull Hill Ghost." And she began to sing.

> *I sit here on a rock, and curse my stupid, bragging tongue,*
> *And curse my pride that would not let me back down from a boast*
> *And wonder where my wits went, when I took that challenge up*
> *And swore that I would go and fiddle for the Skull Hill Ghost!*

As she sang, she exerted a little magic of her own;

warm and loving magic, Bardic Magic and Gypsy magic and the magic of one true lover for another. She sent it, not at the Ghost, but at Kestrel, all of it aimed at breaking the spell of fear that held Jonny imprisoned in his icy silence as she had been imprisoned a moment before.

The warmth must have reached him, for as she reached the chorus, he shook himself, and suddenly his harp joined the jaunty chords of her gittern as his voice joined hers in harmony.

> *I'll play you high, I'll play you low*
> *For I'm a wizard with my bow*
> *For music is my weapon and my art —*
> *And every note I fling will strike your heart!*

That was a change from the original wording of Rune's contest-song; more of a metaphor for the life-and-death battle she had waged to save herself from the Ghost *and* a life of grim poverty than the original chorus had been.

Robin continued in the "Rune" persona, with Kestrel coming in with the Ghost's first line — in a cunning imitation of the Ghost's own voice.

> *"Give me reason why I shouldn't kill you, girl!"*

She watched her audience of one as closely as she had ever watched *any* audience; had she seen the spirit start with surprise at hearing his own words?

She responded as Rune.

> *"I've come to fiddle for you, sir —"*

Kestrel came in — and again, his voice was not a booming and spectral one, as Wren usually sang the part, but in that deliberate imitation of the Ghost's true disembodied whisper.

> "— *Oh have you so? Then fiddle, girl, and pray you fiddle well.*
> *For if I like your music, then I'll let you live to play —*
> *But if you do not please my ears I'll take you down to Hell!*"

The cowl nodded, ever so slightly. And the pressure of *magic* eased off.

Now Robin concentrated on the music, and not the Ghost. She had his attention. Now she must keep it.

The song was a relatively short one, meant for a Faire audience that might not linger to hear an extended ballad. The last verse came up quickly.

> *At last the dawnlight strikes my eyes, I stop and see the sun —*
> *The light begins to chase away the dark and mid-night cold —*
> *And then the light strikes something more, I stare in dumb surprise —*
> *For where the Ghost once stood there is a heap of shining gold!*

Then she and Kestrel swung into a double repeat of the last chorus, laughing and triumphant.

> *I'll play you high, I'll play you low*
> *For I'm a wizard with my bow*
> *And music is my lifeblood and my art*
> *And every note I sing will tame your heart!*

They finished with a flourish worthy of Master

Wren himself. The Ghost regarded them from under his hood with a speculation and surprise that Robin *felt*, just as she had felt the fear he had tried to force on her.

"Well," it whispered, the voice now coming from beneath that cowl and not from every shade and shadow in the clearing. "So, the little fiddler girl survived. Did she thrive as well as survive?"

There was more than a little interest in that question. And not a hint of indifference. He remembered Rune, and he wanted to know about her.

"She continues to thrive, sir," Robin said boldly. "Your silver bought her lessons and instruments, and brought her to the Kingsford Faire and the Free Bards. She got a Master from the Free Bards, and then more than a Master, for she wedded him and earned her title of Master and of Elf-Friend as well. They sing for a King now, and wander no more."

"A good King, I am sure," came the return whisper. "She would settle for naught else, the bold child who dared my hill." Then amazingly, something that *sounded* like a hint of chuckle emerged from beneath the cowl. "It is, I trow, hard to find a rhyme for 'silver' — and that *'heap of shining gold'* tells me why, on a sudden, a fool or two a year has come to dig holes in my hill when they never did before."

"And they f-f-find?" Jonny asked, boldly.

"Rocks. And, sometimes, me." Again the chuckle, but this time it chilled and had no humor in it. Once again, she sensed the power coiled serpentlike behind him, a power that quickened to anger at very little provocation. So before he had time to be angered at the song, at them, she spoke.

"Sir, we came to ask a bargain of our own. Not gold or silver or even gems —"

She was the entire focus of the Ghost's gaze now;

the antithesis of the tropical sun, it fell upon her and froze her in a silence of centuries. Or tried. It was at that moment the Ghost must have realized she was not caught in his web of terror, for the spirit straightened a little in what looked very like surprise. "What — bargain?" it said at last.

"We will tell you anything you care to ask, in as much detail as you wish, if we know the answers," she said, faintly, from beneath the weight of that gaze. "We will sing and play for you until dawn, as Rune did. Information and entertainment, and in return —"

The frigid pressure of his regard deepened. "In return — what? Besides your lives, of course. You have not — yet — earned those."

She tried to answer, and could not. For a moment she struggled in panic, knowing that if she did not answer, he could and would use that as the only "excuse" he needed to take her, Kestrel —

"F-free p-passage f-for G-G-G-Gypsies and F-F-Free B-B-B-Bards," Kestrel stammered, forcing the words out for her, fighting his stutter as she fought the Ghost's compulsion. The Ghost's cowl moved marginally as his gaze transferred to Kestrel and the pressure holding her snapped.

"Exactly," she said, quickly, into the ominous silence. "Free and unmolested passage across your Pass at any time of the day or night for Gypsies and Free Bards. Including us, of course. That's all." She remembered now something else that Rune had said — that the Ghost had heard her tale of being harassed and plagued, and then had said that he and she might have more in common than she guessed. "We're something less than popular with the Church right now," she added, and had the reward of seeing the cowl snap back to point at her. "And with the Bardic Guild. We sing a little too much of the truth, and we

don't hide what we know for the sake of convenience.
We might need —"

"An escape route?" the Ghost hissed, and nodded.
"Yes. I can see that."

He stood wrapped in weighty, chilling silence for a
long time. She studied him, trying to determine what
his race was — or had been. He matched nothing she
had ever seen or heard of. Too tall for a Deliambren, a
Gazner, or a Prilchard. No place under that robe for
the wings of a Haspur —

"I am — astonished," the Ghost whispered at last.
"To dare me and my power simply to assure your
friends of an escape route in case of danger — to dare
me!" He did not breathe, but he paused for as long as
it would take someone to take a deep breath. "Yes. I
will make that bargain. With a single exception."

*Exceptions? Why would he have to have excep-
tions?* Her eyes narrowed with speculation and
suspicion.

The Ghost returned her gaze, but this time without
the pressure of his magic behind it. "I must have the
exception," he said, simply. "I am — bound to a task,
as I am bound to this place."

Now she sensed the full scope of the terrible power
of his anger; once, long ago, she had been in the presence of a dreadful weapon of what the Deliambrens
called *interstellar* warfare. This *interstellar* thing was
something they could not explain to her, but she had
sensed, nevertheless, the shattering potential for
destruction encased within the metal pod-skin of the
object they showed her. The Ghost's anger felt like
that; like the moment before the storm is about to
break, when the earthquake is about to strike, when
some force too large for a mere human to compre-
hend is about to be unleashed.

And yet, it was not directed at *her.*

No — no, his anger is for those who have bound him here. May their gods help them if he ever does get free!

"If your Gypsies and Free Bards are not *sent* here from Carthell Abbey, they may pass," he continued, in his ice-rimed whisper. "But if they are *sent*, I have no choice. I — am bound to slay anyone who is sent from the Abbey. Any other, I shall let pass, freely. This is the bargain; take it, or not. Fear not for yourselves; I shall let you pass without your music if you choose not to take it."

She looked at Kestrel out of the corner of her eye; he nodded slightly. It was the best they were likely to get; the Ghost was giving a pledge within the limits of his ability to fulfill it. Kestrel sensed that as well as she did.

"Done," she said. "I won't hold you to something you can't promise."

The Ghost nodded, ever so slightly, but the atmosphere suddenly warmed considerably, physically as well as emotionally. Although he did not "sit," she felt a relaxation about him, and the chill breeze that had swept through the clearing vanished, to be replaced by a breeze as comfortable as any of early fall, with a hint in it of false-summer.

"I should have given this small comfort to the fiddler girl, had I recognized her bravery and honesty," the Ghost whispered, as Jonny took her hand for a brief, congratulatory squeeze. "But she was the first I had ever seen who deserved that consideration, so perhaps it is not surprising I did not recognize this until after she was gone. So — tell me first of her, in more detail. And of her song. . . ."

She almost smiled at that, and caught herself just in time. *So, he likes being famous as well as any living being! Well, I think I can oblige him.*

She told him Rune's history, or at least as much of it as she knew, from the moment that Rune had left Skull Hill. How she had put his money to proper use, investing it in instruments and lessons, how she had gone to Kingsford Faire to take part in the trials for the Bardic Guild —

How her song of the "Skull Hill Ghost" had won her acclaim and the highest points in the trials —

How the Guild had treated her when they learned she was a girl and not a boy.

That made him angry again; interesting how she could sense his moods now, as if he had let down some sort of wall, or she had become more sensitive. She pitied the next Guildsman, Bard or Minstrel, that might pass this way by accident! He would take out his anger at what they had done to "his" fiddler girl on any of the Guild that came into his hands.

She went hastily on to describe how the Free Bards had rescued her, and what had happened to her then. He asked her detailed questions about Talaysen, Master Wren — and about King Rolend and her position in Birnam. She sensed his satisfaction in the rewarming of the emotional atmosphere.

"Good," he whispered at last. "Very good. I am pleased. Despite her enemies, she has triumphed. Despite fools, she has prospered." He nodded, and the crickets began to sing again, down the hill at first, then up around the clearing. He turned his cowl towards Kestrel. "Now music," he continued. "You, harper. Something with life in it. Warmth. The sun."

Kestrel nodded without speaking, and set his hands to the strings of his harp. As always, he was lost in his music within the first few bars, and as always, he invoked Bardic Magic without any appearance of effort. Robin wondered if he realized what he was doing; the Magic that he called was mild, harmless, and did nothing more than invoke a mood. In this case, in performing a sweet child's song about a mountain meadow, he enhanced it with a mood of sunny innocence.

The Ghost either did not notice, or else since it was not threatening, he simply ignored it. Probably the latter; Robin had the feeling he noticed *everything*.

As Jonny played, she paid careful attention to the flow and flux of powers about them all. About halfway through the song, she knew that there was a pattern to those flows . . . and near the end, she knew what it was.

She had a suspicion when he agreed to the bargain that the Ghost would take power from them, through the music, through the Bardic Magic he hoped they would invoke. And it looked as if she was half right; but only half. He was not *stealing* their power, nor pulling it in. It was as if they were campfires, and he was basking in the warmth they produced. *Taking* nothing, only enjoying what flowed to him naturally.

But she sensed something else as well. This benign enjoyment was the reverse side of something much, much darker. *That* was the side that his victims saw, the icy chill to the warmth . . . as he stole their life-force along with their life.

He chose a Gypsy love song from Robin next; she hid a grin, because she had the feeling he was hoping she'd sing something at and for Kestrel. Well, he would get that — but not just yet. Instead, she sang a song of a night of celebration and tangled lovers who could not make up their minds over who was going to pair off with who, until in the end, everyone ended up sleeping alone, for that night at least! She got the definite impression that her audacity pleased him, and that the song itself amused him.

"Tell me what this quarrel is that the Church has

with your kind," he whispered, as soon as she had finished. "How did you come to this conclusion, and what are you doing to remedy it? All that you know, tell."

She found herself recounting what Nightingale had told them, what she and Kestrel had seen, and Harperus' speculations. He listened silently to all of this, not prompting her by so much as a single word, as she concluded with what she and Jonny were doing — heading to Gradford on the chance that the source of the problem lay in that direction, while Nightingale went in the opposite direction. The anger was back again, but this time she could not imagine what had invoked it. She was only glad that it hadn't been any of their doing.

"I think" — the Ghost began, after a cricket-filled silence — "your searches are like to bear more fruit than hers."

But before she could follow up that astonishing bit of information with a question of her own, he had already demanded a ballad "with free wind in it" from Kestrel.

He obliged with one of the Gypsy horse-trainers' racing songs, and by the time he had finished she knew without asking that question — *how* he knew that Gradford was the direction they must go — that the Ghost would only give them what he chose to in the way of information. It would be enigmatic, they would probably only understand what he meant after they discovered answers for themselves. And he was much too dangerous to play games with, verbal or otherwise.

So when he asked her again for a love song, this time she played one of her own, made for Jonny, and put her whole heart into it.

❖   ❖   ❖

"I think," the Ghost said, tilting his cowl up towards the eastern sky, "that it is not long until dawn."

Gwyna shook soreness out of her weary arms; this had taken a lot more energy than she had ever suspected, and if *she* felt this way with Kestrel and talk to spell her, how had poor Rune ever survived her night of playing?

"I did not lend my strength to you as I did to the fiddler girl," the Ghost said, matter-of-factly, as if he had just read her mind. Perhaps he had; she would not place anything beyond him at this point, and she was very glad that they had both chosen to tell him only the strict and complete truth when he had asked his questions about the outside world. His interrogation had been fascinating to experience; things he had wanted to know, he wanted to know in depth, and things she had assumed he would be curious about, he cared nothing for.

But those things he wished to know — his questioning left her feeling like a rag that had been used to soak up something, then wrung dry. He not only extracted information from her, but as the night went on, he became more and more adept at extracting her feelings about something from her. She was not certain of his motives. It might only be that he had wished to *feel* things, if only vicariously. It might be he extracted some nourishment from emotions, which might also explain why he killed through terror. It might also be that for some reason he needed to understand if she felt strongly about something, and why.

"You did not need that strength," he continued. "There were two of you, and you did not play continuously. So. Dawn approaches. Your bargain is complete. You have given as you pledged, and fully. I shall pledge likewise. From this moment, all Gypsies and Free

Bards that are not sent from Carthell Abbey may pass this way freely." He cocked his head a little sideways. "I may appear, and request a song — but it shall be a *request*."

Kestrel blew on his fingers to cool them, and echoed the Ghost's head-pose. "I th-think s-such a req-q-quest would b-be honored," he said dryly.

There was a whispered chuckle from the Ghost. "You need not give them identifying marks," the spirit continued — which was something that had been in Gwyna's mind. "Such things can be stolen or counterfeited. I shall know them from their thoughts."

She didn't bother to hide her start of surprise. So he *could* read thoughts!

"On occasion," he whispered, and there *was* a hint of humor in his voice. And perhaps, a touch of smugness. "You have been generous in your bargain. I shall be as generous. Spend the morn in safety here, if you wish, or go on. Nothing shall molest you or disturb you while you sleep. My choice of manifestation is my own, for their compulsions were limited in nature — and if I choose to expend myself, the daylight need not hinder my powers —"

And with that final astonishing pronouncement, he disappeared — just as the first light of the dawn-red sun touched the precise spot on which he had been standing just the moment before.

The sunlight glinted on something metallic.

It was Kestrel who climbed down from the tail of the wagon, placed his harp carefully on the floor of the wagon, and walked stiffly across the sun-gilded weeds to the spot that shone with such bright and promising glints.

"Well," he said, carefully, looking down at the small mound. "It's s-s-silver. J-just l-like R-R-Rune's."

She let out the breath she had been holding, and

rubbed her tired eyes. "He said he was going to be generous."

Kestrel tilted his head to one side, and dropped down to sit on his heels beside the pile of coins. "S-so l-let's s-see how g-g-generous, shall w-we?"

She yawned hugely, and blinked at the morning sun. "I can't think of any better way to relax before a good long sleep. Can you?"

He shook his head, and stole a kiss from her as soon as she joined him. Then the two of them knelt down beside the pile of coins that the Ghost had left as their personal reward. They counted with one hand each; their other two hands were clasped together lovingly.

CHAPTER EIGHT

Robin woke to the sounds of birdsong and the soft whistling of a human. She knew by the absence of a warm body next to her that she was alone in the bed; but since the whistling was nearby, she was not alone in the wagon. After a moment, the sound of creaking and tapping told her what was going on.

Kestrel was caching the silver coins in little hiding places all over the wagon. All Gypsy wagons had a few hidden caches for valuables, but none had so many as this one; while it was being built he'd been with the wagonwrights every day, planning hiding places everywhere it was possible to cache even a single tiny copper-piece. Robin knew where some of the caches were, but she hadn't a clue where he hid most of the money they had.

I think he does it so I can't spend it or give it all away, she thought with amusement. *Probably not a bad idea; sometimes I get a little too generous, I suppose. And I know I get a little too spendthrift when I know we have the money.*

Those days when he had not had even regular meals made him more cautious about money and lean times than even old Erdric, so she could hardly blame him. It was just something she was going to have to learn to live with.

She stretched, enjoying the rare luxury of having the bed to herself for a moment, and opened her eyes to stare up at the intricate carving on the underside of the cupboard over the bed. A nice touch, that. It was a sinuous form called "The Endless Knot" that was supposed to aid in concentration and relaxation if you followed it with your eyes long enough.

The encounter with the Ghost had given her more than she had hoped. They had the monetary reward, completely unexpected — and they had the safe-route across these hills for their people and theirs alone. Provided, of course, that none of their people managed to have themselves sent here from Carthell Abbey.

Therein lay the puzzle that kept her lying abed. *Carthell Abbey? Now what in the name of all that is holy could Carthell Abbey have to do with a murderous Ghost?* The Church had never dealt with ghosts at all, except to exorcise them; at least not that she had ever heard.

Well, the obvious answer was a simple one. The Church officials knew that the Ghost had been bound up on the Hill, and they used him, rather callously, as their convenient executioner. The Church was supposed to remand criminals to the civil authorities for trial and punishment, but everyone knew that a criminal Priest was dealt with within the Church itself. And in using the Ghost as their executioner, the Church kept its hands officially clean of blood. Cynical, yes, but the Church was full of cynics.

An obvious answer, except for a few problems. The first was that the minions of the Church *should* have been under spiritual obligation to exorcise the Ghost once they learned he was here — not use him! Especially since he had managed to kill one perfectly innocent Priest already, at least according to Annie Cook.

Well, maybe they did try to exorcise him and that

was how the Priest was killed. Maybe they figured since they couldn't be rid of him, they might as well use him. The Church employs other executioners, after all — this would just be one rather strange executioner.

Maybe. But if the Church was using this spirit, they were *definitely* under moral obligation to warn travelers about his existence! Yet there were no warning signs, and nothing telling a traveler that this was a dangerous road. There was no guard on the way up Skull Hill. What few warnings there were, at least on the Westhaven side, were haphazard at best. If the people of Westhaven had been charged with warning travelers, they were doing a damn poor job of it.

That brought everything back to the same question. Why would the Church have *anything* to do with a spirit like the Ghost? They should do any number of things that they had not; and should not be doing any number of things that they were.

She rolled over and poked her nose through the curtains on the wagon-side of the bed. Jonny was fitting a small pile of silver coins — the last, from the look of things — into the hem of the curtain above the sink. That was one of the caches she already knew about, and as he caught the sound of the bed creaking, he turned and grinned at her.

"All hidden?" she asked. He nodded.

"It's ab-bout noon," he told her. "If w-we move out n-now, w-we should b-be at the Abbey b-by sunset."

She nodded, and swung her legs down over the side of the bed, pushing the bed-curtains back to either side. "And you think we should go there. You think that we might find something out about this vendetta the Church seems to have with us?" she asked, as her bare feet hit the wooden floor with a dull thump.

He handed her a wooden comb, and cut bread and

cheese while she washed her face and dealt with the
tangle of her hair. "Th-the Gh-ghost made a p-point of
m-mentioning it," he said, thoughtfully. "L-like he
c-couldn't t-talk about s-something, b-but w-was trying t-to g-give us a c-clue."

"Hmm." She accepted bread-and-cheese with a
nod of thanks. "There is something very strange going
on here," she observed. "Do you remember, when I
was describing how Nightingale went off towards
Kingsford and I said we were looking towards Gradford, he said that we were likelier to find the source of
our troubles than she was?"

"'M-more l-likely to b-bear fruit,' he said," Kestrel
agreed. "I d-don't know whether he m-meant the
Abbey or G-Gradford, b-but I th-think we n-need to
s-stop at the Abbey."

"It's a start," Gwyna replied, popping the last of her
breakfast into her mouth, and licking a crumb of
cheese from her thumb. "You know the proverb.
'Soonest begun, is soonest done.' Right?"

Kestrel kissed her nose, and gave her a playful
shove in the direction of the driver's seat. As she
crawled over the bed, she saw that he had already harnessed the horses, and turned the wagon so that it
faced down the hill.

"Right" he agreed. "And *y-you* d-drive! I w-was up
early, and I n-need a n-n-nap!"

Jonny had learned long ago the art of sleeping in
odd places and under adverse conditions. A swaying,
jostling wagon was no impediment to his drifting off to
sleep. He had expected nightmares, or at the least,
dreams troubled by the Ghost, but he slept deeply and
soundly, and there was nothing to trouble his sleep.
He woke shortly before suppertime.

He exchanged places with Gwyna, driving while she

rummaged around in their stores for something for them both to eat that was *not* bread-and-cheese. While he recalled only too well the days when he would have been happy to eat bread-and-cheese for a month running, those days were in the past, and if he had a choice, well, the same food for three meals in a row was not going to be his choice.

This was true wilderness, except for the occasional sheep-farm, and by the rocky condition of the hillsides, he wasn't too surprised. Soil here was too thin to farm or graze; basically the only growing things keeping these hillsides from being completely barren were specialized plants suited to driving their roots into rock and holding tight. Two or three kinds of trees, wiregrass, lichen, moss, and some tough bushes; that was about it. Small wonder there were no people out here — the Ghost was hardly to blame for the condition of the land.

Funny, he thought. *Somehow, though, this looks like land that's been worn out, as if people were here a long time ago, but exhausted the soil so much that it couldn't support anything but this wilderness again.*

Well, that could be. Alanda was a strange world, and there were places in it like this, side-by-side with rich and virgin land, or a place like the stronghold of the Deliambrens. Maybe there had been people here, just after the Cataclysm — and maybe they had depended heavily on things coming from far outside *because* they had depleted their own land so much. And after the Cataclysm, when "outside" wasn't there anymore — they had died off, or gone elsewhere, leaving behind the land to recover on its own.

He shook himself out of his reverie as Gwyna reappeared with dinner for both of them. Speculation about the past was all very well, but at the moment he was perfectly willing to put such thoughts aside to concentrate on driving and dinner.

It was to be bread again, but this time with sausage, and an apple apiece. They thriftily saved out the seeds to be given to the owner of the next Waymeet; every Waymeet had some sort of orchard, planted from the seeds the Gypsies brought with them. So you might find apple trees growing side-by-side with Deliambren *pares,* Mintak *tiers,* and Likonian *severins.* Quite often fruits thought to be delicate turned out to thrive in unlikely climates, at least under the careful tending of the Gypsies.

"That's the last of the loaf," Robin told him, as she handed him his dinner through the hatchway. "At least we ate it before it went dry. How's the road?"

"Interesting," he replied, taking a bite. "W-well k-kept."

It was, too; one of the reasons why Gwyna hadn't been tossed all over the wagon while he negotiated potholes and pits. The road had been very carefully patched and graded, and that recently.

She poked her head out, then clambered over the ledge into her seat. "You're right!" she exclaimed. "Now why keep up a road that only leads to a dangerous pass and a nothing little village?"

Kestrel shrugged. "D-don't r-read t-t-too much into it," he cautioned her. "C-could j-just b-be the S-Sire d-doing his r-r-road d-duty r-right. After all, w-we w-were j-just c-complaining that th-the last S-Sire wasn't d-doing his d-duty on the r-roads. So n-no p-point in r-reading something into it wh-when th-the S-Sire's a g-good one."

"It could be, you're right." She settled beside him with her arm around his waist, and smiled up at him. He smiled back and caught her hand in his; a small hand, but very strong, with callouses on the fingers where only a musician would have them. A proper hand, to match the proper lady. Just being with her made him feel so warm — needed and wanted.

Being best friends is the only way to be lovers, he decided, as she rested her head against his shoulder. *Staying best friends is the only way to be married.*

"I th-think the Abbey isn't t-too far," he said, as shadows deepened under the trees, and the skies above the branches turned crimson and gold. "The n-next v-valley, m-maybe."

His guess was correct; as they topped the hill and looked down into the shallow valley stretching below them, it was obvious that they were back in some vestige of civilization. The leafless trees of an orchard lined both sides of the road, immaculately tended. And as the horses stretched their necks out with interest, the sound of bells ringing for evening services drifted clearly up the road.

He flicked the reins to get the horses moving again, for at the sound of the bells they stopped, their ears flicking forward nervously. Long shadows already filled the valley, and as they moved down the hill and went from the last light into evening's mist and blue dusk, the temperature dropped perceptibly. Gwyna huddled against him for warmth as well as companionship, and he shivered as a chill breeze cut through his shirt.

Once they were beneath the trees, they saw the lights of the Abbey shining up ahead of them, at the side of the road. There didn't appear to be any activity at all around it, which was a little odd.

Well, their harvest is obviously over. There's no real reason for anyone to be moving around at sunset, not when they just rang the bells for evening prayers.

The Abbey was fairly small, a complex of two or three buildings surrounded by a stone wall with a heavy wooden gate in the front. Trees grew right up against it, however, and Kestrel could only look at them wryly and remember a certain small boy who had found walls to be no hindrance as long as there were trees nearby. Presumably many generations of novices here had discovered the same truth.

He pulled the wagon up to the gate, handed the reins to Gwyna, and jumped down to knock for admission.

It opened immediately; there was a lantern just outside, and the light fell on a sour-faced Brother in a dull gray robe, who scowled at him as if Kestrel was personally responsible for everything that was wrong with the world. The man had the soft, ink-stained hands of a scholar, and a squint that suggested many hours spent in a library bending over half-legible manuscripts. His mouth was framed with frown lines, and his jowls quivered when he spoke.

"What do you want?" His voice was not pleasant; a harsh and untrained croak. Kestrel smiled encouragingly, and shyly. He tried a ploy that had worked with other officious, self-important men in the past; to look as harmless and humble as possible. This was the one time his stutter might be useful.

He bobbed his head, submissively. "W-we are t-t-travelers, sir, and w-we are s-seeking sh-shelter f-from the c-c-creatures of the n-night w-within the w-walls of the —"

The Brother did not even give him a chance to finish his sentence. "Be off with you!" he growled. "This is no hostel, and we do not take in any ne'er-do-well who comes requesting shelter! This is a holy order of recluses. We have chosen to leave the world and all the sin within it. We sought to leave such as you in our past, not to open our gates to you!"

"B-b-but —" Kestrel began; shocked as well as

puzzled by the Gatekeeper's vehemence. He hadn't said or done anything to warrant such a reaction. The man acted as if they were dressed in rags and covered in filth, yet the wagon was quite clearly visible from the gate, and it was just as clear that they were not penniless wanderers. He had never yet met a Churchman who could resist the possibility of a donation.

Except that it seemed this Brother-Gatekeeper most certainly could and would. "Be off!" he repeated, raising his voice. "No one is allowed within these walls but the Brothers. No one! Find yourself some other shelter — vagabonds and mountebanks are not welcome here!"

And before Kestrel could get another word out, the Gatekeeper slammed the gate shut, right in his face.

He turned, slowly, and walked the few steps back to the wagon, to join Gwyna, who was just as surprised as he was. "What was that all about?" she asked, a little dazed. "What on *earth* made him say those things? Was he quite mad?"

He shrugged. "At l-least he d-d-didn't f-forbid us to c-c-camp up against the w-w-walls," he pointed out. "Th-there m-might b-be a w-w-well or a s-stream where w-we c-can g-get w-w-water."

He took the halter of the horse nearest him and led it off the road, onto the grassy area surrounding the walls of the Abbey, and beyond the circle of light cast into the blue dusk by the lantern beside the gate. Gwyna sat on the seat of the wagon, shaking her head. "I have no idea what could have set him off like that," she observed, dispassionately. "You were the essence of politeness — *he* was the one who was rude. And every single Abbey I have ever seen or heard of has always been willing to take in a traveler or two, especially in the wilderness like this. This is very strange."

He noticed that she was pitching her voice to carry, as if she was speaking to an audience, and he grinned to himself. If Gwyna had her way, her voice would drift right over the walls and just might reach the ears of someone who cared a little more than the Gatekeeper what a couple of "vagabonds and mountebanks" thought of this Abbey.

On the back side of the walls, he found the rear gate, and the path the Brothers took to the orchards and to a small vegetable garden. There was a well beside the garden, as he had hoped there would be; he picketed the horses a little way away from it, in an area where there was some grazing, and left them water and grain to augment the grass.

As he worked, he took in what he could of the area around the walls. The place was unnervingly *ordered*, especially in comparison with the country they had just passed through. The garden had been thoroughly plowed up for winter, leaving not a trace of whatever vegetables had been growing there. He had no clue what variety of tree grew in this orchard of theirs; the thrifty monks had left not so much as a windfall fruit underneath them, and without leaves it was impossible to make any accurate guess as to what they were growing here. While he took care of the horses, Gwyna bustled about the wagon, preparing dinner, heating water for washing, setting up a picture-perfect campsite. . . .

Too perfect, he realized after a moment. This was not like the Gypsy Robin he knew! And he grinned again as he saw what she was up to. She was acting in every way like a proper little wife, a well-trained trader's wife who was a good Church-going woman and a lady who knew her proper place. There was nothing to show that they were Gypsies and Free Bards, and not ordinary, middle-class traders. And if the Free Bards were in disfavor with the Church, the traveling traders were not.

So, they would look like traders; industrious, God-worshiping traders, eh? He silently congratulated Gwyna on her cleverness, and did his best to emulate her, right down to shoving their instruments into hiding when he returned to the wagon. Just in case whoever showed up next from the Abbey happened to look inside the wagon.

There *would* be someone; Gwyna had made certain of that, not only by her words, but by the busy clatter she made with her pots and pans.

But they were left in peace to wash up and eat that hot dinner she had prepared so carefully, and he began to wonder if this Abbey was inhabited by nothing except a single, mad old man. But just as full darkness fell, the expected visitor arrived.

They didn't even notice him, he moved so quietly, with hardly even a swish of his robe against the grass. There were no twigs beneath the branches of these trees to betray him by snapping unexpectedly underfoot; the ground had been swept as clean as the floor in a house. In fact, when the man cleared his throat to announce his presence, he succeeded in startling both of them.

They looked up, to see him standing just within the light of their fire, a thin, diffident man with a pleasant expression and shy eyes. "Oh!" the Brother said, immediately apologetic, and hurrying forward into the light of their fire. "I'm so sorry, I certainly didn't mean to frighten you! I thought you knew I was there! Please, forgive me!"

Kestrel had been sitting beside the fire; he stood immediately, and went to meet the Brother, holding

out his hand, which the man took in a firm and
friendly clasp. "N-no offense. J-just d-didn't notice
you. M-my n-name is J-J-Jonny B-Brede, good s-sir,"
he said, concentrating on speaking slowly and rhyth-
mically as Harperus had instructed him. "M-my
w-wife G-Gwyna and I are t-traders."

"And not vagabonds and mountebanks, I know,"
the Brother said, pulling back the cowl of his gray
robe so that they could better see his ascetic, but
friendly face and his apologetic smile. "I hope you
will find it in your heart to forgive Brother Pierce;
he is old, often ill, and altogether very unhappy. Life
has not treated him well. Most of the Brothers here
are not like him."

Kestrel returned his smile. "Well, I c-c-can s-see
th-that *you* aren't, at any r-rate . . . B-Brother . . . ?"

"Oh! Ah! Brother Reymond, Trader Brede," the
Brother replied, his smile widening when Jonny did
not meet his friendly overture with a rejection. "I
am the Abbey Librarian, and I wanted to apologize
for the fact that we simply have no room for you and
your wife. That is why Brother Pierce has been instructed to tell travelers we can take no one in.
Every cell is occupied, we have no guest rooms, and
since our order has taken a vow to use no beast of
burden, we have not even a stable you might shelter
in. I also wished to be certain that you were warned
about the dangers hereabouts."

"Dangers?" Jonny looked around, nonplused. This
certainly didn't look like a very dangerous area —

But on the other hand, this Abbey *was* a small
island in the middle of the wilderness. They had been
lucky so far; there was no telling what wandered under
the branches of these trees once darkness fell.

"I fear so —" Brother Reymond had the grace to
look guilty. "Of course, to experienced travelers like

you and your wife, these things are likely to be no more than an inconvenience."

"Why don't you tell us what they are, first, before we decide," Gwyna said dryly from her place beside the fire. "Perhaps we ought to move on, after all."

"Oh no!" the Brother said, paling. "No, you *don't* want to do that! There's a Beguiler about, perhaps more than one! What if it found you on the road?"

Jonny shrugged; that was not a threat he took seriously, since they had a wagon to sleep in. Beguilers couldn't get into a closed wagon. "Then I s-suppose we'd d-drown," he replied lightly.

Beguilers were creatures that hypnotized their victims, then lured them into swamps to fall into deep water. Once their victims were safely dead, they feasted on the remains. They cast their "spell" with a combination of sound and light; if you saw them but did not hear them, you were safe enough, and if you heard but did not see them, it was possible to remain in control of yourself. Most often they caught unwary travelers who mistook the light for the lantern of a house or wagon, and were then lulled by the Beguiler's humming to their death. It was not too difficult to evade them, if you knew they were around.

"Oh, don't say that!" Brother Reymond seemed genuinely distressed. "Why, only last week — one of the farm boys hereabouts — not strong in his mind, but still —"

Jonny shook his head apologetically. "I b-beg your p-pardon, B-Brother," he said as quickly as he could. "I d-didn't mean t-to m-make a j-joke of it."

"I know you didn't; how could you have known?" Brother Reymond sighed, and signed himself. "May the poor lad rest in peace. But there are also treekies, an entire flock of them, out in the forest beyond the orchard. I hope you have nets for your horses? If you don't, the Abbey can loan them to you. In that much, at least, we can do our charitable duty."

"With, or without Brother Pierce's permission?" Gwyna asked lightly, and chuckled at Brother Reymond's blush. "No matter, Brother, we do have nets and fitted blankets for the horses, and good shutters on the wagon. We should be safe enough, if that is all we need to worry about." She patted the stool next to her. "Can we invite you to stay for a while? The treekies certainly won't come while the lanterns and the fire are burning, and the Beguiler may not come at all tonight. Even if it does, I see no reason why we can't avoid it."

"I would — yes, I would like to speak with you, if you do not mind," Brother Reymond said, shyly. He settled down onto the stool placed between Gwyna's and Jonny's, and accepted a mug of tea, but waved away a bowl of stew. "Thank you, dear lady, but I *have* supped, and I am not in the least hungered. While your stew smells delicious, our Order regards greed very seriously." He cradled the mug in both hands and smiled at both of them. "I am the Archivist, you see, and I have so little opportunity to speak with outsiders! I try to collect as much information as I can, but —" He shrugged. "My opportunities are few. We do not see many travelers on this road. I can't think why. It is a much shorter route to Gradford than the main trade road, and the Sire tends it well, at least within his lands."

Jonny kept his expression completely under control, but with difficulty. Either this Reymond was the finest actor in the world, or he was completely unaware of the Skull Hill Ghost less than half a day away from here!

"I had heard there was a legend about a haunted hill on this road," Gwyna said casually. "We didn't see anything, of course — but we also traveled between here and Westhaven by daylight. I don't suppose that could have anything to do with the scarcity of travelers?"

Brother Reymond blinked at her in surprise. "I suppose it might," he replied, clearly taken aback. "I should think. But this is the first time I have ever heard anything about a haunted hill!" His expression grew doubtful. "Perhaps the villagers in Westhaven were making a jest at your expense?"

"It c-could b-be," Jonny said, easily. "You kn-know h-how s-s-some of th-these v-v-village f-folk are ab-bout someone w-with an af-f-fliction. I d-do s-stutter. Th-they m-may have th-thought I w-was f-feeble-minded as w-w-well, and ch-chose t-to m-make a f-fool of m-me."

Brother Reymond flushed, averted his eyes in embarrassment, and murmured something appropriate and apologetic. Jonny watched him carefully and became convinced that the Brother was no actor. He really *didn't* know about the Skull Hill Ghost!

"I d-don't s-suppose th-there m-might b-be s-something in your a-archives?" he added. "I'm c-curious now. It w-would b-be n-nice t-to kn-know if I w-was b-being m-made a g-game of."

"Certainly," Brother Reymond said, after a moment of awkward silence. "I can look, of course. I don't remember anything, but that doesn't mean a great deal." He chuckled with self-deprecation. "My memory is not very good. I make a fine Archivist precisely because of that, you know, for I have to index and cross-index everything, or I would never be able to find a single reference."

Jonny laughed, and refilled the Brother's mug. They continued to chat about some of the things he and Gwyna had seen on the road, and inserted a question now and again about the internal affairs of the Church and the Abbey. They continued to talk for some time — or rather, he gradually turned the conversation so that Gwyna was doing most of the talking, and he could simply listen and look wise. The Brother was certainly a guiless sort, and quite transparently enthusiastic about any new knowledge — but he had no notion of any kind about the internal politics and policies of the Church of the present day. Politics and policies of the Church a hundred years ago, now, he knew quite well, but nothing current. It was fairly obvious why he was here; he was so innocent he would never have survived in one of the larger Church installations. The best and safest place for him was out of the way. In some other Abbey, he was far too likely to overhear something he shouldn't, and repeat it to anyone who cared to ask him about it.

Three mugs of tea later, he finally took his leave with obvious regret. Here in the lee of the Abbey walls, there was very little wind, but from the nip in the air, it had gotten much colder while they talked.

Brother Reymond stood, and sniffed the air. "There will be frost by morning," he said, and sighed. "This seems like such a sad time of year to me — and yet, it is such a pleasant season for the farm-folk! Well, so it is — one man's pleasure is another man's melancholy."

Jonny saw Gwyna raise her eyebrow at this unconscious echoing of a Gypsy proverb by a sober scion of the Church, and smiled just a little. "Quite true, Brother Reymond," she said smoothly, accepting the mug he returned to her. "But I can't conceive of anyone finding *your* conversation unpleasant. Thank you very much for coming out, and proving to us that your fellow Brother is the exception within your walls."

Brother Reymond colored up with pleasure, and murmured a shy disclaimer. Jonny had decided after the first mug of tea that he liked the Archivist, as much for his modesty as his eagerness to share knowledge. *And if there were more men like him,* he thought, as Brother Reymond thanked Gwyna for her hospitality and her tea, *the world would be a much better place than it is.*

"Don't forget about the treekies," Brother Reymond reminded them over his shoulder, as he hurried away towards the Abbey. "And the Beguiler!"

"We won't!" Gwyna promised. And as soon as Brother Reymond was out of sight, she exchanged a chuckle and a hug with Jonny.

"I like him," she declared. He nodded agreement.

"I d-do, too," he told her. "He's honest."

She didn't answer immediately; instead, she went to one of the storage bins that contained more of the horse-tack, and opened it, taking out carefully constructed horse blankets that covered everything except the ears and legs, then shook out a pair of nets made of wire-wrapped cord. Treekies, the little nocturnal flying beasts that Brother Reymond had warned them about, were more of a pest than anything else, although their attentions could prove fatal to the unwary. Light kept them away, and any material made of mesh too small for their mouths foiled and frustrated them. But if the bloodsuckers caught an animal out, unprotected, or an unwary human, there would be no next generation. They could drain a poor creature of blood completely, without the victim ever waking up.

They were usually creatures of much milder climes than this; it was the first time that Kestrel had ever heard of them being this far north.

"I trust him, Jonny," Gwyna said, as they fitted the horses with their thick, protective blankets, then hung the nets over them to keep the little monsters off the mares' legs and ears. "I really do. I don't think he's ever told more than a handful of lies in his life, and every time he did, I'd bet he gave himself away. He's never heard of the Ghost."

Kestrel nodded, and shrugged. "I c-can't explain it. M-mind, I d-doubt th-the B-B-Brothers are ever allowed out of th-the Abbey. S-so if th-they aren't f-from around here, th-they w-won't kn-know about l-local st-stories. B-but st-still!"

"Still, he should have heard something." She arranged the net over the patient mare's head. "I can't imagine why he wouldn't have. Unless —"

She paused and Kestrel waited.

"— unless the Abbot was keeping the existence of the Ghost a secret from the Brothers." She raised an eyebrow at Kestrel who had already come to that same conclusion.

"It c-could b-be innocent," he reminded her. "If th-they kn-knew about a Gh-ghost s-so n-near, the d-devout and th-the amb-bitious w-would b-both r-rush t-to t-try t-to ex — ex — g-get r-rid of it."

"Good point," she replied, as they both turned to go back to the shelter of the wagon. "We already know what fate *they* would have. And those who were nei-ther devout nor ambitious would probably flee in terror. That's quite a reasonable explanation. There's only one problem with it. Remember what the Ghost said? About people being *sent* from here?"

He did. Only too well. "It st-still st-stands as an explanation," he replied. "J-just n-not as innocent."

"Hmm." She gave him a long look from under her eyelashes, as they climbed into the wagon to fasten down all the shutters. "You aren't as guiless as you look, Jonny Brede."

He grinned. "N-neither are you."

❖   ❖   ❖

Their night passed with no real disturbance; they heard the Beguiler humming off in the far distance, but it never came anywhere near the Abbey. Eventually they fell asleep without ever hearing anything more sinister than a distant hum, out there in the darkness. Kestrel could not help but be glad that they were *not* afoot on this journey, however. They might have escaped the Beguiler — or they might not. If it had floated up to their camping spot in the middle of the night and begun singing right over their heads, they might have awakened and been trapped by it before they realized what it was.

No, it was a very good thing that they were traveling by wagon. And if the Beguiler was an example of the kinds of dangers lurking in this wilderness area — well, perhaps they didn't have to look for sinister reasons for the abandonment of this trade-road. Who would want to camp in woods where there were Beguilers and treekies?

But the Abbey should *be acting as a traveler's haven and shelter against things like that,* came the logical response, just as he drifted off to sleep. *Why isn't it? And why did the Ghost say that people were* sent *from here?*

And that brought up yet another question — for Brother Reymond had said that this Abbey was full. Why send so many Brothers to such a remote location? Surely there weren't that many men seeking the solitude of the wilderness, and the purity of a womanless existence!

Kestrel loitered over their morning preparations, hoping that Brother Reymond would be able to get away and speak with them before they left, but it was not to be. Instead, they packed up and took to the road without any sign from within the Abbey walls that there was anything or anyone alive within them. Even the bells ringing for morning services could have been coming from somewhere else.

By mid-morning they had passed out of the true wilderness and had struck the same trade road that they had left after the Waymeet. The road was broader and better-tended here than it had been when they left it; there was quite enough room for two vehicles the size of Harperus' monster to pass on this section of the road, and it was very obvious that the local Sire took his road-tending duties very, very seriously. There was scarcely an uneven place in the roadway, much less the size of the pothole that had brought their wagon to grief.

Gradford had no Sire; it was a political entity unto itself, although it owed allegiance to the King of Rayden. The inhabitants referred to it as a "city-state," or a "Free Trade City," and it was very nearly the equal of Kingsford in size and importance.

Located deep in the hills, it commanded an impressive number of resources; water, mines, and an advantageous position on a trade-road. The sole disadvantage to its location was the terrain; the hills grew steeper and rockier with every passing hour, and they often got out of the wagon and walked alongside it to spare the horses. These steep grades were very hard on them; going down, holding back the weight of the wagon, was very nearly as wearing for them as climbing.

They were so caught up with watching the mares for strain that it was almost nightfall before Robin noticed a peculiar lack of traffic on the road, and mentioned it to Kestrel.

He furrowed his brow for a moment, and shook his head slightly, but he waited until they took a breather for the horses before he spoke.

"It's f-fall," he pointed out, but with uncertainty. "It's the off-s-season f-for t-trade."

But she shook her head vigorously. "No it isn't!" she contradicted him sharply. "Not for the variety of trade that Gradford does! Oh, maybe the Faires are over for the year, but there should be a lot of people on this road, and there's no one! We haven't seen anyone all day!"

"W-we might not," he told her. "Th-they c-could be r-right ahead of us, and w-we'd n-never s-see them. N-not with all th-these h-hills."

By the look in her eyes, she clearly did not believe him, or his explanation. "W-we'll s-stop at an inn," he promised. "I w-want a r-real m-meal and a b-bath, if w-we c-can g-get one. Y-you'll s-see."

But when they did find an inn — fortuitously, just over the top of the next hill, for the mares needed a real rest — she was not the one who found her notions contradicted.

Robin finished ordering supper, and went hunting her husband. She found Kestrel out in the stable, making certain that the mares were getting all the care he had paid for. She dragged him away from his inter-rogation of a hapless stable-boy, and into the common room of the inn. Their supper was waiting, but that was not why she had brought him in here.

The dark but cozy common room was half empty, and from the forlorn expressions on the faces of the barkeeper and the serving girls, this was not an anticipated situation. They had been the last travel-ers to seek shelter here tonight, and most of the few patrons had already had their dinner and sought their rooms or wagons — but she had managed to find one man, at least, who was willing to delay his rest and talk to them in return for a pitcher of beer.

The quiet of the common room, holding nothing more than the vague murmur of talk and the crackle of the fire in the fireplace at their end of the room, was relaxing and prompted confidences.

"Kestrel," she said, tugging him towards the table she had taken, in the corner, and away from any other where they might be overheard as they talked. "This is Rodrick Cunart. Rod, this is Kestrel." She did not bother to introduce Jonny as her husband; Rod was a pack-trader, a man whose entire life during trading-season was contained in a single pack carried by a donkey. He knew the road and the life on it; if a Gypsy with a bird-name was wandering the roads with another with a bird-name, it was safe to assume they were "together." And *not* safe to take liberties.

"Rod trades in books in the north, and ribbons and laces in the south," she continued, as Jonny took his place beside her, and gave Rod a nod of greeting. "And he's going up to Gradford, because of some news he got." She was pleased to see Jonny's interest perk up at that. "I asked him to tell us what's going on up there."

Kestrel settled down to his dinner of shepherd's pie without a word, but his eyes never left Rodrick's. The pack-trader poured himself a mug of his beer and took a long pull of it before beginning.

"It's a good thing yer lady found me," he said, slowly, his accent marking him as coming from one of the Southern Kingdoms. "You bein' Free Bards an' all. It could be bad for ye in Gradford. They've gone religious, they have, an' they don't look well on musickers, 'less they be outa the Church itself. Even Guild is lookin' a bit thin there, these days. Not much trade in anythin' but Church music, an' even the Guild musickers get mortal weary of that. As for us" — he shook his head — "thas' why ye see nobbut on road. 'Tis dead to trade, is Gradford."

Even Robin, who had been expecting some sort of bad news, had not been prepared for so bald a statement. "What happened?" she asked, incredulously, the hearty meal before her entirely forgotten for the moment.

Rodrick finished his first mug of beer before replying. "It's all on account of one Priest," he told them, his eyes thoughtful, as if he was putting things together for himself right there on the spot. "*Very* persuasive. They say the birds come down offa the trees t' hear his sermons. He *was* a Count, Count-Presumptive, that is. Count Padrik he woulda been, if he'd waited till his papa died 'fore he joined the Church. But — likely he made the better choice, if ye read him as a man with a bita ambition. He's been a-risin' in the Church like a lark in the mornin'. Fact is, he can't be no older'n me, an' already he's been made High Bishop of Gradford."

Kestrel's brow furrowed. "Isn't th-that a p-p-post th-that g-goes t-to a g-g-graybeard usually?"

Rodrick nodded. "Never heard it go to a man under the age of fifty, that's sure. Well, now he's High Bishop, and seems like all Gradford's gone mad for his notions. Inns — they're closing, 'cause they got no business. Trade in fancy-goods is way down. People are act'lly taking *vows,* an' doin' it like they thought the Second Cataclysm was this Midwinter! Only one trade's doin' any good, an' that's the trade in religious stuffs."

He nodded to himself with smug satisfaction, and Robin took a few bites of her neglected dinner while he basked in his own cleverness.

"I took m'self home, gathered up ev'ry book on the Church list, an' I've got 'em all loaded down on m'poor little donkey. Havna been able t' unload the half of 'em all these years — if Gradford's gonna come down with a plague'a piety, I'm gonna use the chance t' be rid'a this stuff!"

He beamed at them, and Robin chuckled. "Good for you, Rod, and thank you for telling us about this. It may not make us change our travel plans, but we're going to have to change our trades, I can see that."

Rod drank the last of the beer in his pitcher, and stood up to leave. "So long as it be religious, Gypsy Robin, ye'll profit," he said with a nod. "An' on that note, I'll be takin' m'leave."

"And a good night and fair profit to you." She returned the traditional trader's greeting. "And once again, thanks."

"Glad t' be of service," Rod replied, and took himself off, up the stairs to the sleeping quarters used by those who had no wagons to sleep in.

"Well," Robin said, turning to Kestrel as soon as Rod had taken the stairs out of sight and hearing. "Now what do we do?"

CHAPTER NINE

Jonny glanced around, quickly, to make certain there was no one near enough to overhear their conversation. He needn't have bothered; they were the only two patrons left in the common room, and since Robin had already paid for their meal, the serving girls were gone. The barkeeper polished the top of the counter and put clean mugs up on the shelf, obviously there only in the hope that they might order a drink.

If this common room was typical of the rest of the inn, it was one of the better such places Jonny had seen in all of his travels.

Then again, my pocket wasn't up to bearing the price of inns when I was on my own, he thought wryly.

But this was a good, solid place. Immaculately clean, the simple wood furniture was scarred by use and dark with age and many years of cleaning, but sturdily made; the floors were covered with clean rushes, and the smoke-blackened beams above were free of cobwebs. A few lanterns burned along the walls, but most of the light came from the fireplace. There were more lanterns along the walls, but they were not lit, perhaps in the hope of saving a little money on lamp oil.

"Eat," Robin advised him. "No one is going to hear us, or care what we say. They've heard everything in a place like this. They know we're Gypsies and Free Bards, and I rather doubt that the innkeeper is very fond of the Church and the High Bishop of Gradford. Right now, they're more concerned that their custom has dropped off than in anything we might say or do. We're just ordinary musicians, remember? What possible damage could two musicians do to anyone?"

He shook his head, and followed her advice. There was no point in wasting a perfectly good meal, especially not one as tasty as this; the cook had a good hand with pastry, and the tender, flaky crust covered a meat pie rich with brown gravy. But his stomach was a trifle uneasy and it took concentrated effort to calm it; Rodrick's information frankly disturbed him.

It appeared that the Ghost might have been right; certainly this High Bishop was an excellent candidate for the source of the sentiment against Free Bards. An ambitious man — as Padrik clearly was — could look for no better and quicker road to power than through the Church, and no quicker way to rise in the Church than to find *something* to get people upset about on religious grounds.

There aren't too many things that can get people aroused the way religion can, he observed, *and with this outbreak of "piety," sooner or later someone is going to find a "cause" to expend all their energy on. Unless Padrik is a fool, he'll be that someone; it will be the only way he can continue to control his followers. And if the "cause" turns out to be the control of music and musicians by the Church, it's going to be a bad day for the Free Bards.*

There his thoughts might have ended, if he hadn't spoken with Harperus and T'fyrr, but those conversations had opened his eyes to the fact that an attempt to control would not end with music. Control had to begin somewhere, and the best target for the initial stages of control would ideally be someone who was very obviously different, someone who was in the minority. An obvious set of targets for that method of control were the nonhuman citizens of the Twenty Kingdoms.

"So," Gwyna said, as he finished his dinner and pushed the wooden plate away. "We obviously need to go to Gradford even more now than before. What are we going to do? We can't go in as musicians. I have the feeling that we'd better have an obvious reason for being there, or we might find ourselves the center of some unwelcome attention."

"B-but we c-can g-go in as t-traders," Jonny replied. "Even th-the Gh-Ghost's silver won't l-last f-forever. W-we n-need t-to support ourselves s-s-somehow. Th-the only q-question is, wh-what do we s-s-sell?"

She toyed with a bit of bread, and a stray lock of hair slipped over her eye, curling in a most distracting and charming manner. "Religious goods. That would be the most obvious reason to be there. And it would be the safest, really. I don't think anyone is going to accuse a peddler of religious goods of impiety." She tucked the flyaway lock of hair behind her ear, and dropped the bread on the plate. "The quickest and easiest things for us to come up with on short notice are jewelry and display pieces; God-Stars are very easy to make, they're just tedious. And they're the kind of thing that only common, country folk display, so very few craftsmen ever bother with them. If no one in Gradford has thought of selling them, we'll have a temporary monopoly."

Jonny nodded; he had never seen God-Stars until he had arrived in Rayden as a child, for no one of noble blood would ever be caught wearing or displaying one. As wall-decorations, they were simply

four-armed crosses, with colored yarn woven about
the arms to form a solid square. The colors used varied
with the prayers of the owner. Red, yellow, and white,
for instance, meant the Star was a prayer for prosperity. Blue, green, and white meant a prayer for health,
while blue, green, and *brown* was a plea for good har-
vests. He had never heard of anyone making God-Star
jewelry, however.

"How d-do you make S-Stars as j-jewelry?" he
asked.

"It isn't often done, because real jewelers and silversmiths can't be bothered," she replied, with a wry
twitch to her mouth. "You can make them of embroidery thread and twigs, or metal and wire. With the
wire ones, you have to be very careful so the wire
doesn't break — but you use iron, copper, brass, and
silver wire, and two nails for the Sacrificed God as the
cross-pieces. Easy enough, and they make rather
pretty little pendants."

He brightened. "Th-that would w-work. B-but
where c-can w-we g-get materials?"

She thought for a moment, sipping at her mug of
beer. "Well, Gradford's a center for metals and gems;
I'd bet that we can find someone making wire outside
the town and buy up a stock. Nails are easy. It
shouldn't be too hard to find a weekly market to get
dyed wool yarn, and linen embroidery thread, and
sticks are under every tree."

"Wh-why not ask th-the innkeeper?" he asked, with
a sudden inspiration. "W-wouldn't he know the b-best
p-places t-to find things around here?"

She licked her lips, and nodded. "He would, and if
he's like any other innkeeper I've ever met, he'll probably have a relative only too pleased to sell to us. That's
fine; we'll make him happy and get our stock with a
minimum of effort. The amount of money we'll save

looking around for ourselves won't be worth the time we'll waste."

She shoved her stool away from the table, and trotted across the common room to consult with the barkeeper. After an exchange of a very few words, the barkeeper went off, and returned with the man Jonny had seen supervising the stable hands. Gwyna spoke with him for a little, and returned to her seat beaming.

"There!" she said. "It's taken care of. I told him part of the truth, that we were headed for Gradford and just heard we wouldn't be welcome there as musicians, so we need to continue our journey in another of our trades, peddlers selling handcrafted holy objects, since we couldn't afford the loss that going back would mean. He snorted, said, 'Religious trinkets, you mean,' and I knew he'd be willing to help us. He has a brother-in-law who can supply us with wire, and a cousin who can bring us the wool yarn and linen thread. He'll sell us horseshoe nails himself. So we're set."

Jonny shared her grin, and took her hand for a congratulatory squeeze. "S-so far," he replied, "s-so g-good. It's a g-good s-start, anyway!"

Four days later, thanks in no small part to the Ghost's gift, they left the inn with a full stock of God-Stars in several forms. They had bought all of the supplies that the innkeeper's relatives had brought, and still had some of the Ghost's silver left when they were done with their bargaining. There were several trays'-worth of the tiny Stars Robin had made up as pendants, from the cheapest Stars of linen thread and tiny twigs, to inexpensive copper Stars through Stars of mixed metals, to ones made entirely of silver wire and thin silver bars.

Jonny had learned the knack of turning out
wall-hanging Stars at a goodly clip, and he had used
up all their yarn at about the same time Gwyna had
run out of wire.

He was glad to pick up the reins and drive for a
change; they had worked for as long as daylight
lasted all during those four days, and his hands and
wrists were sore from twisting yarn around sticks in
movements he was not accustomed to making. He
knew that Gwyna's hands hurt just as much; working
with the wire was enough to try the patience beyond
bearing, for it broke when flexed too often, and then
it was impossible to mend without the mend showing. She'd been pierced with the sharp ends of nails
and wire so often that her finger-ends looked like
pincushions, and it was just as well that they were
not going to be playing their instruments for a
while, for her fingers needed to heal before she
picked up her gittern or harp again.

They drove off into the dawn, with a friendly farewell from the helpful innkeeper (who had, without a
doubt, skimmed off a commission from his relatives).
The road was going to take them through a series of
steep hills, and if they were going to get to Gradford
before the gates closed at sunset, they needed to get
this early start.

For a price, the cook had provided them not only
with fresh rolls dripping with melted butter for their
breakfast, but a packet of meat-pies for lunch on the
road. With so little traffic about, Kestrel was able to
eat with one hand and drive with the other. He
enjoyed the fresh, hot bread, but Robin was in heaven
over it, sensuously licking the dripping butter from her
fingers until he warned her that if she continued in
that fashion, they were going to have to make an
unscheduled stop!

She laughed, and pouted at him, tossing her long hair over one shoulder in a flirting manner, and he growled at her playfully.

"Ah, well," she sighed. She popped the last bite into her mouth, and wiped her fingers carefully on a bit of rag. "I suppose we'd better behave. If we make an unscheduled stop, we *won't* get to Gradford before the gates close."

"P-precisely," he said, with mock-sternness. "*One* of us h-has t-to have s-some s-self-control!"

She laughed, and folded her hands modestly in her lap under the protective warmth of her coat, looking about with interest. It was a breathtakingly beautiful day, in a stark, monochromatic fashion, but there was no doubt that winter was only a breath or two away. Frost was so thick on the branches and dead, dry grasses that they looked as if they had grown white coats of fur; the cloudless blue sky held a sun that gave very little besides light. As the road wove its way onward, they passed streams that had rims of ice at the edges, and their breath and the mares' puffed out in white clouds whenever they talked or breathed. Crows called occasionally, off in the distance. The hills themselves were covered with forests of hardwood trees that had long since lost their leaves, and made a mist-like haze on the hillsides with the interweaving of their gray-barked, barren branches.

"If it looks like we can pass as 'Church-approved,' we *might* actually be able to play some music," she remarked, when the inn had receded from sight.

"I th-thought about th-that." While they had been hard at work on the God-Stars, in order to get themselves into the proper mood, they had polished up all the ballads about heroes of the Church that either of them knew. If nothing else, those songs were often used as teaching aids by the Priests, and singing them made a painless refresher course in theology and accepted doctrine, not to mention providing a good source of pious quotations to sprinkle over their conversation. "P-purely instrumental m-music ought t-to b-be safe, if it isn't a d-dance t-tune. And even d-d-dance t-tunes c-can b-be *made* s-safe."

"How?" she asked, full of immediate interest. "Oh! Of course! If we slow the tempo so it isn't a *dance* tune anymore, likely no one will recognize it!"

"And add l-liturgical ch-chord sequences, th-the k-kind you hear in h-h-hymns." He was very pleased with that idea; he'd already tried it out in his head, and it made even the liveliest toe-tapper sound as if it came straight from Holy Services.

She nodded, her face full of pleasure at his cleverness. Then her eyes grew thoughtful; he let her sit in silence, knowing that she was trying to work a sudden thought to its conclusion. He listened instead to the steady clopping of the mares' hooves, and the jingle of their harness in the clear, cold air. Finally, she spoke.

"Music isn't going to be forbidden everywhere," she said, slowly. "In fact, the one way to give brothels and pleasure-houses more business than they can handle is to try to forbid pleasure itself. And a pleasure-house is going to be a *very* good place to learn what's going on in Gradford — really going on, that is, and not just what the officials are telling people, or what street-gossip says. Musicians are probably going to be welcome there, if all the places haven't already been taken by Gradford natives."

"B-but it c-could be d-dangerous," Kestrel finished for her. "If Church officials d-decide t-to l-look for s-someone t-to use as an example. S-someone w-with n-no importance. Still. P-perhaps if w-we d-do what

Rune d-did, and have t-two personae, one f-for the s-street and one f-for th-the b-b-brothel."

"It's worth thinking about when we get there," she agreed. "I have to admit I didn't think this was going to be all that important even after listening to Harperus and Nightingale — I thought this was just another bout of petty harassment, the kind we had when we first formed the Free Bards. Something's up though, something is different this time. I don't like what I've been hearing, and I want to do something about protecting our people before it's too late."

Jonny nodded, but did not add what he was thinking.

I only hope it's not already too late.

Their sturdy mares were in fine fettle after four days of rest and good feeding, and made much better time than either of them had expected. The walls of Gradford appeared in the distance in mid-afternoon, and they had plenty of time to study the city-state during their approach.

It had been built on the top of an enormous hill (or very small mountain) and was supposed to be the oldest complex continuously inhabited by humans in the Twenty Kingdoms. The city had expanded several times, and each time it had, a new set of walls had been built to accommodate the expansion. The original structure looked to have been either a military fortress or fortified castle; probably the original Duke of Gradford's holding. Its strange, blocky, angular architecture was at violent odds with the rest of the city, and it was easily the tallest structure either of them had ever seen in their lives. It must have been at least a full twenty stories tall, and Jonny could not imagine anyone climbing all those staircases to get to the top on a regular basis. The building itself, taken over by the Duke, was supposedly a structure that had made it through the Cataclysm intact. But the Duke's line had died out, and no relative could be found to claim the holding before the Mayor of the city below his fortress had claimed independence, supported by the High Bishop.

That had been in the early days, when no one really wanted the remote city, even though it was on a major trade road. Gradford's heyday had come when enterprising souls roaming the hills had discovered rich veins of silver and copper beneath them to the east, and iron-ore and coal to the west. To the south were finds of semiprecious and precious gems; garnet, beryl, amethyst, topaz, peridot, citrine, tourmaline, moonstone, and fine, clear quartz of all kinds.

Suddenly Gradford had something to trade. And by this time, it had the blessing of the High Bishop, a strong Lord Mayor and a Council comprised of Guild Masters from every major trade. The Council immediately let it be known that they were hiring the best mercenaries money could buy, and there were no more rumors of war.

Gradford prospered and grew, but apparently the Mayor and Council never forgot that there were nobles out there who lusted for its wealth. Every building was neatly tucked inside that last wall, and all of the walls sported sentries and guards, tiny as gnats at this distance, but clearly vigilant and visible.

The road did not actually lead through the city, but rather went past the base of the hill it was built upon. Long ago the hill had been cleared of trees, to keep any hostile forces from creeping up under cover of the branches. What remained was rock; rock, and very thin soil covered with tough, wiry grass. The dead brown grass matched the sandy brown rock, the same rock that had been quarried to form the city walls, so that the city rose out of the hillside as if it had grown from the rocks themselves.

A switchback road cut out of the hillside and reinforced with more of the same sandy-brown stone led up to the city gates, which stood wide open at this hour. Hardly surprising, Jonny reflected. The guards on the walls would see enemies coming long before they were any threat, and by the time an enemy force was within striking distance, the gates would already be closed and barred.

The road was wide and even, and so well-maintained that the mares were not even sweating by the time they brought their wagon in under the enormous gates, which had clearly been built to handle vehicles much larger than theirs. There was not one gate, but several, although Jonny suspected that only the outer, wooden gates, banded and reinforced with iron straps, were ever closed at night. Behind the wooden gates was a portcullis of iron bars that dropped down from above. Behind that was another portcullis of thick stakes of wood, woven with iron straps. And behind *that* was a second set of wooden gates, this pair sheathed with iron plates on the inner side. Jonny suspected that there were murder-holes in the floor of the walkway topping the gates, and that anyone who got through the first set of gates would find molten lead, stones, or boiling oil or water rained down on him from above. A truly cruel trick would be to let an enemy pass the first set of gates, then drop the outer portcullis, trapping him between the inner gates and the outermost portcullis, and destroy him at leisure.

They were stopped at the inner gates by a guard; a very brisk and efficient middle-aged man, in chainmail and a tunic with a badge emblazoned on the front. The badge was not one that Jonny recognized; it was not the five coins of Gradford, but a single coin with a four-armed cross superimposed upon it. This guard wanted to know their names, their trade, and where they had come from before he would let them pass.

Gwyna spoke up for them both, although this made the guard frown slightly; evidently women were not supposed to be so forward in Gradford these days as to dare to speak for a man. But neither of them wanted someone as marked by a distinguishing characteristic as Jonny's stutter to be on a guard's list. Gwyna could dye or cut her hair, change her clothes — Jonny could not open his mouth without betraying himself.

So he feigned being mute when the guard made a hushing motion at Robin and ordered *him* to speak up. He hoped that Robin would pick up on his cues; they hadn't had time to rehearse *this* subterfuge! He shook his head as the guard frowned and raised his voice.

"Sorry, sir," Robin said, falling into the part of a woman forced into the role of 'caretaker.' "Me husband's mute, sir. Been so since the storm a year agone —" She sniffed, and the guard's expression turned from one of disapproval to sympathy. "Struck by lightning, he was. Mind is as sharp as ever, but he can't speak a word."

Jonny nodded vigorously, and spread his hands in a gesture of helplessness, thanking whatever god might be listening for Gwyna's quick mind. The guard's expression softened further.

"Then give us the names and all, lass," he said, condescendingly, as if she were just a little feeble-minded. Kestrel clenched his jaw a little, and hoped she wouldn't react to that tone.

She didn't; she kept her temper, and smiled at the guard sweetly. "Jonny Brede and Jina Brede. We're traders in religious keepsakes, God-Stars. We came from Kingsford in Birnam when we heard of the work of your great High Bishop, and how Gradford had turned to pious ways."

Jonny let out his breath in a silent sigh of relief. Evidently Gwyna decided her name sounded a bit too much like she might be a Gypsy — they had taken the precaution this morning of dressing soberly, rather than in their Gypsy or Free Bard finery. Or else she was afraid someone might know the name "Gwyna," even though she called herself Robin in public. She could hardly use *that* name with the guard without branding herself a Free Bard! And she had wisely chosen a city far enough away that no one was likely to send to find out if they *had* been there recently.

"God-Stars?" the guard said, with interest. Gwyna dimpled, and brought out the samples they had stowed under the driver's seat.

"Little ones, for pendants, like, and the big ones, of course." She preened with pride as the guard examined both and praised the work. She started to offer him both, but to Jonny's surprise, he refused.

"That'd be bribery, dear, and we're honest men here in Gradford," he replied. "No, and I thank you, but you keep those in your pretty hands. Best of luck to you. Go right on in; there's no one in Gradford selling God-Stars like these, so you're no competition to a local trader, and that means you can set up in the market whenever you like. There's no tax on religious goods, other than the usual tithe."

Gwyna thanked him, and did not argue; if the guard was too silly to understand that a customer who bought a God-Star would probably *not* buy something else, it was not her problem. Kestrel shook the reins to send the horses forward.

And as soon as they cleared the gates, it was only too obvious that Rodrick had been right. Although this was clearly the start of the market-district, there was not a single busker anywhere. No jugglers, no street-dancers, no musicians. The streets seemed to have plenty of people on them, until you realized that this *should* have been the busiest part of the city. Then it slowly became obvious that there was barely a third of the people here that there should have been.

The undercurrent of music to the chaotic crowd-noises was something that both of them had taken for granted. Now that it was gone, the lack made Jonny, at least, feel oddly off-balance, straining his ears, listening for something that simply wasn't there.

They passed several inns — it was never wise to take the first set of accommodations offered, for such places were invariably overpriced. They shared their side of the street with a number of other vehicles, but none of them were traders' wagons. So Rodrick had been right about that as well; the traders appeared to have deserted the city entirely.

There's no rain that doesn't water someone's garden, Jonny thought. *At least there'll be no shortage of rooms. And probably good prices.* Gwyna had told him that in most large cities it was against the law to sleep in wagons; anyone who wished to camp in his wagon had to do so outside the city walls.

He still wasn't certain which inn to patronize, and when he finally saw *the* sign, he knew instinctively he had found the right place for them. The signboard sported a bird, beak wide open and pointed to the sky, obviously singing for all it was worth. It also, unlike many others, had the name of the inn written under the painted bird.

The Singing Bird. The name seemed a good omen, and Jonny turned the horses into the arched gateway that led into the inn's court.

The lean and balding innkeeper was frantically happy to see them, and a glance at his stable showed them why. No more than a third of the stalls were occupied, and if that was an indication of the number of customers inside, it was no wonder that he was glad to see them and their cash.

He was *not* a Gypsy, somewhat to Jonny's disappointment, but his stables were good, and he saw to their needs personally.

"We'll need to be able to take the wagon out during the day," Gwyna told him. "We'll be using it as our stall in the marketplace."

That stopped him cold, just as he directed the stableboys to put their mares in two spacious looseboxes. "I hope you aren't selling anything — like luxury goods?" he said, hesitantly, the bald spot on the top of his head growing red with anxiety. "There's not much call for such things in Gradford these days."

Jonny mentally gave him the accolade for his honesty. He could have gotten one night's lodging out of them before they found out the hard truth for themselves. Instead, he warned them.

Then again, if we were selling something proscribed, maybe he'd get arrested or fined for giving us lodging. It was a possibility. Given the lack of buskers and all that implied, Jonny was not taking anything for granted.

But Gwyna laughed, lightly. "God-Stars," she said, simply. "As jewelry and as wall decorations."

The innkeeper heaved a very audible sigh of relief, and mopped the top of his head with his apron. "There's no problem then. I'll have the boys ready your wagon and horses at the bell for Sunrise Service from the Cathedral; you come down for breakfast at Calling Bell for Prime Service and you'll find them harnessed and waiting when you finish. Best place for you will be in the market-square in front of the Cathedral, and to get there you just follow this street until it comes out at the square."

They locked up the wagon and took their bags from under the driver's seat, following their host across the yard to the inn itself. It was a sturdy, three-storied affair, substantial and built of dark timbers with whitewashed stone between. "I'm sorry I can't offer you any entertainment," he said apologetically. "But music's not allowed, unless it's from a Church-licensed musician."

His expression said what he would not say aloud. *And those are so bad I'd rather have no music than theirs.*

"Gradford has changed since last I was here," Gwyna replied casually. "There were no restrictions then, on what music could be played and what a peddler could sell."

The innkeeper shrugged, and once again his expression of faint distaste told Jonny that he did not care for the current state of things. But then, what innkeeper would? His custom had been cut down to a third of what it had been; *he* certainly was not prospering.

"I can't sell you strong liquor, either," he continued. "Only beer and ale, and hard cider." By his wary expression, some of his customers had found a great deal to object to in this particular edict, but Jonny only laughed.

"N-never d-drink anything s-stronger," he said, shortly, with a grin that made the innkeeper smile in return.

At that point, they entered the inn, and that was when Jonny realized just how bad things had gotten for the innkeepers of Gradford. Not that the place was ill-kempt, quite the contrary. The common room, with polished wooden tables and real chairs, with hangings on the walls and lanterns or candles on every table, with not one, but *two* fireplaces, was clearly a quality of hostelry they would not have been able to afford in the days of Gradford's prosperity. Or — perhaps, if their music pleased the innkeeper, they *might* have graced this room, but only as paid performers, and then only if a Guild musician didn't want the job. Or if the innkeeper didn't want the Guild musician. . . .

"I'll have a table ready for you as soon as you like," the innkeeper was saying as he hurried them across the waxed and polished stone floor of the common room and towards the staircase at the other side. "It's a good ham tonight, and sweetroots, or chicken and dumplings with carrots, and a nice stew of apples for after. Your room is up here —"

The room, up on the third floor, was obviously not the best in the inn, but it was finer than they *should* have gotten for their coin. It shared a bath with three other rooms; there were good rag rugs on the varnished wooden floor, a plain, but handsome wardrobe, matching tables on either side of the bed, and the bed boasted heavy bedcurtains, a feather mattress and feather comforter. No fireplace, of course, but it did have a small coal-fired stove, and presumably a certain amount of heat came up from the common room below. There were sturdy shutters to shut out the wind, and cheap, thick glass in the windows, full of bubbles and wavy — but in the class of inn they generally frequented, they were lucky to have shutters, much less glazed windows.

They ordered a bath for after dinner, put their gear away, and took the stairs back down to the common room. The ham, as promised, was good, and the room no more than a third full. Small wonder there were only two choices for a meal; with so few customers, this innkeeper could not afford to have several dishes prepared so that a patron had a wider choice.

"You know, we have a few hours of daylight left," Gwyna observed, as they lingered over their stewed apples and spiced tea. "We ought to walk around and see what's to be seen."

Jonny raised an inquiring eyebrow over that remark. Had she seen something he hadn't? He *had* been too busy driving to pay a great deal of attention to anything else.

"There seem to be a lot of street preachers," she said in answer to his unspoken question. "In fact, it looks almost as if the street preachers have taken over from the buskers."

"Ah," he replied, enlightened. "W-we should s-see what th-they're s-saying."

"Exactly." She sighed, and put aside her empty bowl and the spoon. "Much as I hate to ruin such a nice meal with a sour stomach. I think we really need to get a feel for things before we go out tomorrow."

"Right." He rose, and offered her his arm. "W-would m-my lady c-care t-take a s-stroll?"

"Why, yes, I think she would." She dimpled, and took the proffered arm. "The company, at least, will be pleasant."

"Even if th-the s-stroll isn't?" he replied.

She didn't answer him; she only shook her head with a warning look as they walked out into the inn-yard, and joined the thin stream of people leaving their work and going home.

CHAPTER TEN

There were plenty of street preachers, one for every corner, sometimes shouting so loudly that their speeches overlapped, and some of them were unintentionally funny. The trouble was, no one else seemed to see anything humorous in what they were saying.

A chilly wind whipped up the street, tossing skirts and cloaks, and numbing Kestrel's nose. It was a wind remarkably free of the usual stinks of a large city, and the gutters were empty of anything but a trace of water. Perhaps this place was like Nolton, with laws regarding the disposal of garbage, and crews to clean the streets. In a city like this one, with so many people crowded into so small an area and no river to cleanse it, that was not just a good idea, it was a necessity.

Buildings on both sides of the street loomed at least three stories in height, built of stone with tiny windows in the upper stories. Roofs were of a brownish slate, or of sandy tile. There wasn't a great deal of color, even in the dress of the passersby. Only the brilliantly blue sky above gave any relief to the unrelenting gray and brown. Nothing delineated the changes in Gradford quite so clearly as that; elsewhere, people reacted to the coming of winter by bringing out as much color in their clothing as they could afford. Presumably the people of Gradford had once done the same, but no more. The city *looked* sober, as if it already hosted nothing but Brothers and Sisters of various ascetic Orders.

They walked about a quarter mile towards the Cathedral, which loomed over the smaller buildings just as the Duke's Palace loomed over the city itself. They both paid careful attention to each preacher for at least a few minutes at a time; usually a few minutes were enough to get the gist of what each was saying.

Gradually Kestrel began to get a sense that there were three kinds of preachers, and each set shared a common style and a set of messages.

The first kind were the wild-eyed, unkempt street preachers he was used to seeing in every city or town he had ever found himself in. Dressed in strange assortments of tattered and layered garments, they exhorted the crowds passing with wildly waving arms and hoarsely shouted diatribes. They were fairly incoherent, contradicting themselves from sentence to sentence, and full of dire prophecies about the "Second Cataclysm." He'd always thought they were a little mad, and he didn't see any reason to change that opinion now. Interestingly, these men had only the same sort of audiences they got in other cities; people as mad as they were, gawkers, and adolescents who got a great deal of amusement out of making a mockery of them.

But the adolescents making mock were uniformly ruffians, rather than the mix of ne'er-do-wells and ordinary youngsters that usually tried to give these poor old men a difficult time. And the authorities, in the form of the City Constables, ran the youngsters off with warnings, and not the preachers, who would elsewhere have been considered nuisances.

So these days in Gradford, even the lunatics come in for a smattering of respect. Kestrel wouldn't have believed it if he hadn't seen it himself.

The second variety of street sermonizers was a type he normally saw only during Faires: country-fellows who were not ordained Priests and supported themselves through what they could collect on their own. These were men who would say, if questioned, that they felt "called by The Sacrificed God" to preach the Truth as they, and not the Church, saw it. They generally leapt at the chance to preach restraint to a crowd bent on celebration. Their motives were simple enough; perhaps move some of their listeners to moderation, or at least, through a bit of passing guilt, charm a pin or a coin out of their pockets and into the collection plate. Kestrel thought of them as a different form of busker, for they used the same venue as buskers. Their messages were along the line of "repent of your sins and be purified," and "do not waste your lives on short-term pleasures when your energy could better be spent in contemplating God." They urged sacrifice, with the veiled hint that a sacrifice tossed in their direction would find favor with God. More often than not — at a Faire at least — this kind of preacher would manage to "save" some fellow who'd been a chronic drunk all his life and had just hit bottom; having "saved" the fool, the preacher would parade him about like a hunter's prize. And the former drunk, having found a new addiction that made him the center of attention, would perform obligingly.

There were at least two with reformed drunks in tow on this street. And although these men were normally ignored by Faire-goers, who often parted around them like the water in a swift-moving stream avoiding a rock, here their message was falling on more appreciative ears. More than one listener looked both attentive and impressed. Interesting, but not unexpected.

Then there was the third class of preacher — a type

that Kestrel had *never* seen preaching in the street before; real Priests, in immaculate robes, who clearly did not need to be out here and in fact had no collection plates at their feet. These men — they were always men, even though women could aspire to the Priesthood as readily as men — were clean, erudite, and well-spoken, pitching their trained, modulated voices to carry their words over the heads of the crowds.

It was this third type of preacher that had the messages that were very disturbing.

"— come from God are alone pure and righteous," the first of these was saying, as they came within hearing distance. He had a very well-trained and sonorous voice, and he already had a crowd three deep around him. He was brown of beard and hair and eye; his well-kept robe was a dark brown, and he should have blended in with his surroundings. But he didn't — he stood out from them, as if he was a heroic statue, the focus for all eyes. "No matter what the ignorant and unholy will tell you, *all* things called 'magic' are inherently evil. Magic can only be the tool of demons and false gods; there is no truth in it, and none in those who practice it."

He looked around at his audience; Kestrel was very careful to school his features into a semblance of sober interest. This man was no fool; any show of resistance to his words would cause him to single that person out for special attentions and special messages. The onlookers would notice. Things could become very awkward, very quickly.

"Perhaps you have heard somewhere that there are mages within the Church itself, but I tell you that this is *not* true. Whoever has told you this has lied to you," he said, lying gracefully and believably. "Magic is *deception;* magic only counterfeits the real and holy powers granted only to Priests by God. Those powers practiced within the Church come directly by grace and blessing of the Sacrificed God, and they are *nothing* like magic! And only those within the Church, *within the ranks of the ordained* will be blessed with those powers. Those who claim to achieve the same ends through their magic are false, deceptive, and evil. They seek to mislead you, seduce you to muddled thinking and questioning, and then to lead you astray down the paths of darkness."

Neat, Jonny thought, admiring the Priest's command of rhetoric, though not his words. *Redefine magic as anything that is not performed by a Priest, and then you can condemn it without condemning the Priests.*

"Not only is the magic itself inherently and by its very deceptive nature evil," the Priest continued, warming to his subject, "but anyone, *anyone* who uses it *or allows himself to be touched by it* is evil! Magic is a mockery of God's powers! God will not be mocked! He will not permit his servants to be mocked! The day is coming when all those evil ones who practice magic will perish, and those who permitted them to work their magic will perish with them! Those who live by magic will die by the hand of the righteous!"

There was more in this vein, although Jonny noticed that the Priest was very careful not to say *who* would be dealing out this punishment to the "evil magicians." Given the tales that had been spreading of musicians using magic to manipulate their listeners, it was easy to see where *this* was going. He might not have brought up the "evil musicians" yet, but it was only a matter of time.

Nightingale had been only too right, and so had Harperus.

He felt a sudden sickness in the pit of his stomach,

and it didn't take any effort at all on his part to persuade Gwyna away and get out of hearing range. The Priest was still going strong when they left, and as far as Jonny could tell, it was more of the same. No mention, as yet, of musicians. But given the fact that there were no musicians anywhere in sight, perhaps he saw no need to mention them, in his condemnation of every other person who ever made use of magic and mages.

About the only encouraging note in this was that the Priest was losing listeners at a fairly steady rate — perhaps people who had used the services of a Healer, or those who had employed a mage for some minor work in finding a lost object, locating water, or taming a beast that would not respond to normal efforts. It would take more persuasive means than simply *saying* that magic was evil to convince most folk that it was bad.

After all, most people in their lives saw many instances of the use of magic, all of it hired and completely matter-of-fact. How could any of this be evil? Mages created amusing illusions for parties, rid homes of poltergeists and kobolds — they didn't do anything that a Priest couldn't do. And they generally didn't ask as much in return. Priests were often greedy in their demands when someone turned to them for help; a simple mage could only ask the usual rate, and did not care *what* god you followed or whether you were up to date on your tithing.

That was what Kestrel read in the faces of those who turned away from the preacher. But there were some who stayed, nodding in agreement. . . .

A very bad sign.

The sun had turned the sky above the city to a glorious crimson as they came into the "circle" of another of the real Priests out on the street. This man had a much larger gathering of listeners, and fewer of them were leaving with looks of stubborn disbelief on their faces. Jonny steeled himself to hear something unpleasant. This one also wore a brown robe, but he was a much older man, the kind that people would instinctively turn to for advice; clean-shaven with snow-white hair. But there was something subtly cruel and hard about his eyes, and the set of his mouth indicated a man who would never accept any opinion but his own.

"If a soul is the image of God, and God created humankind in His image, how can any creature that does not wear that image have a soul?" the Priest asked, his voice rational and reasonable. "It is there in the Holy Writ, for all to read. *For God then created them, male and female, in His Own image.* Male and female, and human. *The soul is the reflection of God, and is in the image of God.* Human, entirely and wholly. No creature that is not fully human could possibly be in possession of a soul. The implications of this are obvious to anyone who takes the time to study the Holy Book and *think.* A creature that does not have a soul cannot be saved by the grace of the Church; it is that simple, and that profound. Only humans can be saved. Only humans have souls."

This Priest had an interesting demeanor; unlike the last one, who clearly preached *at* his audience, this man kept his voice calm and steady, his tone ingratiating, his expression persuasive. His manner invited his listeners to discover truth for themselves, not just to be told what the truth was and was not. In a village, this man would be the one most would go to for the settling of disputes.

"But there is a much more serious — yes, and frightening — side to this, and one that is not as obvious," he continued, his expression turning to one of warning. "A creature that does not have a soul and cannot be saved by the Church must *by definition* be evil! Oh, do not shake your heads; only think about it. To be evil is to act against the interests of God. But a creature that is soulless cannot know the interests of God, so how can he act in accord with them? They cannot be anything but evil by their very natures. Nothing can change that, not all the good intentions in the world, for it is bred into them, blood and bone, by their very differences. They are the damned and the doomed, and they will always be the enemies of the Church, for their inmost nature will cause them to resist the guidance of the Church." His expression hardened, and yet became sorrowful at the same time. "Surely you, who are thinking men, can see the result of this. The Church's charge is the safety, spiritual and actual, of humanity. The enemies of the Church must become, sooner or later, the enemies of all humankind, and the enemies of humankind will inevitably seek to destroy humanity."

Kestrel had no trouble anticipating the next statement.

"Those who would seek to destroy humankind *must* be destroyed first!" the Priest said fiercely. "There can be no sin in this; it is not murder, for they have no souls! It is self-defense and no more; ridding humanity of their cursed presence is no worse than ridding the city of rats! And *who* is it that has these unnatural magics, that you have been warned against? More often than not, it is these unhuman monsters!"

This time it was Robin who pulled him away, but he was not reluctant to leave; he had certainly heard enough to nauseate him. "God is l-love, l-love is b-blind, I am b-b-blind, therefore I am G-G-God," Kestrel muttered under his breath; something that had become a very unfunny joke. Horrid how the rules of logic could be twisted to make the illogical, irrational, and idiotic sound reasonable. . . .

Robin shushed him, and they crossed over to the other side of the street to return to their inn. The last light of the sun died away overhead; the little canyons between the buildings were already full of shadows, and lamplighters made their way along the street, pausing at each of the street corners. There were not too many people out at this point; those that were did not seem to be in any great hurry to get anywhere. Kestrel noted with thankfulness that the preachers had taken the coming of nightfall as a signal to leave their posts and find some other venue for their speeches. He'd had a bellyful of them, and he was not in the mood for any more.

But he was to get one more dose of Holy Word before they reached the relative safety of their room.

The last preacher of the night was hard to classify; he had the collection plate and the common clothing of an ordinary street preacher, but the trained voice and command of rhetoric of a full Priest. They could not get by, for his listeners had temporarily blocked the street, so they had no choice but to listen for a moment.

And for a moment, it seemed as if his message was no more insidious than any of the other lunatics out here this afternoon. "— idle time, time that is not spent in work or in contemplation, is time spent in evilness," he was saying. Kestrel could not see his face in the shadows; he kept his voice deliberately soft, so that anyone really listening had to lean forward to hear his words. The combination of the darkness, the soft words, the persuasive voice, worked in a hypnotic fashion before a listener was really aware of it.

Unless you were a musician, and had used similar

tricks yourself, to create a mood of quiet persuasion in the middle of a crowded tavern.

"Because of this, anything done purely for pleasure or for simple enjoyment is also evil because these are things done in idleness. The only fit occupation for a true man is work; either the work of his hands and mind, or the work of God and the Church. Those temptations of hollow pleasure must be eliminated, and those who will not give them up must be taught the error of their ways. Gently, if possible, but if not" — he concluded, darkly — "then by whatever means necessary."

At that point the blockage cleared, and Robin and Kestrel hurried on, quickly, until they were well out of range of sight and sound of the final preacher.

"Now I'm glad we were warned," Robin sighed. "If we had come into town the way we usually enter a city —"

"P-playing and s-singing 'The S-saucy P-p-priest'?" Kestrel finished. "I th-think our w-welcome m-might have b-been w-warmer th-than w-we'd l-like."

"That, at least." Robin held his arm, tightly, as much for comfort as for appearances, as they entered the inn courtyard. It opened up like a haven of sanity after the speeches of the past hour. As they opened the door to the common room, one of the serving girls spotted them and hurried over to them.

"Would you like your baths now?" she asked. "The water is hot and ready, and no one has bespoken the room until later."

"Please," Robin said, and lowered her voice a little. "We were just taking a walk outside, and we couldn't help wondering — is every night like tonight? I've never seen so many preachers in one place before. Is there something special about tonight, or this street?"

The girl sighed, and rolled her eyes a little. "Nothing special about tonight, but they do seem to pick this street t' be doing their ranting. P'rhaps it's 'cause most visitors lodge here, or p'rhaps it's 'cause the Cathedral's so near. There's laws, thank heavens; they can't be preachin' long after dark, to disturb folks' rest, or we'd not get any. No offense —" she added hastily.

Kestrel managed a wan chuckle. "N-none t-taken," he said. "We're here t-to p-peddle our c-crafts, and if it's G-god-Stars th-these p-people w-want, th-that's what th-they'll g-get!"

The girl smiled warmly. "I shouldn't've said what I did, but I didn't think you was lunatic religious," she replied. "F'r one thing, they don't bathe near often enough!" And she wrinkled her nose. "Be glad it's 'bout winter! I tell you, some 'f them 'd choke a goat in hot weather!"

Robin shrugged. "We're traders," she said. "We were warned what had happened, and we changed our trade goods for something that would sell under the circumstances. Perhaps it may sound cynical, but if they'd all gone mad for — for some actor who fancied feather masks, for some reason, we'd be peddling those instead of God-Stars."

"But actors don't get y' pilloried — or worse," the girl muttered, then shook herself. "Well, sir an' lady, take y'rselves upstairs, whilst I call th' upstairs wench, an' by the time y' reach the bathing room, the baths'll be ready."

She was as good as her word. The bathing room had two tubs, side by side, and both were full and steaming, as promised, by the time they arrived at the bathroom door. They sank into the hot water with gratitude.

Jonny simply let his mind empty; he did not want to

think about what he had just heard. He wanted to relax, just for a moment, and pretend that none of this was happening.

Church bells woke them; not uncommon in a large city, but they seemed unusually loud until Kestrel remembered the Cathedral was not far away. And they were *very* loud. He hadn't heard bells like this since — since —

Since I was a child, and living in the Guild Hall with my Master. The Cathedral was across the street, and every morning the first bells would wake us, no matter how tired we were, or how late we had been up the night before.

The remembrance was tainted with a little less bitterness now. It helped to know that his beloved Master had not been a crazed and half-witted old man, but a very brave and very frightened one. It helped to know that the Guild had been wrong about both of them.

Robin groaned as Kestrel got out of bed and pulled back the thick, dark curtains. He actually felt rather good, even after those wretched street sermons of the night before — and even though his dreams had been haunted by Priests leading fanatic mobs in chasing him. One thing about being in a city obsessed with religion — there was little or nothing to do after sunset, so going to bed was the only option.

I'll bet they have a population explosion around here in a few months — depending on how long this has been going on, he thought, pulling open the shutters to let the sunlight in. Robin groaned again. *I wonder if the herbs that protect against conception have been put on the proscribed list too?* That would be a logical move, if the Church really was interested in restricting people's interests. If a girl had a real chance of getting pregnant, she might be a bit warier about distributing her favors. And if a wife was burdened with one baby after another, she wouldn't have a great deal of leisure for anything else.

Like thinking for herself. . . .

Robin sat up, her curly hair tousled and a lock dangling over one eye, yawning hugely. "Gods," she moaned, squinting. "Sunlight."

Sun poured through the thick glass and pooled on the floor, catching the reds and blues in the rag rug there and making them glow. Kestrel grabbed clean clothing, while Robin watched, blinking sleepily from her nest of bedclothes. Sober clothing; muted browns and dark grays for him, browns and sand-tones for Robin. No Gypsy reds and yellows here; if he'd had any doubt as to the wisdom of such "disguises," last night in the street had convinced him.

"T-time t-to get to w-work," he reminded her. "W-we're p-peddlers, remember? W-we have t-to be out f-first th-thing when th-the m-markets open."

"I remember," she said, around another yawn. "Well, last night we heard the poison, now we need to find out what the source is. And *why* all these people are suddenly so full of maniacal religious fervor! A lot of the changes here required some changes in the *laws,* Jonny, and that doesn't happen overnight. You have to convince very powerful people to make changes that may not be to their advantage."

"You're v-very articulate this m-morning," he observed, with a bit of a smile, then lost the smile as something occurred to him. "One of th-the p-powerful p-people who s-supported Gradford f-from the b-beginning was th-the High B-Bishop. W-wouldn't he b-be on th-the C-Council? D-did you th-think about th-that?"

"Hmm. I think I was thinking about it even in my sleep." She climbed out of bed to join him in dressing, pulling on linen petticoats, wool stockings and boots, a sober brown wool skirt and sand-colored linen shirt, lacing her brown leather vest over both. "Someone has gotten the ears of anyone important, and has convinced the merchants who are losing money right now that they are better off not complaining about their problems. We should keep our ears open in the marketplace. There are probably some merchants out there that are just as cynical as Rodrick, and we might get them to tell us something. There's a piece missing to this puzzle."

As promised, a breakfast was laid ready for the inn's patrons, a buffet-style breakfast where they could help themselves to oatmeal, sliced bread and butter, honey, fruit, last night's ham, and pastries. And as promised, when they were finished and went out into the court, the wagon was standing ready with several others, mares in harness and stamping impatiently.

They swung themselves up onto the driver's bench, and took the wagon out into the street. All traffic, foot and wagon, was going in one direction this morning; towards the Cathedral. Robin had the reins, and she simply let the press of people carry them along at foot-pace.

"I'm c-curious," Kestrel said, as the Cathedral loomed at the end of the street. "H-how *d-did* you d-do that b-business w-with th-the f-fire in y-your h-hand in W-Westhaven?"

Robin chuckled. "Gypsy trick," she said, lightly. "Meant to fool the stupid. Special paper that burns very quickly, so quickly there isn't any heat to speak of, and it ignites with just a spark. A little misdirection, flint-and-steel and a bit of paper in your hand, and agile fingers, and there you are. I always carry some, and powder of the same sort, good for throwing into a fire to create a big flash."

Jonny watched the faces of the foot travelers around them. They were uniformly eager, clearly anticipating something. "C-can all of you d-do that?"

She nodded. "Useful skill to have, when you need to make someone think that you're more powerful than you really are. We pledge never to teach outsiders, though, so I'm afraid I can't even teach you."

"D-don't n-need it," he assured her. "G-got enough to worry about."

By that time they reached the place where the street emptied out into the square in front of Gradford Cathedral. For the first time they saw the Cathedral as something other than bits of towers and roof, and in spite of himself, Jonny was impressed and moved.

You couldn't get a sense of the Cathedral simply from the bits you glimpsed over the rooftops and at the end of the street. He had no idea how anyone could construct something like this building without it toppling straight over; it looked as fragile and delicate as any confectioner's masterpiece, and just as ephemeral.

He guessed that the four round steeples, one at each corner, must have been at least fifteen stories tall, maybe more. They spiraled up like the shells of some sea-beasts he had seen, coming to a point at their peaks. They were pierced by a fretwork of windows, and looked as delicate as lace. There were no sharp angles in these towers, nothing but curves; curved arches, round windows, spiraling, ramplike exterior ledges that ran from the bottom all the way to the top. The towers were covered with a network of carvings as well, cut in shallow relief into the pristine marble and alabaster. None of the towers were carved alike. The tower to his right was encrusted with waving kelp and seaweed, sinuous eels, spiny urchins, undulating waves, and delicate fish. The one to his left bore clouds in every form, from wisps to towering thunderheads, and among them sported all the creatures of the air, from birds to butterflies. Rainbows arched from cloud to cloud, and the delicate seeds of thistle and dandelion wafted among the flying insects on the lower level.

The other two towers were harder to see since they were on the opposite side of the Cathedral, but on one, Jonny thought he made out sensuous and abstract depictions of flames, salamanders, and the legendary Phoenix, and on the other, carvings of plants and animals crept, climbed, and sported on the curves.

On the top of each tower was a single statue of an angel; they spread wide wings and empty hands over the square below, as if bestowing blessings from on high. Unlike many carven angels Jonny had seen, the expressions of the faces of the two facing him were full of childlike wonder and joy — and there were no weapons on those hands. These angels beckoned the beholder to share in their exultation, neither warning dourly of punishment for sins, nor offering a fatuous and simpering "there, there" in lieu of real comfort.

Within the pinnacle of each tower hung the bells, half-hidden in the shadows, but gleaming with polished bronze whenever the sun struck them.

With those four towers to gape at, it was hard to imagine how the Cathedral itself could be any more impressive than the towers were. But somehow, it was, and it left him gaping.

Though by necessity it had to be square in form with a peaked roof, it had been ornamented in the same sinuous style as the towers. The carvings all over the facade depicted the life of the Sacrificed God, and

the lives of the saints and heroes of the Church. Somehow, even those who had died grisly deaths seemed,
not to be contorted with suffering, but rather dancing
their deaths. Arrows and nooses, torture devices and
instruments of punishment seemed idle accessories to
the dance — wounds mere decorations.

And among the carvings were the windows.

Rather than making pictures with glass, the builders
of the Cathedral had chosen to make the windows a
backdrop for the carvings, so instead of complicated
scenes and designs, there were flowing abstractions —
more curves, of course — of four or five pieces of glass
in harmonious colors. Some echoed the blue and
white of a sky full of clouds, the dark blue and scarlet
of a sunset, the crimson and orange of flames, the
greens of ocean waves, the golds and browns of a field
in harvest-colors. The result was breathtaking, and the
Cathedral sparkled in the sun like a giant box of
jewels.

Jonny found himself thinking only one thing.
*How, faced every day with this, can these Priests be
preaching things that are so small-minded and
petty?* For the Cathedral as a whole was a song, an
expression in stone of the wholeness of man and
the world, however that world was put together.
There was no room in this structure for pettiness
and prejudice. It had clearly been designed,
built, and ornamented by men who loved all of
creation, and felt at one with the world.

It took a conscious effort for him to turn his attention back to the mundane. But the Cathedral would
be here for longer than they would, and there was
business to attend to.

There were many more wagons and stalls here in
the cobblestone square, all of them in a row ringing
the Cathedral, some of the stalls still untenanted,

some with traders setting up. The buildings facing the square were not shops, as he had assumed they would be. Rather, they were private residences; very expensive private residences. The owners of the stalls and wagons had courteously faced their businesses away from these homes, and towards the Cathedral. While waiting for Prime to begin, the first Service of the day that would be open to the public, the crowds gathering here perused the contents of the wagons and stalls with varying degrees of eagerness. Some were plainly killing time; others were in a holiday mood and prepared to buy.

Robin tucked their wagon into a good corner, across from a private home, and beneath a lamppost. No sooner had they tethered the horses, than a City Constable came hurrying over, carrying a board to which several papers were attached.

Jonny let Robin deal with him, keeping up his pretense of being a mute, and set up their display on the side of the wagon facing the Cathedral, following the example of the rest of the merchants. The wall-Stars he hung on the side of the wagon itself, where they caught the sun and made a cheerful display of color against the brown wood. For the trays of jewelry, he propped open the lids to two of the storage compartments and laid two trays each on them; two of the inexpensive thread-and-twig Stars, one of the lesser metals, and one of the solid silver and mixed silver, copper, and bronze.

The Constable went away, and Robin carefully attached the paper he had given her to the side of the wagon. Jonny took a look at it as soon as he was done with his preparations.

It described both of them, their goods, their wagon and horses, and declared that they were "certified" by the authority of High Bishop Padrik.

Clearly, since it described them so minutely, it would do an "uncertified" merchant no good to steal the certification of another. He had to admit, grudgingly, that it was a good idea.

"The tithe here is fifteen percent, not ten," Robin told him in a low voice, as she straightened the Stars in their tray. "It's because of the location; he was nice enough to tell me that if we moved to the rear of the Cathedral, it was the usual ten —"

"If w-we m-move, w-we w-won't see what w-we c-came to see." That seemed obvious enough. "As l-long as w-we c-come out even —"

But already the first of their potential customers was hurrying over, attracted by the brilliant Stars in the sunlight, and within a short time it was clear they were not going to come out "even," they were probably going to run out of Stars before two days were over, if they continued to sell at this rate.

No matter. They could make more. It would be a good excuse to linger around the inn, walk about the town, and *not* go to the market for a day or more.

The jewelry proved unexpectedly popular; somewhat to Robin's obvious surprise, the metal Stars sold as well if not better than the cheaper Stars of thread. Jonny saw why, once he realized what it was that had been bothering him about the wealthier women and their clothing.

The very drabness of it fooled him into concentrating on the color, but as he watched customer after customer *immediately* don her Star, stringing it on her own chain or using the ribbon Robin provided, he saw faces transformed with delight. And he knew that these women had given up *jewelry,* and missed it. After all, Gradford was famous for gemcraft and metals, and it was known across the Twenty Kingdoms that Gradford women all had dowries of lovely jewelry, some of it very ancient, passed down from generation to generation.

The current austere state of things dictated they must give up such adornments. They *missed* their jewelry, and here was a perfectly pious way to get it back.

There had been a number of women and men in finer materials than those coming to the wagon, who had spent some time studying the God-Stars from a distance. *Silversmiths,* he decided, after a while. *Goldsmiths and jewelers. There will be work into the night, tonight, and fine silver and gold Stars by morning. Poor apprentices. . . .*

Then again, considering that the apprentices had probably been doing and learning nothing of late, one long night wasn't going to hurt them. And, inadvertently, he and Robin had breathed new life into a dying business!

With that in mind, he sidled over to her in his first free moment, whispered his suspicions into Robin's ear, and added a suggestion. She nodded, and he went back to hanging up yarn God-Stars to replace the ones sold, confident that his idea was in good hands.

A few moments later, she left the wagon to hurry to the side of a gray-haired man in gray velveteen, who had a young, clever-faced woman at his side. The girl bore a remarkable resemblance to him; most probably his daughter, and possibly his apprentice as well.

Robin spoke to them in a low voice for a few minutes, then waved, inviting them to come to the wagon. They took her up on her invitation, and as they watched, she took apart one of the copper Stars, then remade it so they could see how it was done. The transformation in them was remarkable; they went from interested to animated in a few short moments, finally ending up laughing as she placed the copper Star into the girl's hands.

Jonny saw all this in between sales of smaller and larger Stars; by the time he was finished with the last customer, the two were gone. By this time, all of the wagons and stalls were losing their custom as the crowds left *en masse* and flowed in the direction of the Cathedral. Prime was about to begin, evidently, and no one wanted a place in the rear.

"Well?" he asked, as she sidled up to him and gave him a quick squeeze around the waist.

"Master Tomas and his daughter will be very happy to supply us with base-metal and silver-alloy wire and thin bar-stock at a very reasonable price in return for my instruction just now," she said with the intense satisfaction of any Gypsy who has made a good bargain. "I made some suggestions about chains made of very tiny Stars, and suspending Stars from some of the more elaborate chains they already had made up and couldn't sell. In return, *they* suggested ornamenting the ends of the posts with beads, putting a semiprecious stone or glass bead at the center join, and stringing the Stars on necklaces of beads. Everyone is very happy, me included." She grinned happily. "I could wish we were here just for the profit; we're doing *very* well, even after the fifteen-percent tithe."

She had been the one doing all the talking to the customers and the other traders who had come to see what they were offering that was doing so well; he had played mute, and evidently the customers had assumed that meant he was deaf as well. "Wh-what d-did you find out s-so f-far?" he asked, as the crowds gathered tightly about the front of the Cathedral, and acolytes brought out a portable altar. Evidently, in spite of the cold, High Bishop Padrik was going to hold Prime outside, presumably because there was not enough room in the Cathedral itself for everyone waiting. Jonny wondered how on earth the man expected anyone to hear him. Most Churches were built to magnify the voice; he wouldn't have that advantage out here.

Or would he?

The magnificence of the Cathedral had made him ignore the *structure,* and the two wings of Church buildings on either side of it, inside a walled compound. They weren't on the square, they were *slanted,* like a funnel, with the front of the Cathedral the bottom of the funnel. And the elaborately carved front was in the shape of a shell —

Hadn't he heard of something like this, in an outdoor theater?

It should be just as effective in amplifying a speaker's voice as the interior.

"Well, I'm not sure I believe it," she said slowly, shaking him out of his study of the Cathedral, "but I've heard it from so many different people —" Her voice faltered. "They say Padrik works miracles."

He stared at her, startled. She nodded.

"That's what they say," she told him. "Padrik works miracles. Not just simple Healing, but really impossible things, like straightening limbs that have been malformed from birth, healing people born blind or deaf. Even the most skeptical are really awed by him. *That* is why everyone in Gradford has been overcome with religious fever. Because they're sure the High Bishop is a modern saint."

She was about to say more, when the bells rang out, drowning her voice in their clangor, and the doors of the Cathedral opened. The sun struck something inside, setting up a reflective glitter that made Kestrel's eyes water. An invisible choir saluted the crowd with music that made the heart stop with its pure, measured beauty. And a single figure clad in white

Priest-robes and glittering with gold strode confidently out in front of the Cathedral, and raised his hands.

They were about to discover if the stories were true. High Bishop Padrik had begun the Prime Service.

CHAPTER ELEVEN

Padrik's voice, as beautiful a speaking voice as any Kestrel had ever heard, rang out over the crowd as clearly as one of the bells. It was such an incredible voice that Jonny wished he could hear Padrik sing, and listened closely for any signs that the High Bishop had Bardic training. Padrik was the single most impressive speaker Jonny had ever heard in his life, surpassing even the Bardic Guild Masters and the Wren himself.

Then came the moment in the Holy Services when the sermon was given. If he had not been braced to be skeptical and critical, he might have found himself convinced of the truth of the High Bishop's words, for in comparison with Padrik's superb command of rhetoric and argument, the street preachers of last night were as clumsy as toddlers arguing over a toy.

Padrik's sermon was a combination of all three of the "dangerous" ideas Jonny and Gwyna had heard last night. *Magic is deception and only the miracles of the Church are the truth and therefore magic is evil. Nonhumans are without souls, and therefore the enemies of the Church and humankind. Things done purely for pleasure are evil because they take time away from the work of God and the Church.*

But Padrik made them all seem logical, sane, and part of a whole. Part of a conspiracy, in fact, of nonhumans "and their friends, the betrayers of humanity," to destroy mankind, after first weakening it with magic, and to enslave the survivors. Only the vigilance of the Church stood between the faithful and these "perfidious servants of demons," who sought to bring on the Second Cataclysm and make all humankind the helpless prey of demons. How they were actually going to do that was not specified. But then, most people had no notion how or why the original Cataclysm had occurred.

Padrik completed his sermon with a glorious depiction of the triumph of humanity and a presumably all-human world, dedicated to the glory of God and the Church.

Kestrel shook off Padrik's spell with a shudder, and the cold wind whipping across the square was no match for the chill of fear in his heart. How long had *this* been going on? Long enough, evidently, that now no one openly objected to his ideas. Kestrel had not seen any nonhumans in Gradford, and now he was certain he wouldn't see any.

If they'd had brains worth speaking of, they'd have packed up as soon as the first rumblings of this nonsense started. Probably back when the nonhumans were only "without souls" and had not yet graduated to being the "enemies of mankind." Prejudice could be as damaging as persecution, and there had been outbreaks of nonhuman prejudice before this to act as an example.

The trouble was, they *hadn't* stayed to hear what simple prejudice had become; a call for a crusade against them. If they had, there would be alarms raised all through the Twenty Kingdoms and beyond, to all of the nonhumans across Alanda.

In fact, since only rumors of this had percolated to the outside world as a growing prejudice against nonhumans, it appeared that whoever stayed here long enough was co-opted into Padrik's ranks. Or else —

they were gotten rid of somehow, before they managed to bring warning to the nonhumans.

Oh, *that* was a comforting thought!

But before he got too panicked, he took a moment to think the situation through. Traders looking to buy and sell metals and gems would probably find business mostly as usual, with only a few annoyances — the prohibition against the sale of strong drink, for instance. They would arrive, do their business, and leave, probably without even listening to a street preacher, much less Padrik himself. Most other people didn't travel much in the late fall and winter, not even Gypsies and Free Bards. The Gypsies tended to hole up in Waymeets for the winter; the Free Bards found wintering-over stops, in inns and the courts of minor nobles all over the Kingdoms. Those intending to winter-over in Gradford would have gotten the message last summer that non-Guild musicians were not welcome in the city-state. Why go where you weren't welcome? So one of the best sources of information in all the world was shut out of Gradford *before* all this escalated into madness. As for other visitors — how many would stay in a city that had gone mad for religion? The only people coming here would be those coming specifically to hear Padrik, and would be pulled into his followers immediately.

And as for the citizens themselves — nothing had really happened yet to show them that this was anything other than talk. Oh, the nonhumans were gone, but they'd gone off on their own, surely — and they were taking jobs and custom that could have gone to humans instead, so where was the harm?

Nothing to alarm anyone in that.

The Prime Service wound to its dignified end. And if only Padrik's words had not left such a bad taste in Jonny's mouth, he could have enjoyed it. The music was glorious, and Padrik quite the most impressive clergyman Kestrel had ever seen. As a show alone, it was fabulous.

The trouble was, this "show" was like a tasty candy with poison at the center, a slow-acting poison, one whose effects were so subtle that the poor fool who'd eaten it had no notion of what was happening until it was too late.

Padrik vanished into the Cathedral, and a secondary Priest stepped forward onto the platform. *This* was not a usual part of Prime Services —

"Let the sick be gathered, and the poor be brought," the Priest cried out, for all the world like a Sire's Herald announcing the start of a feast. "Let all those in need come forward into God's own House, for the High Bishop's prayers and God's blessing!"

The entire crowd surged towards the door. Kestrel and Robin exchanged a single look, and in a heartbeat had packed up all their remaining God-Stars, locked up the wagon, and were joining the tail of the crowd as it squeezed in through the wide-open doors of the Cathedral.

The building was as impressive on the inside as on the outside, with the same sinuous, sensuous carvings everywhere, and sunlight shining through the brilliant colored glass of the windows, staining the pristine marble with splashes of crimson and gold, azure and emerald. They were not there to sightsee, however, or to gawk at the statues and glass. What they wanted lay at the front of the Cathedral, where the altar stood —

Their experience in Faire crowds stood them in good stead here; they were able to wiggle and squirm their way up the side along the wall, until they were near enough the altar to hear every word and to see Padrik clearly.

And it seemed that no one was too terribly concerned either about damage to the carvings or to their dignity; people in the rear climbed up onto the pedestals of the carved saints and clung there, hanging onto their alabaster robes like so many children clinging to their mothers' skirts. Robin found footholds for two in the carving of Saint Hypatia the Librarian, and Kestrel joined her there, both of them clinging to the saint's arms, while the alabaster lips smiled down at them as if Hypatia was enjoying their company on her tiny pedestal.

They tried to compose their faces into the appropriate expressions of piety, but only Saint Hypatia was paying any attention. All eyes were riveted to the altar, Padrik, and the young man who had been brought to him on a sedan-chair.

The man seeking Padrik's blessing was in his twenties or thereabouts, dressed in an expensive silk and velvet tunic and shirt of a dark blue that seemed too big for his thin body. Unlike virtually everyone else they'd seen so far in the city, he wore heavy gold chains about his neck, massive gold rings, and matching gold wrist-cuffs. There was a velvet and fur robe covering his legs.

Padrik was young for one with such a high position in the Church; Kestrel judged him to be in his middle thirties, at most. There was no gray in his golden hair, no wrinkle marred the perfection of his face. In fact, he was just as handsome as any of the alabaster carvings in here, a face that matched the glorious voice. In his pristine white robes he was the very ideal Priest, the image of a modern Saint. The white surcoat over his white robes gleamed with gold embroidery, and Kestrel was willing to bet every copper penny they'd made that day that the embroidery had been done with *real* gold bullion.

"What brings you to me for the Church's blessing, my son?" he asked the young man, who was not *that* much younger than he.

The young man's voice quavered when he spoke. "It is my leg, My Lord Bishop. All of my life my left leg has been shorter than my right, and twisted — I cannot walk on it. No one has been able to heal it, and many have tried —"

Padrik's voice grew stern. "Are you saying you have sought the services of the Deceivers, the Unbelievers, those who dare to work that blasphemy they call *magic*?"

The young man did not answer; instead, he broke into tears, sobbing his plea for forgiveness. Padrik's voice softened immediately, and he laid a comforting hand on the young man's shoulder. "God is not mocked, but neither is he unforgiving," he said, his voice taking on the same tones of his sermon. "You have come to God for His blessing and forgiveness, and He shall be generous to you."

He raised his voice. "Let all who see, believe, and let all who believe, rejoice!"

As the crowd held its collective breath, he pulled the lap robe off and laid his hands on the young man's legs. It was very clear that one *was* shorter than the other, although if it was twisted, Kestrel couldn't tell, for the young man wore loose velvet trews with open bottoms instead of breeches or hose, and expensive leather boots. Still, every Healer would be the first to sigh and admit that those born with defective limbs were doomed to live with them; there was nothing any Healer could do to Heal those born with an ailment.

Nothing any Healer could do. Except, it seemed, this one —

As silence held sway over the crowd, Padrik slowly

stretched the young man's bad leg, straightening it and pulling on it until it was exactly even with the good one!

And as the Cathedral rang with cheers, the young man leapt up from his sedan-chair and ran to the altar, to strip off his gold jewelry and place it there in thanksgiving.

There was more of the same, much more. Padrik healed several more people; one blind, one deaf, and one palsied, plus at least three cripples and a leper. Then as the secondary Priests brought forward a group of raggedly clothed folk, Padrik produced a shower of silver and copper coins out of the air as alms for the poor. Finally he singled out one young Priest for a "blessing of the Hand of God." A beam of golden light came from Padrik's upraised hands and bathed the Priest in momentary glory. The young man fell to the ground, chanting in some foreign tongue, while another Priest translated what sounded like prophecies, and messages from "the blessed Spirits and Angels" about members of the congregation. *Those* were all suitably vague enough they could have come from the head of any common fortune-teller at the Faire, but the rest of it impressed and even frightened Jonny.

But Padrik was saving the best for the last.

A shout came from the back of the Cathedral — a cry of "demon!" and "possession!" and shortly several Cathedral guards came forward, dragging a filthy, disheveled, struggling man with them. The man's eyes rolled wildly, and he shouted a string of blasphemies and insults that had Jonny flushing red within a few moments. As they threw the man down in front of Padrik, knocking over one of the many-branched candelabra at the front of the altar, he howled like a beast and spat fire at the Priest, setting fire to his robe.

Someone in the crowd screamed; the crowd surged back a pace. The guards seized him again at that, as one of the secondary Priests beat the flames out with his bare hands. Through it all, Padrik remained where he was, his face serene, his hands spread wide in blessing.

The High Bishop looked down upon the writhing man, whose face was contorted into an inhuman mask, and began to pray, alternately exhorting God to help the sinner, and ordering the demon to release its victim.

The man spat fire again, this time touching nothing, then vomited a rain of pins all over the carpet in front of the altar. Then he howled one final time and lay still.

Padrik directed one of the Priests to sprinkle the man with holy water; presumably as a test to see if he was still demon-haunted.

Evidently he was, for the holy water sizzled when it touched him, and left behind red, blistered places. There were gasps from the crowd, and a few moans.

Finally the High Bishop himself knelt down beside the man and laid his hands upon the man's forehead.

There was a tremendous puff of smoke from the man's chest, and an agonizing screech rang through the Cathedral, a terrible sound that could never have come from a human throat, unless it was a human being disemboweled alive. The man went limp, and Padrik sprinkled him with holy water again. This time it did not burn him, and Padrik declared him free of the demon that had possessed him, gently directing the other Priests to take him to the Cathedral complex to recover.

That, it seemed was the end of the show, for as

Padrik stood, he suddenly swayed with exhaustion, and one of the Priests hurried forward to support him. He leaned heavily against the man, and immediately all of the others but one gathered around both of them, taking the High Bishop off through a door behind the altar. That one Priest announced — unnecessarily — that the High Bishop was exhausted by his ordeal, and there would be no more healing until the morrow.

He did not use the word "miracle," but everyone else in the Cathedral was already shouting the word aloud, praising God and the High Bishop in the same breath. Spontaneous hymn-singing broke out, three different songs at once. Most of the crowd headed for the door, but some flung themselves full-length in front of the altar to pray at the tops of their lungs.

Jonny clung to the arm of Saint Hypatia, feeling dazed and dazzled. In the face of all of that —

Surely Padrik *was* a Saint! And if he was a Saint, how could what he had been preaching be wrong?

All of his earlier convictions went flying off like scattered birds; and if Robin had not pulled him down off his perch and dragged him out, he probably would have remained there, clinging to the alabaster Saint, and wondering if he should prostrate himself as so many others were doing, and pray for forgiveness for his doubts.

He did not really take in Robin's expression until they got outside. Then he got one of the great shocks of his life, for her eyes burned with anger, fiery and certain, and her face was a cold mask donned to hide her true feelings.

She pulled him along until they reached their wagon, then shoved him roughly at the rear door as a hint to unlock it. He did so, hands shaking, and they both climbed in. Once they were inside, and not before, she finally spoke.

"Convinced, were you?" she said, her words hot with rage, although she whispered to keep her voice from carrying outside the wooden walls. "Just like all those other fools out there. *You* saw Padrik perform real miracles, didn't you? With your own eyes! *Damn* the man! May *real* demons come and snatch his soul and carry it down to the worst of his nightmare hells!"

"B-b-b-b-but —" Jonny couldn't get any more than that out.

"Produces alms from thin air, does he? Well so can I!" And before he could say or do anything, she showered him with coins that came from out of nowhere. "I can heal the blind and the deaf, too, if they were never blind nor deaf in the first place!"

"B-but the l-leper —" he managed.

She snorted. "Flour and water paste make the open sores, paint makes the skin pale, and you can wash it all right off. It's an old beggar's trick. Remember how he passed his hands over the 'leper's' limbs? He was wiping them with a damp sponge hidden in the big sleeves of that robe."

"The c-c-c-cripples —"

Her eyes narrowed. "Think a minute. The only one you actually saw 'healed' of anything was the first one. The rest simply showed up on crutches and danced off without them. Here —"

She sat down on the bed and did something with her boots, spreading her skirts over her legs to hide them as the first cripple's trews had hid his. And as soon as she sat down, sure enough, *one of her legs was longer than the other.* The right was longer by far than the left, by a good two inches.

Kestrel felt his eyes goggling. "H-h-how —"

"You'll see in a second. Take my feet in your hands

the way Padrik did." He followed her instructions, taking her feet, one in each hand. "Now, *pretend* to pull on the left one, but *push* slowly on the right one."

He did so; as soon as he began he realized what she had done. She had pulled her right boot down, and as he pushed on the right foot, he pushed her foot back into place within the boot.

The skirts hid most of what was going on; distance would take care of the rest. And because attention had been focused on the *short* leg, it would appear that the shorter leg was being straightened, not the other being shortened. "You see?" she said, jumping down onto the floor of the wagon again, and stamping to get her feet back into the boots properly. "You see what he's doing? Tricks and chicanery, and probably every one of the people his miracles cure is someone from the Abbey here! The light that struck the Priest came from a mirror he had hidden in his palm; I saw him get into position to catch a gold-colored sunbeam coming through the stained-glass windows. Remember how he held his hands over his head when he prayed? He must have the location of every sunbeam in the Cathedral charted and timed!"

"Th-the p-prophecies w-were p-pretty vague," Kestrel said, feeling his confidence and conviction returning with a rush of relief.

"And if you get a big enough crowd of people in a place, *someone* is going to match the 'widow who has lost a sum of money' and the 'tradesman searching for the son that ran away.' Gypsy fortune-tellers work that way all the time, when they don't have the true gift of sighting the future." Her expression was still angry, however. Whatever had put her in a rage, it was *not* that he had temporarily been convinced of Padrik's genuineness.

"B-but the d-d-d-demon —" he ventured, wondering at the truly grim set to her mouth.

"*That* is what got me so *mad!*" she said, gritting her teeth in anger. "Someone has been teaching Padrik Gypsy magic! Everything else is the brand of chicanery that professional beggars and false preachers have been doing for hundreds of years, but he could *not* have simulated that possession without the help of Gypsy magic! Spitting fire — that's done with a mouth full of a special liquid in a bladder you keep in your cheek — remember how close the man was to the candles? He even knocked one over, and that was the one that he used to light the liquid as he spit it out. Vomiting pins is something only we know how to do. The first batch of holy water had a secret dye in it that only turns red after it touches another dye, which you paint on the skin; the water-droplets left behind looked like blisters because you expected blisters to be there. The 'sizzle' came from someone dropping real holy water into one of the incense burners while everyone was watching the show; I watched him and I saw the steam. And the smoke when the 'demon' left the body is another one of our tricks! The howl came from someone frightening a peafowl up in one of the towers — either that, or they've trained it to cry on command." She spread her hands wide, some of the hot rage gone from her expression, replaced by determination and a colder fury. "Some of that Padrik could learn to do on his own, but most of it was done with accomplices. That means that not only is someone teaching him, someone is *helping* him! And I am going to find out who it is!"

Kestrel nodded, remembering she had told him that the Gypsies swore never to reveal their tricks to outsiders. This was an even greater betrayal of that oath than teaching Gypsy magic to *him* would be, by an order of magnitude. He was, after all, a Gypsy by marriage, and he suspected that if he really needed to learn the tricks, Gwyna could get permission from the head of her Clan to teach him. But to teach them to a complete outsider — worse, to one who was using those tricks to promote an agenda that would ultimately be very bad for other Gypsies — that was the worst of betrayals.

"N-not only wh-who," he told her, "but *why*. P-Padrik is already hurting n-nonhumans and F-Free B-Bards; h-how long b-before he s-starts on G-Gypsies?"

"Good point." She straightened her skirts. "We've done enough business already that no one will question our packing up early — in fact, if I drop the right remarks as I pay our tithe as we leave, we might even be considered very pious for not making too much of a profit from the faithful."

"S-so wh-what are we d-doing?" he asked, opening the back of the wagon again, to let them both out modestly, through the door, rather than crawling out the window over the bed.

"We're hunting information," she told him, as he took the reins of the mares, and she counted out the tithe from the bag of coins she'd hidden under her skirt. "Who and what and why."

When they paid the reckoning for the next week in advance, the innkeeper was positively faint with gratitude. Kestrel felt very sorry for him; apparently he'd lost two more patrons who had simply not been able to conduct the business they needed. The nonhuman gem-carvers these men wished to patronize had left in the summer, and the quality of the gems that the humans who had bought their business produced was apparently inferior to the original work.

So the innkeeper was only too happy to learn that *their* business was prospering and that they were prepared to stay some time. But then Robin took him aside for a long discussion in hushed whispers, and the man looked so alarmed that Kestrel wondered what on earth she could be telling him. When she returned, she had a set of written directions in her hand and a smug expression on her face.

"I thought with a name like 'The Singing Bird' this place had to have some sort of connection to the Free Bards or the Gypsies or both," she said, as she took his arm and led him from the inn into the street. "I said as much and frightened him half to death until he realized *I* was both a Free Bard and a Gypsy and not some sort of informer or blackmailer. Then he was frightened because he thought I was going to demand something unreasonable from him." Her tone grew a little bleaker. "I'm afraid that there are already some musicians in gaol here on the charge of 'perverting public morals,' and I think he expected me to ask for help in getting them out."

"Are th-they F-Free B-B-Bards?" Kestrel asked nervously, keeping a discrete eye out for anyone who might be following or listening to them.

"No, they can't be," she told him. "They've been in gaol since early fall, and we would have heard something if they were Free Bards. Someone would have missed them and passed the word. No, I'm afraid they're just ordinary musicians with bad luck. Or else they simply didn't pay enough attention to what was going on with the High Bishop. Wylie says they were arrested for singing 'The Saucy Priest' right at one of the street preachers."

Kestrel shook his head sympathetically. *They* had

performed the same song any number of times, and quite often when there was a clergyman who clearly deserved to hear it nearby. Bad luck, bad timing, and worse ability to observe the situation around them, that was all it was.

"Wh-what's the c-connection t-to the Free B-Bards?" he asked, out of sheer curiosity.

Gwyna chuckled. "Dear old Master Wren again. When Wylie tried to start this inn, he was in a bad case, bills piling up and no customers coming in. Wren offered to play for room and board alone all one winter if he always gave Free Bards the best venue thereafter. He filled the inn every night within the first week and kept it filled all winter. So Wylie renamed his place 'The Songbird' in Talaysen's honor, and he's always kept the bargain."

It was a little past midday, and the street preachers were already out in force. But there were none of the 'dangerous' type, the trained clerics. That confirmed Kestrel's notion that they *were* real Priests; or at least it did in his own mind. Real Priests would have duties during the day that they could not avoid; teaching, performing holy offices, attending to the business of the Church. Only after the workday was done would they be free to come down to the street to pretend to be one of the common-folk, and spread Padrik's word to those who might not come to the Cathedral to hear it.

"S-so what d-did you ask him f-for?" Kestrel asked, grateful that everyone on the street at the moment apparently had somewhere to go. The street preachers were pouring their exhortations out to the empty air. None of them had an audience, except perhaps a few idle children with nothing else to do at the moment.

"Directions. Turn here." She nodded at a side-street that cut away from the main street.

He followed her direction, obediently. "D-direc-
tions to wh-where?"

"Well, I asked him for directions to a place where I
could buy information, and just let it go at that," she
told him. "I told him I had a former friend who'd been
in the Whore's Guild here and I wanted to find out
where she was. *He* was the one who told me what I
really wanted. Directions to the worst part of town."

"The —what?" He felt his eyes boggling again.

"The worst part of town." She patted his hand reas-
suringly. "Dearest, it's broad daylight, and once people
there know I'm a Gypsy they'll leave us alone, unless
we're really, really stupid. That's where you find things
out; and that's where the Whore's Guild moved, after
Padrik shut down the Houses. That's where we'll find
out who's helping him, if there's anyone in this town
who knows outside of the Cathedral."

He felt sweat start up along his back, in spite of the
chilly wind that cut right through his coat. Why did
she do things like this?

But it was too late to back out now.

Robin knew that Jonny was nervous; all the signs
were there for anyone to read, from the way he
clutched her hand to the utter lack of expression on
his face. And she didn't really blame him; despite her
cavalier attitude, she was not particularly comfortable
here either.

This district, tucked away between the tanner's
and the dyer's quarters, was called "the Warren." It
merited the name, for it was a maze of narrow
streets too small for any size of cart to travel along,
with buildings that leaned over the streets until they
nearly touched, blocking out the sun. They hadn't
been built that way, either; the Warren had been
built over ground that had once been a refuse

dump, and was now in the process of collapsing, and as it sank, the buildings leaned, coming closer and closer to falling down with every passing year. Constables never ventured in here; there were not enough of them. It would take a small army to clean out the Warren, and no one wanted to bother.

Sound echoed in here, and it was impossible to tell where a particular sound came from. This early in the afternoon, though, it was very quiet in the Warren. Somewhere there were children playing a counting game, a man coughed and could not seem to stop, babies wailed, and there were two people having a screaming argument. That was nothing compared with the noise and clamor in the inn district. The streets here were always damp, and slimy with things Robin didn't care to think about. The stench was not quite appalling; the horrible odors from both the tanner's and the dyer's district overwhelmed the local effluvia. A few undernourished, wiry children played in the streets — not the source of the childish voices, for these children were playing an odd and utterly silent game involving stones and chalk. But they were the exception here; most children in the Warren were hard at work — at a variety of jobs, some legal, most not. As soon as a child was able to hold something and take directions, it was generally put to work in a district like this one.

She was looking for a particular tavern; one of the few "reputable" establishments down here, and probably the only one boasting a sign. This was where — so Wylie had told her — musicians were wise to come, and where he would have sent them if they had come to Gradford as Free Bards and not as traders.

Finally she spotted what passed for a sign; an empty barrel suspended over a tiny door. It looked nothing like a tavern on the outside, but when they opened the unlatched door and stood at the top of a short set of stone stairs, it was clear they had come to the right place.

Although the enormous room — a converted cellar — was very dark, it was also clean. A few good lanterns placed high on the wall where they would not be broken in a fight gave a reasonable amount of light. The furniture was simple, massive seats and tables built into the walls or bolted to the floor, so that *they* would not be broken up in a fight, or used as weapons. A huge fireplace in one wall with ovens built to either side — an ancient stone structure as old as the building — betrayed that this had once been a bakery.

Wylie's directions included a name — "Donnar" — and when the bold-eyed, short-skirted serving wench sauntered up to them with hips swaying, that was who Robin asked for.

Fortunately they had chosen the middle of the day for this little visit, for "Donnar," a remarkably well-spoken and entirely ordinary-looking man with nothing villainous about him, proved to be the owner of the Empty Keg.

"If ye'd come past supper, I'd'a given ye short words," he said, as he sat down at their table and wiped his hands on his apron. "An' those'd been curses, I well reckon. So, m'friend Wylie sent ye?"

Robin nodded. Kestrel looked as if he felt a little more secure, with a wall to his back, and a fellow who could have been a perfectly ordinary citizen sitting across from them. Come to think of it, she felt a lot more relaxed, herself. "We're Free Bards," she said shortly.

Donnar raised an eyebrow. "Thas more dangerous these days than bein' anythin' but a Buggie," he said, using the rude term for a nonhuman. It came from the term "Bug-eyed Monster," notwithstanding the fact that most nonhumans were neither bug-eyed nor monsters.

"W-we're here as t-t-traders," Kestrel said softly, "in G-God-S-Stars. B-but w-we n-need t-to know what's b-been happening — why-why has G-Gradford g-gone crazy?"

"Ah." Donnar nodded wisely. "Good choice of trade-goods. So, ye want the short an' sorry tale'a what's been goin' on, eh? What happ'ned with Our Padrik, the miracle-worker?"

Robin sighed with relief. "That, and other things. What's it going to cost us?"

Donnar considered this for a moment. "The tale's on th' house, if ye buy some'a m'beer at m'high prices. The rest — we'll see, eh? Depends on what ye want."

Robin and Jonny listened attentively as Donnar described what had been happening, and the measures people had taken to get around the new rules. Virtually all forms of public entertainment and pleasure had been forbidden. No plays, no public performance of music, no Faire-type gatherings. Taverns and inns were not permitted to serve anything stronger than small beer. Extravagance and ornamentation in dress were frowned upon. The brothels had been closed, and the Whore's Guild officially disbanded.

So the Guild and every other form of entertainment organization had moved to the Warren, and the houses had taken on other guises.

"Ye go off t' Shawna Tailor's, fer instance," Donnar said, "an' ye ask fer th' 'personal fittings,' an personal is what ye get! Or there's 'bout a half dozen bathhouses where ye ask fer th' 'special massage.' But it costs more, it all costs more, eh. Outside the Warren,

ye gotta pay off th' Constables an' the Church Guards;
ye gotta bribe th' right people."

Even the Guild musicians had moved on to other
cities, with the exception of the few who had steady
employment with wealthy or noble families, or in the
better class of inn. The few independent musicians
still in the city now played only at "private parties," or,
predictably, in one of the Houses. Taverns did not *sell*
hard liquor; they sold the use of a mug or glass, and for
a little more than the old price of a drink, one could go
to a stall located conveniently near the tavern and purchase hard liquor in tiny, single-drink bottles. The
glass-blowers were the only ones prospering at the
moment; these were the same kinds of bottles that had
been used for perfumes and colognes. If you wanted
to drink with your cronies in the tavern, you bought
your evening's drinks outside, and brought them into
the tavern to drink them.

"Takes deep pockets, though," Donnar sighed. "It
all takes mortal deep pockets. Bribes ev'rwhere ye
turn. An' I tell ye, there's a mort'a folks who just canna
understand why 'tis that last year they was good tax-
payin' tithe-makin' citizens, an' this year they're
criminals. Hellfires, I'm one'f 'em! Had me a tavern
an' didn' have the means t' build me a liquor shop.
Moved in here."

He sighed, and looked so depressed that Robin
reached out to pat his hand comfortingly. He looked
startled, but smiled wanly.

"Well," he continued, "advantage is I started out
with rules here. Don' care who ye be, nor what ye do
— in *here* we got peace. Got th' whole buildin'.
Rented out th' upstairs t' the head'a th' Whore's Guild;
her girls work as m' wenches when they ain't on duty.
An' 'f they decide t' go on duty wi' a customer, 'tis all
right w' me, eh?"

"Padrik — the High Bishop," Robin said, after a moment. "With all the thieves and professional beggars in the Warren, you *have* to know those miracles of his are faked!"

"'Course we know!" Donnar said in disgust. "Trouble is, we can't figger out how he does half of 'em, so what's the good of tryin' t' expose 'im, eh? It ain't no good fer *us* t'do anythin' unless we c'n show ever'thin' is faked! Otherwise, nobody's gonna believe us."

Robin sighed, and agreed that he was right. *She* was going to have to wrestle with her conscience over this one, and she wished desperately for a way to contact the Chief of her Clan. There was no way that she could expose Padrik as a fake without revealing how his "miracles" were performed, which was in direct violation of her oath.

"Does anyone know who's helping him?" she asked, hoping someone did. If she could discover who the Gypsy was that had given away the secrets, she might be able to force him to confess publicly that he had helped Padrik perform his "miracles." That would take care of the problem without revealing any Gypsy secrets.

But Donnar disappointed her, shaking his head. "Not a clue," he replied. "Wish we did. We figger it's got to be somebody in the Priests. Mebbe they found summat in some book somewheres that tells 'em how t' do all that stuff."

That was a possibility she had not even considered! And if anything, that made her quandary worse. If there was no one to blame for revealing secrets, if the Gypsy "secrets" turned out to be something that had already been put in print somewhere, did that make her oath invalid?

She shook her head. This situation was confusing

enough without making it more complicated than it already was.

"Well, the last thing we need is something you can do for us better than anyone else," she said. "We need more information than we have, particularly on the Priests, and the best way to get that —"

She paused significantly, and Donnar grinned. "Is t' go workin' inna House, a'course!" he finished the sentence for her. "I 'spect ye mean as musicians; I tell ye what, I'll get ye an audition at th' place I reckon'll suit ye best. Rest is up t' you." He thought for a moment. "Ye come by in two days, same time as t'day, 'less I send ye a message at th' Bird. I'll have it set up fer ye. A good House; I'd say here, 'cept I already gotta feller who ain't bad, an' he's old. Th' girls spoil 'im rotten."

Robin returned his grin. "So now what do we owe you?" she asked.

He named a price she considered quite reasonable; she slid the coins over to him, and he pocketed them neatly. "That includes safe-passage through th' Warren," he said, as an afterthought. "It'll be 'rranged 'fore ye reach th' door. That means most won't mess with ye. Some will, but th' rest'll leave ye be, 'cause if they mess w' ye, an' I find out 'bout it, well, I got friends in here now." He looked about his establishment, and sighed pensively. "Got so used to it, when time comes I can go back t' runnin' a real tavern again — well, I might not."

And on that odd note, they left him, and made their way back through the Warren's noisome streets completely unmolested. As promised.

CHAPTER TWELVE

There was one truism that Kestrel had always found held up, no matter what happened. Crisis might come and go, war, tempest, disaster — but people still needed to eat and sleep, and somehow, business continued as usual.

And if they were to go on with their ruse, no matter how they felt about the situation, they had to act as if they were exactly what they appeared to be; simple traders. The next day was a repetition of the first; getting up with the dawn in time to be in the square before Prime, selling God-Stars, listening to another of Padrik's sermons, and trailing into the Cathedral to watch more of Padrik's fake miracles.

This time, with Robin's demonstrations firmly in mind, Jonny was able to catch some of the trickery. He *also* noticed that the many of the same people showed up to be "healed" today as had yesterday — only today they were suffering from entirely new ailments! He had quite some time to study them as they lined up for their "miracles." There was definitely a similarity of features among them, as if they were all related.

Or are members of the same Gypsy Clan?

There were no demon-possessions today; evidently Padrik saved his more spectacular tricks to ensure that they didn't lose their impact, and didn't perform them every day. He did produce alms, and heal three cripples, two blind men, a deaf woman, five cases of gout, a woman with palsy, a man with "a withered arm," and a man with running sores on his leg. Today evidently was the big day for "miraculous messages" from angels; he "struck" three different Priests with rays of light, one red, one gold, and one white. They took turns relating messages from departed relatives to the grieving survivors. The one thing these people all had in common were tales of misfortune and woe, and they came seeking answers from those who presumably now had access to all of the wisdom of God.

Kestrel should not have been surprised at the answers, but he was. A great many of these spurious messages claimed that the misfortune that had brought the relatives here to consult with Padrik was due to inheriting "tainted money" and urged the survivors to take what they had inherited and donate it to the Church. Padrik took the occasion to preach an extemporaneous sermon on the subject of the evil magic practiced by nonhumans, and how it tainted even the lives and the goods of those who dealt with them.

"Only by giving selflessly can the taint be washed away," he told the hushed congregation. "Only the Church has the power to cleanse and heal."

And although a scant handful of those who had come to Padrik seeking an answer frowned or looked bewildered and walked away, several dozen more began to weep with hysteria and rushed forward to the waiting Priests. Presumably the Priests were quite prepared to help them with the arrangements for transferring their inheritance into the hands of the Church. . . .

This time the angelic messages were very detailed, relating the circumstances of the person's life and death. Enough detail was included to bring gasps from those grieving relatives they were directed to, people the Priests identified by name. But Jonny had been watching and listening to what was going on in the crowd waiting for Prime Service while he had sold their Stars. His feigned muteness had fooled Padrik's corps of Priests into thinking he was deaf and probably feeble-minded; they had been out among the customers, questioning those who had bought the red and blue Stars for "help in adversity." They had worn ordinary clothing rather than the robes of their order, but something about the way they had spoken had alerted Jonny to the fact that these were no common folk. He had made note of faces — and lo! Here they were, in white robes like Padrik's, though not as elaborate.

So it was no word from "angels" that gave the three Priests "touched by the Hand of God" such detailed information on postulants — it was clever work beforetime by their fellow clergymen.

It was quite enough to make him sick, to see all these innocent people defrauded. And how could a man who was *supposed* to be protecting their souls, who was *supposed* to be giving them good counsel, be preying on them this way?

He left the Cathedral as disturbed as Robin had been angry the previous day. They returned to their wagon in silence; while she went back to her sales, he took refuge from his confused feelings by taking inventory of the Stars they had left, both the wall-Stars and the miniatures.

He knew they had been doing well, but when he opened the boxes and trays they were storing the Stars in, he was shocked. It didn't take a mathematical genius to figure out that they had been doing much better than he had thought. There simply wasn't that much left to count! There was no question in his mind; if they were to continue their mission here and maintain their guise as traders, they would have to take a day or two off and make more Stars. For that, they would need more materials.

Fortunately, just as the noon bells rang, they got a break. The ringing of the bells triggered hunger in the stomachs of those still in the square. Their customers finished their purchases and hurried towards the stalls selling hot pies and drinks, sausages, bread and cheese.

"W-we n-need supplies," he told Robin in a soft voice, as soon as he was certain they were not being watched. "W-we've got enough f-for t-today, and th-that's all."

She ran her hand through her hair, looking tired and distracted. "Already? Well, at least it will give us a break. Do you realize that even after our expenses we've doubled what the Ghost gave us? We could make a fortune here!"

"Unt-t-til someone else s-starts making S-Stars and undercutting our p-p-prices," he said sharply, annoyed that she was thinking only how much money they were making and not what was happening to the poor people Padrik was defrauding.

Or the people who are the sacrificial victims to bring him to power.

But Robin only shrugged. "Then we'd better make money while we can," she said, philosophically. "You know what we need, so go get our supplies. You'll find the jeweler I made our bargain with easily enough, it's Master Tomas and his daughter Juli at the sign of the Three Hearts in Silver Street, and they know what you look like. They can tell you where to go to get the yarn and things. I *have* to stay here, you're supposed to be mute, and it's going to look odd if you start telling people prices and bargaining with them."

She turned back to her task of hanging yarn Stars on the side of the wagon, leaving him to extract some coins from one of the little hoards in the wagon, and get off on his errand.

He wasn't sure how to handle Robin's attitude toward all this. She seemed so callous and indifferent. The only thing that really upset her, so far as he could see, was the fact that Gypsies had imparted some of their secrets to an outsider — and *not* what the outsider was doing with those secrets. He simply couldn't reconcile that with the Gwyna he thought he knew.

Silver Street, the street on which all jewelers and goldsmiths had their businesses and workshops, was not that far from the Cathedral. He met with the jeweler's daughter Juli, currently in charge of the shop, who did, in fact, remember him, and also remembered her father's promise.

"Business has been wonderful," she said, smiling. Her smile had already erased some of the little lines of worry he'd noticed on her forehead yesterday. "And it's thanks to your lady. The other smiths haven't figured out how to make proper God-Stars yet; they've been casting them, and they just don't look the same. You might as well try to make lace by cutting holes in cloth. We stayed up all night working, father, me, and his two 'prentices, and this morning, the *first thing* that happened was that our best patron came to ask if we had any Star Pendants! We sold him one for every member of his family, and he commissioned a chain of them for his wife!"

It was nice to see *someone* happy, for a change. And their silver and gold Stars certainly were beautifully made and impressive. The silver Stars they made were easily four times the size of the little ones that Robin turned out — but then, no one showing up at their stall would ever be able to afford a Star that size. Master Tomas' workers made the silver Stars of three different colors of silver wire, created by alloying the pure silver with different metals. The gold Stars were also made of three colors of wire — red gold, yellow gold, and white gold. Really quite beautiful enough to stay in fashion long after Padrik was gone.

The young woman surprised him then; she and her father were so pleased with the way things had gone this morning, that she had gone out and obtained base-metal wire for Robin as well as the silver that they had promised. And she named him a price for all that was so low he saw no need to bargain. "This is at our cost," she told him, as he carefully pocketed the rolls of wire. "And I dare say that since father and I are well known here, we got you a better bargain on the base-metal than you would have on your own."

"I m-must agree," Jonny replied; she had, especially compared to the price they'd paid for the same stuff back at that inn in the hills. "Th-thank you v-very much."

She dimpled at him, and sent him on his way again with directions to the weavers' and lace makers' street, where he could expect to get his thread and yarn.

While business did seem to be picking up in Silver Street, it was still not what he would call prosperous; and once he got to the area where the seamstresses, hat makers, lace makers and weavers were, the real impact of the new vogue for asceticism was only too obvious. Shops were closed, the windows empty, the doors themselves boarded up. Those remaining showed only the most sober of materials in their windows, and even so, there did not seem to be many folk here buying anything.

Following his directions, he came to a shop — still thankfully in business — which sold not only yarn and thread, but glass beads and crystals. The woman there looked at him askance when he asked for bright colors and beads, but took him into her storeroom and told him to pick out what he wanted.

The room was lined on all four sides with drawers; in sizes from the size of his shoe, to the size of a bread-box. One section contained embroidery thread in silk, raime, linen and wool; one contained sewing thread on spools instead of in hanks like the embroidery thread, and one contained wool yarn of varying thick-nesses. A tall chest of smaller drawers contained beads, and the rest of the room was filled with racks of fabric.

Fortunately he was limited by what he could carry, because the temptations in that back room were tre-mendous — especially a scarlet linen he could easily picture Robin wearing. . . .

Obviously the woman who owned the shop could not imagine what he was going to do with all those proscribed colors of embroidery thread, the sparkling beads, or the bright yarns, but she was too polite — or too politic — to ask.

He paid her, and saw her eyes brighten a little as she put the coins in her cashbox. If only there was a way to help the whole city —

But there wasn't; not short of revealing Padrik for the fraud he was. And they were certainly working on that.

He headed back to the wagon, wondering how Robin was faring.

The moment that Kestrel left, the vultures descended, circling in on her when they realized she was alone.

At least, that was how Robin thought of them. Street preachers began to congregate in the vicinity of *her* wagon (and no one else's) when it appeared that she was alone. It was then that she noticed that of all

the stall-keepers and wagon-vendors within *her* field
of view, she was the only single female.

And evidently single women were fair game,
although they wouldn't trifle with a woman with a
male in evidence.

Some of the preachers confined themselves to looking down their noses at her, or giving her very superior
looks, particularly when she made a sale. But the others were not so polite as that. They took it in turn to
set up impromptu pulpits and preach, not only at the
crowds coming to patronize her stall, but at her specifically.

Now she heard a fourth theme to the sermonizing,
a new one so far as she was concerned and one that
was so clearly calculated to make her angry that she
held her temper just to spite them.

Women, according to these so-wise philosophers,
were by their very nature "primitive, lascivious, and
lewd." This was as God had intended, they said. Their
function as childbearers made them prone to look no
further than the acts that resulted in children; after all,
that was what God had created for them to do.
Women's bodies were created for one glorious purpose; childbearing. Women were inferior to men in all
other counts; in morals, in intelligence, in the ability to
reason — just as their smaller, weaker bodies made
them inferior physically.

Women were nearer to the state of the animal than
the angel, said the preachers. And again, that was as it
should be, God had created them to be dependent on
their partners for the things they lacked. It was up to
men, with their superior intellect and power of reason,
to rule women, to keep their essentially corrupt
natures from overcoming them.

Men should make all decisions for a woman, the
preachers proclaimed, pitching their voices to be

certain that she heard every word. Men should control their every action. Women were not fit to govern themselves, and would be seduced by any creature with a soft word and a clever tongue.

They think I'm alone, she decided, as she continued to smile, thank those who purchased, wish them well with their prayers, and outwardly ignore the preachers. *They didn't do this when Kestrel was here. That's why there aren't any other women out here alone. I know what happens when one shows up. They ring her and start preaching at her before she can even turn around.*

Her blatant and blithe disregard of their words only made them redouble their efforts. And although she continued to ignore them outwardly, she was becoming very nervous.

How long, I wonder, will it be before those words become law here? How long before women in Gradford are forbidden to practice trades, hold property, or do anything at all without the consent and guidance of a man? What had happened to the nonhumans could only too readily happen to women, and to increasingly broader types of men.

It was happening to musicians; it had happened to mages. Once one group was eliminated, Padrik would need another group to focus on as the cause of all troubles. Why not women? There were few enough of them in power, most of whom could be eliminated easily enough.

Why not, indeed. There was no doubt in her mind whatsoever that although Padrik had said *nothing* like this in his sermons, these words were his, in the mouths of the street preachers. *One step at a time, that's how you get people. First you bombard them with the word from a lower source, until they come to think that it might possibly have a little merit. Then you put it in the mouth of a lower authority, so people become persuaded. Then, last of all, you put it in the mouth of the ultimate authority, and their resistance crumbles.*

In fact, some of her customers were beginning to look at her askance, as the meaning of the background hum of exhortation penetrated. She simply put on her most guileless and innocent smile, and hoped she could convince them that she had no idea that the street preachers meant their sermons for *her.*

When Kestrel finally showed up, she greeted him with such enthusiasm that the customers were startled, flying to embrace him, and take some of his burdens from him.

And as she greeted him with the words, "Husband! You're back! I don't know how I managed without you!" the preacher who had been spewing forth a particularly vehement and vituperative version of the corruption and folly of women who attempted to manage themselves alone, choked off his sermon in mid-word, coughed violently, and vanished into the crowd.

Well, she thought with satisfaction, as Kestrel returned her enthusiastic kiss with one rather startled, but just as enthusiastic. *They won't make that mistake again. I just made them look like fools.*

And they would probably hold that against her, too.

She dealt with the remaining customers, then, before any new ones could arrive, she put the rest of the Stars away and closed up the wagon, waving off any potential customers with a smile and a cry of "come back tomorrow!" Jonny was already inside, unloading his packages, and she joined him there with a sigh of relief, closing the door behind her and lighting one lantern to relieve the gloom of the interior. The inside of the wagon was warm compared with the wind-swept square.

Her feet throbbed with pain, and she had been more nervous beneath the steady barrage of the street preachers than she had realized. Her shoulders ached with tension, the corners of her mouth hurt from smiling so much, and she had a headache. Right now all she wanted was a hot bath, a good meal, and bed, the last with Jonny in it.

Jonny greeted her with a smile and a hug, and went back to his work. She took the materials for the miniature Stars from him, and put them neatly away in the trays they'd used to hold the finished products. He'd managed to get turned dowel-rods for the larger Stars, and toothpicks and thin brass rods for the miniatures. After they stowed the contents of his various packages away in the wagon, they took another accounting of their stock.

"We don't have enough for tomorrow," she said, reluctantly. "Good gods, and I thought we'd made enough Stars for a week!"

"B-by t-tomorrow there'll b-be others out here with S-Stars," Jonny pointed out. "P-probably not the j-jewelry ones, though."

"Which is why you concentrated on jewelry supplies; that was a good idea," she told him, standing on tiptoe to kiss his nose. "Well, I guess we're going to have to make some more stock, which means we take tomorrow off."

"Except f-for g-going to s-see about that j-j-job," he reminded her, a slight frown on his face. "I'm n-not sure I l-like th-the idea of w-working in a H-House."

Just what I needed. Being brought up in the Guild Hall must have made him a prude. She was exasperated, but she knew that her temper was probably more than a bit short. She decided not to say anything rather than retorting with a sarcastic comment. Which was rather a new thing for her —

But after her brief stint as a bird, *caused* by flinging insults at a lascivious Priest, she had kept a closer curb on her tongue than she had even done before. It only took one painful experience for *her* to learn her lessons!

Instead, she told him all about the street preachers who had surrounded her as soon as he'd left, and what they'd had to say.

"S-sounds to m-me as if th-the next t-targets are w-women," he said when she had finished, quickly coming to the same conclusion she had.

She nodded. "That was what I thought. And — I'm torn. The money we are making here is amazing. On the other hand, we've already learned *almost* everything we need — and certainly enough to warn Harperus of what's happened. If we return to him, we can warn the Free Bards and he can warn the other nonhumans. You heard what he said; I really think that given enough warning to get out, the Deliambrens can protect all the other nonhumans who care to accept that protection *and* themselves. I'm not sure we need to stay here. . . ." She shivered, as the shrill rants of one of the street preachers penetrated the wooden walls of the wagon, and a chill went up her back in reaction. "I don't like it here, love," she said in a small voice. "It was a Priest that caused me all that trouble before. Padrik has all of the Church and the Bishopric here behind him. There's just the two of us. Shouldn't we leave?"

Kestrel looked down at her, his eyes brooding in the half-light of the wagon. "Y-you w-were th-the one who w-wanted t-to find out wh-what Gypsies were helping him," he reminded her. "W-we still don't kn-know *wh-why* Padrik is d-doing all this — and I d-don't th-think he's even b-begun t-to fulfill his p-plans. And wh-what about th-those Gypsies? Sh-shouldn't *th-they* b-be dealt w-with?"

We have responsibilities, whether you like them or not, his eyes said to her. *We have to live up to those responsibilities.*

As soon as he mentioned the presumed renegades, the heat of anger began to chase away the chill of fear. And while she didn't have much use for people who were not Free Bards or Gypsies — well, this affected both those groups, intimately. She flushed, and nodded. "They should," she said, firmly. "In fact, they *have* to be. First, I can't just report a supposition to the Gypsy Clan Leaders; I have to have proof that I'm not just speculating. And I do have to find out exactly who they are before I can bring punishment down on them. Or rather, before the Clan Leaders do. That's for them to order, not me."

"Punishment?" Kestrel eyed her inquisitively. "Wh-what kind?"

"I can't tell you that," she said, with real regret. "But — it'll be appropriate. Peregrine will probably be the one to handle it. He's done it before."

She saw by the widening of his eyes that she had said enough. Kestrel was only too aware that Peregrine was a mage, possibly the most powerful magician they knew; he was an Elf-Friend, and he might be the ally of many more magical creatures. So any "punishment" would be magical in nature.

"At any rate, we can't do anything about it all now," she continued, and sighed. "I guess we should be trying to stay focused on the things we *can* do, and not worry about the things we have no control over. I'm going to take things as lightly as I can. Otherwise I'd fret myself to pieces in this town."

She sensed his sudden relaxation, as if she had

answered some question in his mind that he hadn't even articulated. Well, whatever it was, there were enough mysteries to solve without trying to figure out what was going on in *his* mind!

"I want a hot bath, a good meal, and a little time alone with you before we start in on making more Stars," she said firmly, as she opened the rear door of the wagon and blew out the lantern. "Which I guess," she added, acidly, "makes me just as 'primitive, lascivious, and lewd' as these preachers claim!"

"I can o-only h-hope," he laughed, and followed her down the stairs, closing and locking the door after her. And wisely, very wisely, he said nothing else.

Practice made perfect, and that was as true with handicrafts as it was with music. They were much faster making this new batch of Stars than they had been with the first batch. Gluing bright glass beads to the ends of the crossbars of the miniature Stars was a good idea; it made them look more like jewelry. Stringing them on chains of matching beads was another wonderful notion.

And the best part — so far as Robin was concerned — was that no one else would have anything like them in the market. Once again, they would have a monopoly of sorts. While they were not here to make money, no Gypsy worth the name would ever have turned down such a golden opportunity.

And if any of the street preachers questioned the presence of the beads, she could blithely point out that there were no *colors* in the miniature Stars to indicate what the owner's intention-prayer was. The beads served that function, of course.

If they can use their twisted logic to prove that nonhumans are demon-inspired, I can use the same rules to my advantage, she thought, making the final wrapping on a miniature Star of copper with red and gold beads. *Let the rooster crow all he wants; it's the hen that lays the eggs, not him.*

They had gotten up early perforce, awakened by the morning bells, but they'd put the time between breakfast and lunch to good use. And when they came down to lunch, the innkeeper himself sauntered over to their table with a note in his hand.

He looked only mildly curious. "This's from m' old friend Donnar," he said. "It come this mornin'. He doin' well?"

"As well as can be expected," Robin replied, opening the sealed note. She noticed with amusement that Donnar had sealed it with a blob of candle wax and the impression of a coin. A rather unusual coin. It was, in fact, one of the silver coins she'd given him in exchange for his information and help, an ancient piece bearing a strange bird with two tails.

"Sometimes I wish I'd'a followed his advice," Wylie said wistfully, without elaborating on what the advice had been; then he shrugged, and took himself off.

The note said simply, "Go to Threadneedle Street, to the shop of Ardana Bodkin. Say, 'I've come to order an alabaster alb and an ivory altar cloth.' Don't bring instruments. It's been taken care of." There was no signature, which was wise on Donnar's part.

Robin memorized the code-phrase, and burned the note in the candle at their table. "Are you tired of making Stars?" she asked. "Could you use a break?"

Kestrel nodded.

"Good. So could I." She stood up, and brushed her skirts off. "Let's go for a walk."

He took her arm and paid their reckoning, and they walked out into the street. "Are w-we g-going where I th-think w-we're g-going?" he asked cautiously.

"Well, probably; since you got to see Threadneedle

Street yesterday and I didn't, I thought it would make a nice walk," she replied. "There might be something down there I could use that you didn't notice."

"Ah." Jonny made no other comment, but his hand tightened on her arm. But he looked a little relieved; evidently he felt a bit better about visiting a House if it *wasn't* in the Warren.

Well, so did she! Donnar's protection notwithstanding, she did not want to visit that place after dark. There really was no such thing as "honor among thieves," and she did not trust anyone in that place once darkness fell.

Ardana Bodkin was the only seamstress prospering at all — the shop front was swept and newly painted, the windows filled with color, silk and satin, and two young women stitching away at crimson velvet inside. But that was only natural — since from the window display, Ardana Bodkin specialized in ecclesiastical robes.

The place was a feast for the eye after the browns and grays of the drab clothing outside. The crimson satin robes of a Justiciar sparkled with rich gold bullion embroidery; the vivid blue silk robes of an Intercessor boasted cutwork of impossible intricacy. Next to that, the emerald green robes for the Service of Vernal Equinox shone with lacework dyed to match. And there were, of course, dozens of the white robes favored by High Bishop Padrik and his Order, all brilliant with embroidery, lace, cutwork, and gems.

"May we help you?" asked one of the young ladies, a plain-faced blonde, as Robin gazed with hungry eyes on all the vivid, soul-satisfying color. She had not realized how much she missed her Gypsy finery.

"I've come to order an alabaster alb and an ivory altar cloth," she said carefully — and a little regretfully. A pity to have to leave all this color. . . .

But the young woman smiled, and said, "Please follow me," then led them both through the back room where a single woman stitched gold bullion to white satin, to a small door hidden behind a swath of velvet. She knocked twice, paused, and three times; the door swung open, and she motioned for Robin and Kestrel to go inside.

The moment they did, Robin swallowed; somehow, Donnar had made a horrible mistake! They were in the receiving room of a convent!

The room held about five or six lovely young women dressed in the robes of the Sisters and Novices of a religious Order; she didn't recognize the pearl gray and white of their habits, but they were clearly religious robes. The room itself was as stark as any in a convent; a few benches, plain white walls, a single bookcase full of books. The young ladies all turned to stare at the intruders.

"I —" she gasped. "Excuse us, we —"

The woman who closed the door behind them laughed. She too wore the robes of the Order, whatever it was, but her chestnut hair was left to stream unbound down her back, like a maiden's, confined only by a headband.

"You think you made a mistake, yes?" she said, in a rich contralto. "But you are Robin, and you, Kestrel; you play the harp, both, and you come from Donnar, yes?"

At Robin's dumb nod, she laughed again. "You have made no mistake. This is the House of the Penitents, and I am Madam — ah, rather, I am *Sister-Mother* Ardana."

Robin blinked — and then she took a second, closer look at the "habits" of the putative Sisters. They were cut to fit like second skins down the line of the torso. The robes left nothing and everything to the imagination, and were certainly teasingly erotic.

"But — why all this?" she asked, as Ardana led them across the room to the door on the other side.

"Well, it is very convenient, for one thing," she replied, tossing her rich brown hair over her shoulder as she opened the second door. "If the authorities were ever to come to this part of the shop, they would find that all of the ladies here are seamstresses — or, at least, they can sew enough to convince a fool Constable of the fact! We have everything in place to make it at least *look* like a convent, so long as we have time to clean the private rooms. There are many convents in Gradford these days, many women establishing their own charitable Orders which support themselves by a trade or a craft, since the miracles began. I have heard that one or two are even genuine."

The door she led them to opened onto a corridor, as austere as the receiving room, with doors on both sides. "Why so many new Orders?" Robin asked, puzzled. "I thought you had to get the permission of the Church to establish an Order."

Ardana laughed again, a good-natured chuckle. "Oh, my dear, no. The Church is indifferent — so long as the Orders find some means of supporting themselves. If they do not attempt to appoint or ordain Priests, collect alms, or usurp any of the privileges of the Church, the Church permits them to do what they will. So many single women in various trades have discovered it is a good thing to form an Order. They need not find convenient men to 'help' them with their businesses, if they do not choose to do so."

Robin exchanged a knowing look with Kestrel. So, it seemed that single women were already under a great deal of pressure here, as she had suspected might happen. And at least some of them had realized that it might not be too long before they lost the right to practice trades or crafts, or to run a business without a man —

— *or without the blessing of the Church. Very clever.*

"My last set of musicians was arrested for street-busking and sent out of the city," Ardana said, as she opened another door, this time to a nicely appointed office, furnished well, and comfortably, and decorated in a modest rose-pink. There were two small harps standing in the corner, beside two chairs. "Donnar said you were looking for a way to pick up information about Padrik; well, many of my clients are either in his employ or in his Order. If any of them are likely to let information slip, it will be here."

She gestured to the two harps. "Consider this your audition," she told them. "If I like what I hear, I will hire you for a few hours in the evening to play in the 'chapel;' you may keep your ears as wide open as you like, and I will tell my ladies to let you know if they hear anything."

She sat down behind her desk, as serene as the statue of Saint Hypatia in the Cathedral, and with that same hint of an amused smile on her lips. Robin passed one harp to Kestrel; she plucked a set of strings experimentally, but someone had done a good job of keeping them in tune. She looked over at him, and somehow, in spite of the tension, they both grinned.

"'Th-the S-saucy P-Priest?'" he suggested.

Ardana laughed.

Kestrel had been very uncomfortable from the beginning about this; when they passed their audition, and Ardana hired them on the spot, he didn't lose any of that discomfort. In fact, it got worse.

It was worse still when Ardana led them to what she

referred to as "the chapel," a room furnished with soft couches and cushions in jewel-bright satins and velvets, and tiny marble tables, where the "Sisters" lounged about in semi-transparent or very abbreviated versions of their "habits." This was where customers came when they wished some entertainment before or after the — main event.

Kestrel had never been in a House before, and he frankly did not know where to look. Or not look. And the ladies obviously noticed; they whispered to each other behind their hands, and cast measuring glances at him that made him flush uncomfortably.

He tried to confine his attentions to the harp that Ardana had loaned him —

Clever of her to know that carrying an instrument openly through the street would get us in trouble, he thought, staring at the ornamental bird-head carved into the support-post of the instrument, as he and Robin put the two harps into perfect tune with each other. *Forethought to the rescue again.*

By mutual consent they had decided to play only instrumentals; voice might give their identities away. And they would try to avoid speaking if they could. Ardana had given them robes that matched the ones the ladies in the receiving room wore, though not so tight across the body; those robes were very effective disguises. Kestrel was so small and clean-shaven he might even pass as a very plain, flat-chested girl.

Which is only fair, since Rune disguised herself as a boy to play. . . .

When the harps were in tune, Kestrel started a tranquil, calming piece; "Fortune, My Foe." Robin joined in on the second verse, playing a lovely descant. He relaxed against the back of his chair and let himself forget his surroundings in the music.

So effective was his effort that he woke from his

self-induced trance with a start, as one of the "Sisters" touched his elbow and offered him a silver-plated goblet of fruit juice. He accepted it, but could not help the blush that burned across his face at the sight of her.

She chuckled, and he burned an even deeper and more painful red. But then she put one hand on his arm, and he raised his eyes to her face, to see that her expression was one of sympathy and not mockery.

"We assumed that this is the first time you've ever been in a House, Kestrel," she said, using his Free Bard name. "It's perfectly fine to feel out-of-place, embarrassed, in fact. I did, the first time I came here. We would *much* rather see a charming blush than a knowing smirk. *You* assume the best of us, and you blush for our sakes as much as your own. The man with the smirk assumes the worst of us, and can't wait to prove it."

Robin grinned at her, and she grinned back, a surprisingly gaminlike grin, full of mischief. "Both of you, consider yourselves as one of us; we're glad to have you," she finished. "I'm Sister Tera; if I can help you in any way, please let me know."

And with that, she delivered the second water-beaded goblet of fruit juice to Robin and took herself out of the room entirely.

The rest of the ladies were clearly "with" someone; offering them bits to eat, filling goblets, entertaining them with conversation. Somehow they had all come in without Kestrel even noticing.

"Don't worry," Robin whispered to him. "You were off in your usual trance, but I've been listening. You wouldn't believe how many of these men are associated with the High Bishop or the Cathedral!"

He gave the clients a second look; they were a well-fed lot, and wore self-satisfaction as if it were a garment. While that particular expression was not

exclusive to the clergy, it seemed the exclusive property of the clergy in Gradford.

"I g-guess we've d-done the right th-thing," he
whispered back, finishing off his juice and setting the
goblet down beside his chair.

"I am very *relieved* to hear you say that," Robin
replied with a sigh. "I was afraid you'd think I'd gotten
us involved with something really repugnant."

He shrugged. "I'm always w-willing t-to l-learn," he
told her philosophically. "Now. L-let's p-play."

"Promise *not* to go off into one of your trances
again," she countered. "We're both supposed to be
keeping our ears open, remember?"

He plucked the first few notes of "My Lady Spy" by
way of an answer, and grinned. She returned it, picked
up the tune within the first bar, and they were off
again.

CHAPTER THIRTEEN

Their next several days settled into an odd routine; a routine Robin even felt marginally comfortable with. So long as she didn't listen too closely to the High Bishop's sermons, that is, and avoided street preachers entirely. They played in the "chapel" by night, and sold their trinkets in the market square by day. Early in the week, Robin took note of the fact that Kestrel had a shrewd business sense. She would not have expected that from someone who had grown up in the Bardic Guild Hall and had been born a Prince. His estimation that they would soon find others duplicating their God-Stars for a lower cost was right. They sold off all their wall-Stars at the same price that the new folks had set and did not bother to make any more. Instead, they concentrated on the miniatures; few people had a delicate touch with the fragile wire, and of those few, no one made them with beads or crystals hanging from the webs or mounted as end-caps on the cross-bars.

They began to see the more expensive versions of the Stars on the breasts of wealthy folk in the Cathedral. They even began to see those same expensive Stars coming into Ardana's "chapel" at night. Many of them stayed with Ardana's ladies, gifts from grateful clients.

They were able to gather quite a bit of information about Padrik and his "special healing services" simply by listening. The most important bit of information came by accident — when one of the people Robin suspected was a Priest let it slip that Padrik had some "special helpers" who were the only ones permitted to assist him in planning the "healing services."

After that, they attended every one of the "healing services" until they began to be able to recognize certain faces, despite disguises. They were even able to put a name or two to those faces, by waiting at the entrance and listening carefully while these "postulants" talked among themselves.

That was when Robin realized that the man who specialized in "being possessed by demons" was a regular client at Ardana's!

She was certain enough that she was willing to put it to a test, the fourth night that they played Ardana's chapel, but she waited until that morning so that she could confirm it with Kestrel.

Robin figured that they were due for another "demon possession" at the healing service — probably today — and she was not disappointed. As they brought the man up to the front, spitting and sweating and breathing fire, she nudged Kestrel in the ribs. "Wasn't he the one with Sister Krystal last night?" she whispered.

Kestrel narrowed his eyes with concentration, and finally nodded. "I think so," he whispered back, "but wait until I get a better look at his face."

It wasn't until "the demon had been cast out" that they both got a really clear look at the man, but the smirk he wore as he was "helped" out of the Cathedral only made the identification surer. He had worn that same smirk last night.

The chapel was empty of clients; a good time to consult the statuesque Sister Krystal. "The client last night?" Sister Krystal wrinkled her aristocratic nose with distaste. "His name is Robere Patsono. Is he one of Padrik's 'special helpers' you were looking for?" At Robin's nod, she grimaced. "I wouldn't be the least surprised to find out he was involved with Padrik's 'miracles.' He's always hinting about how important he is to the High Bishop, but he gets very coy about it when one of us tries to find out exactly what it is he does."

"If his name is Patsono, then he *is* one of the ones setting up the miracles," Robin replied grimly.

Someone lit a sweet-scented candle, and the smell of roses filled the chapel. Krystal tossed her long, ash-blond hair over one shoulder, and pursed her lips with speculation. "Do you think you might be able to — well — put a spike in Padrik's wheels?" she asked, hopefully. "Things were better when the Houses and the Guild were legal."

"Things?" Kestrel asked. He looked puzzled, although Robin had a notion what Krystal was talking about.

Krystal's reply confirmed her guesses. She sighed, and closed her gray eyes for a moment. "Now — well, things can happen to a lady, and the only recourse we have is for Ardana to ban them from the House. She can't always do that, even, because if the client is important enough, he could threaten to turn us over to the Cathedral Constables."

"The Guards of Public Morality?" Robin said, with heavy irony. "Very nice. As if they weren't vio-lating the laws themselves. I've seen plenty of *them* in here too."

Krystal shook her head, and toyed with the silken folds of her robe. "Of course you have. But that wouldn't stop them from arresting us if they were ordered to. They don't care; why should they? We

aren't important to them. *They* can always find
another House."

"Wh-whereas you w-would w-wind up in g-gaol,"
Kestrel said for her.

"Or the work-house, where they make 'honest
women' out of people like me." Krystal tossed her hair,
but this time angrily.

That was new. "What's a work-house?" Robin asked.

Sister Jasmine chimed in. "It's a place where they're
putting women convicted of something called
'immoral idleness.' Basically, it's if they don't have a
husband or father supporting them, or work at a trade
or a job. They do plain sewing and laundry for the
Cathedral and the Abbey here."

"And get paid what?" Robin wanted to know.

"Nothing!" Jasmine said bitterly. "Their so-called
'wages' are confiscated to pay their fines and room and
board."

"I've heard other stories, too, about that so-called
'work-house.'" Krystal's eyes flashed with anger. "It
seems the Priests visit there. Very often. I've heard
they have all of the advantages of a House, one
reserved for the privileged few, but they don't have to
pay for any of them. And not only that, but the laundry
and sewing get done for nothing too!"

"Th-that's s-slavery!" Kestrel said, after a moment of
appalled silence.

Krystal shrugged, and her hair slipped coquettishly
over one eye. "That's the privilege of power," she
replied. "And it's why so few of us have actually been
caught in a raid. We don't want to end up in the work-
house, so we all have ways to escape. If we have to —"
she faltered, then continued. "— well, one way to
make certain Padrik wouldn't want you is to make certain you aren't pretty anymore."

She might have said more, but Ardana appeared

with a client in tow, a rather ordinary and dumpy little man, dressed like a middle-class merchant, with merry eyes. There was nothing about him to fire the imagination, and Robin could not for a moment imagine why Krystal's face lit up with a truly welcoming smile when she saw him. But the lady rose immediately and hurried over, leaving Robin and Kestrel to pick up their instruments and resume playing.

But Robin had everything she needed; anything else Krystal could have told her was of secondary importance, and minimal value. Most of it Robin had already deduced.

It made perfect sense to find the Patsono Clan mired up to their necks in this sordid business. They specialized in being involved in sordid undertakings.

It had never been anything on this scale, though; mostly petty trickery and fraud.

Even among the Gypsies a Patsono was watched carefully, and valuables kept out of easy filching reach. All Gypsies tended to cheat ordinary house-bound folk — who they called *gajo,* or in the Outsider tongues, "rootfeet" from their habit of never leaving a place for as long as they lived. It was not considered cheating so much as a combination of good bargaining and education . . . if the rootfeet learned to be careful, to watch their purse strings or to examine what they bargained for, then they got a cheap lesson in the ways of real life. Sometimes that cheating extended to a bit of outright theft, if the mark appeared to deserve such attentions. Robin had picked a pocket or two in her time. She considered it justice, not thievery; those whose purses she lightened were either far too wealthy for their own good, or they had been particularly noxious, like the bullies in Westhaven.

But Gypsies, as a rule, never made fellow Gypsies

or Free Bards the targets of such thievery and trickery. The Patsono Clan had fleeced or robbed both quite as often as they'd victimized rootfeet.

The only question in Robin's mind was — why? Why were they doing this? What were they getting out of it? Why had they suddenly decided to throw in with a rootfoot — and not just any rootfoot, but a High Bishop? The Gypsies had no shared interests with Churchmen, not even a common religion.

She had personal experience with a Patsono or two; if there was one trait besides dishonesty they all had in common, it was a distinct aversion to cooperate with *anyone.*

There was only one way to find out that "why," and that was to do so in person.

Kestrel isn't going to like this, Robin, she told herself, as she devoted half her attention to her playing, while the other half was wrapped up in thinking up a way to get her into the black heart of the Patsono Clan. *So while you're at finding a way into Patsono, maybe you'd better find a way to talk him into accepting this. . . .*

Kestrel didn't like it. Not at all.

"You're *what*?" Anger had completely obliterated Jonny's stutter. He had listened to her careful explanation in relative calm, but the moment she had told him that she was going into the Clan enclave, he had exploded.

"I'm going to pretend I'm a distant cousin of one of the Patsono's," she explained again, patiently. "That's not at all hard; unless you go through a formal handfasting, there are plenty of Gypsies who don't bother with formalizing relationships, not even when there are children. There usually aren't when there's no handfasting, unless the woman is wealthy in her own right and wants a child. Gypsy women are all taught how to prevent conception."

"So how would you be some kind of relation then?" he shot back, eyes wide with emotion, although she could not tell whether it was anger or something more complicated.

"Because sometimes a woman can choose to have a child, and not care who the father is so long as he isn't a rootfoot," she said, trying not to show her exasperation at having to state the obvious. "And sometimes women are just stupid or careless. It doesn't matter! All I have to do is claim my father is one of the Patsonos, name some city I know the Patsonos were in, and give a vague description of the man. Patsonos have no imagination to speak of; of the entire Clan, at least a quarter of the men are named Robere, another quarter are called Tammio, and the rest are a mix of Berto, Albere, and Tombere. If I say my father's name was Robere and I *don't* try to claim any special privileges or demand one of the Roberes recognize me as his offspring, there shouldn't be any problems or questions. Among the Clans it's basically up to you and maybe the Clan Chiefs to keep track of who you're related to."

If she'd thought that would mollify him, she was proven wrong. "*Shouldn't,*" he scoffed, lip curling in mockery. "Shouldn't cause any problems or questions. Oh, grand. What if it does?"

"It won't as long as you aren't with me," she retorted, her own temper fraying. "Which you won't be. You couldn't pass for a Gypsy no matter how hard you tried, and by now I'm sure there are plenty of Clans who've heard of Robin and her *gajin vanderei.* But when I go in alone, there won't be any reason to connect me with —"

"*What?*" he yelped again. "You're doing no such —"

Her frayed temper snapped. "How *dare* you? You are *not* my master, you do *not* tell me what I will or will not do!" she hissed. "*I* rule my own actions!"

And with that, she whirled, yanked the door to their room open, and stalked away, down the hall, down the stairs, and out into the courtyard, walking as quickly as she could and still preserve her dignity. Once she reached the courtyard, she sprinted across it, and dove into the street beyond.

Evidently her angry defiance caught Kestrel off-guard; if he tried to follow her, he was too late about it, for she quickly lost herself in the early-evening crowds. She wrapped her warm woolen shawl around her shoulders and her head, and slipped through the slower-moving strollers with the agility of an otter in a stream. She knew exactly where she was going now, thanks to those evenings at Ardana's. According to the clients, Padrik's "special helpers" had a little enclave of their own on Church property. There was a walled courtyard on the opposite side of the Cathedral from the market-square, a courtyard that had a guest-house meant for groups of visitors. That was where the "special helpers" and their wagons were, so that was where Robin would go.

Moving at a brisk walk, she kept herself warm, and covered the distance between the inn and the Cathedral in very short order. She actually made better time than she had expected to, emerging into the deserted market-square before she realized that the crowds had thinned to nothing.

She looked up, and could not suppress a gasp; she stopped dead in her tracks to stare.

She had never seen the Cathedral at night; its impact was as great as the first view by daylight had been. The carvings were darker shadows, silhouettes against the colored glass of the windows, and every window shone with its own light. The colors gave the illusion of floating in the darkness of the Cathedral, and now she saw what she had missed before — that the windows themselves, framed as they were by the carvings, formed the simple shapes of stylized flowers and leaves. The Cathedral was a huge bouquet of flowers, made of light. . . .

A cold breeze whipped around her ankles, then blew up her skirt, and woke her to her self-appointed mission. She shook herself out of her trance and hurried across the cobble-stoned square. The windows of the houses surrounding the square were also alight, but this was familiar, homey light, and she concentrated on them rather than on the seductive and hypnotic beauty of the Cathedral. As they had peddled their God-Stars she had amused herself by imagining what lay beyond those windows; now, at least in part, she was able to see how the wealthy of Gradford spent that wealth.

It was often lovely, certainly expensive, but after spending time in the Royal Palace in Birnam, no longer impressive. In fact, the taste in this town tended towards the overblown, over-ornamented. Many of those who had decorated the interiors of these houses seemed determined, not to echo, but to outdo the Cathedral. Where one of the carvings of the sea-tower boasted a single strand of kelp, the gilded ceiling-moldings featured a dozen intertwined strands in a fraction of the space, and fish peeking through the kelp to boot. Where there was a pair of ribbon-tails in mating-flight on the air-tower, the frame of an enormous mirror had three dozen, all getting in one another's way, and looking less like a mating-flight than an absurd crashing bird-orgy. It would surely have embarrassed T'fyrr.

Wallpaper or painted murals featured the same carvings as the towers, but painted in lifelike color — which did not improve the composition any, and made the paintings look overcrowded.

She sighed and shook her head. Sad, that so much money should be squandered on such bad taste. Perhaps this new trend towards austerity would creep over into the furnishings and decorations in these homes . . . if it did, for once Padrik's influence would be of excellent benefit.

The wall around the buildings to either side and to the rear of the Cathedral was an impressive one, and quite blank — which was, in itself, interesting. No carvings, which implied that the wall was new — and no entrances. So, the only way into the compound — unless there were gates in the wall on the other side — was through the single gate she had been told about, and through the Cathedral itself.

Well, if I wanted to keep an eye on the comings and goings of my underlings, that's how I would do it, she thought to herself. *In the robes that most of these fellows wear, climbing the wall would be a difficult proposition.*

Getting in was going to be a difficult proposition as well, unless the Patsonos left the gate open . . . and unless they were so incredibly stupid that they didn't bother to put a guard on it.

Then again, it's the Patsonos. They may be crooked, but they're also idiots.

Still, even idiots could have a moment or two of shrewdness. Plenty of smart people became dead smart people because they forgot that.

But as she rounded the corner, she was able to breathe easier. The gate stood open wide, with yellow light from the courtyard beyond spilling through it out onto the cobbles.

There wasn't even a token guard at the gate. Not even a child, watching to see who came in.

Oh, aye. It's the Patsonos all right.

She simply sauntered through, and once inside, re-arranged her shawl as a Gypsy would wear it, tucked into her belt. She loosened the strings of her blouse a little, and turned her businesslike stride into a slow, deliberately provocative walk.

She saw to her concealed relief that there were plenty of women here — and that, like her, while they might have adopted the mouse-browns and dust-grays of the townsfolk, they still *wore* their clothing like Gypsies. The wagons were arranged around the wall, with a communal fire in a great iron dish in the center of the courtyard. The building formed the rear of the courtyard; by the lights it was occupied, and by the size, there was nowhere near enough room in there for every Patsono here. It must be reserved for the elite of the Clan then, the Chief, his family, his advisors, and their families. There were a fair number of people loitering about; in all ways but the lack of color, music, and dancing, this looked like a fairly typical Gypsy camp situation.

Most of those loitering were young, and by their demeanor and lack of gold jewelry, of fairly low ranking in the Clan. It looked as if she had guessed correctly; the higher-ranked members were granted the greater comfort of the building, while the underlings made do with their wagons. On the whole, this lot was cleaner and better kempt than the majority of the Patsonos Robin had ever been forced to deal with. That made her job of fitting in a little easier.

If I don't stay around the younger and unimportant Clan members, I could get in trouble. The Clan Chief might be smart enough to ask about my "father," and I would *get tripped up by a Chief. Unless I happened by pure accident to pick someone for my "father" who is dead, or simply isn't here.*

She strolled over to a loose gathering beside the fire; someone passed a skin of wine in her direction and she squirted it deftly into her mouth, thus passing the informal "test" that showed she was a Gypsy. No *gajin* had ever mastered the Gypsy wineskins unless they were particularly deft Free Bards.

She let the fire warm her and tried to examine the faces nearby without really looking at them. Light enough came from the fire to see features clearly. Many seemed familiar; they were, perhaps, the people who were "healed" without any outward evidence of being sick or crippled, other than the canes and crutches. Those were simple deceptions that even a child could perform, and in fact, some children *had* performed them.

"So who's on duty tomorrow?" asked a young woman with a remarkably large nose and slender build. "Not me, I know that much." It sounded like the resumption of a conversation her arrival had interrupted.

"Little Robere, Bald Robere, Blind Robere, Tammio Blackbeard, Mindy, and Berto Lightfingers, that's all I know of," another voice said, from the other side of the fire. "There's a special demon-possession up; Padrik has a point he wants to make and a woman he wants to get back at, and people are getting bored with invisible demons anyway. Should be a good show, and it's going to be an impressive enough thing we don't need a big parade of victims."

"Oh, good," the large-nosed girl said with a grin. "That means I'm off. They keep making me play blind, and my legs are black and blue from stumbling into things."

"The bruises make it look good, dearie," said an old woman, with a cackle. "Now I remember when *I* played blind —"

"*Oh* yes, we know all about that, granny," a young man interrupted rudely. "We've heard it all a hundred times, how you broke a leg just to prove you couldn't see a thing. If I hear it again, I'm going to choke."

The grandmother looked mortally offended, and drew herself up with immense, if flawed, dignity. "Well!" she exclaimed. "If me wisdom and experience are going to fall on deaf ears, I will just go elsewhere, that I will!"

She limped off into the darkness, muttering to herself. The thump of her cane on the cobblestones punctuated her grumblings. Several of the younger Gypsies around the fire snickered.

One of the young men looked at Robin curiously for a moment, and she was certain that he was going to ask her who she was. But he only passed her the wineskin, and after she took her mouthful of rather good wine (from the High Bishop's cellars, no doubt), she realized why he hadn't confronted her with a demand for her identity.

"Who's special duty?" he asked instead. "Any magic tricks tomorrow besides the new demon?"

"Only the Chief and that Priest he works with. No one else, not even the peacock," the nose-girl said. Robin laughed a little, with a rueful grimace, and he grinned and winced. She passed the skin back to him.

He *had* seen her — in the Cathedral. And since he was seeing her now, here, he simply assumed that she was one of the other "special helpers." Perhaps there were Patsonos coming and going all the time — Patsono was a small Clan, but she had no idea of the true numbers. Perhaps there was not enough room for all of them here. Perhaps they were still collecting far-flung members as word spread they were needed.

For whatever the reason, she was accepted without question or qualm, and she took instant advantage of the fact, feeling a little smug. Kestrel had overreacted, of course. It was going to be satisfying to point out just how badly he had overreacted. . . .

"Bishop's got good wine," remarked someone, as the skin came around to him. The boy nearest Robin laughed drunkenly.

"Better'n I've ever had, anyway," the tipsy one said. slurring his words a bit. "Good food, good wine, an' trickin' the rootfeet! This's th' best!"

The girl with the nose laughed, just as someone threw another log on the fire, making it flare and casting a ruddy light on her face that made her seem diabolical. She had the most unpleasant laugh it had ever been Robin's misfortune to hear; it wasn't quite a scream, and it wasn't quite a bray, it was a combination of the two.

She sounded rather like the peacock. *Maybe they ought to use her and get rid of the bird.*

"What *I* love," she announced to one and all, "is that it's usin' their own religion to part 'em from everything they got! You seen those sheep when them Priests tell 'em they got cursed money? They can't throw it at us fast enough!"

She got a round of laughter at that. "Like that old goat t'day," the fellow on the other side of the fire said. "Had a bad minute with him, I thought when the priest told him 'bout the curse that he was gonna fall over with a brain-storm. Went purple, he did."

That unleashed another flood of anecdotes, with the nose-girl lamenting that she wasn't a little child anymore, since the children who were "healed" were often showered with gifts from the onlookers.

"Witnesses, Padrik calls 'em." The nose-girl sniggered. "Right. Tell 'em what they're gonna see, an' they sure do see it!"

"I hear that the Chief Robere's working on a really big illusion," the across-the-fire-voice offered. "It'll make the demon look — like a Faire-trick, so they say. Padrik asked him, says he wants a way to get the root-feet to think they got to come up with the money for a hospice. An angel as big's the Cathedral, with, like, a big hospice in its hands. That'll make 'em cough up the silver."

"Gold too, for an angel," the nose-girl mused, the light of greed in her eyes. "How much of that do we get, you reckon? That'd be something."

Whatever else she was going to say was interrupted by the arrival of a much older, gray-haired man with a aura of self-important authority. "Meeting's running long," he said without preamble. "We're gettin' hungry and thirsty, an' we don't want the Bishop's servants carrying tales —"

"So you're lookin' for volunteers t' keep the cups an' plates filled, huh?" the nose-girl sighed. "Gray Tom-bere, I swear you think that's all we were born t' do for you Chiefs. You'd think we was servants."

He gave her a sharp look. "Maybe that's all you're good for, Rosa," he replied sharply. "I don't see *you* exertin' yourself for the Clan. Are you coming in, or not?"

She stretched ostentatiously, and yawned. "I guess. Just as good as bein' out here, an' it's warmer in there."

Robin waited until two more had volunteered before offering herself. Once again, no one gave her more than a second glance, not even the secondary chief who'd come for the volunteers. A moment later she was inside the "guest-house," in a large room heated to semitropic temperatures by an enormous fire in the fireplace. That was the only source of light; either the Clan Chiefs enjoyed this attempt to get the "feel" of an outdoor meeting, or else the Bishop did not trust them around candles and the resulting wax-drips on his furniture and paneling.

If so, he was wise, at least so far as Robin could tell. The carpet had been treated as if it was a dirt floor; the table was crusted with spills that had never been cleaned up, and the sideboard was in the same shape. The Bishop's furniture would never look as good as it once did, and he might have to replace it all after this.

There were platters of food waiting on the side-board, and tall bottles of wine. In the dim light it was difficult to tell just what the food was, other than in the general sense of "meat," "bread," and "maybe cheese." She took the nearest open bottle, and turned towards the table, pouring it in any goblets that were less than full. Rosa took up a platter of meat slices and dropped them on plates with little regard for splatter-ing sauces. The other volunteers picked up platters at random and did the same.

But the owners of the plates didn't seem to care, either. They picked up whatever was on their plates in their fingers, rolled it up, and stuffed the rolls in their mouths without paying any attention to the food itself. Instead, they leaned forward intently, and only a few brushed briefly at the spills on their clothing before bringing their attention back to the words of their Chief.

He was describing exactly the illusion that the boy outside had mentioned, of the Cathedral-tall angel with a hospice in its hands. With additions; the angel was supposed to be real to the touch, in case someone was brave enough to try, and it was to exude an aroma

of incense. It was supposed to smile and nod, as a disembodied voice described the hospice Padrik was
supposed to build.

"So what does the Clan get out of this one?" the
gray-haired man asked as he sat down. "The demon
f'tomorrow was hard enough! Has he got any idea
what he's asking for? That scale of illusion isn't going
to be an easy one to build or hold in place."

"We get a quarter of the take," the Chief replied.
And as a storm of protest erupted, he held up his
hand. "Let me finish, will you? Padrik expects more
than you realize out of this one. Our cut is a quarter
of the take, *or three thousand silver,* whichever
comes out the biggest. *He* thinks we're likelier to
wind up with three thousand in gold, not silver.
Especially if he combines this with a big sermon
about giving up adornments for the sake of God. He
thinks that the jewelry is going to fill the collection
plates, once the angel appears. In fact, his guess is
that within two days, there won't be a piece of jewelry left to anybody with any claim to piety. There
may not be a piece left in the city that isn't some
sort of heirloom."

There was some grumbling, but finally grudging
agreement; after the agreement, there was a pause
while the participants resorted to their wine. Robin
made three circuits of the table, emptying four bottles,
before they got back to business.

They emptied their platters, too, stuffing food in
their mouths as if they did not expect to eat ever again,
and wiping greasy hands on their shirts and tunics. She
kept herself from wrinkling her nose in distaste. It was
just a good thing that the current vogue was for brown
and gray; dark colors that didn't show stains and grease
as badly as the usual Gypsy colors did.

Then again, it looked — and smelled — as if their

clothing had been clean before they sat down to this meeting. Maybe the High Bishop's servants were discretely taking away their soiled clothing and replacing it with clean while they slept, so that their appearance would not arouse suspicion that they did not belong here.

"Now, Gray Tombere, how's the House doing?" the Chief asked. "What's new out there?"

The old man grinned. "Better, since the Guards closed down Lady Silk's and the Snow Maiden. Sale of drink's been real good; new gambling tables are doing well. If we could just get a couple more Houses closed down, we'd be making as much money as the miracles."

But the Chief shook his head. "Don't try to force the Luck," he cautioned. "Most of the Houses are down in the Warren now; you push the local talent down there, and they may come out after us. We can't afford that yet; not until Padrik's got more than Gradford dancing to his tunes."

Robin listened and poured, poured and listened. There was more of the same, rather as she had expected. The Patsonos had basically moved into Gradford and set up their own little network of linked activities. They smuggled in drugs, strong liquor, and anything that had been deemed illegal; they dispensed these things at the House the Chief had spoken of — and Robin had a shrewd notion that if she were to trace the location of this House, she would discover it was one and the same with the "work-house" Krystal had described. They separated the gullible from their money at the gambling tables in the House, and they used their knowledge of who the clients were to extort yet more money from those same clients on occasion.

They had abandoned the usual schemes of fortune-telling and petty pickpocketing. They weren't even involved in horse theft; not here, and not now. They had tied the Clan's fortunes to High Bishop Padrik and his schemes — for just as the Patsonos got their share of the donations resulting from Padrik's "miracles," the High Bishop was taking his share of their income from the House.

And they were completely content with all of this. It apparently had never once occurred to any of them that Padrik and his Priests were observant and clever, and that once they figured out how to reproduce the "miracles" — or managed to find a mage they could coerce into doing the same — they would no longer need the Patsonos. With all the illegal activities the Clan had gotten involved with, it would be child's play to be rid of them.

No one would ever believe that the saintly High Bishop was involved with running a House — and it was doubtful that anyone had anything likely to prove the case. That assumed that the Patsonos would ever make it to a trial, of course. . . .

And with the example of *this* Gypsy Clan to inspire them, how long would it be before the High Bishop persuaded the King himself to legislate against Gypsies and Free Bards?

"*Hey!*" someone said suddenly, breaking into her reverie.

And even as she turned away from the table, wine bottle forgotten in her hand, one of the men behind her grabbed her wrist and wrenched her around. "What're you doin'?" he demanded. "You been *listening*! Who are you?"

"Reba," she said, quickly forcing an expression of vacant stupidity on her face. "Reba, Chief. Gray Tombere, he said come pour wine. Rosa, she say it's warm inside. So I come pour wine. Hey?"

The man examined her for a moment, closely. "Don't I know you from somewhere?"

She shrugged, tasting the sour bile of fear but trying to keep any expression at all from showing. Hadn't she heard of a Patsono that was hung for horse theft when she was a child? Could she remember his name? She made a quick, desperate guess. "Born on road, outside Kingsford. Mam's Clan don' like me, much. Pappy was Long Robere —"

"Ah, she must be that brat Long Robere got on the Ladras woman before they hung him," one of the others exclaimed, and laughed. "That's why you think you know her, old man — she's got that look of his."

As Robin nodded vigorously, the man pulled her a little closer, peered into her face as he exhaled wine fumes into her nose, then let go of her, nodding with grudging satisfaction. Of course, this was probably a fellow who did everything grudgingly. . . .

Robin breathed a small sigh of relief as he motioned to her to refill his goblet. "Yah, that's it, girl. You got your pappy's look about you. Long Robere allus was better looking than he was smart."

"Yah, well I heard that he didn't get his name from bein' *tall*," guffawed another of the men, and as the off-color jokes and comments followed swiftly, Robin turned to get another bottle of wine, too limp with relief to even think straight.

As she turned back to the table, though, the Chief looked directly at her. "You, Reba girl —" he said. "You just get here tonight?"

She didn't know what else to do besides nod. Presumably the Patsonos *had* put it about that their Clan was mustering here. She had better pretend that she answered that call.

"Then you don't know the rules. No hobnobbing

with the rootfeet for girls, 'specially not with the
Priests. You get your tail down the hall to the girls'
room when we're done here," he said sternly. "No Patsono wench runs around loose where *gajin* can find
her. Some of these Priests think our women are here
for *them*. You get yourself a bed where it's safe — you,
Rosa, you show her where, show her where the
clothes is, that kinda thing."

Rosa nodded, and Robin's heart sank. But there was
no help for it. Until she could get away, she was a
Patsono.

Kestrel would be frantic.

And he'd say, "I told you so."

The meeting broke up shortly after that, and
Rosa took her firmly by the elbow and led her down
a long hallway to a huge room, lit by a bare four lanterns, and filled with cots. Most of them held young
women and girls just past puberty; obviously this
was a dormitory. The windows were small; too small
to climb through.

"Chief wasn't joking," Rosa told her in a whisper,
not unkindly. "These Priests, they seem to think we're
just like the girls in their own special House. You just
got what's on your back?"

At Robin's nod, she made a *tsk*ing sound. "Not the
first time other Clan's have turned Patsono get out on
the road with nothing," Rosa said. "Well, no matter.
There's clothes in the closet there we all share; ugly,
but nice make. Servants here take away dirty ones, we
never have t'do no wash. You gotta take a bath every
three days, though, that's a rule."

"Why all the rules?" Robin asked, in a whine. "Why
the ugly clothes, hey?"

"T'make us fit in. Can't look like Gypsy, or the High
Bishop might get in trouble." Rosa shrugged. "It's
worth it; we're getting real money for makin' him look

like a saint. Once you start helping with the services, you'll start getting the money, too."

She led Robin to a cot on the far side of the room — too far to get to the door without waking someone up. There were blankets there already, and a pillow. She patted the cot, and Robin obediently sank down onto it, trying not to show her dismay.

"I'll take you to services in the morning," Rosa said, full of self-importance. "You'll see what we do. Trust me, you'll like it! Even with the rules. This is the *best!*"

"Oh, yes," Robin mumbled, as Rosa went off to her own cot, unaware of Robin's irony. "This is really the best. . . ."

CHAPTER FOURTEEN

Jonny's anger evaporated the moment Robin flung the door open and vanished down the hall, but his indignation remained. He hadn't thought she'd storm off like that! But he stayed where he was, at least in part because he was just as stubborn as she was, and was *not* going to humiliate himself by running after her. He was certain that she would be back in a moment; in two, at most.

She knew he was right; she wasn't stupid. Once she got over being mad about the way he'd ordered her not to go, she'd realize he was right. The idea of trying to pose as some relative of these people was the height of insanity. Surely, if the Clan was as small as she claimed, they knew every single member. Just because she was a Gypsy, that wouldn't make her a believable Patsono!

She would come back. He would apologize for trying to order her around. That was *his* mistake, and he should have known better. Once he got a chance, he could explain that he was only worried about her, that he was afraid that her bravery (better not call it "foolhardiness") would be stronger than her fear, and she would end up in trouble —

No, that doesn't sound right — better say that she would be so intent on finding truth that she might find herself in some situation she hadn't expected.

He didn't even sit down; he stayed where he was,

standing with his arms crossed over his chest, waiting
for her to come back. Waiting to hear her footsteps,
returning. Waiting for her to appear in the open doorway.

And kept waiting, staring at the wood of the hallway
outside the door.

When it finally dawned on him that she really
wasn't coming back, it was too late, of course. She was
long out of reach; he had no idea where this Gypsy
enclave was, so he didn't even have a clear idea of
where she was heading.

His initial reaction was a resumption of his anger.
He stormed over to the doorway, slammed the door
and threw himself down onto the bed. And there he
waited, certain she would not be able to get into this
Gypsy enclave —

*She has no sense of responsibility, dammit! The only
people she thinks are important are Free Bards and
Gypsies — she doesn't care about anyone else. She's as
bad as Padrik! He thinks nonhumans are nonpersons,
and she thinks the same of anyone outside her little
circle. . . .*

Hours passed; the anger burned itself out. Fear
replaced it, turning him sick with anxiety for her. By
the time the bells tolled for midnight, he was certain
something terrible had happened to her. Maybe the
Gypsies had turned her over to the Cathedral Guards;
maybe they had taken matters into their own hands.
Maybe she had been arrested for being out on the
street after midnight. Maybe a common thief had
knocked her unconscious, or even killed her!

Maybe someone had attacked her and she had used
magic to defend herself, and now she was facing a
judge for *that.*

He sat on the bed until the candle burned out. He
was sleepless with tension, waiting to see if dawn

would bring her back. His throat ached; his stomach twisted and churned, sending bile into the back of his throat. His skull throbbed with headache, and his eyes burned with fatigue. And above it all was helplessness — the knowledge that she was in a situation he couldn't discover, with people he didn't understand, and that his damnable stuttering speech would keep him from even asking a stranger about her.

When dawn came without her, his heart plummeted further, and he flung himself off the bed to stare at the rising sun with weary, aching eyes. There had to be *something* he could do!

Too restless with anxiety to stay in the room any longer, he tried to think where the best place might be to hear any news. Ardana's? No, she wouldn't be open for business yet. The Warren? Maybe; but he didn't want to venture in there unless he absolutely had to.

Finally he could only arrive at one answer; the Cathedral. Criminals were often displayed near there, in the stocks — though what she could possibly do to get herself arrested as a common criminal —

She could manage. Just by not going along with a Constable if he stopped her to question her, I suppose —

There was always gossip, the circulation of rumors among the merchants. By now he and Robin were a familiar sight, and many of the other merchants were friendly with the two of them. Maybe one of them would have heard something.

But I am supposed to remain "mute". . . .

He changed, splashed some water on his haggard face, and hurried down to the stable to get the wagon. The sooner he got to the square, the better.

The sun was barely above the level of the rooftops; the courtyard was still in shadow, and frost covered the cobblestones. He was too early for the stable hands and had to wait, pacing, in the frigid courtyard. He could have gone back to the common room to eat while he waited, but he could not even bear the thought of food at the moment. His stomach was so knotted up he was nauseous.

He took the reins of the horses and mounted to the driver's seat as soon as they brought up the wagon. It took all of his self-control to keep from galloping the horses down the street, to the market-square; he wanted to be there so badly that it seemed to take hours for the horses to walk the short distance to the market, and every momentary halt made him want to scream at those blocking the street. It took as much control to set up when he got there, as if everything was as usual; to smile and mime prices and sell the God-Stars as if nothing was wrong.

And there were no rumors, no gossip. Not even about a strange Gypsy being arrested for vagrancy or resisting arrest. Nothing. The other merchants seemed to think that Robin was ill, or resting — several of them took the time to come up and tell him to give his wife their best wishes, or to ask if anything was seriously wrong with her.

The only difference between today and all the previous days they had been here was the number of street preachers in the square itself. They were multiplying like rats this morning.

And this morning their sermons all focused on the same subject; the perfidy of women.

They were not preaching *at* Kestrel, not the way they'd preached at Robin the afternoon she had been alone; the description of him on their license said that he was deaf as well as mute, and most of them read the description and gave him a bored glance before beginning their harangues. Usually the street preachers ignored him entirely. But perhaps because the sun was concentrated here all morning, making this little corner of the square marginally warmer than the rest, there was never a moment between sunrise and Prime Service that there wasn't a preacher delivering a speech within earshot; sometimes there were two or even three, their speeches overlapping and creating aural chaos from Kestrel's point of view.

What was very different this morning, was that their speeches were so similar that they could have been reading from the same pre-written script.

Women are easily corrupted, and spread their corruption gladly. Women are by nature treacherous and scheming. Women are weak, and cannot resist temptation of any sort. Women have no grasp of true faith. Women are inferior, and nearer to the nature of animals than of angels. . . .

Kestrel wondered why none of the women listening seemed disturbed, or even insulted. If it had been *him* —

— or Robin —

— he would *not* have been standing there, listening to some fool claim he was some breed of lesser creature and needed a keeper to prevent him from doing wrong!

Why were they listening to this abuse, and saying, doing nothing? Did they believe it? And why was all this poison specifically directed against women pouring out *now*? What had happened to trigger it?

His anxiety mounted for a moment, if that was possible, as he wondered if Robin could have done something to cause this outburst of venom.

But no; why would they need to prepare people for the punishment of someone they had already *caught* in dubious activity? They wouldn't; more than that, with someone as unimportant as Robin, they'd simply fling her into a gaol-cell, and walk away.

So it couldn't be Robin; it must be that something else had happened, involving some woman of standing and importance. Or was there something *about* to happen?

As the sun rose and the square filled, his questions remained unanswered. And he began to wonder about something else. Could he have underestimated Robin? Could she have gotten herself into the Patsono Clan after all — and had she learned something that had made her stay there with them?

The more he thought about that — well, the more likely it seemed. Robin could well have been angry enough at him to punish him by not sending any word. Or she could have found herself in a position where she was unable to get away. Surely, surely, if she'd been caught, she'd have been paraded like any other common criminal!

But he could not convince himself of that, and he certainly could not convince his gut.

Out of habit, and for lack of anything constructive to do, he closed up the wagon and trailed off with the rest to the Healing Service, hoping that Robin would come to their usual place under the statue of Saint Hypatia. But Hypatia's pedestal was empty, and as the usual show played out in its usual mockery, he was tempted to leave —

Then came a cry that rang over the murmur of the crowd and brought the healing service to a complete halt.

"Demon!"

His head, and everyone else's, snapped around at the cry from the back of the Cathedral. No matter how often Padrik staged these "demonic possessions," they always gave him a shock. Four Cathedral Guards struggled forward with Robere Patsono — who this morning sported clothing that made him look several pounds heavier than he truly was, and a false moustache.

Kestrel sighed with frustration. The way the tension had been building, he had thought for certain Padrik was going to come up with some new revelation before the Healing Service was over. But just as they reached the altar, the expected scenario took an abrupt turn into something completely *unexpected.*

Robere suddenly gave a great cry, convulsed, and went limp in the arms of the Guards. His head sagged, chin against his chest, eyes closed, mouth hung slackly open.

And a thin stream of blue-gray smoke issued from his open mouth.

But it didn't act the way smoke was supposed to. Instead of rising, it snaked down his chest, eeled towards the space between him and Padrik, and pooled there.

He stared, along with every other person in the Cathedral. *If only Robin were here, she could tell me how they're doing this —* It looked real, *very* real. So real that the hair on the back of his neck crawled, and gooseflesh rose on his arms. The Cathedral was so silent that he wondered if anyone was even breathing. The Guards holding the man were white-faced and trembling; *they* certainly hadn't expected this to happen. Only Padrik was unmoved; he watched, face stern, one hand raised in a warding gesture, the other grasping his staff of office.

Then as more and more of the smoke gathered, a vague shape rose up out of the pool of mist —

And Kestrel heard a faint, discordant music. But not with his ears.

Music like, but unlike, the music he always heard when Rune or Talaysen worked real Bardic magic; the music he followed on the rare occasions that he had done the same. Someone was working magic, *real* magic, in the Cathedral!

And if it's not to produce this demon, I'll eat every God-Star I've made!

The shape shivered, thickened, grew opaque — and took on a clear, defined form. Then more than a form.

It became a demon; a real, three-dimensional being, that looked exactly as the demons portrayed in so many Church paintings and carvings. Pale gray, the color of stone. Manlike, but clearly not a man. Naked, except for a loincloth, clawed feet and hands, huge bat-wings, horns, a raptor's beak where a mouth should be —

— strangely similar to T'fyrr —

People nearest the demon screamed as it snarled at them, then turned its attention towards the altar, and hissed. But before Kestrel had any chance to wonder about that resemblance to T'fyrr, Padrik spread both his arms wide and over his head, his staff of office held between them. A white-gold glow surrounded the staff and the hands that held it.

"Begone, foul fiend!" he thundered, his voice filling the Cathedral and drowning the cries of panic from the crowd. "Begone, be banished, and trouble us no more!"

The fiend laughed, and Kestrel felt his knees turning to water with fear. He couldn't have moved; like everyone else in the building he was paralyzed with fright. He shivered with cold, drenched in an icy sweat; he shook as if he was trembling with fever, and started to sink to the floor in abject terror —

When he suddenly felt the internal music intensify, and a new melody join it, and realized that the fear he felt was not coming from within him, but from the music!

Once he knew that, he was able to shunt the music away, and fear vanished, exactly like a soap bubble popping. With it went the paralysis that had held him helpless.

He remained on his knees, however; if he had stood, he would have been terribly conspicuous amid all the rest of the grovelers. Padrik was the only man standing now, for even the Guards had dropped to their knees, leaving their "prisoner" to lie on the floor like a dead thing. The High Bishop glowed with hazy, golden light — light that was no more divine than the demon, Kestrel suspected.

"In the name of God and His Angels, begone!" Padrik cried again, his voice rising over the demonic laughter. "Begone, lest the wrath of God be unleashed upon you!"

The demon's only answer was to leap upon the High Bishop, claw-hands reaching for his throat.

Padrik brought down his staff just in time; the demon's hands closed upon it rather than flesh. The moment that it touched the wooden staff, however, the real show began.

The two combatants lurched in a bizarre circle-dance, linked by the High Bishop's staff, never once leaving the clear space before the altar. Coruscating lightnings of eye-searing yellow and blood-red lanced from the demon, grounding everywhere except on Padrik, whose golden glow had hardened to a visible shield about him. The demon's shrieks of rage echoed through the Cathedral, further terrifying the congregation. Now that Kestrel was no longer in the thrall of the artificially induced terror, he was able to admire the artistry, and wonder who among the Priests or the Gypsies was responsible. As a show, it was the best he'd ever seen; a truly professional illusion on the mage's part, and a truly fine acting performance on

Padrik's. It really *looked* as if he was fighting something!

At first, the struggle appeared to be completely even, but gradually the tide turned in Padrik's favor. The High Bishop was back in his former position, where he'd started when the fight began. His back was to the altar, with his face to the congregation, and the demon's back to them. There he stopped and held his ground.

The demon cried out, and for the first time there was something like fear in its voice.

His face shining with well-simulated righteous wrath, Padrik forced the demon to its knees, and with a tremendous shout, wrestled the staff out of its hands and struck it across the head! A soundless explosion of light covered the lack of any sound of impact. It collapsed at his feet, and he planted the tip of his staff firmly in the middle of its back.

It groveled on the marble before him, whimpering.

A collective sigh passed through the crowd at the successful conclusion to the "struggle." Kestrel was impressed, Robin's disappearance momentarily forgotten; this was going to enhance Padrik's reputation no end! It was one thing to "banish" a "demon" no one could see — it was quite another to actually defeat such a creature in a battle anyone could see with his own eyes!

Even if it is as phony as glass diamonds.

But surely now the show was over. He expected the High Bishop to "banish" the creature as he always had before, though probably in a much more spectacular manner.

But once again the little play took an entirely different turn.

"Who sent you?" Padrik demanded, his voice booming and echoing in the silent Cathedral. "Who sent you to possess this man, and to attack me? What vile magician is it that you serve, creature of darkness? Answer! Or you will feel the might of the weapon of God once again!"

He raised his staff in threat, and the demon groveled and wept and whimpered so convincingly that Kestrel almost felt sorry for it.

"*Lady Orlina Woolwright,*" the demon hissed, its voice harsh and hoarse. "*That isss my missstresss, the lady I sssserve —*"

Kestrel started with surprise, and he was not the only one to do so. *Orlina Woolwright?* He knew that name — and so did every native of Gradford, and every merchant who had been here more than a day or two.

She was one of the Mayor's Councilors, appointed by her Guild, for the Mayor surely would never have appointed anyone as outspoken as she was on his own. A few days ago, she had made a public speech or two of her own in the Cathedral square from the vantage of her own balcony, concerning the rights of tradesmen, with carefully veiled references to all the restrictions that Padrik had been attempting to have signed into law. She was beautiful, wealthy, a Master in the Weaver's Guild in her own right, and perhaps not so coincidentally, the only person on the Mayor's Council with a sense of humor. She'd certainly been able to make a mockery of some of Padrik's more outrageous statements in those speeches of hers. She had — unwisely now, it seemed — been flaunting the new wave of piety, by dressing as a woman of refinement and fashion, rather than a woman of the "new" Gradford.

She had been too prominent a target for Padrik to attack in the Council or in any other conventional, secular venue. That was what the other merchants had said, anyway. She held too many debts, knew too many secrets.

So has he chosen this way to bring her down?

"Orlina Woolwright? So be it!" Padrik raised his staff above his head, and gazed out over the heads of the crowd. "You have all heard it! You have heard the testament of the witch's own creature, sent to slay me! I now denounce Orlina Woolwright as a sorcerer, mage, and witch of the blackest and darkest! I declare her Anathema in the sight of all good Churchmen! Let no man aid her, let no man succor her, for the wrath of God is now against her!"

A bolt of lightning lanced down out of the ceiling of the Cathedral, and struck Padrik's staff with a *crack*. He pointed the staff down at the demon, and another bolt crackled down to strike it —

This one was so bright it brought tears to Kestrel's eyes, and when he blinked them clear again, gasping, all sign of the demon was gone. Padrik stood triumphantly before the altar, alone.

Was he the only one to notice that there was no sign *literally* of the demon — not even a blackened spot where the "bolt of lightning" just hit?

Silence for a moment, then a single voice rang out over the crowd, as a single, discordant chord of jarring music rang through his head.

"Get the witch!"

Before Kestrel could blink, the crowd had turned to a mob, a raging, maddened mob. He tried to stay where he was, tried to cling to the statue, but the press of people surging towards the exit was too great, and his grip was torn loose as the mob carried him away. It was all he could do to stay on his feet and not be trampled!

Now he was afraid, really afraid; frightened that he would stumble and fall, frightened that the mob's anger *might* turn against him for no reason at all. The brief glances he took at the faces of those around him only frightened him more. There was no sense in those dilated eyes, no sanity in the twisted mouths that spouted shouts of hatred.

He could only hold to one thought. *If I try to leave now, they'll turn on me and tear me to shreds along with whatever they do to Orlina Woolwright.*

Orlina Woolwright's home was one of the many fine houses on the square facing the Cathedral; the mob did not have far to go for their victim.

Two burly men at the front of the crowd sprinted ahead and broke in the door just as the main body of people got there. The house could never hold them all; and only part of the mob surged inside; the rest waited, shouting, for the first group to find their prey. Jonny could only watch helplessly as one poor servant who tried to stop them was beaten half to death and left beside the splintered remains of the door. Other servants ran for their lives; some crawled away with the marks of more blows upon their faces and bodies.

Within moments, glass shattered as something was thrown out of a window — a beautiful silver candelabra. A woman snatched it out of the air, and screamed, *"Take the witch's wealth! Strip her as naked as she was born!"*

That was the signal for all-out looting. Windows shattered as goods came tumbling out of them. The mob surged forward and people snatched at anything that the righteous looters inside pitched out a window — lengths of fabric, paintings, furniture, clothing and jewelry — a fork, a glass paperweight, an ornamental letter-opener —

People snatched their prizes and ran, and no one did anything to stop them. The City Guard had vanished; there wasn't even a Cathedral Guard to be seen.

Jonny was quite certain that there was nothing left but the bare walls by the time Orlina appeared, herself bundled up like so much loot, bound and gagged and carried in the ungentle hands of the two men who had first broken down her door. And now the mob parted to let them through, then surged along behind them as they carried her off to Padrik. Strangely, they had not stripped her literally; that seemed odd in the light of their lack of restraint so far — she remained clothed in her fine gown of mulberry-colored wool; not even the badge of Master on its chain around her neck had been taken from her.

Once again, the mob surged forward; somehow, this time, Jonny managed to get to the edge near the front. If he got a chance to bolt for the wagon, he was going to take it!

The High Bishop met them at the foot of the staircase in front of the Cathedral doors, his face the very essence of a grieving saint. The two men tumbled the woman at his feet and forced her to kneel before him. Jonny could not see her face, but her back told him that if she had one hand free and so much as a letter-opener in it, Padrik would have been eviscerated before anyone could blink.

"You are a witch, Orlina Woolwright," Padrik thundered, as the mob quieted. "You are a dark mage, and a foul demon-lover. Your own acts condemn you, as should I. And yet" — his face softened, and his tone took on new sweetness — "and yet I cannot do other than forgive you."

Gasps came from everywhere, and one woman began to weep. Jonny had been nauseated before, but now his gorge rose, and he fought down a wave of sickness.

"Yes, I can forgive you, for you are only a woman, and by your very nature you are weak and need to be led in the proper path," Padrik continued, magnanimously. "And I, as man and as your spiritual leader, failed to give you that guidance. I shall remedy that lack now."

He took a pendant from around his neck, a peculiar piece of jewelry that Kestrel did *not* remember him wearing before. It was made of iron, black wrought-iron, in a lacy filigree design in the form of a double circle or an orb. That was all Kestrel could see of it — but something about it made his stomach twist, and he suddenly did *not* want to look any closer.

Padrik put the pendant around Orlina's neck, removing the chain that held her Master's badge — and that rigid, unyielding back went limp; she sagged forward in her bonds, bowing her head before him.

Padrik's smug smile of triumph made the hair on the back of Jonny's neck rise, and he forced back a snarl. "Here then, is your only sentence. You must make a pilgrimage, alone and unaided, on your own two feet, without benefit of carriage or beast. You must go to Carthell Abbey, place this token of your obedience on the altar with your own two hands. Only then can you return, and resume the proper duties of a true woman and a daughter of the Church."

He expected the woman to fight — or at least to defy the High Bishop. So Orlina's submissive nod made Kestrel's mouth fall open with surprise.

The mob, however, was not going to give her any opportunity to display that submission on her own.

The same two men hauled her to her feet and half-dragged, half-carried her along the street of the inns to the city gates. Once again, Jonny was forced by the press of bodies to go along, and so it was that he saw the end of the incident.

Once the mob reached the city gates, the two men who had carried her all this way cut her bonds and set her free, shoving her out of the gates and onto the road leading downward.

She stood up, shook off the bits of rope, and brushed her hands absentmindedly across her hair. And without so much as a glance behind her, as if she was setting off on a stroll across the street, she strode down the road that led eventually to Carthell Abbey.

Robin's stance, not in the least submissive, gave her away, even though she wore the same drab clothing as every other woman in the square. When Jonny saw that familiar figure waiting for him beside the wagon, he was torn between giddy relief and wanting to strangle her with his bare hands.

Relief won easily. He shoved his way through the crowd towards her. At the very last moment, though, he remembered that Robin was "supposed" to have been a little ill, not missing, and kept himself from running towards her and flinging his arms around her as if she had been gone since last night.

That did not, however, stop *her* from doing the same.

"I'm sorry, I'm sorry, you were right, I shouldn't have —" she babbled — and before she could say anything that might betray them to listeners, he stopped her the only way he could think of. With a kiss, and a hug that squeezed the breath out of her.

"Inside," he whispered into her ear, quickly. "Preachers."

She started, and took a quick glance around, her eyes widening at the sight of all the street preachers around. She nodded, and followed him inside the wagon.

She waited until he closed the door before finishing her sentence. "I'm so sorry" — she babbled, as they threw their arms around each other and hung on as if they would never let go again — "I'll never be that stupid again, I was an idiot, you were right —"

"But n-not r-right to act as if I c-could order y-you about," he interrupted, caressing her hair in the soft semidarkness. "Y-you w-were r-right, t-too. I'm s-s-sorry."

"Not half as much as I am," she replied, ruefully, calming down and chuckling a little. "I was a little *too* convincing. They thought I was a real Patsono, all right — and they put me up in the dormitory for their unattached women! I couldn't get out all night, and in the morning I had a self-appointed guide that glued herself to my elbow right up until that mob broke loose to go after that poor Woolwright woman!"

He shuddered; he couldn't help himself. He could all too easily imagine the same thing happening to himself, or any of the Free Bards. "I s-s-saw it all," he said, locking both his arms around her to stop her sudden shivering. "Th-the d-demon and everything. S-s-someone w-was using m-magic in th-there, of c-course. How d-did you g-get away?"

She put her head against his shoulder, until her shaking died down. "The girl who was watching me couldn't resist a chance at the loot, and she left me as soon as those brutes broke down the door," Robin told him, after a moment. She put her head back a little, so that she could see his face. "I didn't get any good looks at the demon-show —"

He smiled, wanly. "W-well, I d-did," he said, and proceeded to describe everything he had seen and heard, in as much detail as he could remember. She shook her head in disbelief several times, and her lips and chin tightened in anger long before he was done with his narrative.

She hugged him hard, then pushed him away gently when he had finished. "That's it," she said firmly.

"That's all of this I can take. I don't know about you, but I've seen everything I need to; I can tell the Gypsy Chiefs who is betraying our secrets, we can warn the Free Bards, the nonhumans, and the Gypsies about what is starting here. Now I want *out* of here, before they do something like that to one of us!"

Kestrel nodded. "There's n-nothing back in our r-room at the inn th-that c-can't b-be replaced," he told her. "W-we k-kept everything important in th-the w-wagon. How ab-bout right n-now?"

Her face lit with a smile of relief. "That's the best idea I've heard in a long time!" she exclaimed. But then her face fell.

"What about Orlina Woolwright?" she said, hesitantly. "She's innocent — and we know that, and we didn't do anything to stop them —"

Jonny paused for a moment, hand reaching for the door, then turned. "W-we g-go after her," he replied. And wondered if Robin was going to argue with him. "W-we c-can take her t-to one of the J-Justiciars. Wren kn-knows one —"

He expected Robin to object, but she nodded with enthusiasm — a change in her that made *his* spirits rise. "I know her too!" she exclaimed. "And I doubt she'll have forgotten me! That is the perfect solution — surely what Padrik is doing can't be legal, even by Church standards. And — well, the Justiciar we both know is impartial enough that she has made judgments against Priests before this."

"All r-right, then," Kestrel agreed, opening the door. "Th-then let's g-get out of h-here b-before s-something else happens!"

CHAPTER FIFTEEN

Getting out was easier said than done.

Robin noticed that the square was filling up with people as they readied the horses and headed for the street of the inns; and that was odd, because at this hour, things were usually winding down and people were going home. But the moment they maneuvered the wagon out of the Cathedral market square and onto the street itself, it seemed that everyone in the city was determined to go *towards* the Cathedral while they struggled to move *away*. One or two folk struggled against the growing flow-tide of Gradford citizens, but most were trying to get to the very place she and Kestrel wanted to leave.

A pity that they weren't real merchants; they'd have sold everything they owned with a crowd this big!

I'd be doing my best to stay out of the street in this part of town, if I lived here, Robin thought grimly, a headache starting to form in both temples, *I'd lock my door and not open it until morning. It must be that they've heard about the demon and all the rest of it, and maybe they're trying to stream in to show their piety. Come to evening services and prove that you aren't a sorcerer! What a clever way to make certain no one ever decides to oppose your will! Surely every Councilor by now has seen the proverbial handwriting on the wall. Get in Padrik's way and he'll see that you wind up being accused of demon-summoning!*

And there would be no proper court of law for those who were so accused. Padrik had just set a precedent; *he* was judge and jury for those he accused — and his mobs would see that punishment was dealt out with a heavy hand.

Their wagon was forced to the far side of the street and kept there by the press of bodies. A blind cripple would have been able to walk faster than the horses could, and every time there was an intersection, there was a City Constable there, stopping traffic to let another stream of people onto Inn Street.

In the end, it was full dark long before they reached the city gates, and they had actually been able to retrieve their belongings from the Singing Bird after all. Robin simply hopped out and shoved and elbowed her way through the crowd when they were two buildings away; by the time the wagon reached the opening to the courtyard, she had gathered everything up and was waiting for him. It had been easy, and she hadn't even needed to give a parting explanation to the innkeeper, for the Singing Bird was so full of people she couldn't even see him. Not that she thought he'd be the loser in this; he was going to have the money they'd paid in advance for their next week. She was glad of that; it made leaving a little less distasteful. In fact, the only thing she regretted was leaving Ardana without entertainers, with no notice whatsoever. But if Ardana had heard what had happened tonight — well, she would probably understand.

She might even be thinking about a swift relocation herself right about now. What was the cost and difficulty of packing up and leaving, when compared to waking up to find yourself accused and convicted of dark sorcery?

Robin tossed the bags of their personal things up beside Kestrel and climbed onto the driver's bench, pushing open the doorway over the bed and shoving the bags in there quickly.

A good thing I went back, too, she reflected, as they inched along, both of them trying very hard to look relaxed and completely unconcerned about the press of traffic. *If Padrik or someone in his train is working magic, and he gets an inkling that we were something other than what we appeared to be, any mage can use our belongings to find us. Or to send things after us! I don't want to have to test Bardic Magic against that!*

She took mental stock of what provisions were still in the wagon; not a lot, unfortunately. They hadn't been planning on running. And she had no notion what they were going to do when they finally got out of Gradford; camp at the bottom of the hill and hope that the area was safe, probably.

Poor planning. Next time they did this, they'd have to make certain they were *ready* in case they had to make a run for it.

Next time! she thought, suppressing an hysterical giggle. *If there's a next time like this, I'm becoming a washerwoman!*

They reached the gates just before they were about to close for the night. There was no one else waiting to get out, and a thin stream of people coming in at the last minute. The Guards there looked at them a bit askance; usually people wanted to get into a walled city before the gates closed, not out of the place. But now that they were leaving, Robin didn't particularly care what they thought; she didn't bother to offer any excuses or make up any explanatory story. If luck was with her, she'd never have to visit Gradford again in her life!

Well, luck was with them enough that there was a high, full moon tonight. The switchback road down to the bottom of the hill stretched out before them, clear and pale gray in the bright moonlight. The horses were able to make their way down the road to the bottom of the hill with very little difficulty, and only a stumble or two over a rock or a hole.

Once at the bottom, though, it was clear that it would not be possible to go any further tonight. The valleys were deep in shadow, and anything could be hiding there. The horses could easily break legs over unseen obstructions. So they made camp; not a very satisfactory camp, as Robin had foreseen.

The provisions still in the wagon left a lot to be desired. The horses had grain and water, but not as much of the former as they wanted. There wasn't much to eat for the humans, either, no lamp oil, and only enough charcoal for the stove to warm the wagon and cook a scanty meal, not enough to keep the wagon warm all night. So Robin made unleavened griddle-cakes, two each, and generously loaded them with honey. Not enough to do more than tantalize. Then they went to bed still hungry, with only the blankets and each other to keep them warm through the night. That wasn't as bad as it could have been, though; they both had belated apologies to make to each other and a quarrel to mend. It was an argument that had proven to bring misery to both of them — but the reconciliation made up for the horrible night before.

Roosters high in the hills woke them at false-dawn, stiff with cold and muscles aching. There was nothing to eat, and only work to warm them. But they set off again as soon as the sun rose, with Jonny catching up on his missed sleep, and Gwyna driving, knowing they would easily reach the wayside inn by noon. The horses knew this road, now, and they remembered there was an inn on it, which meant a real stable, hay, and grain; they made very good time with no need for urging on Robin's part, setting off at a brisk walk when she gave them the signal.

Robin kept her eyes sharp for foot travelers. She expected at any moment to see Orlina Woolwright, limping along the side of the road. The woman was wealthy and not used to walking, after all; she was afoot, and they were in a wagon. Granted, the advantage of the wagon was somewhat negated by the fact that they were in hill country, and a man walking could make roughly the same time as any beast pulling a vehicle; only a person riding would outpace either. But as the hours passed, and Orlina did not appear, Robin began to wonder just what had happened to the woman. The only foot travelers she saw were a couple of shepherds and a farmer or two.

"Where can she *be*?" she wondered aloud, as the inn appeared on a hilltop in the distance, and there was still no sign of Orlina's mulberry-colored dress. Surely the woman hadn't just dropped out of sight! Robin hadn't heard of any robbers on this road; the local Sire kept it as well-patrolled as it was tended. And if she had fallen over from exhaustion, she should still be on the grassy verge. . . .

But Jonny didn't answer her; he was still asleep. She swallowed, and glanced back at the closed door behind her, feeling rather guilty. His red-rimmed eyes had told her more than he himself had about how *he* had spent the previous night. Well, she hadn't exactly enjoyed herself, but she had known where he was, and that he was safe enough in their room in the inn. He'd had no idea where she was, or what had happened to her — and likely, if they both hadn't been mistrustful of anything that passed for an authority in Gradford, he'd have had her name and description up with the Constables before sunrise.

That bewildered her a little, and touched her a

great deal — and made her feel horribly guilty for making him so miserable. She wasn't used to having someone *worry* over where she was and where she had gone. Or at least, not since she was old enough to leave the family wagon and go out on her own. And to have someone worry himself sleepless over her . . .

But if it had been the other way around — hmm. I think I'd have done the same. If I hadn't known he would stay where he was, I still might have fretted myself into a lather —

She shook her head and gave up on it. She had promised she would never be that stupid again, and she meant to keep that promise. Too much going on, and not enough time to think about it all, that was the problem. Too many things happening too fast, and they had completely neglected to make plans together. Next time they'd do better. Weren't they partners? That was one meaning of *vanderei;* "partners on the road." Partners didn't leave one another in the dark. *He* never forgot that; it was time she started remembering.

And where on earth was that Woolwright woman? Surely no wealthy rootfoot could have *walked* this far — surely she wouldn't have walked all night!

But that assumed she was walking of her own will. She might not be; hadn't Jonny said something about how the woman had looked after Padrik put that curious "token" around her neck? Yes, he had; he'd been adamant about it.

Spell-struck, that was what he said. As if something had just thrown a spell over her, and had taken over her body, mind, and will.

If Padrik really didn't *care* if she returned or not, casting a spell on her mind to make her keep walking until she reached Carthell Abbey would be no great problem. What would it matter if she walked herself into exhaustion and collapse? What would it matter to him if she walked over a cliff? Why should he care? Any misfortune that befell her would clearly be the will of God.

So the least he had done, probably, was to make certain she *would* walk straight to the Abbey with no pause for rest. For a moment, Robin felt guilty again — they hadn't done anything to stop Padrik, and they could probably have used Bardic Magic to cancel the spell on that token. Had they stood by and con-demned an old woman to death-by-exhaustion?

Maybe not; when she made that speech, she didn't look very frail to me. She's a Master in the Weaver's Guild; that's a lot of hauling, walking, lifting . . . even for a Master with a shop full of apprentices. She could be more fit than I had thought.

She could, in fact, have the reserves to walk a full day and a night without collapsing. And if that was the case — she would be a full day ahead of them by now!

Robin sighed with resignation, her guilt lost in a moment of self-pity. Last night had not been very comfortable, and she had been hoping to intercept the woman and enjoy a good rest at the inn. But this meant no warm bed in the inn tonight, and no supper cooked by someone else. Only a brief stop to properly re-provision the wagon —

At inn prices. She winced. While she was hardly parsimonious, a Gypsy was never happy without a bar-gain. There were few bargains to be had at inns as remote as this one.

So. It had to be done. Once they had restocked, they could go on, and hope to catch Orlina before she actually reached the Abbey.

And try to figure out what sort of spell they have on her, and how to break it, she realized, as the horses mounted the final hill and quickened their pace, with the inn in clear sight. *They* knew what was up there! *Otherwise, if we don't break it, she's going to keep right on walking to the Abbey, no matter what we do.*

The innkeeper was very happy to see them again; as she pulled the horses into the dusty yard in front of the door, he came out himself, beaming a cheerful greeting in the thin winter sunlight. "Well, my travelers!" he called out. "You return! And did you prosper in Gradford?"

"Ai," Robin said, sadly, and made a long face, as she halted the horses. "Everywhere one turns, there are hard times, and everyone is a thief. How can any honest craftsman prosper in times like these?"

"How, indeed." The innkeeper wiped his hands on his apron, and made a mock-sober face himself. "The times are hard. But you have come to stay, surely —"

His face truly fell when she shook her head; with custom already thin along here, the coming of winter must be hitting him hard. "No," she replied regretfully, "but we will have to reprovision here. We will need everything; horse-feed, oil, charcoal, food — we are down to nothing but a handful of meal and a few cups of oats. And I don't suppose your cook has any of those little meat pies that keep so well — ?"

His expression regained its former look of cheer. "Why, he made a batch this very morning! And for you, of course, my prices on provisions will be so tiny, I shall make no profit at all!"

"I'm sure," she told him dryly, then settled down for a serious bargaining session.

Jonny slept all through the stop; he didn't even wake up when she entered the wagon to store everything she had bought, nor when the innkeeper's workhands clambered atop the wagon to store waterproofed sacks of charcoal up on the roof.

The horses might not have gotten their warm stable, but she did see that they each got a good feed of grain, and bought more to store under the wagon. Their profits for their God-Stars paid for all of it; would, in fact, have paid for it all three times over. But she wept and wailed and claimed that the innkeeper was cheating her; he blustered and moaned, and swore she was robbing him, and in the end, they both smiled and shook hands, satisfied.

He had been able to unload some stocks that he clearly wasn't going to need this winter, and she was at least as satisfied as she was ever likely to get, buying provisions at an inn set out in the middle of nowhere.

The innkeeper hadn't seen anyone even remotely resembling the description of Orlina Woolwright, neither walking nor riding. None of his stablehands and servants had, either, and Robin wondered then if they had gone off chasing a phantom. Still, she reminded herself that their main reason for leaving hadn't been to run off to her rescue — it had been to escape while *they* still could! If they couldn't find her, they couldn't help her, and there was no getting around it.

But as Robin set the horses on the road again, reins in one hand, meat-pie in the other, that rationalization felt rather flat.

The woman isn't a Gypsy or a Free Bard, she told her uneasy conscience. *We don't owe her anything. We're doing our best for her, but how can we do anything until and unless we find her? We can't; and that's it.*

Except that both she and Jonny *knew* Padrik's demon was a fraud, his accusations completely groundless. They'd had the proof at the time, and they hadn't done anything to stop him. Robin had been in an even better position to do so than Jonny; she had, after all, been among the Patsonos. She could have done something to disrupt the illusion, or drugged the chief participants' wine, or —

Or something. I probably would have gotten caught, but I could have done something. She bit into the flaky crust of the pie, pensively, licking a bit of gravy from her fingers, as the horses plodded up the slope of yet another hill. The fleeting, fragile beauty these hills had held only a few short weeks ago was gone now; the trees were bare, gray skeletons in the thin sunlight; the grasses sere and brown. Only the evergreens provided a spot of color, and even their greens seemed washed-over with a thin film of gray dust. She wore her coat and a thick knitted sweater, woolen mittens, and a knitted hood, and still she was cold. She wondered how Harperus was faring, and T'fyrr. The winged Haspur hadn't seemed equipped to take the cold.

Then again, neither do hawks and falcons, and they do all right. Unless the hard weather came early, there wouldn't be any real snow yet for weeks, but by the time it came, the ground would be as unyielding as stone, and the ponds frozen over. She made soothing sounds at the horses, and longed for summer. Or at least, a good, weathertight room somewhere, with a big, cozy bed and a fireplace.

And hot meat-pies and wine. Or a great roast of beef, nicely rare, and fresh bread. Or a roast goose with stuffing, or better still, a duck, and yams. And while she was wishing, why not servants to wait upon her, and comfits and cream, and —

She shook her head at her own folly.

Uphill, and down; uphill and down. The horses plodded onward in resignation while the sun westered, and the trees cast ever-lengthening blue shadows across the road. The air grew perceptibly chillier.

Finally the little door behind her slid back, and Kestrel poked his tousled head out. He blinked at the light. "Are w-we th-there yet? Or c-close? How l-long d-did I s-sleep?" he asked, yawning.

"We've been there and gone. It's late afternoon," she told him. "I got supplies at the inn, but you were so tired you slept right through it all. We're on the road to Carthell Abbey, and I expect to get there about sunset at the rate the horses are going. There's no sign of Orlina Woolwright, though, and no one at the inn saw her."

Kestrel frowned. "Th-there might n-not b-be," he said, "if sh-she's b-bespelled, sh-she m-might n-not s-stop for anything. If sh-she p-passed the inn at n-night —"

"Of course!" Gwyna replied, disgusted with herself. "She would have passed the inn last night, about midnight, if she just kept walking."

"N-no reason n-not to," Jonny pointed out. "If sh-she's under a s-spell, she w-won't b-be able t-to s-stop, even if she f-feels t-tired, and l-last n-night was a f-full m-moon. Plenty of l-light t-to walk by. N-not likely she'd f-fall off the r-road."

He crawled out over the sill, and into the seat beside her. He'd fallen asleep coat and all, and looked rumpled head to toe.

"How l-long t-till s-sunset?" he asked.

She squinted at the sun. "Three hours," she said. "Roughly. Want a pie?"

She pulled a pie out of the sack under her seat; it was cold now, and not as tasty as it had been when it was warm, but the pies were still good even cold, and far, far better than the bannocks they'd eaten last night. And he must be ravenous.

Jonny took it with a nod of thanks, not *quite* snatching it, and devoured it in a few moments. She handed him another, and took one herself.

So, this time we make a plan first, and stick to it. A plan we can both agree on. "How are we going to approach the Abbey?" she wanted to know. "The last time they weren't very friendly to us, and I don't think that's going to change. But if that's where Padrik sent Orlina Woolwright, she'll probably be inside. Or at least they should know where she is."

"I've b-been th-thinking about th-that," Kestrel replied, around a mouthful of pie. "I have a p-p-plan. If y-you l-like it t-too, that is."

She grinned; they must have been thinking identical thoughts. "Just so it's better than one of *my* plans!" she teased. "Going in there in disguise as a Brother, for instance, is probably not a good idea. The last thing I need to do is have to rescue you from an Abbot who thinks you're one of his novices — or have him discover that I'm *not* a boy!"

"I'd th-thought of th-that," he admitted. "It w-would s-serve you r-right, after all, t-to b-be on the other s-side of th-the w-w-worry!"

She slapped his knee with the ends of her reins by way of an answer. "So what's the real plan?" she asked.

He finished the last of his pie, and licked his fingers. "Th-there *is* a d-disguise, b-but n-not a d-dangerous one —"

It seemed to take forever to reach their destination, though perhaps that was anxiety and not reality. Finally the road dove down into the valley that contained Carthell Abbey; it was just before sunset, and the sky above the western hills glowed flame-streaked and glorious. Too bad the valley did not match the view — bare trees on either side of the road stretched riblike limbs toward them; a clammy, spectral mist rose from stagnant pools of water as they passed through the Beguilers' swamp. It was very cold and damp here, and the deep shadows of the surrounding hills made it colder still. But at least by now the treekies and the Beguilers would have gone into hibernation for the winter.

Now just so that there aren't any gellens or varks in this valley as well, Robin thought. Kestrel must have felt the same way, urging the horses to a faster pace. *Be just our luck that there are nocturnal winter monsters here as well as the ones that hibernate.*

Kestrel had taken over the reins shortly after he awoke; he stopped the horses well out of sight of the Abbey, and Robin climbed down off of the passenger's seat. She was dressed in her warmest and drabbest, and she only hoped that Brother Pierce, the surly Gatekeeper, hadn't gotten a good look at her the last time they were here. Right now, she looked like a very respectable young woman straight out of Gradford, and that was what she wanted him to think she was.

A very respectable, very wealthy, and very assertive young woman. The kind Brother Pierce would *have* to answer, whether he liked it or not.

They unhitched one of the horses, and threw a blanket over it, hoping that in the semidarkness, it would look like a saddle. She trotted up the road to the Abbey afoot, leading the horse, for she did not know if it had ever been broken to ride, and now was not the time to find out! The brisk pace warmed her thoroughly, her breath puffing out in front of her in clouds of white. There was going to be a hard frost here tonight, and perhaps a light sprinkling of freezing rain . . . not ideal weather for camping. There wouldn't be a choice, however; not tonight. Far safer to camp than trust to the safety of any

shelter offered by the Church. Assuming they
would offer it.

Not bloody likely.

The Abbey loomed up around a bend in the road,
lanterns beckoning with a promise of warmth that she
already knew would not be kept. She hurried her pace
a little; the horse tugged on the rein in her hand, and
whickered. Poor thing; it thought she was taking it to a
stable. If there *were* varks out here, she wanted to get
back to the wagon as fast as she could!

She stopped, a few paces away from the door, to
compose herself. The horse pawed the ground with
impatience. When she had caught her breath, she
rang the bell with an imperious hand, hoping to sound
like the sort of person who was not used to being kept
waiting.

When Brother Pierce did make his appearance, he
gave no sign of recognizing her as anything other than
a female, and thus, a major intrusion into his life. He
frowned at her, his face taking on all the look of someone who had bitten into an unripe plum.

"What do *you* want?" he asked, rudely. "Be off! We
don't house vagabonds —"

"I'm no vagabond, you insolent knave!" Robin said,
with shrill indignation. "If this were Gradford, I'd have
my servants horsewhip you to teach you manners!"
She had heard enough of the wealthy women of Gradford and the way they spoke to underlings who
offended them to enable her to produce a pretty fair
imitation of their mannerisms. She drew herself up
tall and proud, as he gaped at her, clearly taken aback
by her rude response. "I am Rowen Woolwright, sister
to Master Orlina Woolwright of Gradford, and I
demand to know what you have done with my sister!
That cur of a High Bishop sent her here on some fool's
errand and —"

Brother Pierce's wizened face flushed as she began her harangue, but a sly smile crept over his features when he heard who it was Robin claimed to be. He made an abrupt gesture, startling the horse, and cutting off her torrent of words.

"Shut your mouth, woman, before it condemns you to a fate like hers!" he snapped, interrupting her. Now it was her turn to stare at him in simulated surprise that he should even *dare* to interrupt her. "We'll have no truck with the agents of darkness here, nor heretics, either! She's not here, the sorcerous bawd! She conjured a demon and sent it to destroy the Holy High Bishop, but he was stronger than her dark magic, and the Hand of the Sacrificed God protected him. He defeated the demon, as a hundred witnesses can attest, and the demon itself betrayed its mistress."

Robin hoped that she looked appropriately stunned. Evidently she did, for Brother Pierce smiled nastily.

"High Bishop Padrik had every right to condemn her, but he forgave her and sent her on a pilgrimage of penance to this Abbey," he said, his voice full of glee. "She's been sent to a holy shrine in the hills by our Abbot, as is his right and duty. She was unrepentant when she came, and he has sent her on to be judged. The Sacrificed God himself will be her judge once she reaches the holy shrine of the hills; if she returns from the shrine, well and good, she will be restored to her former position by the High Bishop himself."

"And if she doesn't?" Robin asked, sharply, "What then? How will you protect her —"

He smiled, displaying large, yellowing, crooked teeth. "God will protect her, if she is innocent. If she doesn't return, well, then she is clearly a witch, guilty of the charge the blessed High Bishop laid upon her, and the God has sent her where she belongs. Her property will be confiscated, since all witches are traitors, and it will be turned over to the Cathedral and Carthell Abbey."

She did not have to feign the shock she felt. No wonder Padrik was a wealthy man, able to give an entire clan of Gypsies silver and even gold! If he was getting monies this way, as well as from the gifts of the faithful —

"The shrine —" she said, gasping out the words. "Where is this shrine?"

Brother Pierce grinned again, overjoyed to see her so discomfited, and obliged with a description.

"Ye follow this road *here* —" he said, pointing to the Old Road that led on to Westhaven. "Not the newer route, but this 'un. Ye take it into the hills, till ye come to a bare-topped hill. If ye get to a village called Westhaven, ye've gone too far. On top of the hill, that's the shrine. But I wouldn't go there —" he added, as she turned to go.

"Why not?" she asked, belligerently.

He laughed, the first time she had heard him do so. It sounded like an old goose, honking. "Because, woman, if you go there, ye'll be judged too! And be sure, if you don't return to your home and the duties of a proper woman, it'll be because demons have taken you like your sister!"

She turned away from him as he slammed the gate shut, feeling chilled, and not by the wind. The Old Road — a bare-topped hill? Between here and Westhaven? There was only one place he could possibly mean.

Skull Hill.

She ran back to the wagon as fast as her legs would carry her, the horse running alongside, but looking back over its shoulder with longing; there was a painful stitch in her side before she got there. "They sent her to Skull Hill," she said, panting, as she harnessed the horse up again, and flung herself into her seat. "I don't think she's very far ahead, not if they wanted to time her arrival for midnight —"

"R-right." Kestrel didn't waste any words; he simply slapped the reins against the horses' backs to get them moving again.

It was terrible. They wanted to gallop the horses and knew they didn't dare. It only took a single hole in the road to send both horses down — and at a gallop, that would mean broken legs and dead horses for certain, and if the wagon overturned as well, *they* could wind up dead.

It took a few moments for the pain in her side to leave; she breathed the cold air in carefully, holding her side, and waited, before the pain eased enough that she could speak again. "Now we know what the Ghost meant," she pointed out. "About people being sent from here."

"Y-yes," Jonny replied, urging the horses to a faster pace than a walk, until they were moving as fast as even Gwyna considered safe. "P-put one of th-those p-pendants on an enemy, it m-makes them c-come here. And it identifies th-them t-to th-the Ghost."

"He'll kill her, of course," Robin replied off-handedly. "He won't even hesitate. He told us that himself."

But Jonny only turned and flashed her a feral grin, teeth gleaming whitely in the moonlight.

"N-not if w-we f-find her f-first!" he said. Robin returned his grin, but uncertainly, then peered through the darkness ahead of them. She was hoping to spot Orlina Woolwright quickly, for at this pace, they could defeat their own purpose by accidentally running her down.

Through the valley of Carthell Abbey they raced, and out the other side into the hills; Robin could hardly believe that a woman on foot had come so far, so quickly. It seemed impossible — but the road was wet and muddy here, and they kept coming across the tracks of a human, pressed into the mud and visible even at a distance. They both knew how seldom anyone used this road, so who else could it be?

They were deep in the hills again before Robin realized it. And now she had the answer to another question — why tend this road so well if no one used it?

To make it as easy as possible for your victims to reach the place of ambush, she thought grimly. *It isn't the Sire who tends this road; it's the Abbey, I'd bet the Ghost's silver on it.*

But they were very, very near Skull Hill now; one more hill, and Orlina would be within the Ghost's grasp.

"There she is!" Kestrel exclaimed, his stutter gone in the tension and excitement. He slapped the reins over the startled horses' backs; they jerked into a canter, and she finally saw what he had seen. A fast-moving shadow ahead of them, a shadow that fluttered near the ground, with a flurry of skirts. It was Orlina, indeed, and she paid no attention whatsoever to the horses bearing down on her. Kestrel cracked the whip, startling the horses into a dangerous gallop; the wagon lurched as the horses bolted.

A few yards more, and it would be too late!

Heedless of her own danger, Robin launched herself from the seat of the wagon as Kestrel pulled the horses to a halt; the wagon slewed sideways with a rasping screech of twisting wood and grinding stone, blocking Orlina's way. Robin flew through the air and tackled the woman, knocking her to the ground. The song of the pendant rasped like an angry wasp in her mind as soon as she touched

Orlina's flesh. They tumbled together into the underbrush; the thick and springy bushes alone saved them from broken limbs. Together they tumbled back into the road, and Robin yelped with pain as her shins and elbows hit rock.

She didn't even think, she simply grabbed the pendant, and jerked, breaking the chain, before the woman could get to her feet again. If Orlina ran, they might not be able to catch her before the Ghost took her.

The song in Robin's head whined — then faded. Orlina Woolwright sat up slowly, blinking, as if she had been suddenly awakened from a deep sleep. Moonlight poured down upon her as she frowned, looked quickly and alertly about her, and focused on Robin, who was sprawled in the dirt of the road beside her.

"What am I doing here?" she demanded, in a strong, deep voice. "What has been happening?"

Jonny came around the front of the wagon, first pausing long enough to soothe the bewildered mares. He reached down his hand, with a courteous grace Robin had seldom seen in him — except when he had been in his uncle's Palace. In one heartbeat, he had gone from the vagabond, to the Prince in disguise.

A useful ability. Orlina Woolwright recognized that grace for what it was, and took his hand. He helped her to rise; she accepted that aid, and when she next spoke, her voice was softer, less demanding.

"I last remember being hauled before that dog of a High Bishop," she said, her words clipped and precise. "What happened?"

"It's a l-long s-story, my l-lady," Jonny said, carefully. He helped Robin up; she moved carefully, but although she felt bruised all over, and had her share of scratches, there was nothing seriously damaged. Jonny gave her a quick hug, then led Orlina over to the back of the wagon, and opened the door for her. She got in as gravely as if it had been a fine carriage. "W-we'll t-tell you all, if y-you have the t-time."

As he lit the lantern inside and Robin climbed up the rear steps, she saw Orlina Woolwright smile as she took a seat upon their bed. It was not a condescending smile, and she took her place in their wagon as if they were both royal and she was honored to be there.

"High Bishop Padrik has left me little but time, young sir," she replied. "And I think he tried to take that, too." She gestured for the two of them to join her. "I would be very pleased if you would tell me the whole of it."

CHAPTER SIXTEEN

Robin was glad they had reprovisioned; with the stove going, the wagon seemed a cozy island of safety in all the darkness. She made hot tea for all of them, served up the last of the meat-pies, and tended to her own scratches and bruises — or at least the ones that she could get to without disrobing. Orlina did not seem to notice hers; perhaps some of the numbness of the spell that had been on her still lingered — or perhaps she was tougher than even Robin had thought. She was certainly younger than Robin had assumed, given her rank — in early middle age at most. It was the lady's leanness that had fooled her into thinking Orlina was older; there was not even a single strand of gray in her hair, and the muscles beneath the dress had been as strong as an acrobat's. But she ate like one who had been starving for a day, and drank so much tea Robin had to make a second pot. The tale was a long time in the telling, and it was well past moonrise before they finished it. They had a great deal of explaining to do; the lady believed them, but Robin had the feeling that if she had not found herself on a road in the middle of nowhere, with no memory of how she got there, she would not have.

She examined the pendant with interest, but did not touch it. "A nasty thing, that," she said, then looked thoughtful. "Guild lore has it that silk will insulate magic —"

"Gypsy lore too," Robin told her. "I'd like to wrap it up, but we don't have any."

"Allow me," Orlina said, and pulled a silk handkerchief out of her sleeve like a magician. Robin accepted it with gratitude, and quickly shrouded the pendant in its folds. At last the annoying mental whine of the pendant's "music" stopped.

Only one thing Orlina had no trouble believing; that the High Bishop had such a convenient way for disposing of those who caused him trouble.

"I've long suspected something of the sort," Orlina said grimly; there were dark circles under her eyes, and a bruise on one prominent cheekbone but she showed no other outward signs of weariness or damage. Except, of course, for her dress, which was as muddy and brush-torn as Robin's, and her disheveled hair. "He rose to power in the Church with amazing speed, and those who opposed him or were simply in his way found reasons to take themselves away from Gradford." Her lips compressed to a thin, angry line.

"Straight to the Skull Hill Ghost, I would guess," Robin replied. "But the immediate question is, what of you? Have you anywhere you can go?"

"Th-the Abbey isn't s-safe," Kestrel told her, quickly. "Th-the Abbot's in th-this."

"He's probably waiting for a messenger from Gradford to tell him what his share of the loot will be," Gwyna added. "If you go back there, he'll just find another way to be rid of you, and blame it on the Beguilers or the treekies."

Orlina looked down at her hands. "Other than my office of Master Weaver, I have nothing," she said softly; but she did not sound vulnerable, she sounded detached. "Padrik took it all from me, with a few moments of lies and some shoddy magic tricks." She looked up again, and there was fire in her eyes. "I should go back there and confront the dog! I —"

"Do that, and another mob will get you," Robin said firmly. "You haven't a chance against him."

"And you do, I suppose." She lifted one ironic eyebrow.

Kestrel shrugged. "S-some c-contacts. P-people wh-who w-will b-be interested in hearing th-the t-truth."

Orlina looked as if she was about to give them an argument, then looked down at her hands again. They were shaking with the fear she would not show, and this outward sign of her weakness must have convinced her, for she abruptly collapsed in on herself. "I have nowhere to go," she said, a new hesitancy in her voice. "A few relatives that I haven't seen in years, decades —"

"Then go to them," Robin urged. "Petition the King for justice from a position of safety."

"Or m-move t-to another K-Kingdom," Kestrel added, flatly. "If w-we c-can't d-do s-something about the s-situation in G-Gradford s-soon, th-that's wh-what w-we're d-doing. It w-won't b-be safe here for anybody."

Well, that was news to Robin, but it was news she agreed with. *He who flees, lives. Better a live fox than a dead lion.*

"You're still a Master of the Weavers, lady," Robin continued, as another idea occurred to her. "He didn't take *that* away from you, because he can't. Your Guild isn't one of the ones supporting him in Gradford; it should give you shelter that you're entitled to. You *earned* it, by your own work."

Some of her color returned; some of her pride as well. "That's true, young lady," she said after a moment, the fire returning to her hazel eyes. "And the

Guild does take care of its own." She sat in thought for
a moment. "I think I have enough gold and jewelry on
my person to purchase transportation to the nearest
Guild Hall." She smiled slyly. "And what that fool
doesn't know is that the Master's *pendant* does not
identify the Master, at least in our Guild. The ring
does, made for the Master's hand."

She held out one of her trembling hands to display
a ring, gold, with an inlaid carbuncle featuring the
Weaver's shuttle. "Anyone who sees this will know me,
and the Guild will protect me."

"Good, we can do that," Robin affirmed, as Jonny
nodded.

"I'll t-turn the h-horses," he added. "W-we've a
l-long r-road ahead of us."

Fortunately, the lady didn't ask him to elaborate.

They left her at the door of a shepherd's home —
one which providentially housed a member of her
own Guild, as designated by the shuttle burned into
the wood of the door. The family welcomed her with
sleepy enthusiasm and some hearty curses for anyone
who would dare damage a Guild Master.

They left the entire group listening to Orlina's tale,
after first making certain that these people had no
great love for the Abbot of Carthell Abbey.

"Greedy and grasping, I call it," the weaver said
with a snort. "A bargain's one thing, but he cheats with
short measures. Got so we make special trips up the
road to trade, rather than trade with *him*. And that
Padrik was no better when he was at Carthell Abbey."

They offered a good place to camp, and Jonny
headed back in the direction they indicated.

"Are you thinking what I think you're thinking?"
she asked, after the silence became unbearable.

"S-something h-has t-to be d-done," he said, flatly.

"I'll bet th-there's s-something at the Abbey th-that'll t-tell us h-how t-to g-get rid of th-the Gh-ghost."

"Are you planning on breaking into the Abbey?" she asked softly.

He gave her a sideways look. "G-got a b-better idea?"

"Not at the moment." They drove on in silence for a while longer, the horses' weary hoofbeats clopping dully along the dusty road. "The worst that can happen is we can pretend to be looking for holy books. That we've been overcome with a terrible case of religion."

His sudden bark of laughter released the tension in both of them.

"Tomorrow night," she replied. "Not tomorrow during the day. We're both tired, and so are the horses. We can sleep as much as we need to, get rested, and get into the Abbey tomorrow night." She tilted her head toward him, coaxingly. "Hmm?"

For answer, he turned the horses off the road as soon as they reached the camping spot that the weavers had offered; just beyond a small bridge over a stream. The mares were more than glad to stop, and so was Robin.

"N-not afraid of t-treekies?" he teased, as she jumped down to unharness them and get them hobbled for the night.

"Not treekies, nor Beguilers, nor varks," she replied, her hands full of leather straps. "But I *am* afraid of your food, and it's your turn to fix dinner."

"S-so it is." He laughed, and went around to open up the back of the wagon. Presently she smelled lamp oil and bacon. By the time she finished with the horses and came around to the door, he'd warmed the wagon completely, and had hot tea, with sausages wrapped in bacon slices waiting for her.

And something else as well; which left her too

weary to ask him anything more about his new plan before she drifted off to sleep.

Jonny had moved the wagon to a point just outside Church lands, and hidden it in a thicket off the road. They were still within easy walking distance of the Abbey — and more importantly, from here they could hear the bells as they rang for the various Holy Services of the day.

"It isn't m-much of a p-plan," Jonny told her the next day, as they waited, rested and fed, for the sun to sink. "B-but I used t-to b-break into Ch-Church b-buildings all the t-time when I w-was on my own. Only p-places they g-guard are th-the T-Treasury and th-the k-kitchen. I w-was l-looking f-for s-safe p-places to s-sleep. N-nobody g-guards the L-Library."

Robin took up the mass of her hair to braid it so that she could bind it around her head, out of the way. She gave him a puzzled look. "The treasury I understand," she replied, "but why the kitchen?"

"B-Brothers are always h-hungry," he told her. "N-novices are always *s-starving*."

They were both wearing dark breeches, close-fitting sweaters, and soft boots; all clothing they had gotten for Gradford, so all of it a drab charcoal gray. Gray was better than black for hiding in shadows, as Jonny well knew.

They waited after the sun set until the bell for Sixte, the last of the day's Holy Services rang; then they waited another hour or so for the Abbey to settle.

Just before they left, Jonny impulsively picked up the silk-wrapped pendant; he had the feeling it might be useful, although he wasn't certain how.

He recalled noting certain trees beside the Abbey, easy to climb, with boughs overhanging the wall; they were just as easy for the two of them to climb as he had thought. The Abbey itself was dark, with not even the single lantern at the gate alight. That was both inhospitable and unusual; but he reflected, as he inched along the bough he had chosen, that he already knew that Carthell Abbey was both. With luck, they could come and go and never leave a sign that they had been here.

They took their time; no point in hurrying and possibly giving themselves away with an unusual sound, or worse still, a fall. Kestrel straddled the bough he had chosen, lying on his stomach, and pulling himself along with both hands, while both legs remained wrapped around it. If he lost his grip, he would still be held by his legs. Gwyna was behind him; he hoped she had chosen a similarly safe way to cross. Excitement warmed him; now they were finally *doing* something. It felt good, after all this time of simply sitting back and watching things happen.

The bulwark of the wall lay below him — then behind him. If this had been summer, this would have been a bad place to come in, for the soft ground would have betrayed him by holding his footprints. But the ground was rock-hard, and any tracks he left in the frost would be gone with the first morning light.

Bits of bark caught in his sweater, and the bough sank towards the ground. Good! That meant less of a drop.

But now he would have to carefully gauge the strength of the tree-limb he was on. If he went too far, he was in danger of snapping it.

The limb creaked a little as it bent — then it came to rest on the top of the wall. Enough. It wasn't going to get any better than this.

He clung with his hands, and slowly lowered his legs until he was hanging from the limb; then let go, flexing his knees for the fall.

He landed on turned earth; a tumble of frozen clods that made footing uncertain and gave him a bad moment as his ankle started to twist. But he managed to save himself by flailing his arms for balance, and a moment later Gwyna landed beside him.

He tapped her on the shoulder; she followed him to the building, where they crouched in shadow for a moment, listening intently.

Nothing. All was silent.

There were some advantages, he reflected, to trying to break into a building in a place where there were treekies at night. No such place would ever have guard dogs or sentinel geese; the treekies would happily make a meal of them.

This was probably the kitchen garden; the rear door into the kitchen itself would be to his right. But he didn't want that door — for as he had told Gwyna, the kitchen might well have a guard on it. *He* wanted a side door, preferably one that led into a meditation garden.

He went to the left, with Robin following. He left one hand on the wall to guide him and tried to feel how the ground changed under his feet. Here in the kitchen-garden, it would be gravel between the plots and the building; once he reached the meditation gardens, the gravel should give way to grassy lawn.

From time to time his hand encountered the frame of a window; when that happened, he warned Robin, and crouched down below the level of the sill, crawling on hands and knees to get past it. All it would take would be one sleepless Brother staring out at the stars, and seeing a man-shaped shadow pass between him and them, and it would all be over.

Finally, his foot encountered grass; thick, well-tended grass, by the feel of it. In the summer it must be like a plush carpet. Very difficult to achieve and maintain that effect; now he knew what the poor novices here spent their disciplinary time doing.

Praying and weeding; praying the weeds don't come back. He smiled a little, but it was a smile without humor. What need had an Abbey for a lawn like that? He wondered if the surly Brother Pierce was permitted to walk in this garden; such a lawn would make a barefoot "penance" into a sensual pleasure.

Two more windows — then his hand encountered a frame that did not mark a window, but a doorway. Exactly the place he wanted!

The door was unlocked, and swung open at a touch, without the creaking that the kitchen door would likely have emitted. A tiny vigil-lamp burned beside it on the inside wall. He slipped inside, Robin followed, and they closed the door lest a draft give them away.

This doorway gave out on a short hall; they followed it to the end, where it intersected with a much larger hall. He thought for a moment, trying out the pattern of most Abbeys in his mind.

The Library was always next to the Scriptorium, where the manuscripts and books were copied. The Scriptorium needed very *good* light, which generally meant a southern exposure; the Library demanded much less, lest the manuscripts fade. He thought that the wall they had come in on faced south —

There were two doors to the left; none to the right. He went left, and opened the one to the room that had an outside wall.

The smell told him it was the Scriptorium; wet ink and paint drying.

So the room across the hallway should be the Library.

He tried the door; it was locked. He smiled to himself in great satisfaction. He knew from all his other clandestine forays that if the Library was locked, it would definitely not be not guarded or watched. Locked, because every Library had *some* "forbidden" work in it that the novices spent their entire novitiate trying to get at to read. But it would not be guarded, because, of course, novices would not dare to remove the treasured tome, lest they be caught with it in their possession.

But the locks of Libraries, as he had reason to know, were built to impress, not for efficiency.

Gwyna might be skilled at picking pockets, but he was a Master of Library Locks.

It was a matter of heartbeats with the help of a long, slender wire and a bit of wood. The lock fell open, and the door swung inward.

To his relief, there were more of those tiny vigil-lamps burning here; they would not have to work blind. As Gwyna closed the door behind him, softly, he studied the bookshelves, and suddenly realized with dismay that he had no idea where in all of this to start!

There were *hundreds* of books in here, not the mere two or three dozen he had expected! Book-shelves filled the room, reaching from floor to ceiling, and all of the shelves were full. If they were cataloged in any way, *he* didn't know what it was. The key to all this probably resided in the Librarian's head —

As he gazed at the wealth of books in an agony of despair, he shoved his hands down into the pockets of his breeches — and encountered a small, hard lump wrapped in silk.

The pendant!

In a heartbeat, Talaysen's lessons on the laws of magic flashed into his mind. *What once was one is always connected. Things that are related are connected. Things that are similar are connected —*

It was the second law that he needed to use now. Things that were related were connected, and under

the proper circumstances, they would attract or reso-
nate with each other. Since the pendant had
something to do with the Ghost, it followed that the
pendant could lead him to something else that related
to the Ghost.

He hoped.

As Gwyna watched him curiously, he took the pendant out of its silk wrapping, wincing a little at the
discordant "music," and held it in his hands, tuning his
mind to find more of the same "music."

There was music of various sorts all around him;
many, many of these volumes had something to do
with magic. Some of it was pleasant; some absolutely entrancing, the kind he could get lost inside
for hours.

But he didn't have hours, and he wasn't looking for
anything pleasant.

Then he heard it; a thin, evil trickle that could not
by any stretch of the imagination be called a melody. A
discordance of which the pendant was only a small
part.

He turned and followed it; it led him to a panel on
the back wall, to one side of one of the enormous
bookcases. It was a panel like many others in the
room, but when he tapped it slightly, he thought it
sounded hollow.

The only trouble was, he couldn't open it.

He tried everything he could think of; pressed anything that looked like it might be a release, and all to
no avail. Gwyna took her turn at it, but her skill was
not in this, and she was no more successful than he
was.

He was about to make another attempt, this time at
forcing the panel open, when he felt a presence
behind him.

He turned; Gwyna whirled at the same instant.

Brother Reymond stared at them in dumb shock, his mouth agape with surprise.

Robin didn't wait to see what he'd do; she muffled his mouth with both hands, as Kestrel grabbed his arms. Together they wrestled him around and stuffed him in a corner.

He looked at her; she looked back at him. "Now what?" she mouthed at him.

He shrugged. "We t-try to convince him," he whispered back, then looked into the frightened eyes of the Brother.

Robin only rolled her eyes skyward, and tightened her hold on Brother Reymond's mouth.

Afterwards, Jonny wasn't certain how long it took him to convince Reymond simply to stay quiet until he had heard them out. It felt like forever, and he was certain that Robin's arms were aching with strain by the time Reymond nodded a frightened agreement.

Things went a little faster, after that. She told him in detail about the Skull Hill Ghost, and the curious exception he had insisted on making to his promise. Then Kestrel told him about Padrik and his Healing Services.

Reymond's eyes grew larger and larger, the more they spoke, but his mouth betrayed, not fear, but dismay. When Robin related her little stay with the Patsonos, his brows drew together in anger — but when Kestrel finally told him about the demon-summoning, and the fate of Orlina Woolwright, he could hardly contain his agitation.

"Dear and gracious God!" he exclaimed in a hoarse whisper when they were done. "I never thought — I didn't want to think — but this explains all those visitors to the Abbot, the ones who seem to be in a trance, and who disappear, never to be seen again! They *all* wear pendants like that one" — he indicated the wrought-iron pendant in Kestrel's hand — "and that alone would convince me that you are telling the truth! But I have learned other things since you were last here. . . ."

"Like what?" Robin asked harshly, as his voice trailed off. He flushed with shame.

"About your Ghost," he said, unhappily. "I have found manuscripts that told me he was bound there by the first Abbot, some fifty years ago or so. I also learned that there are other manuscripts that would tell me more, much more, if only we could find them."

"What do you mean?" Robin asked, her face puzzled. "Are they lost? Were they taken away?"

He shook his head, growing more and more distracted with every word. "No, they were hidden, somewhere in this Library, but I cannot for the life of me find them, and I have been trying —"

Jonny cleared his throat, very delicately, and Brother Reymond started. "C-could they b-be b-behind this p-panel?" he asked, touching the offending bit of wood.

Brother Reymond looked at the panel curiously — then suddenly lost all his color. He reached out with trembling fingers, and did something complicated among the carvings.

The panel swung open. Behind it was a deep recess; in the recess was a bound manuscript.

They all reached for it at the same time, but Brother Reymond's reach was longer and he got it first. He removed it from the recess, hands shaking — but he did not hold it as if it was something precious, but as if it was something vile that he did not wish to contaminate them with.

He took it to a reading stand and lit the lamp from one of the vigil-lights. As the steady flame illuminated his face, he began to read, scanning the contents quickly.

"This is what I was looking for," he whispered. "This is the journal of the first Abbot of Carthell. He was a mage as well as Abbot, but he had been rejected as a Justiciar, and the rejection made him an angry and bitter man. He saw this appointment as an exile — I have read his first journals, and they are full of bile in the guise of piety."

He turned away; Robin moved belatedly to stop him, but he was only relocking the door. "Now we will not be disturbed," he said. "There may be some other restless souls abroad tonight."

He returned to the manuscript and scanned a little further. "Ah, here it is. *I have uncovered a new spell, one that will bind the spirit of a being to a particular place, and make it to do the will of the binder.* There, that's what we were looking for. *I must have a living being for this, for the spell will not work on the dead, not even the newly dead.* Dear and blessed God, he is contemplating murder here! *There are many travelers upon this road who are not human. I mean to use one of those. It would indeed be a grave and mortal sin to kill a human, but these monsters and monstrosities are beyond the Church pale and law, and therefore, it is no murder to do one to death.*"

Reymond was so white that Kestrel feared he might faint at any moment, but his voice was strong enough as he turned the pages.

"Here is the spell itself — no, I shall *not* read it, I had rather burn it! Here he selects his victim — *I have succeeded! My spell has worked beyond the wildest of my dreams! I drugged the creature's food, and carried him out to Bare Hill upon my own donkey; there I wrought the spell which slew and bound him all at once — and the spirit arose a hundred times more powerful and deadly than the monster had been alive!"*

Reymond's eyes flickered across the pages, as his voice filled with agony. "Here he tells how the Ghost he created killed at his command, destroying 'sinners' he sent to it for penance . . . here he tells how it also began to kill anyone who dared to cross its Hill after sundown. Look, here is the list of victims that the Abbot sent — and here the list of those who died 'accidentally'! One of them is the Priest of Westhaven who tried to banish the poor creature! And he says — oh, monstrous! Horrible, horrible —"

Now his voice broke, and he buried his face in his hands for a moment. Kestrel dared to place a hand on his shoulder, trying to offer some sort of wordless comfort. Reymond's shoulders shook, and when he removed his hands, his face was wet with tears.

But his voice was strong again. "This *fiend* wrote here, in his own hand, that he told the Priest only 'some things were better left to the hand of God,' and the Priest ignored his warning. His *warning*! That was no warning — that was not even an attempt at a warning! This man was a monster, a demon in human guise —"

He shook his head, violently. "And to not only leave that abomination in place, but to continue to *use* it! This is *not* the Church I joined; these are *not* the deeds of a good and God-loving man! This man was a monster of the basest sort, and the current Abbot is no better, cloaking his crimes, using what the other created!"

Robin broke the silence that followed his outburst. "Was Padrik educated here?" she asked, quietly.

Reymond nodded. "We thought it a matter of pride, that he should rise to be High Bishop," he whispered brokenly. "And now I find it to be not a cause for pride and rejoicing, but for shame. . . ."

"My people have a proverb, that two bad grapes don't mean all grapes are bad — but two spoiled grapes contaminate the whole bunch," Robin told him. "He and the Abbot together are doing terrible things in Gradford —"

"And if they are not stopped, those terrible things will spread." Reymond's back straightened, and his expression went from horrified to determined. "We must put this right, the three of us," he said, finally, and firmly. "I am not a mage, myself, but I have studied magic in the course of my work for some time. I may be able to free this poor spirit — I must study the binding spell, vile as it is. If there is a physical link, I need only break it to break the binding spell. If the spell can be broken at all, I can do so within the next two days. I can wait here for those who Padrik may send, and free them once they reach the Hill, by taking their pendants as you took Orlina's. And if I can, I will go with further victims to the Justiciars at Kingsford, lay this before them, and ask them to deal with Padrik."

Kestrel silently applauded the man's courage — he *knew* that the Ghost had killed dozens of people, and yet he was willing to dare its anger to free it! And then, not content with that alone, he would go petition the Justiciars as well, a long and uncomfortable journey in the heart of winter. His regard for Reymond rose, and he tried to put his admiration into his eyes, for he knew that his words alone would not convey it, poor and limping as they were. Now, *this* was a man of the Church who could restore his faith in the Church's honor!

"Y-you are a *g-good* man, B-brother R-Reymond," he said, warmly. "As g-good — as the f-first Abbot was evil."

Reymond blushed, and smiled shyly. "Thank you for those kind, but inaccurate words," he said softly. "I don't know if anyone could be good enough to counteract this evil."

"D-don't ever b-believe that, please. E-ever."

Robin had gone into the Scriptorium for pen and paper when Reymond made his declaration; she had been scribbling furiously ever since. Now she blew on the ink to dry it, folded the note, and handed it to Brother Reymond. "Give this to the first Gypsy you see on the road and tell him it *has* to get to a Gypsy named Peregrine, immediately," she told him. "I've left notes in other places for him, but you may be my fastest courier. When he reads it, he'll deal with the Clan that is helping Padrik with his frauds."

Reymond nodded gravely, and put the note carefully inside the pouch hanging on his belt beside the keys to the Library. "And what of you?" he asked, faltering just a little. He clearly wanted to hear them say they intended to *do* something, but he also was obviously afraid that they weren't going to.

Robin smiled, a smile that dazzled the poor man. "We're going to do the obvious," she said, simply, an abrupt turnaround from her earlier attitude that took Kestrel completely by surprise, and left him openmouthed with amazement. "We're going back to Gradford, to see if we can't expose him as a fraud without getting ourselves thrown in gaol or hung. If you can free the Ghost, that's the least we can do."

Reymond blinked, and well he might. That was a tall task for anyone —

"Can you do that?" he asked.

Robin shrugged. "We can try," she replied.

Jonny grinned, with a combination of relief and approval that made him want to cheer. "One th-thing w-we c-can do," he said, "is m-make sure as m-many

p-people as p-possible learn P-Padrik is p-playing
t-tricks. And w-we c-can p-prove it by s-showing that
anyone can d-do them."

"Oh, now that is an excellent idea!" Brother Reymond applauded.

"That's probably one reason why he's forbidden
public entertainment," Robin mused. "If some sleight-
of-hand artist duplicates one of his 'miracles,' people
are going to start wondering out loud." She frowned at
that. "It's a pity we couldn't arrange a show."

"H-he m-may have f-forbidden p-public entertainment," Kestrel said slowly, "b-but he *can't* s-stop
p-people from d-doing a t-trick or two t-to amuse th-
their f-friends in p-public!"

Robin visibly brightened, and snapped her fingers.
"Now *there* is an idea! And by the time any Constable
gets there, well, the party has broken up and there's no
one to arrest! I can think of a *lot* of people who would
like to be in on that plan!"

So can I, Jonny thought, remembering Ardana's
girls, and wondering if any of the unofficial Houses
would welcome a trickster as entertainment instead of
a musician. For that matter, a party made up of a few
of the young ladies and their favorites could well wander the inns every couple of nights . . . or better yet,
every couple of afternoons, so the ladies would not be
losing any income.

With all the lovely ladies in such a party, eyes would
naturally be drawn to it. And when someone offered
to do a trick for the amusement of the group —

Oh, yes, that would work very well indeed. *Very*
well.

He was so lost in his own musings that he missed
part of what Robin was saying.

"We'll leave at dawn, and we should reach Gradford
in a few days," she was saying to Reymond. "I know

where we can leave the wagon, so we aren't recognized, coming in a second time."

"And I will do my part as soon as I believe I have mastered the binding spell," Reymond said, solemnly. "That will be two days, at the most. I *will* work this release by daylight; I am not brave enough to face your deadly spirit by night." Then he blinked. "You are braver than I, friends. The only foe I face is one who will likely help me if he can, when he learns my task. You face an entire city."

I wouldn't place any money on the odds of the Ghost helping you, Kestrel thought, and shrugged. "Th-that m-many p-people c-can work against each other," he only observed.

"May it be so," Brother Reymond said, making the words into a benediction. "Go with the blessing of God, my friends. I shall see you to the kitchen gate; no one will question *my* walking about so late."

"Thank you, Brother Reymond," Robin said, then grinned. "From a good heart, the blessing of your God is worth a thousand from anyone else — and I have the uneasy feeling we're going to need all the blessings we can get!"

CHAPTER SEVENTEEN

"This place is worse than it was when we left," Robin muttered under her breath, as they waited in line at the city gate for a Constable to get to them. "And I didn't think that was possible."

There was one advantage to returning to a city you knew something about; you also knew where things were, and the best way to disguise yourself as harmless. They had entered this time with a crowd of farm-folk, carrying simple packs. The wagon and horses had been left at the inn, along with most of their possessions. It had been a long time, nearly six months, since Robin had been forced to walk to get where she wanted to go, and she'd forgotten what a luxury it was to ride. . . .

Now her legs and back ached, and so did her arms; the last part of the journey, taking the switchback road up to the gates of Gradford, had nearly done her in.

But the shock of seeing the changes in the city they had left only a few days ago was enough to make her forget her aching legs.

It started at the gates; they were informed as they entered that their packs were going to be searched for unspecified "contraband." Robin suspected that "contraband" included money, and was very glad that she and Kestrel had hidden the horde of coins they had brought with them in the hems of her drab skirts and petticoats. That was where they had hidden the silk-wrapped pendant as well. It was a good thing they had taken that precaution, as it turned out. Even the clothing in their packs underwent an examination; one woman was found to have a pair of breeches in her bag, and was informed that "decent women are to be clothed decently in Gradford." The Guard gave her a long lecture on what a "decent" woman was and was not — and that if she were found "dressing against her sex" she would be thrown in the stocks for it.

The poor woman was in tears before he had finished with her. She was a simple farm-wife, here to see the great High Bishop and visit a sister who had just given birth, and it had never occurred to her that the wearing of breeches to do the heavy chores could possibly be considered "immoral" by anyone's standards.

Well, she wasn't alone; it hadn't occurred to Robin, either. Now she was very glad that she had left her breeches in the wagon. She was even gladder that they had left the wagon — nearby, a simple farm-cart had been stripped down to the bed in a search for "contraband," and she did not even want to think what kind of inspection their wagon would have gone through.

But these Guards were oddly reticent about touching women, although that reticence did not extend to their baggage. They never even laid a finger to her sleeve; they shied away from her as if simple contact might contaminate them.

Fortunately this very prudery concerning women kept them from searching Robin as they did Kestrel; he submitted to the humiliating search with a bored look on his face, and they found nothing more incriminating than a handful of Mintak copper coins, which were confiscated for bearing the images of nonhumans upon them. "Portraits of unbelievers," they were called.

To be fair, they did give him a chit for the supposed

"value" of the coins, which could be redeemed at the Cathedral. Which they did not intend to do, for the Guard made it very clear that only those whose piety was in doubt would do such a thing; the rest would consider their lost coins a donation to the Church.

So much for the "honest men of Gradford." Robin wondered how that particular Guard, the one who had refused a gift of a God-Star, was doing now. Did actions like these bother him — or had he been persuaded like the rest of them?

As they waited for the endless questions and inspections to be over, Robin watched the street of the inns beyond this Guardpost. There were Guards and Constables everywhere. One was posted at the entrance to every inn, taking down the names of everyone who came to stay there. The street preachers had real podiums now, erected beneath the street lamps, from which to harangue the passersby.

There were rules now, endless rules. So many they made Robin's head swim, then ache. Things that could not be worn, eaten, drunk, said, or done. And they were informed that there was something called a "curfew," that once the bell had rung from the Cathedral signaling that Sixte was over, they had one hour to get inside. After that, only folk with emergencies or official passes had leave to be on the streets.

Public gatherings were prohibited. Public parties were prohibited. Gathering in an inn for the purpose of "idleness" was forbidden. Only those living in an inn were permitted to eat and drink in the inn. Strong drink was prohibited, as were gambling and music.

Except in that special House that Padrik owns . . .

And women must not be "forward," must always be "modest and unassuming," in word, deed — *and thought*. There were more rules about the proper conduct for a woman; Robin let them all wash over her without really noting them. If she did take note, she knew she would become so enraged she would give herself away.

Forewarned by the lecture to that poor, hapless farm woman, Robin let Jonny do all the talking, which he did in very slow monosyllables, constantly pulling on his forelock, and mumbling "yessir" and "nossir." Their story was as simple as his words. He was "Jon Brede," she was "Jen Brede." They "farmed." Their purpose in coming to Gradford —

"Same as them," Jonny said, nodding at the rest of the group. "Visit the Cathedral."

Not a lie, not at all; only a tiny part of the truth.

There was another new innovation — a little piece of pasteboard with their name, occupation, reason for visit, date of entry, and description written on it.

She and Jonny made no pretense of being able to read or write, and made a pair of marks — a scythe for him, a flower for her — where they were required to sign these "papers." Besides the physical description, Robin's said she was "meek and wifely." Jonny's described him as "simpleton." It was not very difficult to keep her face straight; she was so knotted with tension she could not have smiled if she wanted to.

Probably they would have to present these "papers" anytime anyone demanded to see them. People in authority would know where they stayed, where they ate, what they did.

Had it only been a week since they left? What could have happened in the interim?

They made their way down the street of the inns, but Robin had absolutely no intention of staying here. Not with Guards at every door — and if they were only farmers, there would be questions about where they had gotten the money to stay in a good inn. There couldn't be Guards *everywhere;* that wouldn't be feasible. Only people with good money would come here — poorer folk went elsewhere, and Padrik would have no real interest in poorer folk.

This was where the knowledge gleaned from their previous visit was invaluable. They did *not* have to search for lodging; they knew where to go. "Elsewhere" was all the way across the city, in a section not far from the Warren, a place Robin had noted against future need. Inns there sold sleeping space on the floor of the common room; they would have two or three large chambers above, where people would sleep in rows of cots, and perhaps four or six tiny chambers, hardly larger than closets, for those who wished a little more privacy. Their coins would go a long way in this section of Gradford.

All things considered, though, it was a good thing that their silver all bore the stamp of the King and not of any nonhumans. Otherwise, those coins would go straight to the coffers of the Church. Robin rather doubted that anyone in this town would accept a coin with the nonhuman stamp.

Her stomach was already in knots, and she had the feeling that things were going to get a lot worse.

They had to cross the Cathedral square in order to get there; it appeared that Padrik had decided that business was too good for the small merchants who *had* been setting up there. There were small stalls set up facing the Cathedral, selling the same merchandise as before, but they were all manned by young men in Novices' robes. There was even a stall selling God-Stars, both the pendants and the wall-decorations! But Robin noted that the workmanship was distinctly inferior, and from what she could see, so were the materials. A small victory, and a petty one, but this was the only bright spot so far.

"I guess the licenses weren't enough for him," she said in a low voice, after a quick glance around showed no one close enough to overhear a careful conversation.

"Aye," Kestrel replied sardonically. "L-look at the h-houses, th-though —"

Something about the square had struck her as odd, though she couldn't put a finger on just what was different about it. But once he said *that,* she took a closer look at the fine mansions that faced the Cathedral —

The outsides looked the same as before — but the windows were black and empty. It was getting dark, and there should have been lights in those windows, curtains across them. There was nothing, and there was no sign of life about them. Only bare, blank windows, like the empty eyes of a madman, staring at the Cathedral.

"They're deserted!" she exclaimed, keeping her voice to a surprised whisper.

"My g-guess," Jonny confirmed.

She could only wonder why. Had their wealthy owners decided that what had happened to Orlina could all too easily happen to them and cut down on their households and visibility — or had they decided that Gradford itself was no longer a healthy place for them and gone off elsewhere?

Or had Padrik decided that where Orlina had gone, others could follow? Were the prisons full of other "heretics," waiting to receive their own pendants?

If so, Padrik was going to get a big surprise eventually, when all of them surfaced to testify against him in Kingsford.

Always providing, of course, that the Justiciars at Kingsford did not consider High Bishop Padrik too dangerous a man to cross . . .

❖   ❖   ❖

Robin was glad to be out of sight of the Cathedral, and away from a place where so many Guards and Constables were patrolling. The far shabbier quarter where they found themselves had fewer figures of authority in it — and even the street preachers were the kind they were familiar with; the disheveled, ill-kempt, near-lunatics. They found the class of inn they were looking for, as full night descended and the lamplighters made their rounds, giving the street preachers light to see and be seen by. It was small, nondescript, with the barrel that signified an "inn" hanging over the door, in a building flanked by a shop and a laundry. Both of those were, for a miracle, still open.

Robin stopped in the shop long enough to buy candles, sausage, cheese and bread, and despite Jonny's obvious nervousness and impatience, went to the laundry as well, for a spirited bargaining session. It was nice to do something as normal as bargain; for a moment she was able to forget her tension, and stop watching over her shoulder for Church Guards. When she came out, she had several old, but clean, blankets folded over her arm, and it was obvious from Jonny's expression that he did not understand why she had bought them.

"If they give us any bedding in here, it's not going to be much, and it'll be full of fleas," she said, very quietly. "This is stuff that was sent to be cleaned but never picked up. We can get clothing that way, too. That's why I wasn't worried when we didn't have much appropriate clothing. We'll be able to buy things that already look worn, not new." His eyebrows rose, and he nodded shortly.

They went in; the common room had a bare earthen floor, pounded hard and covered with rushes, with the only light coming from the fireplace at one end. That fireplace evidently served as the rude "kitchen" as well, since there was a large pot of something hanging over it that smelled strongly of cabbage, and a stack of bowls over the mantle. Furnished with crude trestle-tables and benches that had seen a great deal of hard use, it held two or three dozen people who looked to be the same class of farming folk that Gwyna and Jonny pretended to be. As Robin had expected, there were no Guards at the door here, but the innkeeper perused their "papers," reading slowly and painfully, with his finger under each line and his mouth moving as he spelled out the words. Then he required them to make their "marks" in a book, copying their names beside the marks, before he would rent them their room.

A scrawny boy, summoned from his station beside the fireplace, led them to it. It lay on the third floor, at the top of a steep and rickety stairway, in a narrow corridor with seven other rooms, and was lit with a single lamp. The lamp did not give off much light, which was probably just as well; Robin wasn't certain she wanted to see just how derelict the place was. They were allotted one tiny stump of a candle for light, given to them by the boy, who flung open the door and vanished after shoving the candle end at Kestrel.

The room was barely large enough for the bed; as Robin had expected, it was nothing more than a thin mattress on a wooden platform. Jonny lit the candle stub at the lamp in the hall, and stuck it on top of a smear of waxy drips, on a small shelf by the door. Robin closed the door, and looked around.

In the better light from the candle, it seemed that her worst fears had been groundless; the place was clean. The thin pallet held no fleas or bedbugs. The floor wasn't dirty, just so worn that there wasn't even a hint of wax or varnish, and gray with age and use.

There was one window, large enough to climb out of; that was good, if they ever had to make an unconventional exit. She dropped her pile of blankets on the bed, and opened the shutters — there was, of course, no glass in the window itself. The window overlooked a roof, and a bit of the alley in back of the inn; a rain-gutter ran beside it up to the roof, and the roof of the laundry was just below.

She smiled tautly in satisfaction. Curfew or no curfew, *here* was a way to come and go at night without being seen.

She closed the shutters again, and turned back to Jonny. "It isn't the Singing Bird," she said, apologetically.

"It's also n-not th-the g-gaol, or a d-dry s-spot under a b-bridge," he replied. "And it s-seems c-clean."

"Very true." She bent down for the blankets, but he beat her to them, unfolding them deftly and helping her make up the bed. "We'll have to take everything with us whenever we go out openly," she told him, "or it likely won't be here when we come back."

He turned to pull the latch-string in, barring the door to anyone who wasn't willing to break it down. "I t-take it w-we w-won't b-be d-doing a l-lot of th-that?"

"Probably not." She spread out her purchases on the bed. "The food here is going to be pretty dreadful, that's why I bought all this; since neither of us can afford to be laid up with a flux and cramps, we'd better buy our dinners elsewhere. They tend to buy rather dubious foodstuffs for these places — well, look at the candle, they buy these stubs in lots from the Cathedral and the homes of the rich, who won't burn a candle down to the end. The food'll be like that. There won't be any facilities here other than a privy in the alley. The laundry has a bathing room we can rent." She sliced up bread while Jonny dealt with the cheese and sausage. "One of us should stay in the room when the other leaves officially. That probably ought to be you."

He nodded. "B-between th-this st-stutter and th-the f-fact th-that you m-might n-not b-be s-safe here alone, I th-think you're r-right. J-just d-don't let any P-Patsonos s-spot you."

She winced, but he had a perfect right to remind her of that. *And a few weeks ago — I would have been angry that he had. Now it simply seems practical. . . .* "Right. Well, it looks as if our plans just got thrown right out. We can't take pleasure parties around to the inns doing magic tricks . . . and I'm not sure that any of the Houses are still in operation, except in the Warren itself." She frowned with thought. "I'll have to go in the Warren and start spreading the word about how Padrik actually works his 'miracles.' Maybe the people in there can do something. I'll start with Donnar, and see if there's anywhere I can go from there."

He ate several bites before replying — and as their candle-stub threatened to flicker out, took one of the new candles and lit it from the last flame of the old, pushing the unlit end down into the melted wax from the stub. "I d-don't l-like you g-going in th-there alone. B-but th-there's n-no ch-choice." Then he smiled shyly. "B-besides, you're p-probably more c-competent in there th-than m-me."

She glowed briefly with pleasure at his words, but then sighed, and ate a piece of cheese, pensively. "I only hope we aren't too late to do anything at all."

Donnar was willing to see her, but as she shared a jug and a plate of fried dough-bits with him, he listened to her brief explanation and shook his head.

"Ye're too late," Donnar said, flatly. "There's not a thing ye can do, now."

She glanced around his establishment, which was

only half-full. The customers drank with one eye on
their liquor, and one on the door. The Guards and
Constables had not yet "cleaned up" the Warren,
but rumor had it that they were getting ready to do
so, and those rumors had every petty thief and free-
lance whore jumping at shadows. No one had
molested Robin in any way on her way in; no one
had any time to worry about one small, drab female,
when there was so much more threat from other
sources.

"What happened?" she asked, feeling desperation
creeping into her voice. "Has everyone here gone
mad?"

Donnar shook his head. "Ye'd think so," he sighed.
"Padrik's got the Mayor an' the whole damn Council in
'is pocket. Couple three days ago, all of a sudden, like,
comes all these new rules — an' all these new Guards
an' Constables t'enforce 'em, an' the Mayor an' Council just back 'em right up. Padrik must'a been plannin'
on this fer a while; most'a these clods ain't from Gradford. I heard they been in trainin' since summer, off
on Church land somewheres. But whether that's
true —" He shrugged. "I dunno where th' copper
came t'hire 'em, but I'd bet it's from Church coffers,
an' not the town's."

"So even if I could tell you, not only how Padrik
does all his 'miracles,' but *who* showed him how, it
wouldn't do any good?" she asked, tension and fear
putting an edge to her words. How could this have
happened? Never for a moment had she thought that
there would be *nothing* they could do!

Donnar stared at her for a moment, then said,
slowly, "Evr'one in th' Warren is a lawbreaker; either
he started out like that, or th' Church an' th' law
forced 'im into it. Who's gonna listen to *us*?"

He had a point, and she stared at her mug, utterly

deflated, and all in a single moment. "No one," she replied, dully.

He nodded. "Tha's 'bout the size of it. He's got ev'thing but th' Warren, an' now there's rumors he's gonna take it, too. I dunno if Padrik's really gonna clean up th' Warren or not. Thing is, I kin think 'f one way he could do it, if he didn' give a fat damn what happened t'nobody, an' didn' have th' men t' do th' job."

She stared across the table at him. "How?" she whispered, rather certain that she was not going to care for the answer.

She didn't.

"Burn it down," he replied, succinctly, and a chill left her frozen in her place. "An' thas' why I'm leavin', soon's I can. Tomorrow, mebbe next day, at th' latest. Out through the Back Door, what I tol' you about."

The Back Door was a way out of the city via the sewers. Only the desperate took it, but it did avoid the Guards at the gates, who were stopping not only those going into Gradford, but those trying to leave. If things had gotten bad enough that Donnar was going to take the Back Door out, then they were bad indeed.

And the average citizen is probably pleased with all the new Constables to guard him and his property — so pleased, he doesn't realize he's been locked into a prison he can't escape.

She thanked him, in a daze, and went back out into the street. She still had a few errands to run; things to buy —

Like a couple of sets of lock picks. She hadn't wanted to bring any into the city; there was only so much she could fit into the hems of her clothing. But there was certainly a locksmith here in the Warren, and in the Warren, he wouldn't be selling just locks, he'd be selling the means to open them.

It took her a while to find the man she wanted, but for once in Gradford, her sex worked *for* her in convincing him that she was not an agent of the Guard or Constables. Apparently, no woman would ever be considered by Padrik's people for any important job.

The lock picks were expensive, but some of the finest she had ever seen — and if it turned out that they *needed* them, they would have been worth any price.

Those she hid under more prosaic purchases of food and drink — as she had expected, the food in the inn *was* dreadful, and the beer was worse, awful beer to start with, now gone flat and stale.

While she walked back to their inn, Donnar's last words kept coming back to haunt her. He was right. If Padrik didn't care about how much damage was wrought, or how many people died, that *would* be the easiest, perhaps the only way, to "cleanse" the Warren. All he had to do would be to set Guards in the streets to arrest anyone boiling out of the district, then set fire to buildings in a ring around it. With real mages working with him, the fire could probably be confined to the Warren and perhaps a few buildings nearby.

Padrik could even have the fire set "accidentally" and the Guards stationed there "coincidentally." Or, for that matter, he could have one of the mages create that Cathedral-tall angel, and this time, give it a sword of flame, and make it appear that the Sacrificed God Himself had set the blaze going.

And the average citizen would think him a hero, for clearing out all the "criminals." It won't occur to the people that the same weapon could be used to threaten his home, his family, if he ever opposes Padrik.

She shivered inside her shabby, warm coat. Padrik had already proved, many times over, that he cared for nothing except the path to power. She could only hope this scheme had not yet occurred to him; that he was whipping up a state of panic in the Warren by spreading rumors with no substance behind them.

And meanwhile, now that their best plan for uncovering the High Bishop's fraud had gone awry, she and Jonny would have to think of something else. . . .

There had to be something, some solution. There was *always* something else that you could do.

Wasn't there?

In the next several days, they spent most of their time in their room, trying to think of that "something else." In the meantime, the rumors of the cleansing of the Warren had not yet come true —

But the Cathedral-tall angel put in his appearance, right on schedule.

Neither of them was there to see it, but while the vision had many people who had seen it speaking of it in awe, there were some who were just a trifle less than enthusiastic.

This was the first time that Robin had ever heard Padrik's devotees speak of him and his works with a little less than full enthusiasm and belief. Evidently Padrik had overstepped himself this time, for the angel only called to mind other illusions that these folk had seen, put on for the purposes of spectacle at festivals and other city-wide celebrations.

And when they were asked to describe what it had looked like, they told the tale in just those terms.

"Kinda like that red an' green dragon th' Mayor had conjured up fer the Midwinter Faire ten, fifteen years ago," one grizzled oldster said in answer to Gwyna's questions. "Yah, that's what it was like. Like that big ol' dragon. Ye could see through it, ye know, an' *it* didn' seem t' see anythin' — just smiled an' waved its wings, lazy-like."

Contributions to the hospice-fund were reported to be disappointing, although attendance at the Healing Services remained high. But Gwyna took a little more heart; if people would only start to *think* instead of simply following along like so many sheep —

There was no sign of whether or not Brother Reymond had managed to free the Ghost; but then, there probably wouldn't be. The spirit had no interest in staying around, after all. In all probability, the only interest it had was in getting rid of the men who had kept it bound all this time; the Abbot and Padrik — the former was within reach, but how would the Ghost know how to reach the latter? If Robin had learned anything on Skull Hill that night, it was that the spirit bound there was a great believer in expediency as well as revenge.

By now, he's gone, she thought more than once, but with only a feeling of relief. For even if Padrik was sending poor victims outbound with spell-laden pendants, Reymond was waiting at the other end of the road to free them.

She decided that it was time that the two of them started attending the Healing Services again. Perhaps, if they studied what was going on, they could get some notion of how to disrupt one of the services. Hopefully without getting arrested afterwards — they wouldn't do any good stuck in a cell, after all.

Jonny agreed.

"I'm g-getting t-tired of sitting around h-here, d-doing n-nothing," he told her. "At l-least, if w-we g-go w-watch, w-we'll b-be *t-trying.*"

So they tucked all their belongings into their packs, wearing what wouldn't fit, and rolled up the blankets and tied them atop the whole. The Cathedral was not heated — it would have cost more than even the Church had to heat such a huge stone barn in the dead of winter. They would be glad of the extra clothing before the Service was over.

Gwyna put the lock picks where she could get at them quickly, just in case — in a pocket in the side of one of her boots. Jonny slipped the silk-wrapped pendant into his own pocket.

They set off for the Cathedral, joining a growing stream of people who trickled out of the inns and hostels along this street with their belongings on their backs. But they had the advantage of knowing the way, and knowing where to go when they got there; they beat most of the crowd to the Cathedral itself, and wormed their way very near the front, by working along the side wall.

Coincidentally enough, they found themselves in their old places, beneath the benevolent eye of Saint Hypatia. Gwyna took that for a good omen; Jonny had told her that Hypatia was the patron saint of knowledge and of truth-seekers.

Maybe she'd look kindly on their current task.

We can certainly use any blessings we can get, she recalled, uneasily, as she and Jonny took their places on either side of the saint's pedestal. Although they didn't plan on doing anything tonight, she was still nervous and distinctly jumpy. She kept looking out of the corner of her eye at their neighbors. Were there Patsonos who could recognize her nearby? Or Guards that would take exception to the way they acted?

There was a large, draped object on the platform near the altar; very bulky, and covered with a heavy dark cloth. Robin wondered what it was. Some new construction, perhaps? A new pulpit for Padrik to speak from? It was bigger than the old one; perhaps the old one wasn't grand enough anymore.

Finally, after every last bit of space had been filled by an eager observer, Padrik made his usual dramatic appearance from behind the altar, resplendent in his white robes, with an even bigger train of Priests following along behind than he'd had before.

And even though it was *not* appropriate for a Holy Service, the assembled crowd began cheering and applauding as soon as he appeared. They behaved more as if he was some sort of popular entertainer; perhaps, deep down inside, some of them *did* realize that was all he really was. A showman.

A fraud.

He smiled graciously, nodding his thanks — and *long* past the time when he should have tried to quell the outburst, he finally raised his hands for silence.

He got it; the cheers cut off immediately, leaving only the echoes of voices playing among the spires.

"My friends," he said, his beautiful voice making a melody of his words. "My children in God — I can see that there are no doubters among you *this* day!"

Which only proves he's not infallible, Robin thought wryly. *And that he can't read minds, no matter what other magic he's using. Didn't find us, and we're doubters for sure.* That was something of a relief, anyway.

Padrik's smile faded, replaced by an expression of deep sorrow. "I have heard rumors, though — terrible rumors. There are stories in the town that the vision of the Hospice Angel was no vision at all — and that if the angel is an illusion, then so are all the rest of the miracles you have witnessed here. This grieves me deeply, more deeply than I can express."

Robin kept her face stony-still, but she was astonished that he would have brought the subject up at all, much less addressed it so directly.

The crowd began to murmur uneasily, and with the same surprise as Robin. Padrik continued to look out at them, gently, benevolently.

"Oh, do not deny that you have heard those rumors — and perhaps, have been tempted to believe them! But I say unto you, that not only are those tales the basest of lies, but the temptation to believe them was *indeed* a *temptation,* a snare set by dark forces to lead you into disbelief! There are those out there among the unbelievers who only wish to spread dissension and lies, so that the truth will be obscured! There are those who would wish you to think that what is truth is a lie, and lies are truth!" His voice rose, just a little. "And today, I have the means to show you the agent of those rumors!"

He gave no sign that Robin could see, but suddenly the heavy drapery fell away from the construction near the altar — and it was not a new bit of building at all.

It was a cage.

A hanging-cage, to be precise; with a loop on the peak of its domed top, clearly meant to receive a hook. Spaced around the cage were iron loops, where bindings could easily be attached, and manacles and closed-hooks already hung from them.

There was something inside the cage, huddled on the floor. One of the guards prodded it to stand with the butt of his spear, and as it did so, both Gwyna and Jonny stifled gasps of recognition.

It was T'fyrr!

Robin's heart stopped, and Kestrel went completely white. Never in their worst nightmares could they have imagined this!

"This vile creature, this half-demon, was sent to spy upon the godly people of Gradford, and to lead them astray with false tales and rumors," Padrik proclaimed, as T'fyrr pulled himself up to his full height and glared at him through the bars of the cage. His beak had been clamped shut with some iron and leather contraption; he looked half-starved. "He was sent by the evil and decadent Deliambrens, who seek to destroy us and all humankind, to make us into their pets and slaves for their lusts and their amusements — and here is the proof!"

One of the Guards brought out a couple of bewildered-looking rustics, who twisted their hats in their hands, and said, yes, that they had seen this bird-man with a Deliambren. Oh, they knew it was a Deliambren; they'd seen the fellow before, and besides, only a Deliambren would have such a mucking great wagon, with all manner of strange things hung on it. They'd seen the two talking — and then the bird-man had flown off —

Padrik nodded wisely, and cut the last one short. The Priests hustled the puzzled men out, discreetly, as Padrik turned back to his audience.

"So you see!" he called, in stentorian tones. "Those honest toilers of the earth would not lie — nor would they produce such things out of their fantasies. But this creature is not only a half-demon himself, *he* is a mage, a mage of dark and terrible evil and —"

"Look!" cried someone in the audience, pointing at T'fyrr's cage.

A demon appeared in a puff of black smoke, a demon that looked a *great* deal like T'fyrr. It shot a bolt of red lightning at the lock on the cage door, as if trying to free the Haspur — though why it would do so *now*, in full view of hundreds of people, did not make any logical sense. But then, these people were not thinking logically. T'fyrr didn't move, didn't flinch; Robin wondered if perhaps *he* couldn't see the illusion, if it was meant for the eyes of those in the congregation alone.

But the demon only got off the one shot; Padrik

whirled in an artistic swirl of white robes that made part of his costume stand away from him for a moment, like a pair of great white wings unfurled. He raised his staff of office over his head, and a beam of light shot from the top of it to strike the demon, who vanished without even a "pop."

The cheapest illusion there is! Done with mirrors, for heaven's sake! You don't even need any magic to pull it off! Only good for a few seconds — the type of illusion that anyone with any experience has seen at a dozen big Faires — but this lot is eating it up!

"You see!" Padrik exclaimed. "You see how he summons his evil minions to aid him! But they are not proof against the power of the Sacrificed God —"

There were shouts now, of "Kill him!" and "Destroy the beast!" Robin went cold with fear. They *had* to get to T'fyrr to free him — but how could they get past a mob in a killing mood?

But Padrik held up his hands, and the crowd calmed instantly. "*We* are not animals, *we* are not monsters, to tear apart our enemies in the heat of anger," he proclaimed, as Robin added nausea to her fear. "The power of God is sufficient to hold this evil, vile creature in his bonds. Nor shall we permit him to disrupt the work we are truly here for, God's own work of healing! We brought him here only that you might see the true face of your enemies, and know them for what they are."

"G-give me one of your p-pick-sets," Kestrel whispered, under cover of the speech. "I th-think I can g-get th-them t-to him."

And then what? she thought — but she handed him the set of lock picks anyway. He slipped off into the crowd, and if she hadn't seen him vanish, she wouldn't have known he was even there in the first place.

While Padrik continued to pummel the congregation with examples of *his* benevolence and the nonhumans' perfidy, she kept a watch on T'fyrr's cage. And in a moment, she "heard" that little thread of "melody" that meant someone was using magic. This was familiar enough — magic meant to rivet the attention to the speaker, and make his words seem the acme of truth. She was ready for it, and she was not caught like the rest. Padrik's sermon had mesmerized his audience to the point that no one, not even the guards, was watching T'fyrr.

And Jonny had taken advantage of that.

He'd taken advantage of something else, too.

There was another thin thread of mental "music," weaving with Padrik's siren song. Free Bard Kestrel was invoking Bardic Magic.

Don't look at me, the song ordered. *Don't see me. I'm not here. Ignore me. . . .*

And since it not only didn't interfere with Padrik's spell, it actually worked *with* the High Bishop's magic, no one noticed it except her.

She added her power to his, humming under her breath, following that "melody" in her mind with a real melody meant to reinforce the magic.

Once again, if she hadn't been watching, she would never have seen that shadow slipping among the statues of the saints, the movement down near the floor as something was tossed into the bottom of the cage, and T'fyrr's quick bend to retrieve what had been thrown in.

As Padrik wound down, Kestrel reappeared on the pedestal of Saint Hypatia, looking as calm as if he had never been gone. But he was breathing carefully, hiding the fact that he had been exerting himself, and he looked very, very tired.

Just about as tired as she felt. He flashed her a

quick glance and a hidden gesture of approval; she gave him a strained and nervous smile in return.

Well, now T'fyrr had lock picks, hidden in his feathers. Whether or not he could use them was another story entirely. Whether he would get an opportunity to —

But Padrik's Priests were assembling those in the crowd who felt in need of healing — and with a quick glance and a nod, they both slid down from the pedestal to crowd up a little further to the front.

She bit her lip as her mind accelerated through plan after plan, shuffling bits of foolhardiness with honest fear. Wasn't there something they could do?

Suddenly Jonny grabbed her hand, and whistled a soft phrase of melody — that of "The Skull Hill Ghost."

She stared at him in puzzlement for a moment, completely baffled, as he shook her hand with impatience, and whistled the chorus. Then, as if dawn had suddenly broken over her, she *knew* what he was trying to tell her.

If the Ghost was free — oh, surely it was by now! — it would be only too happy to see Padrik again. And if it was free, well, couldn't they *call* it? They'd called an Elf before, just by thinking about Bardic music and magic and wanting to have an Elf answer them.

How could it hurt to try?

She nodded frantically, and began to hum Rune's tune under her breath, concentrating very, very hard on how *much* she wanted the Ghost of Skull Hill to appear right now —

Faintly, she heard Kestrel do the same. And as his melody joined hers, the internal music that sang of the power of Bardic Magic took on life and strength.

The line to the altar was long, but the two of them

were so short that the Priests might have mistaken them for children; somehow they found themselves in the first rank when Padrik began the first "healing." Robin's teeth chattered unexpectedly and the melody she hummed broke for a moment. They hadn't expected to be up *here* —

Oh no — what am I supposed to be sick of? she thought in a panic, T'fyrr momentarily forgotten. *What can I fake? Infertility, maybe* —

Padrik had his hands on the head of a "cripple," one of the Patsonos, of course, who stared up at him in carefully simulated admiration while the High Bishop prayed. And just as Robin decided that infertility was probably a good choice —

Every light in the Cathedral suddenly blew out.

Then the windows darkened abruptly as well, plunging the interior of the Cathedral into thick gloom.

There were screams from outside, as Padrik stopped in mid-sentence, and looked up at the windows, a most unsaintly expression of annoyance on his face.

"What is going —" he began.

But before he could complete his sentence, his final word was obliterated, as a bolt of lightning struck the roof of the Cathedral directly over his head.

The thunder that accompanied it flattened everyone to the floor. Glass shattered and showered the people with tiny slivers and specks; Robin's eyes swam with tears of pain from the burst of light, and she tried to blink away the spots obscuring her vision. Now there were people screaming inside the Cathedral as well as outside, but only the loudest could be heard above the ringing in everyone's ears the thunderclap had caused. The crowd surged towards the exit; she stayed where she was. Trying to move in any direction at all could get them trampled.

Something made her look up, as soon as she was able to see anything at all. The lightning had torn an enormous hole in the roof; she glanced at Padrik, only to see that he was just as surprised as everyone else.

So this isn't *one of his miracles? Is this — could this be the Ghost?*

She hardly had time to do more than frame the thought. In the next heartbeat, a terrible, chilling wind rushed in through the hole in the roof, a wind that chilled the soul as well as the body, and howled like all the nightmares that had ever walked herded together. It formed into a whirlwind in front of the altar, picking up bits of everything from within the Cathedral and sucking them up into itself. The debris began to glow with a spectral, greenish-white light, and the whirlwind spun tighter, faster, forming a column —

Oh dear gods. I've seen this before!

— and then into a manlike shape, a shape that wore a deeply cowled robe, a robe that had never contained anything like a human form.

But this time the shape was five times the height of a man. And the posture of the Ghost of Skull Hill said without any need for words that he was *not* happy.

And that he saw, and recognized, his enemy.

Padrik made a hasty motion, and a ring of fire sprang up around the Ghost, confining it, momentarily at least. Robin couldn't hear anything above the screams, but she saw Padrik's lips moving, and she didn't think he was praying.

So he is a mage!

The Ghost looked down at the ring of flames surrounding him, and moved towards them, but the bottom of his robes flared and flickered as he advanced. The barrier held against him. Padrik's expression brightened for a moment — but in the next instant, the Ghost made a gesture of his own, and the whirlwind formed around him.

The wind whipped the flames, and the flames thinned, threatening to die away altogether.

Padrik gestured again, shouting now, words and incantations that Robin didn't understand, but which hummed in the back of her head like a hive of poisonous wasps. The flames rose up again with renewed strength.

The Ghost spun his whirlwind faster still, staring at Padrik across the barrier of fire and wind, his hatred a thing so real and palpable that it, too, was a weapon.

Behind the more dramatic action, T'fyrr worked frantically at the lock of his cage with the lock picks Kestrel had passed him. Robin noticed him — at the same time as the only one of Padrik's guards to remain standing fast.

The guard's mouth opened in a shout that simply could not be heard over the howling of the Ghost's eldritch winds. He ran towards the cage with the keys in his hands —

T'fyrr looked up at the movement, and froze, dropping the picks. Before Robin had blinked twice, the guard had reached the cage —

And had put himself into T'fyrr's reach.

T'fyrr's taloned hand shot through the bars, and grabbed the hapless guard by the throat, plucking the keys from his hand and tossing him aside like a discarded doll.

In a moment, the Haspur had the cage unlocked and kicked open the door. But the guard was not giving up on his responsibilities so lightly.

The guard rose to his feet, drew a sword, and charged the open cage door; the Haspur didn't even pause. His eyes were red with hunger-madness and he was quicker than she would ever have believed. He slashed out with his clawed hands, using them as his weapons, before the man could even bring his blade up to guard position.

He caught the Guard across the throat, tearing it open with a single blow.

Robin turned away, sickened, as blood sprayed across the white altar-cloth, and the man collapsed with a gurgling cry.

There was a thunder of wings, and when she looked again, it was to catch sight of T'fyrr in flight, vanishing up through the hole in the roof, fighting the magic-brought winds. A moment later, and he was gone.

Movement at her side caught her attention, and she glanced back over at Jonny just in time to see him fumble at his belt and drop the pendant he had carried out of his pocket, along with a few coins. It fell out of its silk handkerchief and onto the floor, although there was so much noise that the sound it made hitting the marble was completely lost.

He snatched it up, cocked his arm back, and flung it with all of his might, hitting Padrik square in the chest.

It struck hard enough to distract Padrik, and broke the High Bishop's concentration — and it caught in all the gold embroidery decorating his robe, becoming entangled there. Padrik froze in mid-gesture, staring open-mouthed down at his chest.

The ring of flames vanished, blown out as easily as a candle —

And the Ghost reached forward with a howl of triumph, and seized Padrik in both clawlike hands.

The sound of the Ghost's laughter did not — quite — drown out Padrik's screams.

Blackness as thick as a moonless night descended

on the Cathedral, and the crowd went utterly mad. Gwyna and Jonny simply huddled on the floor for a moment, then slowly crawled towards the altar, hoping in that way to avoid being trampled. But before they reached that haven, light returned, pouring through the shattered windows. Padrik was nowhere to be seen.

The screams died, and Robin looked up.

"*Witches!*" someone cried out in despair. "*That evil creature slew the High Bishop!*"

She saw the face of a nightmare, a crowd ready to tear anything and anyone apart in sheer, unadulterated panic. In a moment, they might very well remember seeing Jonny fling that pendant at the High Bishop —

They'd kill him, and her — and then do exactly what Donnar had feared; run wild through the streets looking for evil mages, killing, and burning. They'd certainly run rampant through the Warren — and if they found T'fyrr, they'd tear him to pieces, too.

They weren't going to listen to *her* —

"You're a man!" she shouted at Kestrel. "They'll listen to you! Say something! *Stop them!*"

Jonny knew the face of the mob when he saw it; he'd already had a taste of what they could do. They were poised to act — and someone had to give them direction, or it would turn into hate, fear, and destruction. Someone had to say or do something before one of them pointed *him* out as the one who'd broken Padrik's defenses and let the Ghost through.

But *him*? He could hardly say two words without stuttering!

Fear held him paralyzed for a moment. Then, in his mind, he heard Harperus. "*You can't say it? So sing it.*"

He did not even waste a moment on consideration; he leapt to the top of the altar, and held up both his hands.

And gathered, reached, desperately, for the melody he needed. For the Magic . . .

"*Stop!*" he cried/sang, his voice ringing out like a trumpet.

The mob obeyed.

People froze in place, staring at him, mouths agape with astonishment.

Words poured from him as if from some supernatural source; he told them everything, as their faces gazed up at him, expressions dumbfounded. How Padrik was a fraud, working his "miracles" with the help of criminals. How he had truly used their donations — the House he ran, the luxuries he enjoyed. And before anyone could challenge him, he signaled to Robin, who began to reproduce some of those "miracles."

She started with bursts of flash powder, and then "magical appearances" of the altar-decorations by sleight of hand. She worked her way around the altar and made a couple of quick movements; Kestrel heard a muffled thump. She then found the mirror-rig, and used it to reproduce the "demon" — a puppet hanging slackly among the sculptures of angels up above the altar, out of sight of the congregation.

He told how Padrik had bound the spirit of a poor nonhuman, murdered by an evil Abbot of Carthell, to become the High Bishop's own personal executioner.

He stretched the truth a little, describing Reymond as a "holy mage of the Church," who had discovered this and had freed the Ghost, sending it to take its own revenge on Padrik.

He poured his heart into his words, falling into the same kind of trance he invoked when playing his music. Behind his words, he heard another strand of melody, as Robin wove her magics in with his. She was singing an accompaniment to his rhapsody, steadying his lips, giving him strength beyond his own. As if the words came from someone else, he heard himself eloquently describing how Padrik had taken over all the trade in the Cathedral market — how Padrik confiscated the goods of those he sent off to be slain by the Ghost — how he had been collecting more and more money, and doing less and less for the poor, the sick, those to whom it was supposed to go.

Somewhere in the back of his mind, part of him gave an astonished cheer as the crowd began to pay more and more attention to him — and as their mood, staring at Padrik's chosen Priests, turned uglier and uglier.

"Go!" he heard himself urge, as his voice rang out in a triumphal call-to-arms. "Go and look in his quarters! See what luxuries he has hidden there! See the place where those vagabonds he consorted with are living, how they eat from silver and drink from crystal! These things were bought with your money, and with blood-money! He has been living off of you and off the stolen goods of the innocents he has sent to their deaths, and all falsely in the name of God!"

A long silence filled the Cathedral for a moment.

It was broken by a single whisper of sound; the rustle of robes as one of the Priests tried to edge his way out of the Cathedral, ducking behind the statue of Saint Tolemy —

"*They're running away! Get them!*" someone shouted.

The false Priests broke and ran, holding up the skirts of their robes in order to run faster, fleeing into the Church buildings behind the Cathedral.

Robin plastered herself up against the altar as the

mob flooded past her, storming after the fleeing Priests, brushing aside the guards. Kestrel just watched them go, sinking wearily to the surface of the altar. Padrik's quarters were in there, somewhere, and he had no doubt that they were as luxurious as he had described. The mob was going to have something to vent its rage on, after all.

When they had all gone, their shouts fading as they passed into other parts of the complex, he looked over at Robin and held out his hand. She smiled, exhausted, walked over to him, and took it.

Sunlight poured down through the hole in the roof to pool around the altar. Kestrel saw that there was someone lying behind the pulpit, quite unconscious, next to an obviously broken and jammed trapdoor. The back, and the clothing of the figure seemed oddly familiar.

Robin grinned, and turned the body over.

"Who is it?" he asked.

She straightened. "The Clan Chief of the Patsonos," she replied, her voice filled with glee. "Come give me a hand with him —"

She had grabbed one arm and tugged him, none-too-gently, across the marble floor.

"Why?" he asked, taking the other arm, and blinking in bafflement. "What do you want to do with him?"

They hauled the Gypsy up the altar stairs, as she panted out her answer. "Someone — ought to be here — to answer questions," she said, her voice and face brimming with malicious enjoyment. "And we have — a nice big cage here — to make sure *he* is the one to answer them."

"And not us," Kestrel supplied, in complete understanding and agreement. "Good idea!"

They locked the Gypsy in the cage that had held T'fyrr, first making sure that the Haspur had not left his lock picks behind, that the Patsono Chief did not have a set of picks on his person, and — with a judicious thump on the head with the pommel of Kestrel's dagger — that he would probably not wake up until after there was someone here to deal with him.

"That should do it!" Robin said, as they slammed the door shut on him. "Prey for Peregrine." She looked around the ruined Cathedral, thoughtfully.

"You know, things are going to get very interesting here for a while," she said, nibbling her lower lip. "And they just might be looking for more people to blame. . . ."

"I've always wanted to see Trevandia," Kestrel declared, even though he had no such longing until just that moment. But Trevandia was the farthest place *he* knew of from Gradford that still had welcomed Gypsies and Free Bards.

"Why, so have I!" Robin exclaimed. "You know, another kingdom seems like a very good place to be right now!"

They looked at each other for a long moment — then broke into only *slightly* hysterical laughter.

"Trevandia it is!" Kestrel said, when they could catch their breath. "As soon as we get the wagon."

There was a growling sound in the distance — growing nearer. It was that of an angry crowd returning.

"How about now?" Robin asked, innocently.

He did not bother to reply; only seized her hand. Together they ran out into the square, and did not stop running until they were past the gates of Gradford — and they did not once look back.